ANY MEANS NECESSARY

Also by Jenny Rogneby

Leona: The Die Is Cast

A LEONA LINDBERG THRILLER

ANY MEANS NECESSARY

JENNY ROGNEBY

Translated from the Swedish by Agnes Broomé

Other Press   New York

Copyright © Jenny Rogneby 2016

Originally published in Swedish as *Leona: Alla medel tillåtna*
in 2016 by Wahlström & Widstrand, Stockholm.

Published by arrangement with Partners in Stories Stockholm AB, Sweden

English translation copyright © Other Press 2019

Production editor: Yvonne E. Cárdenas
Text designer: Julie Fry
This book was set in Quiosco and Founders Grotesk
by Alpha Design & Composition of Pittsfield, NH.

10 9 8 7 6 5 4 3 2 1

LIBRARY OF CONGRESS CATALOGING-IN-PUBLICATION DATA

Names: Rogneby, Jenny, 1974- author. | Broomé, Agnes, translator.
Title: Any means necessary : a Leona Lindberg thriller / Jenny Rogneby ;
    translated from the Swedish by Agnes Broomé.
Other titles: Alla medel tillåtna. English
Description: New York : Other Press, [2019]
Identifiers: LCCN 2018027098 (print) | LCCN 2018028480 (ebook) |
    ISBN 9781590518854 (ebook) | ISBN 9781590518847 (pbk.)
Classification: LCC PT9877.28.O44 (ebook) | LCC PT9877.28.O44 A7813
    2019(print) | DDC 839.73/8—dc23
LC record available at https://lccn.loc.gov/2018027098

ANY MEANS NECESSARY

He adjusted the heavy belt strapped around his hips, relieving the pressure from the steel cylinders that made the waistband of his trousers chafe against his skin. The wire connecting them to the detonator shifted on the outside of his right trouser leg. He grabbed the trigger. Squeezed it hard. His hand was damp. Sweat? He didn't know.

The only thing he cared about was his mission.

His final mission.

One push of a button and everything would be over.

His eyes were fixed on the low-set, four-wheeled police robot slowly approaching him. Despite the sirens and the roar of the police's Eurocopter 135 hovering above his head, the sound of his own breathing was loud in his ears. Shallow. Irregular. The shadows cast by the rotor blades swept across the grand, sunlit facade in front of him.

Parliament.

He studied the coat of arms above the entrance, the watchful Mother Svea, an ancient symbol of Sweden. All around the perimeter of the leafy park, now encircled by police cordons, he could make out the silhouettes of armed men. Sniper rifle barrels on the roof of the Royal Palace flashing in the sun.

The police robot had reached the lawn now and was trundling toward him.

"We put it right up front."

The tinny voice of the negotiator rang out between the rhythmic sound of the helicopter rotors.

He could see it.

The pliers taped to the top of the robot were meant for him. For cutting the wire. For making everything right. Like that was an option.

When he let his unbuttoned coat fall to the ground, revealing the entire belt, and grabbed hold of the trigger once more, the solitary voice of the negotiator gave way to the barked commands of police officers.

"No! Drop the trigger! Drop it! Hands up! On your knees! On your—"

He tuned them out.

Stopped listening.

Nothing mattered anymore.

It was time.

He lifted his hand up and fumbled along the chain around his neck. Found the silver pendant that had stuck to his chest. Clutched it hard while he moved the thumb of his other hand to the trigger.

He inhaled. Pulled the air deep into his lungs. Then raised his eyes to the dazzling, clear blue summer sky one last time.

Closed his eyes.

And pushed the button.

ONE

I closed my eyes, fully aware I was being watched. Every expression. Movement. Reaction. Everything was noted and analyzed. I, Leona Lindberg, had done it myself a thousand times. As a detective with the Violent Crimes Division of the Stockholm Police, I was no stranger to interviewing people. Scrutinizing their stories for inconsistencies. It was a familiar role I was comfortable with.

But this time was different.

This time, I was the one being scrutinized.

My therapist, Aimi Nordlund, watched me intently from her armchair. Her office consisted of a single room, decorated to encourage conversation. The walls were a cool shade of green, the somber upholstered armchairs had cushions that guaranteed a soft landing in an ergonomically correct position. The color palette made the office feel like a homey living room, but I still had a hard time breathing whenever I was in there. It was as if there was a heavy weight on my chest. Pushing me against the backrest of my chair.

I never thought I would one day find myself in a therapist's office, talking about my life. Just a few months ago, it would have been unthinkable. Seeing a shrink wasn't my bag. But after everything that had happened, I had officially hit rock bottom.

No, I had fallen even lower.

Financially.

Even physically.

Five months after returning from England, I had woken up one morning and been unable to get out of bed. My body had felt like it was strapped to the mattress. It had taken me an hour to get up. I have no recollection of going to work. Apparently, I had gone about my business as usual, even though I had been completely switched off mentally. When I wasn't at work, I stayed home. Sat in the dark, curtains drawn, just staring into space.

During my first therapy session with Aimi, I had barely managed to put two words together. Hadn't known where to start. A thousand thoughts had been swirling around in my head. Sorting through them by myself had proved impossible. Solitude only seemed to give them free rein. They flapped around like bats in the night, never more than briefly glimpsed, impossible to corral. But here, in Aimi's office, for some reason, they slowed down and stopped.

She asked me questions. The kind of questions no one had asked me before. About my background, who I was.

So who was I?

Most people would say I was a normal, divorced mother of about thirty-five, some might mention that my profession, police detective, was a bit unusual, but that aside from that, I was more or less like everybody else. My colleagues considered me a skilled investigator. One who often challenged authority and tended less toward teamwork than some, granted, but an otherwise upstanding member of society who shared the Police Authority's values and respected the laws of the land.

Few knew who I really was.

That I had rejected the ordinary, honest life of the average Swede. Had stopped trying to conform and started living instead.

For real.

Without a safety net.

I had sacrificed a lot and crossed lines few ever even stray near. But it had been necessary in order to escape a life built on lies.

The select few who knew I was a crooked detective with one foot in the criminal underworld had every reason to keep that to themselves.

I looked up at the ceiling in Aimi's office. Thought about what she would say if she knew that a few months previous, I had framed another detective for a crime I had committed. Wondered if that would make her reconsider her approach. It hadn't been my intention to set him up; it had been a last resort. He had started poking around my business, screwing me over for his own personal gain. Only afterward did I find out that he had been tapping my phone. He was arrested while trying to collect enough evidence to nail me.

I got away with it by the skin of my teeth, but didn't have to wait long for his demands. When he realized just how much money was involved, he opted to blackmail me, rather than rat me out. I was forced to hand over all my ill-gotten gains, several million. In return, he was prepared to spend a few years in the nick. He reasoned that even if he appealed his sentence and was exonerated, he would never be able to regain the trust of his superiors at the Police Authority and continue his career. He was probably right. Rumors about his sketchiness had been floating around for years. Lots of people had heard him complain that the salary wasn't worth doing the job for. My millions had simply been too tempting. Now he was behind bars at Hall Prison outside Södertälje.

Forking over the money had stung, obviously. I had gone through a lot to get it. I had planned to use it to start a new life.

But crying over it was pointless.

I had made new plans.

Which would make me even richer.

The only thing I needed now was the strength to pull them off.

I needed help to get back on my feet and Aimi was the right person to talk to. I studied her. Apparently, therapists prefer not to talk about themselves, so I only knew what I could glean from her appearance. Her straight, dark brown hair, light brown skin tone, name, and the rings on her left hand told me she was in her fifties, of Japanese descent, and married to a Swedish man.

I took a deep breath, pushing the weight away from my chest. Had to fight to get the words out, more than ever now that I was preparing to tell her about the thing that nearly suffocated me every night. I closed my eyes.

"I'm in a church. Dressed all in black. A veil over my head that I'm trying to remove so I can see. It's all I can do to keep moving down the aisle. I put one foot in front of the other, but it's like I'm not getting anywhere."

I spoke quietly and calmly. Made an effort to recount the dream as accurately as possible.

"The pews on either side of me are full of people in black robes. When I look down at my body I realize I'm wearing one too. They all have their hoods pulled up. I manage to pull mine down and turn to catch a glimpse of the people's faces, of who they are, but the hoods make it impossible. They all stand there, swaying gently, like tall, black phantoms. I don't know why I'm there. Someone must have died, I think to myself, but I don't know who. Not knowing makes me feel desperate."

Even though I could feel my heart pounding, I pressed on.

"There's a terrible feeling in the pit of my stomach. My legs are heavy. I can hear organ music. I drag myself all the way to the end of the aisle to see if there's a coffin up front. It's like moving through molasses, but I slowly get closer. Seven rows left. Six."

I had never described this dream to anyone. Now that I was, it felt almost as real as at night.

"Everyone suddenly sits down as one. There's not a sound. Then I see it. It's to the right of the altar. A tiny, blindingly white coffin. At the same time, the person in the front row turns to me. Even though his hood hides parts of his face, I can see who it is. My husband. His eyes are red from crying. When I move closer I realize he's holding our five-year-old daughter Beatrice's hand. She's sitting next to him. Looks up at me with those clear, blue, innocent eyes. The space next to her is empty. At first, I fail to put two and two together. I look around for Benjamin. My darling son. Where is he? When my eyes fall on the coffin again, I stop breathing. I'm falling. The church floor disappears from underneath my feet and I plummet into a bottomless, black abyss."

I looked up at Aimi. Her facial expression radiated kindness and calm. She urged me to continue.

"I wake up in a panic, fighting for air. Can't breathe. Like I'm drowning. Then I hear Benjamin."

Not a night went by when I didn't hear Benjamin crying. Calling out for help when his stomach pains overwhelmed him. Even though he was gone and no longer cried in the night, it was as though he didn't want to let go. Or maybe I didn't want to. It hurt that I could no longer help him. I usually didn't catch myself until I was halfway out the bedroom. He wasn't there anymore.

"It's a horrible dream, but the worst part is waking up and realizing that…it's not a dream. That he's gone forever. My son was…"

It was difficult for me to put my thoughts into words. To talk about him. I would really have preferred not to. And yet, I knew I had no choice.

"…he meant everything to me."

My eyes welled up. Tears blurred my vision. When I closed my eyes, there was no room for them; they rolled down my cheeks, fell onto my black blouse. I could hear Aimi rustling the box of tissues on the table. I reached out to take one.

"And then there's the memories from the hospital," she said.

I nodded. The memories from the English hospital often ran on a loop in my head. Waiting for Benjamin's complicated intestinal transplant to be over. For the doctors to come out and tell us that everything went well, that our beloved son was going to survive his Crohn's disease and that we would be hearing his thin little voice again before long. Instead, I watched the surgeon walk up to my husband. Peter, my stable, composed husband, collapsed on the floor right there in the corridor. The doctor had told him they had done everything they could, but that they had been unable to save Benjamin's life. I hadn't heard the words from where I was standing; Peter's reaction was enough.

My throat had closed up. I had wanted to scream, but hadn't been able to get so much as a sound out. Hadn't been able to pull air into my lungs. Reason had told me I had to go over and listen to what the doctor had to say, be there for Peter, but my body refused to obey. Stunned into some kind of trance, I had started backing away from Peter and the doctor. I needed to get out of there. Needed air. The only thing I can remember after that was that I ran. And ran. Until my legs wouldn't carry me anymore. Then I collapsed. Cried. Sobbed.

"How were things between you and Peter afterward?" Aimi asked.

I didn't reply. The weeks and months that followed were a haze. The days had all blended into one. My new boss, Alexandra, had forced me to take a week off against my will. I had been worried about what would happen if I had to be on my own. Work had been a refuge. The only thing keeping me upright. Until everything came crashing down and I was no longer able to get out of bed.

"Peter wanted to talk about him all the time," I said. "It was unbearable. I couldn't even say his name. It was too much for me. Peter had already told me he wanted a divorce, so I moved out. Did my best not to think about everything that had happened. It was the only way I knew to survive."

In a way, you could say Peter's and my relationship has carried on much the same since I moved out; Beatrice was the only thing we ever communicated about. I didn't miss our marriage. While we were together, I had strived to be a loving partner to Peter and a good mother to the children. In the end, our family life was more like running a business. All of Peter's and my conversations were about pickups and drop-offs, buying groceries, driving the children to various activities, cooking, reading stories, organizing family outings; the list went on and on. Our day-to-day was all about the rat race, about running as fast as we could to keep our robotic lives from coming off the rails.

That was what people expected life to be.

Even as a child, I had discovered that it was vital to do what was expected of me. As long as I did that and never stood out, I survived. It was easier at work; I never got particularly close with anyone there, but with Peter things had been more complicated. Having to keep up appearances within my own family had gradually worn me down. When I realized I no longer had it in me to be the loving wife Peter wanted, or the perfect mother my children deserved, I knew I had no other choice but to leave the life I had spent years building.

That was when my journey toward a new life began.

I was conscious of the fact that my decision ran counter to what a woman, mother, and officer of the law was expected to do. But I refused to let others dictate my actions. Was no longer going to adhere to their rules.

I went my own way, and I improved the lives of the people I worked with. One of them was a half-Finnish father of young children, who had now gone back to Finland, a few million kronor better off. Another was a prosecutor, who after teaming up with me was able to quit her job and move to the French Riviera.

I had come so close to getting what I wanted, but because I had lost my share of the money, I had been forced to go back to square one and come up with new schemes.

If not for the fact that most things felt meaningless without Benjamin, the serenity and silence that enveloped me whenever I stepped into my apartment would have made things easier. I no longer had Peter to think about and no one to keep up appearances for in my own home. I tried to be there for Beatrice, but was overcome with restlessness during the day and sleeplessness at night. Thoughts of Benjamin kept me awake.

Aimi slowly leaned forward in her armchair. Looked me right in the eye and said in a calm voice: "Leona, have you given yourself permission to grieve for the loss of your child?"

I looked away, gazing out the window while tears streamed down my face. I had done everything to avoid grieving. To function normally. Do my job. Sort out a new place to live. Try to look after Beatrice. Before, changing my focus had always been an effective tactic when I encountered resistance.

But not this time.

I was afraid of myself. Didn't understand what was happening. I still didn't know. That was why I was here, talking to Aimi.

"What would happen to you if you did?" she asked.

The silence was broken by my mobile phone going off. It was Alexandra, my boss. I picked up but couldn't get a word out.

"Leona, where are you? I need you to come in ASAP."

I stood up. Quickly dried my tears. Explained to Aimi that I had to go. I couldn't bear to stay anyway. I was looking for help to find strength, not weakness. Aimi usually had a calming effect on me, but I didn't like that I sometimes felt worse when I left than when I came. Or maybe that was exactly it; she made me feel things. It scared me. If I opened up too much, I would fall into a big, black hole and never be able to climb out.

I didn't want to go back to that.

TWO

In my car on the way from Aimi's office, I turned the call from Alexandra over in my mind. From her tone on the phone, it was clear she had something important to tell me.

Alexandra Risberg was the new superintendent at the Violent Crimes Division. That was still her official title. Next year, the Police Authority was set to undergo its biggest reorganization in fifty years. After that, the divisions would no longer be called divisions and Alexandra's title would change. Even though she was new in her job, there could be no doubt that she wanted to climb the ladder.

Alexandra had explained to me that the division had been allocated additional funds earmarked for counseling, which she had offered me several times after Benjamin's death. I had declined every time. When I told her I had decided to see a private therapist, she had been very encouraging and given me permission to go during work hours. Now she had called to ask me to come back as soon as possible, knowing full well where I was.

I turned the police radio off and skipped through the regular channels in an attempt to find something upbeat to help me shake the heavy mood from my therapy session. After browsing through a number of uninspiring talk radio stations, I gave up and listened to the monotone drone of a newscaster:

Today's headlines. The bomb that exploded outside Parliament last week triggered extensive police action, involving

the National Task Force, the National Bomb Protection Unit,
and officers from several police forces. Snipers and specially
trained negotiators were also called to the scene. A total of two
hundred officers were active during the acute phase, which
lasted approximately ten hours. The national police commis-
sioner predicts that from now on, Sweden, like other countries,
will need to dedicate more significant resources to fighting
terrorism...

I turned it off. Couldn't bear to listen. Over the past week, the media
had been utterly dominated by the suicide bomber outside Parliament. You couldn't turn on the TV or radio, browse the Internet,
or flip through a newspaper without being bombarded with information about and debates on the subject. Every expert felt compelled to have a theory about it. Even at work, the event was the
topic of fervent discussion. People speculated about whether the
Security Service really did keep an eye on all potential terrorists
in the country, and whether it had been right to heed the recommendation of the National Center for Terrorist Threat Assessment to raise the threat level. I stayed well out of it. The whole
thing just made my longing for a different kind of life more urgent.

I didn't notice the faint smell of smoke in the car until I
stopped at a red light on Sveavägen. It didn't take me long to
locate the cigarette butt on the floor next to my feet. I rolled
down the window and was about to throw it out when I heard a
child crying.

"Mommy, mommy."

A woman was holding a little boy by the hand, walking so fast
down the sidewalk that the boy, shuffling behind, was unable to
keep his balance. His legs wouldn't carry him. His mother pulled
and tugged at him. Shouted that they were in a hurry. I rolled the

window back up. Felt sick. From the smell of the cigarette. From seeing myself in that woman. My previous life.

The boy was no more than a year or so older than Benjamin. I recognized the stress. If only I hadn't rushed around like that woman. If only I had had more time with my son.

That life was like a hellish hamster wheel.

People always complained about the everyday niggles, but never spotted the bigger patterns. Maybe they didn't want to see them. They preferred doubling down and staying in their point-less, regimented, stressful lives to doing something about it. Change was too difficult.

I had had my reasons for living like that. I had done it because I knew society doesn't accept nonconformity. If you deviate from the cookie-cutter norm, you are left out in the cold. Worthless. From there on out, you're on your own.

I wondered how long it would take the woman on the sidewalk to realize that fighting so hard to fit in is pointless. That she was part of a competition that has no winners.

Only losers.

She had come to a stop on the sidewalk, bending down and yanking at her son, who was now putting up more determined resistance. He refused to stand up and was crying so loudly I could hear it clearly through my rolled-up window. Maybe the woman would wake up one day. Realize that a single minute with her son was infinitely more precious than whatever she was in a rush to get to.

I accelerated, drove much too fast, and slammed the brakes when I spotted two colleagues on the beat. Since the events of the previous week, a wave of officers had been ordered out onto the streets; there were more uniformed officers in the city center than usual now.

Back at headquarters, I went straight to the break room, poured myself a glass of water, and washed down a painkiller on my way to Alexandra's office. She was on the phone but waved me in when she spotted me through the glass wall. I entered and went over to stand by the window. Aside from a few potted plants, the room looked the same as it had when it belonged to my former boss Claes. Some of my colleagues had figured having a female manager would be radically different. Claes had a temper on him and was often loud. Alexandra was calmer, but that's not to say she was at all conflict-shy.

I took a seat by the round conference table until she was done. As always, she spoke in calm, collected tones. Yet even so, the tiny furrows on her normally smooth, tanned forehead revealed that something was troubling her. She hung up and studied me.

"Are you still having trouble sleeping, Leona? You look a bit tired."

I shrugged. That was an understatement, but I didn't exactly feel inclined to discuss the state of my health with her. Either way, she clearly wasn't inquiring out of concern alone; she would hardly have asked me to cut my therapy session short to discuss my well-being.

I poured a glass of water from the jug on the table and took a sip. Thought it tasted of iron.

"There's a new case I need you to handle," she said. "They've managed to wake up the bomber who blew himself up outside Parliament last week."

I gritted my teeth. Of all the ongoing investigations I could have been assigned to, this was the worst imaginable for me right now.

"He's still in the hospital. Refuses to talk to SÄK," she continued.

That he didn't want to talk to them was hardly shocking, I thought to myself. SÄK was the abbreviation traditionally used internally for Sweden's Security Service, known externally as SÄPO. An attack like the one outside Parliament was considered a threat to national security and consequently within the purview of the Security Service. What any of it had to do with me was unclear.

"The chief prosecutor at the National Security Unit and the head of SÄK have both been in touch. I just spoke to the commissioner as well. They all requested you specifically," she went on.

I sighed. Time and again I was reminded of the drawbacks of having won an award for best investigatory achievement six months ago. It was ironic, to say the least, that the award had been given to me for framing a fellow detective for a crime I had in fact been the brains behind. Either way, I had, since then, been handed a number of difficult cases. But nothing like this. Once upon a time, the challenge would have amped me up, but these days I needed whatever energy I could muster for other things than work.

I had been in my office last week when the event Alexandra was referring to took place. A man blew himself up outside the main entrance to Sweden's Parliament building. Even though central Stockholm had seen a similar attack once before, it was hard to accept that there really had been a suicide bomber. The first responders had recounted the unsettling course of events during which the man's body was torn to pieces before their eyes. He had lost limbs but survived. Luckily, no one else had been in the vicinity, but security had been stepped up in the wake of the blast and half the city center was cordoned off because the threat level in and around all political buildings was judged to be elevated. Even at that early stage, I had been grateful I didn't work for SÄK and so wouldn't have to have anything to do with it. Taking on an investigation of this magnitude was something I had neither the energy nor the motivation for.

"But Alexandra, that case is enormous. If we bring it over to Violent Crimes there's bound to be a media frenzy. Is that really—"

"I'm not asking, Leona," she said. "It's already been decided that we'll be conducting the preliminary interviews. I know you have a lot on your plate right now, but we're all convinced you're the right person for the job."

I knew there were more than a few detectives at Violent Crimes who would kill for a chance to do those interviews, but at the moment, it was nothing but a burden to me. I was neither physically nor mentally fit enough.

"As you know, the negotiators failed to get through to him at the scene. I want you to head up to the hospital and talk to him and then we'll take it from there."

She pulled out her cell phone. Glanced briefly at the screen. After pushing a button, she put it down again. I let my eyes wander across her desk and the conference table.

"Where's the file?" I said.

"Since this is an act of terrorism, the investigation is going to remain with SÄK. You just have to interview the man. That's all."

Any detective would know that it was not going to be a matter of "simply" interviewing him. Being the lead interviewer in a case as serious as this one was going to be challenging. Nor was it particularly common for us to work so closely with the Security Service.

I sighed, hand on hip.

"Are you telling me they're not planning on sharing any more information?" I asked.

SÄK not only concealed their doings from the public, but from the rest of the police as well. To a virtually ridiculous extent. Since they wouldn't even give me enough information to do their work for them, I personally felt they were welcome to do it themselves. In Alexandra's position, I would have hung up the phone after saying a few choice words to clarify to the head of SÄK that he needn't be in touch again until he was willing to share the necessary facts. But then, that was likely why I was not in Alexandra's position. Keeping on the good side of the higher-ups was not my forte. I refused to kiss up. Especially if there wasn't even a reward for it at the end of the day.

"They want you to go in with an open mind, without a bunch of background information. And besides, you already know some things about the case."

So that was what they were calling it, "an open mind." Even Alexandra seemed to realize how stupid that sounded.

"So how am I supposed to get my information, the media?"

She frowned at my sarcasm.

"This is how it's going to be," she said and stood up. "We have to make our peace with SÄK's methods."

Ever since I made the decision to live my life differently, I had found the kind of thing Alexandra had just said more and more annoying. Saying "this is how it's going to be," as though we were nothing but passive spectators to things that "just happened." I was aware that everyone was terrified of classified details leaking, especially in an investigation like this one, but this was absurd.

"This is the man's personal information and the results of our database search," Alexandra said. "Bring Fredrik along; he can drive while you read up on...well, I guess it's just the initial report."

"Oh, so they've been generous enough to surrender the police report, have they? Swell!"

I was being sarcastic. We were perfectly able to print out the report ourselves, and either way it would tell me nothing about the man's background.

"He's already been informed of the charges, I take it?" I said.

"I think so, but inform him again anyway, the usual procedure. The correct charges are in there. It's unclear whether he's able to take anything in at this point."

I shook my head inwardly.

"So it's me and Fredrik? With him assisting in the interviews?" I said.

"That's the thing," Alexandra said and walked around her desk. "They actually want you to do the interviews on your own. They also want a—"

"Excuse me?!" I cut in and stared at Alexandra.

She looked up at me without answering.

"The head of SÄK told you I'm supposed to interview him on my own?" I pressed.

She nodded.

"They also want a pre-interview meeting with you to go over what you should ask him."

"What the fuck?" I exclaimed.

This was unbelievable. With a case of this magnitude, using just one interviewer would normally be out of the question. Personally, I had no problem doing interviews on my own—I actually preferred it—but it was not standard procedure.

"I explained to them that you like working independently. But the interviews will be filmed and you will write a summary report they can go over."

I pondered this for a second. Was working independently suddenly okay now?

"Alexandra, if you're all sure I'm the right person to interview this guy, and you want me to do it on my own, I'm going to assume you're going to let me do it my way. I don't want to have to take meeting after meeting with condescending jerks from SÄK looking to give me instructions on how to do my job."

Alexandra nodded.

"Make sure you get the first interview done," she said. "Go up there and feel him out and report back to me as soon as you're finished."

"Can you tell me what really happened?" I said. "How did he survive that blast?"

"The explosive belt slipped down his hips the moment before he detonated the bomb, which ripped both his legs off. According to the paramedics, the man was conscious and trying to crawl away when they arrived at the scene."

I nodded. This case was going to require my undivided attention. Then it hit me that I could demand to be relieved of my other assignments. If I was taking over the whole bomb case, it would be a given that everything else would be taken off my plate, but since I had only been tasked with doing the interviews, and since this was likely not going to be a protracted process, the situation was much less clear. But I was going to give it a shot. Having only these interviews to worry about would make my life a lot easier.

"Hey, about my other investigations...," I said. "It's going to be difficult to fit everything in."

Alexandra looked at me and frowned. She could glare as much as she wanted. If they insisted I was the only detective in town, or, actually, in the country, who could do the interviews with the bomber, and also thought I needed to do it on my own, I was in a position to make one or two demands. I was going to have to spend late nights watching the recorded interviews to analyze them, turning over every damn word the bomber had said.

"To be able to give this the time it needs, I want to ask you to reassign my other cases," I said and looked back at Alexandra.

Not an unreasonable demand, quite the opposite, a prerequisite for doing the job properly.

She sighed. No superintendent ever likes reassigning cases. Even though all investigators log their actions meticulously these days, knowledge is always lost when a case changes hands. Some information simply can't be recorded, which means that it risks being lost entirely when someone takes over a case from someone else.

She nodded and raised an admonishing finger at me.

"But don't think this gives you license to go AWOL, Leona. You're still part of this division. You're going to make sure you attend staff meetings and meet your other obligations."

I nodded.

"You will, for instance, be giving all the lectures you have scheduled. Anything else will be considered unacceptable," she said.

I was barely out of training when my superiors discovered that I was not only quick to take in new information, but that I also had the "ability to convey knowledge pedagogically to others," as they put it. Disseminating knowledge throughout the organization was one of the Police Authority's persistent challenges. Consequently, I had frequently been dispatched to conferences and key information meetings, tasked with passing on knowledge by giving lectures to my own division as well as to colleagues up and down the country. It goes without saying that no financial compensation was given for this, no, it was considered part of a detective's job description. Anyone who objected was labeled backward and a hindrance to the Authority's improvement efforts. Which made internal promotion impossible. Personally, I viewed the lectures as a nice break from my investigative work. They also came with a certain amount of status.

"Fine," Alexandra resumed. "If you give me your other case files, I'll redistribute them."

I started moving toward the door.

"Leona," Alexandra said. "I want you to be aware that a lot of people are invested in seeing this case solved, both here and internationally. We're counting on you."

I left Alexandra's office and walked toward the elevators. Felt a quick vibration in my pocket. I didn't want to check. Didn't have it in me. I knew what it was about. It was a text from a French banker named Armand. I had first come into contact with him via Ronni, the half-Finnish man I had partnered with for my previous robberies. Armand, who for many years had loaned, collected, and laundered money for criminals, had made a name for himself in the underworld with this side business. These days, he was in a position to be picky about which jobs he wanted to be involved in. The few he did accept, he liked to be very involved in, as I knew from experience. Far more involved than I was comfortable with. I had hired him to launder the money from my heists. For that, he wanted a 5 percent cut. He had tried to control me from the first. Demanded updates via text about whether everything was going according to plan.

I had only met him in person a handful of times. He wore a suit and was absurdly polite. Other people had told me he was not someone you wanted to rub the wrong way. There were rumors about what he did to people who refused to pay up. How much truth there was to those rumors, I couldn't even begin to guess.

It's not unusual for criminals to cultivate a reputation for being deeply dangerous.

According to our agreement, the total sum was to be delivered to him for laundering when the last heist was done and dusted. At that point, he would take his cut, 150,000 euros. Naturally, I hadn't planned on losing all my money to a blackmailer. When I tried to explain the situation to Armand, he gave me a look that chilled me to the bone. He squinted and asked me in his formal, French-accented English to repeat what I had just said about the money I owed him. Said that he thought it had sounded as though I no longer had the money, but that he was certain he must have heard me wrong.

That man had the ability to make even me nervous.

Not until I told him that I was planning a big new job did his eyes soften. As an experienced banker, he understood my thinking immediately. Very large sums in several different currencies. Which meant I would be in even greater need of his services to handle the conversion and laundering. I had been careful, however, not to be too specific about the timing and method.

After that he had left me alone for a while. But now he was back, demanding his money.

I rubbed my temples in an attempt to ease my headache while I waited for the elevator. As if that wasn't bad enough, another problem had now been dropped in my lap.

The bomber.

Alexandra and the entire senior management would be all over me, querying my work. As would a number of foreign security services and Europol. Swedish and international media would hound me with questions. I slumped against the elevator wall. Exhaled.

I had to try to get out of this assignment.

THREE

David Lind stared at the TV screen behind the man sitting across from him in the café. The news was showing pictures from Parliament. Police officers filed past, then footage of the x-ray screeners and metal detectors all visitors now had to pass through. David heaved a sigh. In addition to the officer in front of him, the city had been swarming with police since last week. Everywhere there was talk of how terrorists could strike at any time.

He glanced at his watch. He was supposed to be in the boxing ring, changed and ready to go, in forty minutes.

"I have to dash. Boxing," he said.

Sven Malmström, who was sitting across from him, glanced at his watch as well, as if to double-check that David was telling the truth, that it really was time for boxing.

"We're in agreement?" Sven said.

David shrugged. Do I have a choice? he thought. Sven had called when David was on his way to the boxing club, asking him to step into the nearest café and wait for him there. Sven loved pastries. Was digging into a jelly-covered thing with berries on it right now. It seemed odd to David. It didn't mesh with his view of Sven. David had long wondered how a detective of about fifty could be so enthusiastic about his job. He didn't know much about Sven's background, other than that he liked pastries and that his surname was Malmström. Since he was never slow to respond and had made it abundantly clear from the first that David could call him at any hour of the day or night, David assumed Sven didn't have much of a home life. He also had a very intense demeanor. Gray eyes that always seemed to search and dissect.

Sven opened his tattered bag, which looked like a cross between an old-fashioned briefcase and a laptop bag. Pulled out a mobile phone that he placed on the dark brown café table in front of David. Apple's latest model. David stared at it.

"I need cash, not a new phone."

"Give me your old one," Sven said and held out his hand.

David didn't understand what Sven was getting at.

"But I have all my contacts on it," David said.

Sven kept his hand extended.

"But how the fuck am I supposed to get in touch with people?" David said. "And who is going to pick up if someone from the Blood Family calls, you?"

"I'm just giving it a quick once-over," Sven said.

"You're just too fucking much sometimes, you know that? You still don't trust me?" David put his hand into the pocket of his jeans, pulled out his phone, and pushed it across the table.

David had been put in contact with Sven two and a half years earlier, after a friend had had his apartment searched. The police had stormed the place and found drugs. Arrested everyone present and driven them straight to detention. Everyone except David. Him they had shoved in an unmarked police car and driven around town, telling him they had been watching him for a good long while. They had told David they knew he secretly wanted to walk away from his life of crime and asked how he would feel about being put in touch with a handler. In that moment, in the police car, on his way to a detention center and with a prison sentence hanging over him, he had said yes. Figuring it was now or never. This would be his chance to straighten his life out.

Later on, Sven had visited him in his cell. David had immediately started telling him about the things happening around him in the hopes of being released from custody and avoiding prison. But it turned out Sven wasn't able to help with either of those things. He told him that wasn't how it worked. David had to serve his time, but afterward he could choose to start working as an informer.

By the time David was released from prison, he had done a lot of thinking. He had agreed to become an informer and knew that from now on, he was always going to have to be on his guard. With the police as well. They were not to be trusted, that much he knew. Sven tried to make out as if he cared about David, but David knew he would never be able to tell Sven everything. He had heard about informers who had accidentally had their covers blown by the police. It had put them in mortal danger and they had been forced to leave the country. David had to look out for himself.

If this was a way for Sven to try to keep David sweet while he waited to be paid, David was not impressed. A new phone was the last thing on his mind right now. He flipped through the apps for a bit and then slipped it into his pocket. After poking around David's phone without seeming to find anything interesting, Sven handed it back to him.

"You pick up when I call," Sven said. "Give me the old one when you've transferred your contacts."

David stood up, grabbed his gym bag, and left.

At first, being an informer had been about telling Sven where certain criminal elements hung out, who they hung out with, and what type of business they were involved in. The payments David got for this didn't come close to a full-time salary, but he was paid extra for particularly good info. He needed the money to prove to his girlfriend, Saga, that he had straightened himself out and had an income. She thought he worked full time for a moving company, but he only did casual work for them when they needed extra hands. He couldn't tell anyone about this gig. Not even Saga. Sven had been pretty fucking clear about that.

Not long after David was released, Sven had asked him to sound out the situation among the city's criminal gangs, one in particular, a gang that had been growing stronger and the police were apparently having a hard time with. It was called the Blood Family and differed from the others in several ways. They came from the northern suburbs and didn't stoop to things like debt collection and blackmail like some motorcycle gangs and various other groups. They thought of themselves as businessmen, plain and simple. Their main cash area was selling cars, drugs, and weapons. They were also the only criminal gang in town that accepted female members. David had managed to get in closer with the Blood Family than he was actually comfortable with. The leader of the family had taken notice of him early on and asked him to do minor errands on the gang's behalf. Sven had been very excited when David told him this and urged him to accept and keep reporting to him. The minor errands had then gradually been replaced with far riskier assignments.

As David crossed the street, the new phone buzzed in his pocket. He pulled it out and looked at the display. Immediately turned around and looked back at the café. Sven nodded to him through the café window.

FOUR

"The counselor's in with him just now," the suicide bomber's doctor said, pointing for me to take a seat on the chair in his sterile examination room.

I glanced at the nametag pinned to his white coat. Dr. Nair, it read. He wasn't much taller than me. Probably around fifty-five. A faint accent told me Swedish wasn't his mother tongue. He pulled out the glasses he kept tucked into his breast pocket alongside a couple of pens. Placed them on his nose and opened the folder he was holding.

I wasn't comfortable sitting down or chatting calmly with a doctor in the clinically clean yet still somehow sickly hospital environment. Instead, I restlessly paced back and forth, pretending to read the text on a poster showing skeletal parts, but not actually seeing what it said. I've always had a hard time with hospitals. Especially after my most recent experience in England a few months ago. I hadn't set foot in a hospital since then.

"I'm very concerned an interrogation might be too much for Fred…"

"How is he doing?" I interrupted.

"He lost both his legs in the explosion. On top of that, he has a fractured pelvis and burns and fragment injuries to large parts of his body. He was lucky to survive."

"How long has he been conscious?" I said and studied a pelvis on the wall poster.

Skeletons, corpses, severed body parts, anything to do with dead people made me feel sick. Memories of torn tissue, strips of clothing, and blood from people throwing themselves in front of trains, being dismembered, dying in fires or traffic accidents filled me with revulsion. Older people passing away in their homes and not being discovered for weeks. The police were often the first to enter after a neighbor called to complain about the stench in the stairwell. Bodily fluids leaking out, almost gluing the body to the living room floor. Not to mention people who hanged themselves, jumped from bridges or balconies, died in workplace accidents, and then, of course, all the murders.

"Two days," Dr. Nair replied. "The Security Service has tried to get through to him several times. I don't think they've had much luck, but I wasn't given any information about it."

"Can he talk?" I said.

"The counselor has had some form of communication with him. I've only seen faint nods myself. But that's hardly surprising. What he's been through over the past few days is very traumatic. No one should have to go through something like that."

"Don't forget that he is very likely a terrorist who chose to strap on an explosive belt and probably wanted to kill a lot of innocent people."

He shook his head. "We don't make distinctions here. Everyone has a right to the best possible care." He stood up and started walking toward the door. "I'll go with you. Go easy on him. He's very weak, and mentally fragile."

Even though I was aware my emotional responses might be different from those of other people, I found it hard to understand how anyone could feel sympathy for people like the bomber. Expressing your dissatisfaction by killing yourself and a lot of other people seemed pointless to me. What's more, this suicide bomber had failed. I sighed. It didn't help matters that I had to conduct this interview in the hospital.

I walked down the hallway, one step behind the doctor. Ghosts in white clothes with masks over their mouths and noses walked toward us. The smell of sterile solutions pricked my nostrils. Made me feel sick.

The bomber's room was easy to spot. Two plainclothes police officers were posted outside the door.

"Violent Crimes," I said, and showed them my badge.

They let me and the doctor in without a word. As usual my SÄK colleagues didn't deign to say hi or even nod when greeted. Always with the damn hierarchy. I was going to interview their suspect for them, then I was out.

In the doorway, I turned to the doctor.

"I'm going in alone. I don't want him affected by other people before or during the interview."

Dr. Nair stopped.

"I'm responsible for his health as long as he's —"

"I'm sorry," I told him. "Police protocol doesn't permit you to be present during the interview."

One of my colleagues from SÄK moved a step closer to us. Crossed his arms, gave Dr. Nair a level look, and nodded out toward the hallway. When Dr. Nair realized there was no arguing, he shook his head, turned around, and walked off.

Without knowing what to expect, I slowly opened the door and entered.

FIVE

The hospital bed was hovering a foot above the floor. Fred Sjöström had been floating around in a kind of dreamlike, hallucinogenic state for days. Maybe weeks? He didn't know. He had vague memories of being transported through corridors. White tunnels that never seemed to end. Bright ceilings rolling by high above him. Spinning every time they turned a corner. Bare walls. Diffuse shadows cast by people in white coats that floated past.

Then the pain. During his years abroad, he had endured enormous physical pain. Wandered through scorching deserts, slept outside in subzero temperatures in cold, damp clothes. Lived with open wounds that wouldn't heal, even been shot. Unspeakable pain. And still that was nothing compared to what he was going through now. The pain that had washed over him when he woke up felt like electric shocks pulsing through his body. His legs were the worst. Last night, he had woken up and screamed until a nurse came in and gave him even more morphine.

He looked down at his body. He had seen torn-off limbs and truly gruesome wounds as a soldier, but what was hidden under his own covers knocked the air out of him. Everything was gone. His feet. Ankles. Calves. Knees. They had clamped two big white tubes onto his upper thighs. They looked very strange. Like two shapeless lumps of plaster. So heavy he couldn't move them so much as an inch. And then the pain. How could nature have set things up this way? What was the point of feeling pain in body parts that were no longer there?

At the moment, the morphine had him numbed. His sinewy arms lay like heavy logs along his sides. He could turn his head a bit, but lifting it off the pillow was impossible.

A lot of people had been in and out of his room. White coats wandering in and out. Doctors with concerned looks on their faces. A few men in dark clothes had been by as well. At first, he hadn't understood who they were. They had demanded information. Asked questions about who he was and what his affiliation was.

A counselor had been there, too. Her voice was calm. Pleasant. Almost dreamy. Her words had been comforting. She had talked about his condition. And his illness. The diagnosis he didn't want to talk about.

He had known for a long time that something was wrong. He had lost weight and had a hard time eating. His usually strong, robust body had come up short for the first time ever. After collapsing at work, he had been taken to the hospital in an ambulance. That was when he was told. Pancreatic cancer. Stage three. Surgically removing parts of the gland was pointless since the cancer had been discovered too late and had already spread.

Fred had received the news in silence. Just stared vacantly into space. The doctor had repeated the diagnosis. Told him he was going to explain it several times, as many as Fred needed to grasp the implications of his disease. Fred had grasped it the first time, but hadn't been able to think of anything to say. In the end, he had calmly held his hand up and nodded to the doctor to show that he had understood. Then he had left the hospital.

He had made up his mind that day. Known what he had to do to give his life meaning, despite everything that had happened.

He wasn't going to let the illness kill him; he was going out on his own terms. With a message. He had nothing left to lose.

Talking to the counselor about his disease was pointless, but he liked her presence. He had heard a nurse tell the others that his blood pressure was lower after the counselor's visits. That his breathing was more regular. Her calm voice had given him a feeling of harmony that he couldn't remember ever having before.

He thought his war years had prepared him. He and his comrades had laid down their bodies, their lives, for what they believed in. Or to get away from their previous lives. They had all had their own reasons for joining up. Some had done it for a higher power, or to feel alive. Because even though he knew he might not survive the war, he had felt strong. Immortal.

Living close to death made you feel more alive.

He had been ready to die. But that was then and there. What he was going through now, no one could ever be ready for.

The only thing that made him feel better was that he didn't have long to go. Soon, everything would be over.

The room to his door had opened. The hinges squeaked. The sound hurt his ears. Metal against metal. Lifting his hands up to cover his ears was impossible. Just opening his eyes was an effort. He raised his eyebrows as a first step, in the hopes of making the next step easier. His eyelids covered his eyeballs like two-ton blast barriers. He gave up. Let them stay closed. Focused on his breathing instead. His lungs. Oxygenizing his blood. That was important. Slowly. In. Out.

They had removed the respirator. Ever since, his throat felt scratchy and dry like sandpaper. He tried to clear it. In his weakened state, it turned out to be impossible.

Just like the night before the explosion, he felt separated from his body. As though he were someone else. Someone standing next to himself, observing. Noting his suffering. His desperation. His disappointment at still being here. Being conscious. And yet, sometimes he was unsure if he really was.

The footsteps walking over from the door were light and unlike the other ones that had moved through his room, these feet wore high heels. They fell silent at the foot of his bed.

"Fred Sjöström. My name is Leona Lindberg."

From somewhere, he found the strength to push his eyelids up. He studied the woman in front of him. Once he managed to focus, he saw a pair of weary eyes looking back at him.

"I'm a detective with the Violent Crimes Division. I've been ordered to come here to interview you."

So this is what she looked like. Leona Lindberg. He didn't know what he had expected, but it wasn't quite this. Half her face was illuminated by the light from the window, which made the other cheek look ghostly pale. Her dark, unkempt hair seemed to have a mind of its own. He mused that the combination of such dark hair and pale skin was unusual. She was young, probably around thirty, but still looked haggard somehow.

He'd been unable to speak, had only barely had the strength to hold a pen, to scribble a few words on a piece of paper for the men from the Security Service. "Will only speak to Leona Lindberg," his note had read. He had been unsure whether her surname was Lindberg or Lindblom, but now she had confirmed that he had got it right.

"I have no interest in dragging this out and hate hospitals to boot, so you'll be doing us both a favor if you continue to refuse to talk. Then we don't have to waste each other's time."

He continued to study her. Her eyes were darting around the room. Seemed to be taking in the tubes, racks, and machines around him.

"I have a duty to inform you that you are still charged with committing a terrorist act of causing devastation endangering the public outside the east wing of Parliament on 30 May at 1:55 p.m. You have a right to legal representation during both the investigation and at any subsequent trial. Do you have a lawyer in mind?"

She paused, waiting for a reply. He made an attempt to speak to her. Tensed his stomach and his lungs, but the only thing he managed to get out was a noise that sounded more like a faint clearing of the throat than a word.

"If you don't want to communicate with me, that is, as mentioned, perfectly fine by me," she continued, and picked up the purse she had placed on the floor by the bed.

He made another attempt at speaking.

"I am in fact obligated to inform you that you have the right to remain silent during this interview, if you so wish."

He did his best. Dug in deep. No sound at all this time. A wave of darkness and anxiety washed over him. He was unable to move. To speak. He wanted to scream but couldn't summon the strength. He was trapped inside his own body.

She slung her purse strap over her shoulder and started walking toward the door. He gave it everything he had.

"You…"

His voice disappeared. But she had heard him. Turned around. Looked at him with a frown. Walked over and leaned in closer. He didn't try again until her face was mere inches away. On his next exhalation. He breathed in.

"It's…you…"

New breath. One more. He braced himself again.

"…est sacrée."

She stopped and studied him before turning around once more and leaving the room.

SIX

"I want to speak to Fred Sjöström's doctor, Dr. Nair," I told a nurse while rubbing one of my temples.

My head was throbbing. I rummaged through my purse for painkillers.

"He just left for the day. But you can probably catch him if you—there he is!"

She pointed out into the corridor in the direction of the elevators. On the other side of the glass door, I spotted a man's back. I set off at a brisk pace. If the nurse hadn't pointed him out, I would never have recognized him from behind. Seeing doctors in their normal clothes was always weird. It was like they lost their identity. I ran to catch up with him.

"Dr. Nair!"

He looked up at me just as the elevator doors opened. I stepped in after him.

"I need more information about Fred Sjöström's condition."

"I'm on my way home. Can it wait until tomorrow?" he said and pushed the button.

The doors closed. I went to stand at the opposite end of the elevator.

"He seems confused, could it be that he doesn't remember what happened? I mean, is that possible?"

"Long periods of unconsciousness are almost always accompanied by memory loss. How far back and for how long varies from patient to patient. Some remember everything except the accident, others have trouble remembering several weeks before. Memory loss extending as far as years is unusual."

The elevator descended slowly.

"I would recommend waiting at least a week before asking detailed questions, if you want him to be able to give useful answers," he said.

"A week?!" I said and laughed. "The Security Service is going to be real pleased."

As usual, health care professionals lived in their own bubble. Dr. Nair seemed completely unperturbed by the pressure the world was exerting in order to extract information from this man. I had no objection to the interviews being postponed, it gave me more time to see to my own plans, but I would be surprised if Alexandra consented to wait a whole week to talk to him again. That said, it was worth a shot.

"Fred has a lot of things to work through," Dr. Nair continued. "It's going to take time to accept and come to terms with the loss of both his legs, and if he has other traumas in his past, chances are he is dealing with repressed memories. Waking up after an attempted suicide often comes with a sense of disappointment that is difficult for an outsider to understand. Waking up in the hospital is further confirmation of their view of themselves as worthless, incapable of accomplishing anything, even ending their own lives."

The elevator emitted a scraping noise that made me look up at the display that showed which floor we were on.

"He reacts very strongly to needles as well. Keeps ripping out his cannulas. He's been giving the nursing staff a hard time."

The doors opened. I exited with Dr. Nair. Felt my phone buzz in my pocket. Pulled it out and checked the screen. A text.

"It must be hard for him," I offered.

A pretty banal insight given everything that had happened and what Dr. Nair had just told me. Even so, he gave me a surprised look. As though I were the only police officer who had ever listened to him.

"Nice to hear one of you people have some kind of understanding of the medical context. His situation is exceptional and his recovery is not aided by police officers pestering him with detailed questions."

Delay means consequences, the text read.

It was from Armand. I had tried to delay paying him the money I owed. If I hadn't been saddled with this mess of a case, I would have had more time to raise money through my planned scheme. Money I could have used to keep Armand at bay. I wouldn't have been able to give him the full amount up front, but paying in installments was better than not paying at all. Now he was trying to threaten me.

"Even if he speaks a word here and there, his physical condition is still very serious, and there is a significant risk of infection," Dr. Nair continued. "Psychologically, he needs to process his situation, accept that he's alive, understand what it means to live without the legs he lost and be given help to work through the whole series of events."

"I understand," I said, nodding to show my concern.

Normally, I would have interrogated the man for hours, until he didn't have it in him to withhold the truth any longer. Not completely by the book, since exhausting an interviewee wasn't allowed, but the rules weren't always completely clear and sometimes it was necessary in order to get salient information as early as possible. If you just made sure the suspect was fed and allowed a decent amount of sleep, you were usually okay. But in this case, I had good reason to listen to Dr. Nair.

"I assume a smoother healing process means more information for us at the end of the day?" I said. "I'm not going to have an easy time explaining that to my boss and the Security Service, but if you stand by your opinion that he shouldn't be interviewed until next week, I will let them know that we have to wait to question him until he's more stable."

Dr. Nair looked at me in surprise.

"It's important we work together here," I continued. "He barely talks and we don't know how much he remembers, so there are going to have to be a lot of interviews before we're done. Which means it's important for you and me to get along. There's been enough conflict between the police and health care professionals about these things. I don't want to work like that."

I held out my hand to him. He seemed almost shocked as he slowly took it.

As soon as we had parted ways, I called Alexandra. Now I could tell her the truth and didn't have to concoct a story about him saying a few words but leaving out the most important part, as suspects so often do. They go on and on about all kinds of irrelevant trivialities, but once it comes to the part about accountability, about the crime they have committed, most of the details are almost always left out. My second idea was to tell her he didn't remember. It wasn't unusual for suspects to claim to have a poor memory or strange memory lapses. Such claims were extremely tedious to an interviewer. Especially when the suspect could remember countless details about the time right before the crime was committed, and just as many from the time right after, but the exact moment when they stuck a knife into some stranger's guts, for example, they often inexplicably forget. But in this case, it wasn't needed. A doctor had deemed it necessary to postpone further interviews. Not a formal verdict, true, but still a recommendation based on a medical assessment. With luck, that would be enough.

SEVEN

"Leona Lindberg, could you tell us what the suicide bomber is saying in interviews?"

A reporter shoved a microphone with the biggest windshield I had ever seen in my face as soon as I stepped out the hospital door.

"Has he told you his motives?"

I shook my head and walked briskly toward the parking lot. The woman followed.

"Is he a member of ISIS, al-Qaeda, or some other terrorist organization? Should the public be concerned there might be more people like him in the city?"

The questions kept coming. I walked on without a word, hoping she would give up. Before I had reached my car, a second reporter had caught up.

"Can you tell us anything about what the explosives belt looked like?" he asked.

I realized SÄK must have registered me as the lead interviewer for this case since the journalists had caught wind of my involvement. I avoided them. Didn't answer phone calls from withheld numbers or numbers I didn't recognize. One word from me would energize them enough to ask fifteen more questions.

Without responding, I got in my car, reversed out of the parking space, and drove back to headquarters.

When I stopped at a red light, the tabloid headlines outside a 7-Eleven caught my eye. The evening papers were determined to squeeze every last drop out of the incident with their oversized black block print.

YOUR NEIGHBOR COULD BE MAKING A BOMB, they warned.

I snorted derisively. Tabloid journalism was despicable. I had to stay far away from that madhouse. The interview had been short, just as I had hoped. Given that, I hoped the suicide bomber with the severed legs would now be a closed chapter as far as I was concerned. I had completed my task. Whatever he had tried to tell me, I wasn't going to mention it to Alexandra. A mix of Swedish and French words. I couldn't help but ponder what they meant. *Sacrée*, I looked up a translation on my phone while giving way to an elderly man at a pedestrian crossing. "Holy," it meant. Not much of a clue for me. Committing a crime like his required a great deal of conviction, but that was hardly reason enough to assume some kind of terrorist cell was really behind it all. What puzzled me more was that he had said, "It's you." What had he meant by that? He may have just been high on painkillers, but the way he said those words, and his eyes, they had wanted something. Even though he was barely able to keep his eyes open, I thought I had seen something in them. I just couldn't quite put my finger on what.

I called Alexandra as I set off again.

"I didn't expect to hear from you so soon," she said on the other end.

Her voice was deep and monotonous as usual. She never raised her voice, but I had no problem picking up on her displeasure.

"It's unlikely this guy is part of a terrorist network," I said.

I couldn't be sure, but I had a strong feeling I was right. Besides, I had a better chance of getting out of conducting the interviews if I refuted the suspicion that the attack was part of a larger plot.

"What makes you think that?" she said.

I glanced in the rearview mirror. A dark car that had been following me for a while made the same turn as me, again. I squinted but at this distance I could only see the dark outline of the driver.

"Trust me. My judgment is rarely off," I replied.

"I know you're an accomplished detective, Leona. The fact that SÄK requested you specifically shows that a lot of people trust your judgment. But do you mean to tell me that I should explain to SÄK, who in turn should explain to various foreign intelligence agencies and Interpol, that we don't need to worry about this being the act of a terrorist organization, based on nothing but your gut feeling?"

A skilled detective always knows how to pose a question in a way to make people feel uncertain. But I was secure in my assessment.

"I do."

I said the words with greater conviction than in church when I married Peter.

"The suicide bomber is likely nothing more than a psychologically unstable, lonely man," I said. "Besides, he refuses to talk."

"Not a word?" Alexandra asked.

"Not really, no."

I instantly regretted saying it. Why did I have to slip up like that? I prayed Alexandra wouldn't pounce on my tiny equivocation.

"What's that supposed to mean, Leona?" she immediately retorted. "Surely he either said something or he didn't? If he didn't speak you can hardly have any inkling as to whether he is part of a terrorist network or not. I take 'Not really, no' to mean that he did in fact speak and that you therefore will have the pleasure of working overtime."

"I got him to say a few incoherent words, that's all," I told Alexandra.

"And? What did he say? Who does he work for? Are they planning more attacks? *What?*" Her tone was still calm, articulating some words very clearly.

"Alexandra, he's not a terrorist in the normal sense of the word. This is something else. But he's confused. His doctor tells me he needs to rest, that we won't get anything out of him for another week on account of his physical and psychological injuries."

She laughed on the other end. "A week! Yeah, right."

"It's too much for him right now," I said. "You don't understand the state he's in, Alexandra. He's only awake for brief periods and can barely open his eyes even when he is. Don't you trust the doctor's expertise?"

"Since when do we trust doctors? If it were up to them, no suspect with even the tiniest injury would ever be interviewed. We have solved a lot of serious crimes by not listening to doctors. Like Fredrik's case with the little boy who had witnessed his father stab his mother to death. We interviewed him just hours after the event. It's what secured the father's conviction. And that boy was five. What's the matter with you, Leona?"

"I actually believe the doctor is right in this case," I replied. "We should wait. The guy's completely out of it. Dr. Nair says his medical condition means we can't expect any answers from him yet."

That wasn't exactly what Dr. Nair had told me, but I filled in the gaps as needed. I turned onto Hälsingegatan, pulled into a parking space, and looked back. The dark car was still behind me; it slowed down farther up the street. Stopped.

"Who does he want representing him?" Alexandra asked.

"I don't know. He didn't say anything," I replied, and turned my head to try to make out the license plate number of the car.

"He can have one day. You'll be going back in for another interview on Wednesday; let the doctor know," Alexandra continued. "Make sure you question him properly. I'll let SÄK know you're on it, but that so far, nothing points to a terrorist organization being involved. I sincerely hope you're right."

As usual, Alexandra hung up without saying goodbye. I sighed and spat out a few choice curses while staring at my rearview mirror. The car reversed back to the intersection and turned right. With a few quick motions, I backed out, turned around and drove after it. When I reached the intersection, there was no sign of the car.

EIGHT

A faint, unfamiliar smell greeted me as I unlocked and opened the door to my home. It was already half past ten at night. It had taken me a good long while to tidy up my ongoing investigations so I could hand them over to Alexandra, but now the case files had been cleared of random notes and Post-its. To aid whoever was taking over from me, I had added a clear description of what was left to do in each investigation. There was nothing more annoying than being handed a messy, poorly documented investigation.

I had planned on eating a simple tomato soup and then hitting the hay. Was hoping to be able to get to sleep at a decent hour. But the smell in the hallway made me stop dead and look around.

The coats and jackets hanging underneath the hat rack were all in order. The shoes on the floor. The chair with a few items of clothing thrown over it in the corner. Everything looked the same as when I had left in the morning. And yet something was off. I put the bag of groceries down on the floor. When the front door quietly closed behind me, the room went dark. Instead of turning on the hallway light, I carefully felt my way along the wall under the hat rack. Groped around for the baseball bat I kept in the corner. My hand closed around the handle and slowly pulled it up from behind the shoe rack. I grabbed it with both hands and slowly walked toward the kitchen. I opened my eyes wide to help them adjust to the dark quicker. The kitchen was quiet. The closed blinds stopped almost all light from outside from seeping

in. When I was sure no one was in there, I walked back to the hallway on my way to the living room.

"Don't even think about it, Leona."

I flinched. The shadow of a strange man loomed up in front
of me in my living room. The warm streetlights outside shone in
through the window, framing his dark bulk with a golden con-
tour. His face and the middle part of his body were impossible to
make out, but my eyes quickly slipped down to his knees, where
the light fell across him. One hand was motionless on the armrest. In the other he held a gunlike object. Pointed straight at me.

I could feel my heart racing. I stared at him. Who the fuck
was this? I still couldn't see him in the dark. I was overcome by
a sense of unreality. I was an officer of the law and even though
I had been at the wrong end of a gun on several occasions, it
had never been like this. Never in my own home. He had clearly
let himself in with a key. The door had shown no signs of being
forced. I slowly lowered the baseball bat onto the floor, keeping my other hand in the air all the while. When the tip of the
bat touched the floor, I let it drop. The sound of wood clattering
against the hardwood floor echoed in my ears. I slowly straightened back up, now with both hands raised in front of me where
he could see them.

He nodded for me to move farther into the room. I took a few
steps in from the doorway, hugging the wall.

"Sit down!" he said.

His voice was steady. He was clearly not a madman about to
start shooting indiscriminately. That did little to calm me down,
though, since from that distance he would have no trouble plug-
ging me.

Without taking my eyes off him, I sidled toward the armchair
on the other side of the coffee table. He kept his gun pointed at

me by turning his own chair as I walked. As the chair gradually angled toward the window, the light revealed more of his face. I concluded I had never seen this man before. It didn't appear to be a perp who had decided it was my fault he had ended up behind bars and come to exact his revenge. He looked remarkably polished for a person who broke into other people's homes. He wore a black sport coat, necktie, and white shirt. I noted a thin black mustache and glasses.

I slowly bent my legs and sat down in the armchair. Still with my hands in front of me, palms out.

"What...do you want from me?"

I would have preferred to speak in a firmer, maybe even cocky tone, but my voice quavered. Few people know what it feels like to have a gun pointed at you. In your own home. The terror of realizing your life is in a stranger's hands makes it difficult to function rationally.

"Armand is tired of you not paying," he said.

So Armand had sent him. I should have known. He shared Armand's strict sense of style.

"You will start paying. He will let you know how much and where to deliver the money."

He stood up. Stuck his gun inside the waistband of his suit trousers and started walking toward the hallway. As he reached the door, he stopped. Pulled a note out of his breast pocket and placed it on one of the shelves of the bookcase.

"Consider this a payment reminder, Leona."

Without saying another word, he walked out into the hallway. Opened the front door and stepped out. A few seconds later, I heard a key turn the lock from outside.

I stayed where I was with my jacket still on. As though I were stuck in the armchair. My heart refused to slow down. I knew he had used the key to demonstrate his power. To signal that he could come back anytime.

I forced myself over to the bookcase in the dark. It wasn't a piece of paper he had left there, it was a photograph. For some reason, I didn't want to turn on the ceiling light but, rather, preferred to walk over to the nearest window to look at it. I angled it toward the light. The picture was grainy. Looked like it had been zoomed in from a considerable distance. Outdoors, by a gate. In order to see more clearly, I held it up closer. Squinted and focused on a person in the middle of the picture. What I saw paralyzed me.

I stopped breathing.

Dropped the photograph as though it had burnt my fingers.

My daughter, Beatrice.

NINE

I immediately walked over to the window in Aimi Nordlund's office at Subrunnsgatan 32 in Stockholm. Looked down at the street. Both directions. Tried to do a thorough inventory of the cars outside.

"Would you like to sit down so we can start?" Aimi said in her usual placid tone.

It was afternoon, but even though it was getting close to rush hour, the street was quiet. A car parked directly below the window had a flat tire. On another one leaves and bird droppings on the roof showed it hadn't been moved in a while, either. The other cars seemed recently parked, but as far as I could tell, there was no one sitting in any of them.

"Leona!?" she urged.

"Oh...I'd rather stand," I replied curtly.

Aimi had recommended I start coming more regularly. Felt I needed it. I wasn't planning on staying the whole hour this time, though. Didn't have the peace of mind to sit around and chat. Just wanted her to prescribe something to help me sleep at night.

I knew she tried to be discreet about it, but it was always obvious when she thought my reactions provided clues to my inner workings. Whenever that happened, she immediately looked down and wrote a few words in the notebook lying open on her lap.

"Would you like to tell me why you don't want to sit down?" she continued. "Are you looking for something out there?"

I heaved a sigh. To keep these precious minutes from simply being about why I preferred to stand, I walked over to the armchair and sat down so quickly it tipped backward slightly. There was a small thud when the front legs landed on the floor again.

"There!" I said in a stressed voice and drummed my fingers on the armrests.

I inspected my nails. Chewed down to the quick. I had even started in on the cuticles and the skin of my fingertips. Not out of nervousness but rather something akin to restlessness. Madeleine, the nail technician I used to go to, would have shuddered to see my hands now.

Aimi looked back down at her notebook. What did she write in there?

My phone buzzed in my pocket.

"I'm sorry," I said. "I have to take this."

"Hans Nilsson from SÄK," the man on the other end said. "You've interviewed the suicide bomber. Can you give me the headlines?"

Fuck, were they going to start calling me directly now?

"Hasn't Alexandra been in touch with you?" I said.

She was supposed to liaise with SÄK.

"Either way, he didn't say anything during the interview," I continued.

"Another interview then," he said. "We need to establish whether the suspect has connections with—"

"Look, this is kind of a bad time. Alexandra will update you on the situation."

When I hung up, Aimi was studying me.

"Turning our phones off might be a good idea."

I tried to ignore how much it annoyed me when she said "our," like I was a child. I turned off my phone.

"What's going on, Leona? I can tell something's different today. Would you like to talk about it?"

"I'm just a bit stressed," I said. "There's…a lot going on right now."

"A lot of what?" she asked in that quiet voice of hers.

I searched for the right words. At the same time, a thousand thoughts whirled through my mind. Armand's actions made it imperative for me to get my new plans underway as quickly as possible. In order to do so, I had to seek out some more suspects from old investigations of mine. I needed to find out more about them. Where they were, what they were doing. Explain that I had a proposition for them. I had already been in touch with a couple, but I needed more. My plans required eight, nine people.

Aimi looked at me inquiringly. I usually felt relaxed during our sessions, but not today. The calmer her voice, the more stressed I felt.

"Nothing, I've just been assigned a tough case. My bosses, journalists, and fucking everybody is all over me about it."

"Then maybe we should talk about that today?" Aimi said.

I shook my head. Really didn't want the case eating up all the time and money I invested in these sessions. Besides, confidentiality precluded my saying much about it.

She flipped back a few pages in her notebook.

"You mentioned before that you've stopped gambling," she said and looked up. "Can you tell me more about that?"

I knew what she was getting at. I shrugged.

"I just quit…don't feel like I get much out of it anymore."

We had spent a lot of time on what she called my "addiction." The effects poker had had on my life. On my family's economic stability. On my marriage with Peter. On my work. For my part,

I had always been convinced I could stop anytime I wanted. Aimi seemed to think otherwise. She claimed the first step was to admit to yourself that you had a problem. That it was part of the addict's nature to deny the addiction. To me, that seemed illogical, since in that case, everyone was an addict. If you said you weren't, you were simply living in denial, according to her. But if you just weren't addicted, then there was surely nothing to admit, to yourself or anyone else. Admitting to something you weren't guilty of was just plain stupid.

If Aimi was trying to hide her skeptical look, she was failing. Her lips stiffened and she squinted at me in response to my statement. She was jotting something down in her notebook when there was a loud bang. I jumped.

"What was that?" I said, halfway out of the armchair.

Aimi reached her hand out to reassure me.

"The door to the next building. The hinges are broken. It's the sound of the door closing."

When I heard languid footsteps coming up the stairs, I leaned back again.

"What did you feel you got out of gambling before that you no longer need?" Aimi pressed.

"A thrill, I guess," I replied. "Now I just want my life to be calm."

I had started playing online poker at night because my life was full of predictable routines. The gambling gave me excitement and a hope of a different life. I got a kick out of winning and carried on. Granted, I had lost a lot, but who didn't spend money on their hobbies? I knew colleagues who sunk hundreds of thousands of kronor into golfing equipment, golf trips, skiing equipment and trips to the Alps, and whatever else, but in those cases, no one raised an eyebrow or complained about how their interests were expensive. And they didn't even have a chance to win all their money back.

My gambling had had unpleasant consequences, I wasn't denying that, but if I had had the energy to carry on and more time to learn about the game, I would have won most of it back. After all, I had made a lot of money from time to time. The problem was I could no longer focus. My entire body refused. I was weakened in a way I had never experienced before.

"I'm so tired, Aimi. Worn out but still restless somehow. Can't sleep at night."

It wasn't just the poker; I no longer really felt like doing anything. I needed the strength to put the things that had happened behind me and move on.

I wished I could tell Aimi everything. She would probably never truly understand, but right now, at this moment, it would have been nice to be able to trust at least one person. To be able to talk about what was buzzing around my head like flies. That because of crimes I had committed, I was being threatened by a person I owed money, who would hurt my daughter if I didn't pay up. That poker was the least of my problems.

I had called Peter and Beatrice's preschool several times to make sure she was okay. Peter was probably going to have me committed if I carried on like that.

"I need to get my strength back, get back to being my old self again. Be able to be a functional mother to Beatrice again."

Aimi nodded.

"It takes time, Leona. Losing a child is the hardest thing a parent can go through."

I hadn't always been able to be that warm, stable parent the children needed, but my love for them had always been the only truly real thing in my life. Bea's childhood was better than mine.

That was important to me. She had a stable, considerate, caring father who loved her more than anything. The kind of father I had dreamt of as a child.

"And when Beatrice visits, how do you feel about that?"

Before I could answer, a loud ring echoed through the room. A doorbell. I instantly sprang to my feet. Whipped around and scanned the room for a way out if needed. There was no other door and even though the office was on the first floor, it was quite a drop down to the street.

"I'm sorry, Leona. It's probably just one of my other clients," Aimi said and got out of her armchair.

She walked into the hallway that led to the front door. I silently padded over to the doorway and listened. I lifted up my shirt and pulled out the service pistol I carried tucked in the back of my pants ever since Armand's collector had visited my apartment the day before. Aimi hadn't closed the door to the office, so I could hear what they were saying over by the front door. It was a woman who seemed very confused. Aimi was calmly trying to explain to her that she didn't have time to see her until tomorrow because she was with another client at the moment. The woman refused to accept this and said she could pay more so long as she could come in. I slipped my gun back into my waistband and was on my way back to my armchair when Aimi's closed notebook on the table caught my eye. I walked over to it. Listened to make sure she wasn't on her way back. When I heard them still talking at the other end of the hallway, I opened the notebook. At the top of each page was a name. The names of clients, I assumed.

I quickly turned the pages and glanced at the door. They were still talking out there. I kept flipping. Looking for my name. It was at the very back. At the top of a page. "Leona Lindberg" followed by some words that looked like they'd been scribbled down in a hurry. Diagonally across the lines.

I stared at the words.

There must be some mistake.

I looked again at the top of the page to see if I had got it wrong. If those words were actually about someone else. A client who was a lot more screwed up than me. Because I was there to process the grief I felt at my son's death. To get my life back on track after my divorce. To cure my insomnia and what Aimi referred to as my gambling addiction.

But there was no mistaking it. The name at the top of the page was mine. Underneath it, Aimi had written:

Delusions
Psychopathic tendencies
Antisocial personality disorder?

TEN

Not a single light was on in the apartment when David opened the door. Was Saga not home yet? The smell of home-cooked food puzzled him. He turned on the hallway light, put his backpack down on the floor and stepped out of his sneakers.

"Hello!" he called.

No answer. Without taking off his jacket, he walked through the hallway. When he got closer to the living room, he saw the candles. The table was set with plates, the fancy glasses Saga's grandmother had given her, and napkins.

"Happy our day, honey."

Saga emerged from the darkness. Fuck, he'd forgotten. She put her arms around his neck, pulled off his jacket and let it fall to the floor. Their lips met in a warm kiss and he put his arms around her, breathing in the smell of her hair. Closed his eyes. She was lovely. His comfort. She had been there for him during some of the toughest periods of his life. He often wondered what she saw in him.

Saga came from a rich family. Had grown up in the posh suburb of Täby. She had worked abroad as an au pair after high school and was now at college, majoring in social work. They had met several years ago at a party on Riddargatan, which David had ended up at mostly out of sheer happenstance. Saga was the kind of girl he'd never been able to bring himself to hit on. Wouldn't have thought he had a shot in hell. That was why he was surprised when she came over, wanting to talk. They had started dating and everything had been good until she realized just how different their backgrounds were. David had grown up in the projects in Skärholmen with a single mom and two siblings. His dad, who was from Ghana, had moved back there when David was little. After his mom died of cancer, David and his siblings had been placed in foster care in different cities and had lost touch.

"It's all right, honey. I've made dinner."

David studied Saga's table setting. Three red roses in a vase and rose petals scattered across the tablecloth. She was an excellent cook. Made up her own recipes that she shared with her friends. Luckily, his boxing kept her tasty cooking from showing on his body.

The ringing of his phone in his pocket made her let go of him. It was Sven. David declined the call. Saga looked at him questioningly.

"Just a friend," David said.

He wished he could tell her he worked for the police, but it was way too risky. He trusted her implicitly but knew there could be situations when she would want to tell just one of her friends, or that she might let something slip after a few drinks. If he got burnt, neither one of them would be able to stay in the country.

Saga was the kind of girlfriend every man wishes for. When she and David became an item, it raised his status among his friends. Back then, things like that had mattered. Now, the important thing was for him to prove to Saga that he could turn his life around. He wanted to prove it to her family, too.

The first and only dinner he had been invited to at her parents' had been stiff and awkward. Their disappointment in her choice of boyfriend had been palpable. Saga tried to claim it had nothing to do with David's skin color. Insisted they weren't racists, just generally conservative and suspicious of anything different. She didn't care what they thought, she loved him and that was all that mattered, she told him. David had not expected her to actually mean it. It hadn't been clear to him just how much she loved him until he was arrested. She had stood by him through the trial and during his prison sentence. Visited whenever they would let her, and when he came out, she had been waiting for him outside the prison walls. After that, he had started working for the police and got a part-time gig with the moving company. The work was good for his physique, but since they only gave him work when they needed extra help, there wasn't much money in it. He had stopped selling drugs, even though it was a lot more lucrative. Drugs were a highway to hell, he had seen plenty of examples of that among his old crew, so he was staying well away from that. He owed a number of people money from before and he would never be able to raise as much as he needed from working for the moving company. Using the money the cops gave him, he had been able to pay off some of his debts. That was something he opted not to share with Sven. Once he was debt-free, he wanted to quit the informer racket. Live a normal life. Maybe have kids with Saga. He had been with her longer than with any other girlfriend.

"How did the interview go today?" she asked, looking up at him.

He bent down to pick up his jacket.

"I think they were looking for someone different," he replied, and started walking toward the hallway.

David hadn't been to a job interview. He had been to see an annoying and demanding cop called Sven.

He hung his jacket up on a coat hanger in the hallway and went back into the kitchen. Saga opened a bottle of wine.

"You just have to keep trying. Sooner or later, you'll find the right place."

She poured two glasses of red wine and handed him one.

"Three years, honey. Here's to us!"

ELEVEN

A nurse was holding a glass of water with a straw up to Fred Sjöström's lips when I entered the room. He was clearly in better shape than the day before last, when he had been so doped up I'd been unsure he even knew I was there.

As usual, I hadn't slept much; I noticed the sandy feeling in my eyes was making me squint. I didn't like popping pills, but I wished I had something to calm my racing mind. Yesterday's therapy session with Aimi had not made things easier. I was doing everything in my power not to think about the words she had jotted down in her notebook.

A gurgling sound came from the straw as Fred sucked down the last of the water. The nurse pulled the glass away and left the room when she noticed me.

"At least you're drinking a little," I said, and put my purse down on the visitor's chair by the window. "I'd almost expected a full-on hunger strike as well. Since you seem to want to annihilate yourself."

If there had been anyone else in the room, I wouldn't have put it that way. Nor if I had actually wanted to get something useful out of this interview. But right now, I had everything to gain from him disliking me.

It might seem cynical, but I almost wished he hadn't failed to blow himself up. Not that I had anything against him as a person—I didn't know him—but because of what this case entailed for me. That I of all people was being forced to conduct these interviews, and in the hospital to boot. God knows I didn't like police stations and prisons, but I would have been more than happy to swap the hospital environment for the corridors of a detention facility or the cramped, windowless interview rooms of the Police Authority. But that was never going to happen. He was hardly going to be released anytime soon. My only option was to try to make him not want to talk to me. What little energy I had, I needed to carry out my own plans and create a better life for myself, far away from people like him, not waste it on complicated investigations that would suck the energy out of the most experienced detective.

"It seems you and I are stuck with each other for a while longer," I said as I removed my damp jacket.

He turned his sunken eyes toward me. His facial expression was dour, frowning, the corners of his mouth pointing straight down. His gray hair fanned out across his pillow like little half moons set at an angle. He wore a white, long-sleeved hospital gown. Over that, a yellow hospital blanket. And then there were his eyes. They were an almost unbelievably light gray.

I hung my jacket over the back of the chair and avoided looking at all the tubes and machines in the room.

"You were unconscious for a week. I figured I might clue you up on what happened while you were out."

I had brought some of the newspapers they had saved at work. The lead investigator had imposed full restrictions on Fred, which meant he wasn't allowed access to news of any kind, since that could compromise the investigation. I had chosen what to show him very carefully.

"'Man blows himself up outside Parliament,' writes the morning broadsheet *Dagens Nyheter*," I told him.

I placed the newspaper on the bed next to him so he could see the big black headline.

"'Terrorism finds foothold in Sweden—suicide bomber in central Stockholm,' wrote the evening tabloid *Aftonbladet*. They obviously have a flair for the dramatic," I continued.

Fred glanced at the papers impassively.

"*Expressen* kept it succinct with 'Suicide bomber outside Parliament,'" I continued. "But you also made the headlines far beyond Sweden's borders, in case you're interested. The foreign media have painted Sweden as a haven for political extremists. And all of it is thanks to you."

He didn't say a word.

"As I'm sure you can understand, there was a lot of fuss in the wake of your attack, which means everyone's demanding explanations. For example, people want to know which organization you're a member of."

He turned his head away from me. Was it really going to be this easy?

"Maybe you don't remember much?" I said.

I wouldn't actually buy total amnesia. It's only in the movies people wake up not knowing who they are. But in this situation, it could work out well. People would be annoyed, but no one could reproach him for having trouble remembering things after an explosion like that one.

He made no reply. Screaming outside made me look out the window. A little boy was running around down below, chasing a dog with a stick in its mouth. So carefree. Happy.

"I wonder what the real difference is between the silent game and the angry game?" I said and sat down in the visitor's chair with my back against one armrest and my legs over the other. "Like you're not silent when you play the angry game too, am I right?"

He remained expressionless.

I reached for an out-of-date glossy magazine sitting on the windowsill. Giving him access to old gossip rags wasn't going to undermine the investigation. American actors Brad Pitt and Angelina Jolie were on the cover, with a picture that looked like it must've been taken years ago. Around Angelina's left hand was a big red circle with a line drawn to a second circle with a zoomed-in shot of her ring finger.

"Did you see that Brangelina filed for divorce? Were they even married?" I asked him and pondered how old the magazine must be.

No reaction. The suicide bomber was probably as indifferent to gossip and the private lives of celebrities as I was. I checked my watch, wondering whether I could claim to have wheedled him for long enough.

"Seriously, Fred Sjöström, if you don't want to talk, there's not much else I can do."

I looked at him inquiringly. If he didn't respond now I could tell Alexandra the man was refusing to talk, without lying. I pulled on my jacket and gathered up the newspapers. Put them in my purse and was just about to leave when I remembered something. I turned to him.

"What was it you told me when I was leaving last time?"

He slowly turned his head to face me. Looked at me with his light eyes and said in a deep, gravelly voice: "I will tell you…everything…And you will listen."

TWELVE

Leona had left the room with a look on her face Fred Sjöström found hard to interpret. What he had managed to get out was more words than he had been able to string together since waking up.

She was a letdown, Leona Lindberg. Her attitude. He was starting to think she was just like all the other fucking pigs. But Ronni had assured him she was all right, the only one worth trusting. He had said that if Fred was ever in a tough spot, or needed a cop for some reason, he should contact Leona Lindberg from Violent Crimes.

Ronni Åberg was a Finnish-Swedish veteran jailbird Fred had got to know on one of the Finland cruise ferries he'd worked on. Ronni lived in Sweden for the most part but had an ex-wife, daughters, and various relatives in Finland. He often took the boat across the Baltic. Ronni was considerably younger than Fred. They didn't really have much in common, but he was a good guy and okay drinking company and that was enough.

Ronni had been very secretive about how he actually knew Leona. Had just said they'd had dealings with each other. If Fred ever contacted Leona, he wasn't allowed to mention Ronni, he'd said.

Ronni rarely spoke well of people, especially not cops, whom he hated as much as Fred did. Which is why Fred had been surprised when Ronni had started talking about some lady cop he claimed was all right. He had also said Leona was respected in law enforcement circles and often handled cases that were in the public eye. When Fred woke up in the hospital, he had thought to himself that she was the right person. A cop other cops would listen to. Who could make the media listen. He had no choice but to trust Ronni. He needed her and refused to talk to the other pigs.

Through Leona, he would make people understand. This was just the beginning. They'd see.

He was going to tell her everything.

Fred slowly turned his head to the window. Looked out at the sky. It looked bluer from inside than he remembered it being outside. The last time he'd seen it this crystal clear had been outside the Parliament building. He would remember that sky forever. He would never see it from outside again, he knew that. His days were numbered. Feeling the wind against his skin, squinting at the sun, having rain trickle down his face, those were all things he would never do again.

There he was, riddled with cancer, with two legs blown off and full of shrapnel. In pain so severe it was unbearable from time to time. Morphine made him feel even worse.

He had nothing left to lose.

He instinctively put his hand to his throat. Fumbled around for his necklace and instantly recalled it was no longer there. It had been his first thought on waking up.

My necklace.

The pendant that had been with him ever since that day. Hung there like a reminder of what had happened. He had not been without it for even a second all these years. He had gone through a lot to keep it. Fought for it. Even been forced to swallow it once. No matter how bad his life had been, he had been able to hold that pendant in his hand, close his eyes, and find his strength. It was as though it radiated mental energy that gave him the will to keep going, for her.

Without the necklace, he was empty inside.

THIRTEEN

"Planning," I said. "Most criminals are bad at planning the crimes they intend to commit. They can't estimate how many people they're going to need, what equipment's required, what the escape routes should look like, and how to handle the stolen goods afterward."

I looked out across the audience before me. With all the lectures I'd given in recent years, I was an experienced speaker. I had given talks to colleagues up and down the country. To veteran detectives, officers in training at the Police Academy, and beat cops. Mainly on the subjects of interview technique and investigatory methodology but also on police tactics and other things. Interest levels and involvement tended to vary. Sometimes, it was abundantly clear it wasn't the police officers themselves who craved to improve themselves, but their department heads who felt the skill level among their staff had to be raised. In those cases, I was met with skeptical looks from many of my colleagues. Primarily my male colleagues. It didn't sit right with some that a female detective from inner-city Stockholm had come to tell them how to do their jobs. They had years of experience and knew how to get things done.

I had popped two painkillers on my way to this lecture, but a headache still throbbed at my left temple, radiating out toward my forehead. I was on edge. Couldn't stand still. Paced back and forth while I talked. Shot a quick glance behind the white, semi-sheer sheet that covered the window. Nothing unusual out there.

I moved away. Tried to stay calm and collected. Cleared my throat and spoke up to show through my voice and body language that I knew what I was talking about.

"Which of course the police exploit," I continued.

I looked at my watch. I had been at it for twenty minutes. They may have been looking at me skeptically, but no one had started shifting or yawning. I was a bit surprised by that. These were not the kind of people who would normally just sit still and listen. They were doers and preferred to be out in the field.

I took a sip from the glass of water I had placed on the table behind me.

"If we were being completely honest, we detectives would have to admit that fairly often, our solving a case has less to do with our skills and more with the mistakes criminals make. In other words, you could say the police should be grateful criminals aren't better at what they do."

A clock mounted on the wall at the other end of the room, next to one of the windows, caught my eye. It was stuck. The red second hand was twitching in place.

"And as far as the psychological part is concerned, there are a lot of tough, macho perps out there who have no idea how they'll react in really tight spots. If things go sideways, which is usually the result of bad planning, they get stressed out and act without thinking, which is a recipe for disaster. It's in those situations thugs sometimes turn their guns on us. And I don't need to tell you that those situations can have really bad outcomes. Lethal."

"So what are you saying we should do?" a man in the front row asked.

I was glad he had asked that particular question, because this was the most crucial point.

"Make sure that we, the police, never even come to the scene of the crime. Without us there, you can work in peace. It's a simple equation."

Lecturing to my fellow police officers was something I had done to death by now. They were actually fairly boring people. Rarely offered any kind of perspective on life other than rigidly black-and-white worldviews. To give a talk to criminals, as I was doing now, was something else entirely.

Instead of a swanky, taxpayer-financed conference room, this workshop was held in a cold, grimy abattoir in the Meatpacking District near the Globe Arena in Stockholm, but it would have to do.

I knew what I was doing.

My business plan was to charge money for teaching people how to commit crimes without getting busted, and without hurting anyone.

My target audience: midlevel criminals.

You couldn't just pick any old thugs for this kind of venture. The men sitting in front of me had been carefully selected. I had gone through the people I knew from my own or my colleagues' old investigations, meticulously mapping out their criminal activity, childhood experiences, and family relations.

I had homed in on midlevel criminals for several reasons. They were the easiest to deal with. The most hardened criminals had already invested in their own criminal personas, with MOs and lifestyles that I would have a hard time influencing. More often than not, they also surrounded themselves with other hardened criminals. Blundering into the strict hierarchies of a criminal organization was more trouble than it was worth. Besides, those guys already felt that they knew all there was to know about the world, that they didn't need the kind of knowledge I offered. I avoided the lowest, least sophisticated class of petty criminals as well, since they mostly shot their mouths off and caused general trouble. It was the midlevel guys I had gathered here. A bunch of young, hungry men who had not been in the game long enough to turn mean and bitter, but who still retained a somewhat positive drive, and who, just like me, dreamed of a better life.

The sticky situation I found myself in had forced me to think of new ways to make money. Even though I occasionally did well at poker, the risks associated with gambling were too big.

My skills and experience as a detective were the ace up my sleeve.

My weapon.

I was going to make use of it. Before, it had mostly been about escaping my phony, mediocre existence. Now it was more than that.

I was under threat.

As was my only daughter.

I was going to use any means necessary to protect my child and continue my journey toward finally being free.

To criminals, I was a repository of valuable information. Facts that no one other than a police officer could provide. The authorities that attempted to discipline them, reform them, and make them upstanding family men with summerhouses in the archipelago and honest employment at a bank, had failed.

Not everyone was cut out for that kind of life.

Nor did everyone want it.

These guys were clear proof of that. At the same time, they were not short on zeal, strength, or determination, that much was obvious. They just didn't share society's notion of what a worthwhile goal in life was.

The state still had no good alternative to locking criminals up; some people probably still thought prison made them less recidivist. Figured that if the criminals were just made to sit and ponder their sins for long enough, they'd have a change of heart. But prison was nothing but counterproductive. In many cases, inmates were more likely to reoffend after a spell behind bars. Because how could it be otherwise? They had spent years in an environment where everyone defined them as criminals and the only people they interacted with were other criminals. Once they were released, they had nowhere to live, no job and no money. Instead, they faced debts with the Swedish Enforcement Agency, broken relationships with parents and children, former friends who had been replaced with drug addicts and criminals, and people they owed money. There were long gaps in their CVs which they had to explain when they looked for work. Getting a loan to buy a home was unthinkable, they couldn't even get a phone contract. These guys didn't go back to square one when they were released, they were in the red. To turn their lives around and become productive citizens was completely impossible. Many of them realized as much and quickly found other paths forward, outside of society. They often ended up in a destructive existence where they hurt the people around them both physically and psychologically. In their desperate attempts to get their hands on money, they committed ever more unplanned crimes, which in turn led to violence against innocent civilians, feuds with other criminals, trouble with the law, new arrests, criminal charges, and longer prison sentences. The guys sitting in front of me had all been in and out of jail in recent years.

I was going to show them a different path. Naturally, I had no way of knowing what they would think of my business model, but so far, they were listening attentively. It was important that what I told them held their interest and that they understood the potential applications. Guys like these often looked up to more advanced criminals. Now they were being given a chance to reach the next level of criminal sophistication themselves. Instead of studying for their MBAs so they could work in a bank, I could teach them how to rob a bank, without being arrested and sent down.

"In order to pull it off, you need knowledge. That's where I come in."

I would understand if they were surprised. When I had looked them up, one at a time, I hadn't told them what the meeting was about, just explained that they were going to have an opportunity to make serious money. That it wouldn't hurt them to come find out how. Like most people, and criminals in particular, they were curious about ways to make a quick killing.

"If you want to be involved in the kind of game that nets you the big bucks, millions at a time, you need capital. You need to buy services and equipment. For example, tools and a number of firearms, a couple of getaway vehicles, an insider, and someone to plan the job. This could normally run to upward of several hundred thousand kronor. But if you choose to participate in my business venture, everything you need will be provided, free of charge."

I had five guys so far; a few more were needed to make this profitable.

This was not a charity project.

If they wanted my knowledge, they were going to have to pay for it.

I needed money. Fast.

But they could count the cost of accessing my knowledge as an investment. It would pay for itself many times over, so long as they learned what I had to teach them. Just like me, they needed money and were to a significant extent driven by thrill chasing.

Living on the edge was like a drug.

Criminals and police officers did have a lot in common after all. On either side of a fine line.

"Those of you who've had run-ins with me on the street or in an interview room probably don't doubt that I know what I'm talking about."

I brandished my police badge. The chain I normally wore around my neck dangled down my arm. When they looked up at the emblem I couldn't help but be fascinated. These hardboiled criminals who normally showed a frightening lack of respect for the police were now still and attentive.

"I have years of experience as a detective and have seen most of the mistakes criminals make. From the most inept crimes to the smartest. I've also seen a lot of guys like you waste their lives. Both the ones from good backgrounds and the ones who never had a real chance."

I paused for a moment.

"I know where you're from. I know your lives have been tough. I want to see you get back on your feet. Get really good at what you're already doing. I'll teach you how to do it. I'll give you a unique chance to do what generates cash. Serious cash. And you know how soon it could be yours."

I grabbed hold of the chain and spun it around until the badge ended up in my hand.

"You also know how quickly you can end up in a cell if you don't know what you're doing. Everyone sitting here today has had one of these shoved in their face more than once."

I had planned to hang my badge around my neck, but I knew it was a red flag so I shoved it into the pocket of my jeans instead.

It had caught their attention, thus serving its purpose. They still looked slightly baffled and were glancing at one another as if to see how everyone else was reacting to what I was saying. Some of them knew each other and had done jobs together.

I walked over to the window again to make sure no unauthorized people were lurking in the area. Only Lasse, the landlord, knew I was there, and he obviously didn't know what kind of business I ran.

"Now listen up. Before we can really start getting into it, I want to make a few things clear. I didn't pick you just because I want to help you."

I turned around and opened my laptop on the table.

"I've looked up each and every one of you. Checked you out pretty thoroughly and found some stuff I know you don't want the police to find out about."

While they sat in silence, watching me, I browsed through my saved documents.

"Zack, Liam, and Marc! I've found a couple of unsolved crimes it turns out you were behind."

I looked up at them. They stared back at me.

"I know about the weapons heist from the army stores in Norrtälje, where a number of automatic rifles went missing just over a year ago. As you know, a lowly private was busted for stealing one of them; the other people involved were never identified. I happen to know that was you. And what's more, I can prove it too."

They exchanged looks. If I had been even slightly unsure about my claims, their reactions confirmed my assumptions. I moved on.

"Eli and Sam," I continued.

"All right, seriously, what the fuck is this?" Sam said and stood up.

"*Sit down!*" I said firmly and held my hand up. "There's no need to worry. Sure, these things have become known to the police, which is to say to me, and normally I'm obligated to report it, but I haven't...yet. Sit down and I'll explain."

Sam slowly sat back down. Crossed his arms.

"I know about the drug racket the two of you are running. You've already been busted for parts of it, but there was a big bust where the charges were dropped because a witness claimed not have seen anything. But I've talked to him and know what he saw. I could convince him to talk."

I smacked my laptop shut.

"But so far I haven't had a reason to pursue any of these things. The reason I took the trouble to find out is that I'm about to tell you things about myself that you will keep to yourselves, the way I keep the things I know about you to myself. Are we clear?"

It had taken some effort to gather info about all of them, but I had known it was there. These guys had obviously committed more crimes than they had been charged with, so for me it was all about going through unsolved cases and finding details my colleagues had missed.

It was time to give them some information about me.

"Remember the incidents that were all over the news last fall? When two banks and a currency exchange lost large sums of cash?"

No one spoke. I looked at Zack Stenborg, who was slumped in his chair. I had included him in my select group primarily because I knew he was good with explosives. He was black and had dark brown hair in short dreadlocks. A scar diagonally across the bridge of his nose, stubble, a slate gray, washed-out T-shirt with a rumpled shirt over it. Jeans and white sneakers. His tattered look was deliberate. When our eyes met, he said, "That little kid pulling bank jobs?"

"Exactly," I said. "A seven-year-old girl. You don't remember?"

Now several of them nodded.

"Wasn't it Smokey Ronni's daughter?" Zack said.

Ronni Åberg, the girl's father, had spent some time behind bars many years ago for helping a friend burn down his restaurant. An attempt at insurance fraud that ended with severe burns, debts, and a prison sentence. Ever since, other criminals called him Smokey Ronni.

I nodded.

"His daughter was seven at the time and executed the heists perfectly, according to my instructions. She did good."

They looked at me wide-eyed.

"But didn't some guy go down for that?" Zack said.

I nodded.

"A detective. But it was actually me behind the whole thing."

"Fuck me!" Liam said, staring at me.

In these circles, elegant crimes gave you status. Gave you respect. That I had let another cop take the fall was further proof I had stepped over to their side. Telling them this was a risk, but at this point, some risks were unavoidable.

Without risks I would never be able to change my life.

It was interesting, not to say amusing, to watch their faces when they realized that I, a detective, was a more serious criminal than they were. And more skilled. I sat down on the frontmost chair. Put on the sweater I had brought. The fluorescent light from the ceiling lamps on the dazzlingly white wall tile and the tools and aluminum workbenches did nothing to make the room feel warmer. It was not the kind of location I had imagined. I couldn't remember ever being in a slaughterhouse before walking in here today. It had looked like the lair of a serial killer, but I had cleaned it up. Thrown stuff out and moved tools aside and put chairs out in the middle of the room. The guys had looked around, slightly taken aback, when they first came in, but had all sat down without question.

"How much did you make?"

Zack seemed very interested. That was good. I considered telling them the total amount. Decided I might as well. Getting them to trust me and what I could do was my most important job right now.

"All in, about three and a half million euro. A few people were in for a cut."

There was no reason to tell them the rest. All they needed to know was that, aided by my knowledge, they were in a position to make big money.

"This is obviously no cooking course at the Learning Annex. You've been selected because you have something special."

There was a noise from outside. I walked over and peeked out the window from behind the plastic sheet again. Two taggers were standing by the building across the way, spray cans in hand. I resisted the impulse to storm out and catch them in the act. I pushed the plastic sheet back into place.

"If you follow my instructions, you won't get busted. You'll learn how to calculate risk, choose appropriate targets, plan and execute crimes in a professional manner."

The second hand on the clock refused to stop. It was distracting.

"But as ever when you're dealing with people, there's the risk that things go wrong. Which is why you will also be trained in what to do if by some incredibly unlucky break you still end up arrested. What to say in police interviews and what to do to be declared not guilty in a court of law."

They looked at me as if what I was saying was too good to be true. It wasn't. It was all about knowledge and logic. As police officers, we were often baffled by how unprepared criminals were. We often mused that if criminals could just be more on top of things, they'd be a lot more successful.

"But if you want to learn these things, there are rules to be followed."

There were a few important conditions I wanted to inform them of straightaway.

"How many of you sell drugs?"

Dead silence. I nodded toward my laptop on the table.

"There's no point trying to keep things from me. I'm just a click of a button away from getting all that info about you."

I'd already seen that they all either had drug convictions themselves or were linked to known dealers.

"How many of you take drugs?"

Still no reaction. I waited. Knew that most of them didn't think it was a big deal, especially if it was marijuana. It was considered perfectly normal. I shook my head.

"Quit!"

Zack rolled his eyes as though he'd heard it before, which they all certainly must have. Many times. From family members, friends, the police, social services.

"Quit," I said again with more emphasis. "Those of you who take drugs won't be able to do this. You may have gotten away with small-time crimes or possibly even pulled off something bigger under the influence, but the really big jobs, the ones that mean something, are beyond you if you're high. At least if you don't want to get caught.

They looked at me skeptically.

"I could spend the rest of the year lecturing about biology, the effect of various drugs on human organs, and how incredibly fucking bad your decision-making skills are when your body's full of those chemicals, but you'd probably get bored. Which is why all I'm going to tell you is this: if you want to be really high-end and successful in your criminal ventures, stay as far away as you fucking can from drugs of any kind. And that's true of all crime categories, okay?"

I was starting to come into my own.

"In the coming days, I'm going to select a few of you for a big hit. A carefully planned heist that will financially change your lives and entire future."

The plan was ready and I had already acquired the equipment that would be needed. But I wasn't about to share any details with them yet. And only the ones I selected would be told at all.

"But I don't work with junkies. No way am I standing there when the heat's on, when it's life or death, together with some-one who might lose his shit. Because that's exactly what usually happens to people with drugs in their systems. The only thing those people are capable of is violence. If you think otherwise, you've watched too many movies. No drugs if you want to make it big. It's up to you."

No one spoke. I pressed on:

"My number one requirement is another rule that you can't deviate from so much as a millimeter, if you want in."

I could clearly see some of them sighing, as though they were thinking to themselves that I was about to reveal the catch. The thing that made everything I had just told them impossible to do. That all these things that had seemed too good to be true in fact were.

"No physical violence!"

I wanted to let that one sink in. I held off for a few seconds before continuing.

"Those of you who have some sort of fondness for punching people in the face can leave this group right now. This is no Fight Club you can use to vent your aggression or hate toward society.

For some, that might be the hardest part.

"You've all been convicted of various violent crimes. Stabbings, shootings, bar fights, one of them even fatal. I want it to be perfectly clear that violence is unacceptable. You might think there are times when you have to use violence, but those days are over now."

I carried on.

"Aside from the fact that it harms people, there are other reasons why you should never assault anyone. If you end up in a fistfight or you shoot someone, you'll leave traces that will be used as technical evidence. It could be DNA, blood, shell casings, clothing fibers, and so on. Those are the kinds of things the police use to identify you and tie you to the crime and the crime scene."

Maybe it was dawning on them that they were not going to get to be as suave as their potential role models from whatever gangster movie. That my business plan wasn't culled from some Hollywood TV show with a fetish for gratuitous violence.

"You will avoid physical contact with the victims if at all possible, self-defense being the only permittable exception. The smartest crimes involve no violence."

They were listening. If they didn't give a fuck about my first argument, this one should be getting through to them.

"You have to start acting like serious professionals. Not primitive thugs running around beating each other up. It's beneath rational individuals."

That was how I wanted them to start thinking of themselves.

"Besides, it's absolutely unbearable to imagine a family member or friend hurt or killed. How many of you have a loved one or close friend who's been the victim of violence?"

Everyone nodded or raised a finger in the air.

"So it's not hard for you to figure out that all people are someone's family member or friend and just as important to them as your loved ones are to you."

No one spoke.

"I don't know what kind of faith you belong to, and I don't care, but if you assume, as I do, that we have only one life, we have to respect that and accept that everyone's life has equal value."

That was the end of my sermonizing. Time to lighten the mood.

"Besides, as far as I'm concerned, violent macho men are an incredible turnoff."

Several of them cracked a smile.

"Don't believe what they tell you in the movies, that girls like those ruthless, brutish, coldblooded guys. It's not how it is. Girls just want you to *look* ruthless, brutish, and cold, they don't want you to *be* those things. On the inside, it's the soft, warm, loving guy they want. The combination of a hard outside and a soft inside is a winner with the ladies, believe me." Now they were starting to look at me as if I'd said something they'd never considered before. None of what I had just said was true for me, I chose my men according to a completely different set of criteria, but I knew a lot of other women were like that.

"And speaking of looks..." I looked them up and down. "...that's a topic for our next meeting."

The most important points had been covered. It was getting to be time to wrap things up.

"As I said at the start, you'd be wise not to talk to people about me. Remember that I know a lot about you."

I slipped my laptop into its case.

"It's been a long time since I stopped following the rules, but I still have access to the police's resources. An unbeatable combination you will both benefit from and have trouble with, if you don't stay sharp. I could easily nail you and use coercive measures against you if I wanted to..."

It obviously wasn't that simple, but the important thing was to make it seem like it was. I wasn't really all that worried. The risk of these criminal gentlemen running to a police station to file a report against me was extremely low. For obvious reasons, they didn't want to draw the police's attention. But I didn't want talk about my venture to spread in criminal circles.

"...but in exchange for your silence I'll refrain. I'll also resist the urge to arrest you for the petty crimes I can see right here and now. After all, I have a duty to report these things, you know."

I went around the room. Looked at them all in turn.

"One look is enough..."

I bent down and looked Liam in the eyes. They were bloodshot.

"Possession," I said.

"The thing is, I—"

"Spare me the bullshit, Liam. I've heard it all a thousand times. I can tell you're high. It's the last time, if you want in on this."

I moved on to Eli. Gently tugged the gold chain around his neck.

"Grand larceny? Or maybe robbery? That's a unique-looking chain. It would be a snap for Property to trace it back to its rightful owner. I don't understand why you haven't sold it, but hey, none of my business. Or, wait, let me guess, it was a gift from grandpa?"

I was being flippant. I might have been a bit amped up, but I wanted to underscore that there was no point trying to trick me. I stood in front of Liam, who I could see had something hidden under his shirt. It wasn't hard to figure out it was a weapon, probably a knife. I explained that he was breaking the knife law, which he of course already knew.

I looked at the clock. The second hand was still twitching. It was time to wrap it up. But first some info about our next meeting.

"The perfect crime, is there such a thing?" I said and looked at them.

No one spoke.

"That one heist that is so meticulously planned and that could make you so rich you never have to worry about money again, does it really exist, you think?" I pressed.

The corner of Liam's mouth twitched and he tossed his head to get his blond bangs out of his eyes.

"If you want to know the answer to that and really learn how to commit crimes without getting caught, it's going to cost you three thousand kronor per session."

"Fuck me," Zack said, staring at me.

The others didn't react to the price. Some of these guys were used to having large sums of money at hand sometimes and no money at all at other times.

"Calm down, Zack, not this one. This is an introduction, no need to pay for it. The first hit is free," I said and smiled.

Eli and Marc chuckled.

"We're also going to talk about what kind of equipment you'll need, and how to handle it. But this is no charity scheme. So you'll have to pay."

I walked over to my bag.

"You've all been arrested for crimes you've committed. It's unavoidable, plain and simple. Without knowledge, it's only a matter of time before you get caught. Now you can choose to carry on like you have and rely on luck..."

I slipped my laptop into my bag.

"...or you can choose to become experts in your field. What I'm offering you is a unique opportunity. The information I give you will be tailored to you. There's no school or course book that teaches what I can teach you in Sweden, or anywhere in the world for that matter. With my knowledge, you will make so much money off your crimes, you'll no longer have to commit any."

After everyone had left, I sat down on the table at the front. Looked out across the room. Smiled to myself.

The clock on the opposite wall caught my eye again. I got up, grabbed a chair, and briskly carried it across the room. Climbed onto the seat and pulled the wall clock down. The spring in the back shot out when I ripped out the battery, killing the red second hand.

FOURTEEN

As ever, when the leader of the Blood Family wanted to talk to David, he was escorted from the front door of their clubhouse by a guy who was a head taller than him and looked like he had been raised in a boxing ring. Folds appeared on the guy's neck, which was about as thick as David's thigh, when he walked. As usual, he had patted David down for weapons as soon as he stepped inside. David knew the president, Simon Hall, liked him, but this was a place where you didn't trust anyone who didn't belong to the inner circle, which David didn't. Nor did he have any desire to be admitted to it. Besides, the road to the inner circle was long and difficult. If you chose to start down it, there was more or less no way out. It was a life decision.

The heavyweight waddling in front of David always seemed to have all the time in the world. Spoke tersely, if at all. After opening the door to Simon Hall's room, he took up a position, arms crossed, in the doorway, and motioned with his head toward the room inside. David entered.

"Good," Simon said softly when he spotted David, and nodded for the guy in the doorway to leave the room.

Simon was sitting in a high-backed office chair behind a mahogany desk. The clubhouse was on the basement level. Light came in through tiny, barred windows just below the ceiling. Simon nodded again. This time for David to take a seat on the wooden chair in front of the desk.

David was unsure what this was about. For his previous

assignments, he hadn't been allowed to sit down and talk to Simon. And he had never been alone with him, without any of his bodyguards in the room.

David slowly walked over to the chair. Sat down.

"You've been doing good," Simon said.

David tried to look casual. Being called in by the head of the Blood Family could make the most confident person nervous. They would never ask him to kill anyone, that much he knew. In order to earn the trust needed for an assignment of that magnitude, even if it was just a fake one to test him, you had to be much higher up the hierarchy than David was. He was only on the gang's outermost periphery. There were countless other, serious tasks they could ask him to do, though, things they didn't want to do themselves for whatever reason. If he said no he would never be asked again and his chances of getting closer to the gang, which he needed to be in order to give Sven more information and earn more money, would be slim.

"I need you to go get a car from Copenhagen," Simon said.

Driving the cars the gang stole from one place to another was something he had done before. It had always been about transporting a car from Sweden to another country. The gang made some of its money stealing exclusive cars and exporting them. It was a low-risk venture with big profit margins. But this time, David was apparently supposed to go get a car abroad and drive it back to Sweden. Not such a big deal. But Simon was unlikely to call David in like this just to tell him to drive a car across the border. There must be something else.

"The car's pretty much worthless," Simon continued. "The contents are what matters. Not a job I'd give just anybody. You in?"

David was silent. Asking questions about the cargo was pointless. Simon would only give him the information he considered necessary. Besides, questions would only serve to make David anxious and that was the last thing he wanted in this situation.

"Sure," he heard himself say.

"We'll be in touch about the details. But hey, when you're in Copenhagen and they deliver the car to you, you wait for a call from me before doing the handover, got it?"

David nodded. He relaxed on his way out. He wanted to quit crime, but even so there was something inside him that liked the excitement. The feeling of completing a dangerous mission. Testing your own boundaries.

That Simon had chosen David for something like this instead of someone from the Blood Family's inner circle meant he trusted David. Sven would be very pleased to hear that.

FIFTEEN

With my elbows on the conference table, my hands folded, and my chin resting on my fingers, I sat with my eyes fixed on the PowerPoint presentation Alexandra was giving. I wasn't following along, just staring vacantly at the white screen until the letters and images blurred into a gray haze.

Having not really known what to expect, I was happy with how my first meeting with the guys had gone the night before. That being said, I did need to find a few more.

Even though I hadn't been sitting in my current position for more than a minute, my fingers were growing numb. I stretched them out and balled my fists a few times to kick-start my circulation. Leaned back and let my arms dangle down the outside of the armrests instead. Imagined that gave my blood a more unobstructed path. When my forearms started throbbing against the edges of the armrests, I put them in my lap instead.

My body was aching.

Sometimes it was confined to specific spots, but more often the pain seemed to move between body parts. I caught my mind wandering and did my best to focus. After all, the staff meetings were a lot more effective and to the point under Alexandra's leadership than they had been back in Claes's day. The Police Authority required more of its superintendents nowadays. Alexandra had trimmed the meetings down to a crisp half-hour instead of an hour, which before had often stretched into an hour and a half. Most people were relieved not to have to sit through long meetings. The issues that were brought up again and again were enough to make anyone break out in hives. One of them was police conduct in connection with lineups. Not so much about how they were supposed to be done, most people knew that well enough, but rather in what situations it made tactical sense to use them and which pictures should be used. Sometimes, the persons in the reference pictures from the photo registry looked so much like the suspect it was virtually impossible to tell them apart. In other cases, one person was too different from the rest. These things could be pivotal in deciding whom a witness identified as the perpetrator of a crime, which had been discussed on several occasions. It was rehashed yet again before Alexandra started talking about a conference she wanted us to learn more about by logging onto Intrapolice.

Intrapolice, the police intranet, was a cause of griping for most. It was impossible to navigate, yet it was where we were supposed to find important new information about everything from new legislation, political decisions, and assessments from the parliamentary ombudsman to how to fill out forms to order, for example, technical analyses. Everything was there, but impossible to find, even if you typed in exact search terms. Alexandra was talking about an upcoming conference about the reorganization of the Police Authority, which was going to be implemented at the start of the new year. More information about it could be found on Intrapolice.

"We have selected the delegates we want to send from VCD. It takes place on July 23 on Silja Line MS *Galaxy*. The conference participants will subsequently present what they have learned to the rest of the division."

I didn't want to be selected. The mere thought made me want to stand up and walk out of the meeting. But I stayed in my seat. If she said my name, I would refuse point blank. But I also didn't want to cause a scene. Hopefully she realized I had my hands full already.

"Primarily, we want Åse and Anette from admin there."

They both smiled and exchanged looks.

"That's great, thank you!" Åse said.

Their colleagues smiled at them. The few times Åse and Anette had been away at the same time, like when they had been granted vacation time simultaneously, had impressed on the rest of us how instrumental they were to the division.

"We obviously prefer to keep one of you here at all times, since we can barely get by without you, but it's just one day. We'll make sure we stay afloat," Alexandra continued and smiled. "The administrative work is going to change quite a bit after New Year's, so pay attention and take lots of notes."

Anette nodded and flipped through a small calendar.

"Of the detectives, we're sending you, Fredrik," she continued.

Fredrik had always been clear about wanting to get on. Taking initiative in meetings and volunteering to participate in the planning of the further development of the division. He had taken courses to master the very popular waste minimization method LEAN, which he was now busy trying to get the rest of the staff to implement. He smiled. No one could have thought they would have picked anyone else. They were probably going to send a female detective as well. I held my breath.

"And the last person we want to nominate is you, Cilla."

Alexandra looked at Cilla, who beamed like the sun. She was that girl at the office who was always twittering happily in the hallways, seeing to things no one else could be bothered with. Back when Claes was still our boss, I would see Cilla in his office from time to time. Talking and laughing.

Neither Fredrik nor Cilla could hold a candle to me when it came to investigative chops, but I found the social aspect of the job more challenging. I had made a habit of mimicking the others. If I had seen Cilla chatting away in the boss's office in the morning, I found a reason to go in that afternoon. And I usually brought a cup of coffee as well. Some felt it was beneath a woman's dignity to make coffee for her boss, but it didn't bother me. All I had to do was stick a mug into the machine and press a button. Going into someone's office with two cups of free coffee and handing them one often produced surprising levels of appreciation. Funny how little it took. It was all about finding those little things that had low energy investment but big rewards.

Now that Alexandra was our boss, however, there was less of that. She drank tea. There was no tea in the machine; you had to fill the kettle, wait around for two minutes while it brought the water to a rumbling boil, choose a teabag, get a spoon out, stir and throw the teabag out before the tea got too bitter. More work, in other words. It may come with certain rewards, but it was simply too much hassle. Compliments worked better on Alexandra anyway. A tiny throwaway comment was all it took. Telling her she'd handled a problem well always paid dividends. In fact, those kinds of comments made most people happy.

If you were a person who constantly needed validation, law enforcement was not the right profession for you. On the contrary, within the police, you usually had to take shit from almost everyone around you. From your superiors and people on the street, in interview rooms and in the media.

I could relax. For the first time in a long time, I caught a break and failed to get picked. Going on an overnight cruise with only a handful of lectures, having to spend the rest of the time mingling with a bunch of drunken colleagues, was not on my wish list right now. I was happy to be off the hook. Maybe I should consider having a cup of tea with Alexandra from time to time after all.

SIXTEEN

It was Monday morning and I had forced myself to go to the hospital. I had to wrap this up. This was going to be my last interview with Fred Sjöström. After that I wouldn't have to deal with the sterile walls, the hospital smell, the tubes and the machines.

Fred had claimed he wanted to tell me everything, but I wasn't about to spend hours dragging the information out of him. He had been given plenty of chances already.

I had set up the camera so that I would finally be able to show Alexandra, once and for all, that my sitting in his room, listening to the three words an hour he deigned to squeeze out, was an indefensible waste of the taxpayers' money.

My eyes were feeling tight, which made me squint. One side of my head was pounding. As usual, I had tossed and turned all night. Got up. Turned on the TV. Been bored to death by what was on. Paced around my apartment. Eventually fallen asleep. Slept for an hour and woken up completely exhausted.

I went to stand by the foot of the bed. Waited to turn the camera on. It would take at least a few minutes to prepare him.

"Right then, Fred, here we go again."

He glanced up at me. Tried to move and winced when he couldn't. Both of his arms were full of puncture wounds and bruises. I looked down at the legs that weren't there.

"Must really hurt," I said.

He made no reply. I walked over to the visitor's chair and

opened my bag. I wasn't there to kvetch about his medical condition. I was just going to finish what I had been ordered to do.

Suddenly he replied, in a dark, raspy voice: *"La douleur est une forme supérieure de plaisir."*

I froze. Quickly turned to look at him. From his eyes, I could tell he knew what he had said would cause a reaction. I put my bag down on the floor, moved the chair closer to the bed. Sat down. What he had said was not something just anyone would say. I recognized it. Had heard it before.

"The Legion?" I asked.

He didn't respond. I knew quite a lot about the French Foreign Legion. The information available to the general public was very scant and few people really knew what their work entailed. Those who had served in it were generally not particularly interested in talking about their experiences. What I knew, I had learned from a friend of mine who had signed up. He had been thrown in the Legion's prison and had in the end deserted.

I had heard my friend say the French phrase Fred had just uttered many times. It meant "Pain is a higher form of pleasure."

Who was this man? The normally abundant information about suspects contained in the police's many registers was far from sufficient to form a comprehensive picture of him. His criminal record consisted of a conviction for a bar-related assault and a couple of minor offenses in his youth. Aside from that, he had been taken into custody for being drunk and disorderly on a couple of occasions, but that was all. I hadn't felt butting heads with SÄK to extract more information had been worth the trouble, since I didn't intend to stay on this case, but what he had said intrigued me. The French Foreign Legion was the reason there was a gap in his Swedish residency between 1985 and 1994.

Put another way, in front of me was a former mercenary who had tried to blow up Sweden's Parliament building. I continued to study him. More intently now. Trying to read his expression. He closed his eyes as though he wanted to escape my gaze.

"There's no point in trying to hide. Whatever happens you can count on every detail of your life being scrutinized. All the little events that led up to your attack."

I walked over to the camera. Pushed play and started by stating the date and time.

"So this is another interview with Fred Sjöström. The charge of terrorism still stands. Fred has declined to have a lawyer present during these interviews. Information about potential public defenders for any future court hearing will be provided in due course."

Then I turned to Fred.

"Fred, why don't you start by telling me which organization you work for."

Normally, an interviewer would never start by asking the most sensitive question. You'd never open an interview with a question that risked making the suspect clam up and refuse to cooperate. But in this case, that was, of course, exactly what I wanted. What's more, I had asked him whom he worked for several times without getting an answer. The risk of getting one now was marginal at best. The difference was that the camera was rolling this time so I would be able to show Alexandra that he didn't want to talk, at least not with me. I would come across as a slightly inept interviewer, but I didn't care about that.

To my surprise, he didn't look at me but rather straight into the camera, and he appeared to be about to actually say something. He took a few deep breaths.

"The fact that I'm still here…" He spoke slowly, his eyes fixed on the lens. "…shows that the first one failed…"

"The first one," what was he on about? The bomb?

In a monotonous drone, as though he were in a trance, he continued: "…but the next one won't."

What the fuck?! I suddenly felt cold. Acted instantly. Took two quick steps over to the bed. Grabbed the hospital blanket and ripped it off him so I could see his body. Looked for something to explain what he'd just said. Saw nothing but his hospital gown, the medical tubes, the bandages on his amputated legs. Nothing else.

"What the fuck are you saying?" I said.

I was clammy with perspiration now. He slowly looked up at me with a crooked smile and reached out for his alarm button. Before I could stop him, he had pressed it.

I was unable to stop myself.

Everything went blank.

I completely lost control. I grabbed hold of the collar of his gown with both hands and pushed his neck and shoulders into the mattress. Shouted at him: *"What the fuck are you saying? What do you mean the next one? WHAT DO YOU MEAN THE NEXT ONE?"*

Two seconds later, the door was thrown open. Out of the corner of my eye, I saw my colleagues from SÄK burst through it. A couple of nurses dressed all in white in their wake. My colleagues grabbed me, pried my hands off Fred and tore me away from him. Away from the bed.

"I'm fine," he said between coughs. "Leona just got a bit excited. I'm okay."

Leona? Suddenly he was calling me by my first name. And that was the most I had ever heard him say.

"Get your hands off me," I hissed at my colleagues, and I tried to pull free.

They let go. I snatched up my jacket and bag, grabbed the camera, and stormed out of the room. My heart was pounding in my chest. Another bomb? When? And where?

If this leaked to the media, all hell would break loose. When my superiors and SÄK found out, I would never be able to get out of this shit.

"*Fuuuck!*" I shouted loudly as I hurried down the hallway with my bag and jacket flapping around me and one of the tripod legs scraping against the floor.

Fred had the upper hand.

SEVENTEEN

"Leona!"

The elevator doors were just about to close when I heard Fredrik call me. I pushed the button to keep them open while he dashed over.

"Heading up to VCD, are you?" I said as he squeezed through the doors that were trying to close again.

"No, I have to go over to Property," he said. "Some colleagues submitted one of the guns used in my casino robbery before I had a chance to get photographs and prints. Fucking incompetents."

I pushed three.

"How's the suicide bomber case coming?" he said.

I shook my head.

"I wish I had nothing to do with it," I said and quickly averted my eyes after catching sight of myself in the mirror. "That case is nothing but trouble."

It would get a lot worse if there really was a second bomb planted somewhere. I would have preferred to pretend I knew nothing about it, but that was impossible now.

"I'd take over in a heartbeat if I could just get rid of these two casino robbers. They're going to hang for it for sure, but it's a boring case. No challenge. A lot of admin. I don't know how I'm supposed to make time for the police conference cruise and prepare lectures on top."

He stepped out of the elevator when the doors opened.

"I'd love to hand off the bomber. I'll put in a good word for you with Alexandra. I'm heading up to talk to her now. Surely someone else can do the casino thing."

The doors slid shut between us and I continued up to the sixth floor.

As soon as I stepped into the hallway, I could hear agitated voices. I continued on toward the reception and Anette's room. Stopped in the doorway and looked at her inquiringly.

"A suspect has assaulted both Cilla and Marcus in the interview room," Anette told me. "They're in with Alexandra now."

I raised my eyebrows. For a suspect to add assault against police officer to their crimes as they were being arrested was not unusual, but to attack detectives during an interview was definitely novel. After watching American crime movies, people might be excused for thinking lots of suspects were rowdy during interviews, but that wasn't how it really worked. On the contrary, most were very calm. Some had really bad attitudes, but resorting to violence was rare.

"They're both fine, but they're discussing who is going to do the interviews going forward," Anette said. "The suspect seems to be something out of the ordinary. Alexandra put Cilla in for Marcus, but that just made it worse."

"Thanks for the heads-up," I said.

If I hadn't needed to speak to Alexandra, I would have slipped into my own office and closed the door. The risk of my being stuck with that troublesome interview was considerable.

"Leona, great!" Alexandra said and stood up when she spotted me in the doorway to her office.

"Alexandra, I need a word," I said.

Cilla was sitting by the window, wiping her nose with a bloodstained tissue. Marcus was standing next to her, looking at his phone. Seemed to be studying a bruised welt on his jaw.

"You look like hell!" I exclaimed.

"I need you to do an interview, Leona," Alexandra said.

"I don't think I can fit that in right now. As you know, I've got the suicide bomb — "

"It's just a few quick questions," Alexandra interjected. "We're short-handed. I would ask Fredrik but he's got his hands full with the casino robbery. Everyone else is busy with other things."

She looked at the clock on the wall behind the conference table.

"There's not a lot of time. We need to conduct a proper 24:8 interview immediately so the prosecutor can make a decision about further detention. You're doing this, Leona."

Marcus rolled his eyes at me and sighed as though he wanted to apologize for sticking me with their bullshit. The whole thing was tragicomic. I pictured what it must have looked like when Alexandra sent them into the interview room, one after the other, and they came out bleeding and limping. Like the Keystone Cops. The only thing keeping me from bursting out laughing was the knowledge that I would pay dearly for it. I leaned back against the wall and crossed my arms.

"Alexandra, I really do need to talk to you. Alone," I said.

I had to be careful about sharing this information. The press must not catch wind of it. That's why I had to keep it from as many people as possible, colleagues included. I didn't trust Marcus and Cilla. Granted, the people I did trust were few and far between these days, but I could pretty much count on anything I told those two being passed on.

Alexandra heaved a sigh.

"Wait outside," she told Marcus and Cilla.

Cilla gathered up the tissues on the table and walked toward the door with her head tilted back and a tissue pressed against her nose. Marcus closed the door behind them.

"We have to give the suicide bomber case back to SÄK," I whispered.

Alexandra frowned and put her hands on her hips.

"I don't have time for this, Leona. We have been tasked with doing the interviews for reasons I'm not going to discuss with you right now. You can't question it because you don't like the —"

"There's another bomb, Alexandra!"

I cut her off. Had to prove that this wasn't just about my opinion of the bomber, but because his plans could hurt innocent people. Alexandra stared at me openmouthed.

"He told you that?" she said.

"He implied it."

"Implied? Is there a clear bomb threat?"

"Sort of…," I said.

"Leona, what the hell's wrong with you? What exactly did he say?" she said and fixed me sternly.

When I told her what he had said, verbatim, she walked out from behind her desk and sat down in a chair. After a few seconds, she said: "I'll handle it. You're going to drop it for now and go sort out the interview Cilla and Marcus bungled. Meanwhile, I'll talk to SÄK."

She got up from the chair and went over to the door.

"The interview is about a jewelry store robbery that took place on Kungsholmen yesterday," she said as she opened the door and waved Cilla and Marcus back in.

Alexandra nodded for Marcus to take over catching me up about the case while she went back to her desk and pulled out her phone book. Marcus chewed the air and moved his jaw from side to side, one hand clapped to his cheek.

"There were three perps," he said. "Ran in and threatened the staff with gunlike objects. Got away with gold and cash. Two of them are still on the lam. The driver of the getaway car was arrested and—well, you can see the rest for yourself." Marcus pointed to his jaw.

"Just the one interview for me?" I said and looked at Alexandra.

She nodded. Robberies of this kind were not particularly complicated. Normally, I would have taken over the whole investigation if I was interviewing the suspect anyway. That way, I would have scored another point in the registry, but since I didn't know what was going to happen with the suicide bomber, I had no desire to volunteer for more work. If I could get away with just an interview, I was going to consider it a win and move on.

I sighed and held out my hand. "Give me the file."

Marcus handed it over. As soon as it was in my hands, I could tell it was heavier than just the papers would be.

"So, seized goods?" I said as I opened the folder and only just managed to catch one of the two zip-lock bags that tried to slide out.

"For fuck's sake, Marcus," I said. "I could have dropped that on the floor."

"I'm sorry," he said. "Those two pieces of jewelry were found in a bag in the van the suspect was driving. All seized items have already been submitted and catalogued. There are some clothes as well. Probably for them to change into after the robbery."

I studied the jewelry.

"I suppose you can use the jewelry in the interview, if you…uh, get that far," Marcus continued and poked at one of his upper canines with his thumb and index finger.

I started walking toward the door.

"Have you opened an investigation into the assault on a police officer yet or should I stick with the robbery charges to start?"

"Lay it all out," Alexandra said. "There's also threat against and assault on a police officer during the arrest. Two of the beat cops got a pummeling as well. All right, now get out. And close the door behind you."

I shot Alexandra one last look before exiting with Marcus and Cilla.

"She seemed to be in a weird mood," Marcus said about Alexandra. "Problems with the suicide bomber or what?"

I ignored his question and kept flipping through the case file. The suspect's name and personal identity number caught my eye. I was surprised. It was an unexpected name.

"Previous convictions?" I said.

Cilla, who had wiped all the visible blood from her nose and shoved two new tissues up her nostrils, said stuffily: "Doe, just a decisiod dot to prosecute a shopliftig. Fuck, I'b goig to look like a boxer wid a swolled dose ond de bolice cruise."

"Mental illness?" I asked.

Marcus shook his head.

"Just really fucking furious."

"Did you get anything useful at all?" I said.

"Not a word," Marcus replied. "I can check if there's someone on call who can accompany you in the interview room if you want?" Marcus said.

"Huh? Not a chance," I said. "If I have to do it, I'm doing it on my own."

Before going down to Detention, I went past my office. A few registry searches confirmed that this suspect could be useful to me. Maybe I could turn the interview to my advantage.

On my way to detention, I continued to study the case file. The apprehension had been performed flawlessly by the arresting officers. And yet, I could tell that, as usual, a lot of questions would have to be answered before a prosecutor could charge the suspect. Questions that in this particular case I might do well to compound.

I left the newly installed CCTV cameras and monitors you could use to record the interview turned off. Contrary to what people thought, far from all interviews were recorded or filmed. Especially in cases of simple holdups like this one.

Vibrations in my pocket made me take out my phone. A text from Armand: *100,000 SEK. Wednesday. Confirm.*

Fuck! I hadn't counted on him wanting that kind of money in one go. My plans for getting the money together were going to take longer than six days. I needed to come up with something. Pondered whether there was someone I could borrow it from. I was just about to call my friend Larissa when the detention officer appeared. A text was all I had time for before he had ushered in the suspect and left the interview room.

I stayed seated, staring openly without saying a word. Amazed at what I was seeing. So this was the young, angry driver who in spite of a number of police officers, handcuffs, and pepper spray had been almost impossible to restrain when the arrest was made. A very unusual robber. Not only because of those circumstances.

This robber was a woman.

Short and of slender build.

And she'd already done away with two interviewers.

Now she was sitting calmly on the other side of the desk, looking down at the floor.

I opened the case file and read the report again. Suspect: Vikki Dimberg, it said. She wore black sweatpants and a gray hoodie. I noticed the white drawstring had been left in the hood. Someone had clearly been sloppy during booking. Suspects were not allowed to bring things like that into the cells on account of the suicide risk. If they objected to having the string pulled out, claiming that would ruin the sweatshirt, they were given a smelly detention center sweater to use while their own garment was placed in a locker along with the rest of their possessions.

I hardly thought this girl had any plans to kill herself, however. Obviously, I had no way of knowing what was going on behind her facade, but that was my educated guess. Her body language signaled a certain amount of attitude, but other than that she looked pretty well put together. Clean hands and nails, washed hair, no visible bruises or needle pricks. She didn't seem to be the kind of broken young girl who sooner or later ends up in our care. So far, she hadn't shown any signs of aggression and at this moment, she didn't look like she had any plans for attacking me physically. This might be a girl I could use.

Now all I had to do was make her say something. So far, she hadn't uttered so much as a grunt. I realized I was going to have to try something beyond the regular interview techniques to get through to her.

I waited.

When she had still not spoken after three minutes, I double-checked that the camera light wasn't on. I shifted in my seat. Leaned against the backrest, making the chair tip back and forth, crossed my arms in front of me, looked at her, and said calmly, "You should have used more violence."

She looked up for the first time. Stared me straight in the eye. Her eyes were a deep blue with sharp, dark rings framing the irises. The whites of her eyes were slightly bloodshot, probably from the pepper spray my colleagues had used on her during the arrest. Her pupils were normal. Nothing suggested she had been under the influence, which was unusual for someone behaving that way toward officers making an arrest.

After that line, I was planning to wait her out. The one who spoke first had lost. Interviews were always a power struggle. I waited. Silence was a very effective tool. Most interviewees were uncomfortable with silence, found it unbearable even. They often started talking out of sheer frustration when they couldn't take it anymore. Often that was when the most important information slipped out. Normally, I never had trouble waiting out an interviewee, but this time I was feeling stressed. Even so, I forced myself to sit in silence, since I was convinced it was the most productive method in this particular case. I looked down at the floor where it met the wall. Giving her a chance to study me without our eyes meeting. There was a discarded saliva sample wrapper in the trash can. It occurred to me that I hadn't checked if the girl had been swabbed. It was up to me as her interviewer to check if she was in the DNA database. If she wasn't, I was obligated to ask the lead investigator to make a decision about sampling and then execute the decision. A laborious and tedious task. In this case, I would be forced to act like some kind of nurse, put on plastic gloves and dig around some stranger's mouth with an extra-long cotton swab until I could squeeze out enough saliva. Press the swab against a chemically prepped pink paper so drool could trickle onto it and dye it white, fill out seventy-five different boxes with information about the suspect's identity, tester, case number, and so on, and then send it by normal post to the National Forensic Center in Linköping for analysis. The results were then crosschecked with various databases. Sometimes, you got a hit for other crimes the suspect had been involved in where the perpetrator had previously been unknown. In the case of this young girl, I wouldn't be surprised if more crimes popped up. A robbery committed together with several other criminals is hardly the first crime a person commits. But I had no time to mess around with a swabbing right now.

I looked at her. Maybe it was just happenstance that I was on this side of the table and she on the other. It struck me again how fine the line was between law enforcement officers and professional criminals.

The thrill seeking.

The feeling of having power over others.

The underlying violence.

A lot was the same, but the ideologies underpinning them were, naturally, fundamentally at odds.

And if you looked at it from a purely financial standpoint, a skilled detective was always poorer than a skilled criminal.

Police work had been exciting the first three or four years. At that point, I had rubbed up against its main constraint. That you were so limited by the regulatory framework that the chance of making a real difference was nonexistent. In the criminal underworld, you answered to yourself. Set your own boundaries.

I let the chair fall back onto all four legs. Put my forearms on the table and leaned in closer.

"You're done. You know that, right?" I said.

Vikki looked away again, as though she figured I was just a regular fucking cop after all.

"You've been arrested on the way from a robbery, in a van identified by witnesses that contained a bag of clothes for the robbers to change into. The van was also caught on CCTV at an ATM nearby. The bag, moreover, contained gold jewelry, and it doesn't look like it's yours, put it that way."

I pulled out the bags containing a one-and-a-half-inch gold bracelet with crisscrossed gold bars and a thick gold ring with diagonally set diamonds all around. Not the kind of jewelry a young girl would normally wear. They were in separate ziplock bags, tagged and numbered. I realized Marcus and Cilla hadn't mentioned whether the gold was being sent in for technical analysis. The officer who had confiscated them had put them in zip-lock bags, which wasn't exactly optimal storage if they were going to be checked for fingerprints, but none of that mattered. I was planning to take over the case and had no intention of sending anything to the lab.

Good thing the confiscated items were documented and registered properly in the database. Someone had even taken the time to photograph them. If swabbing was a tedious part of the job, it was nothing compared to handling seized goods. Gold jewelry might be okay, but confiscated things like drugs, dyed bills, alcohol, bats, bloody clothing, guns, knives, and whatever else was unpleasant to deal with, even with gloves. Few people ever thought about all the bodily fluids the police have to handle. Saliva samples, urine samples, vomit, sweat, and general grossness. Luckily, you were done with most of the disgusting parts of the job once you moved on from field duty and worked as a detective. But instead, you had to slog through tedious, time-consuming admin work, like managing inventories of seized items and writing requests for technical analyses. Most detectives felt that shouldn't be part of a detective's job description. And it wasn't unusual for seized items to disappear. Some things ended up floating around the police station for days without anyone knowing where they'd gone. Sooner or later, they usually turned up, but running around looking for items that had not been entered into the system correctly was frustrating, to say the least.

I might as well not have shown her the gold. She looked at it but remained impassive. Pretty impressive. There was something about this girl.

"The others are still on the lam," I said.

I had no idea what her relationship with the other robbers might be.

"I suppose you've already pondered how it happened that you were the one left behind. Arrested with just a few stray pieces of jewelry while your so-called pals made off with most of the gold and the cash. I would give that some thought if I were you. If I were in your position, I would reconsider my friendships."

She looked down at the floor. Maybe this was how I could get to her.

"I don't suppose I need to tell you how seriously courts take robbery?"

Being reminded of that at this early point could hardly be particularly uplifting. I wasn't going to torture her with more statements about how useless her life was and how many poor decisions she had made to end up here. She would have enough time to ponder those things on her own. Instead, I was going to throw her a life raft.

"You and I could be useful to each other."

I gathered up my documents and closed the folder. Held it up to her and said, "I can make this disappear."

She looked at me with slightly raised eyebrows.

"If you convince your friends to cut me in on whatever they made away with, I'll make sure none of you go down for this."

She stared at me like she'd seen a ghost. I flipped through the case file in front of me. Looked for a memo that more accurately outlined how much the robbers had made away with. Maybe it was enough to tide me over for now. Unfortunately, there was just a note that the lead investigator would contact the jewelry store owner for detailed information about the total value of the stolen merchandise and cash.

"You will obviously have to persuade them. If you don't, you're going to have to spend a few years inside. The sentencing guideline for robbery is a minimum of four years in prison. And you've added a few crimes along the way as well, threat against police officer, assault on police officer…"

It was a good deal; we both stood to gain. For a young girl like her to serve time for robbery was a real waste. It would destroy her life. She had made bad decisions, that much was clear, but to have your whole life destroyed because of it, that wasn't fair. It also irked me that the other robbers seemed to have conned her.

"I'd suggest you explain to your pals that you're going to start pointing fingers if they don't agree to your terms. Just a tip. I think they'll listen."

There was a knock on the interview room door. Alexandra stuck her head in and motioned for me to join her in the hallway. I looked at Vikki.

"Think about what I've told you. I'll be right back."

After pulling my pass out and picking up the case file, I walked out to join Alexandra.

"I just wanted to check how it's going," she said.

Vikki hadn't said much, but given Cilla and Marcus's results, I had to consider my attempt successful. Vikki Dimberg was going to take me up on my offer, I knew she was. What choice did she have? If I was going to be in a position to make sure this investigation was dropped, I had to be the lead investigator.

"I can take over the whole thing," I said. "She seems to trust me."

Alexandra brightened up.

"You're a team player, Leona," she said. "Come by my office afterward and we'll talk more about the suicide bomber."

When I went back into the interview room, Vikki was staring at the tabletop. I walked up to her and put the case file in front of her.

"Have you contemplated your sins?"

She looked at it, then up at me.

"Who the fuck are you anyway?" she said.

I smiled and walked around the table. To unequivocally signal that she didn't have to worry about the police report, I picked it back up again, along with my notepad and pen.

"I'm going to write that you deny any involvement in the robbery, but that you admit to the threat and assault. It just won't look very credible if you deny that too, you know? According to the paperwork I have here, you were given plenty of opportunities to calm down, but you refused, were very amped up. You're going to have to apologize in court and say that you panicked and thought you were going to die or whatever."

"But then I'll end up with a criminal record anyway," she said.

"And do you want that record to say robbery as well, or what? That'll obviously net you a longer prison sentence, as I'm sure you understand. This has to sound believable, otherwise they'll never release you. Your choice. On a different note, you should seek help for that temper of yours."

She lowered her eyes.

"I'll make sure you're released as soon as possible and that your confiscated phone is returned to you. I'm going to text you an address. Talk to your friends and bring the money to that address at 10 p.m. tonight."

I started walking toward the door. Turned around.

"And hey, bear in mind that there's no point trying to trick a cop, especially one who no longer plays by the rules."

I opened the door, nodded to let the detention officer know we were done and went back to the department. Vikki Dimberg wasn't going to make trouble, I could feel it. All I needed to do now was fabricate an interview report where she gave her version. That, however, was going to require a bit of thinking. Convincing the prosecutor to let her go wasn't going to be easy, since from an investigatory perspective there was a risk of collusion, or in other words that Vikki could destroy evidence or in some other way undermine the investigation if she were set free. Since two other robbers were still on the loose, and most of the stolen goods were still unaccounted for, the prosecutor was going to consider that risk significant. I was going to have to make up a story that showed Vikki had nothing at all to do with the robbery and didn't associate with criminals. That her record was clean aside from a shoplifting case many years ago in which the charges had eventually been dropped made my job a lot easier.

In the interview report outlining her version, I was going to make something up about the van having been borrowed and Vikki having just been asked by a friend to drive it back, and to pick up a person in town on the way. About how she hadn't known who she was picking up, that she was just doing a friend a favor. Maybe that the guy she was picking up turned up and threw a bag into the van and told her to hang on while he went to get another one. When Vikki heard sirens, she started feeling antsy and left without checking what was in the bag. Then the police caught up with her. I needed to polish the narrative a little, but something along those lines. I was also going to have to show that the other two robbers had left no traces behind if I was going to be able to make sure they got off scot-free too. The CCTV system in the store had been out of order, which was not unusual. Normally I would curse at all the stores that didn't keep their cameras in working order. They were either old, had bad resolution, were installed at the wrong angle, or just didn't work. For once, though, I was grateful for it.

The case against Vikki was pretty flimsy anyway. Even if I was sure she had been involved, it would have been hard to prove. There was no witness placing her in the store. She was arrested several blocks from the scene of the crime and was not in the company of either of the two guys witnesses had seen. As of yet, there was nothing to prove that the jewelry in the van she was driving was from that particular shop or that particular robbery. I could explain her odd reaction to being stopped by the police by saying she was scared. Besides, courts still tended to think of women as victims, even when they were the perpetrators. Flimsy evidence combined with a tearjerker of a story in which Vikki explained that she had acted in good faith, had thought she was helping out a friend by promising to pick up a person in town and that she was shocked and panicked when so many police officers suddenly swarmed her. That it would go from that to a conviction for robbery was not very likely.

This was going to work.

Vikki was going to stay out of prison.

And I was going to get money.

"Have you talked to SÄK?" I said once I was back in Alexandra's office.

Alexandra pursed her lips and glared at me.

"Why did you attack him?" she said. Of course someone had told her about that. "The head of SÄK just told me," she continued. "What the fuck are you doing, Leona? Have you lost your mind?"

I looked at the floor. The way you were supposed to when you'd been caught doing something you shouldn't. But then I realized this in fact provided something of an opening. Another chance of getting out of working on the case. With my eyes still fixed on the floor, I said falteringly, "I think it might be better if SÄK took over the interviews. Or that someone else did them. Maybe Fredrik."

"But I was asking you why your colleagues had to storm in and pry you off a disabled older man in a hospital bed. Answer the question, Leona."

She wasn't going to relent. I sighed and rubbed my forehead.

"Eh...I just snapped."

"You're going to have to make this right," Alexandra said.

"So you're not going to bench me?" I blurted out.

"I'm afraid it's not that simple," she replied.

"What did SÄK say?" I asked.

She leaned back in her chair and made no answer. I suddenly understood.

"You didn't tell them?" I said.

"What was I supposed to say?" she wanted to know. "That the suicide bomber might have planted a bomb several weeks ago but that we have no idea where? A bomb that might go off at some point but we have no idea when? That he hasn't even made an explicit threat but only offered vague hints about planning some kind of attack? We don't even know if it's a bomb. That's not going to fly, Leona."

She was right. The information was vague, but I still felt the bomber's hints should be enough for Alexandra to seriously consider handing back interview duty.

"The threat level is raised nationally and SÄK is already working on the assumption that he is a member of a terrorist organization that could strike again. Security has been upped for politicians and political and religious targets, and extensive intelligence work is already underway. We need to get more out of the interviews to help them take the next step."

"He has worked as a mercenary, Alexandra. The French Foreign Legion. He's obviously not one of our run-of-the-mill criminals. Interviewing him the regular way is pointless. He may have been a prisoner of war and tortured for information, what do we know? He can't be brought to heel, okay? We either have to accept his terms and let him say two sentences per interview, or we can give up and hand the work back to SÄK."

She looked more concerned than I had ever seen her. It was clearly important to her to maintain good relations with SÄK, but I still didn't understand why it was so important that I do the interviews.

"SÄK's bright idea that I go into this without any background is just odd," I ventured. "I don't understand the point of it. I can't conduct interviews without background information. I don't know which direction to take it. If I'm going to stay on the case, I need access to the whole file."

Every police officer knew that good prep was crucial for a successful interview. It was so obvious it went without saying.

Alexandra kept staring at me without saying a word. Studied me as though she were looking for something in my eyes. Then she walked over to the desk and picked up the phone.

"Hans, this is Alexandra at VCD. The suicide bomber has started talking. We need the whole thing."

I tried to figure out what Hans Nilsson, head of SÄK, was saying on the other end from her expression, but her face was impassive. A good poker face, I caught myself thinking. She obviously knew I was watching her. When she looked in my direction, I looked away. I pulled my phone from my pocket and checked the screen again, as I'd been doing every fifteen minutes. Larissa still hadn't replied. But thanks to Vikki Dimberg, my financial situation was hopefully going to work itself out anyway.

"They're sending the whole case file over immediately," she said after hanging up.

Suddenly it was no problem getting them to hand everything over. Odd. She hadn't commented on Fredrik. To hand the case over to him was apparently out of the question.

"Go over the documents from SÄK carefully and come up with a strategy before you see him again. And bear in mind that he seems keen to get his message out."

"And SÄK?" I said.

"Let me handle them. You just do your job. As quickly as possible and as well as you always do."

I nodded.

"We're done," she said and started walking toward the door. "And hey, the next time I'm told about violence against an interviewee, I will report you myself."

I went into my office. At least I had told Alexandra there might be a second bomb somewhere and she had accepted the situation.

It was on her now.

EIGHTEEN

"I'm just popping out for a smoke," David called to Saga from the hallway. He had already pressed "accept" on his phone to make it stop ringing, but hadn't said anything, just listened.

"Where are you? I'm here now," Sven Malmström had said.

David pulled on his sneakers and snatched up his jacket and a baseball cap on his way out the door. Not until he'd jogged down both flights of stairs and was on the street did he put the phone to his ear again and say he was on his way. David had been in touch earlier that evening, asking to talk to Sven. Now Sven was parked a few blocks from David's house.

"What do you have?" Sven said when David pulled the car door shut.

"Frihamnen. One shipment," David said.

"When?" Sven wanted to know.

David slumped farther down the seat when he spotted a neighbor he knew walking by. He didn't want to be seen with Sven.

"They seem to have sussed out that the cops have tails on some of them, so they're laying low for a while. I'd guess a few weeks from now," David said. "Seems pretty big. Several pounds."

"Find out exactly when and who's involved."

Sven always sounded excited whenever David gave him more concrete information.

"I obviously can't offer you a financial inducement, but if the shipment is as big as you say and we pull it off with your help, you know you'll be getting a —"

"Considerable sum," David finished his sentence for him and sat back up.

He'd heard it so many times before.

"I need more cash," David said.

"You'll get more when you deliver," Sven replied.

"I've given you names of people you had no idea were in these circles and info about deliveries and deals you would never have heard about if it weren't for me," David said.

"You think we have access to endless funds, do you?" Sven retorted. "The big money is paid out for major busts. Find out more about that cocaine deal and let me know."

David fell silent. Pondered whether he should tell Sven about Copenhagen.

"Is that all?" Sven asked.

"I've been given a new assignment," David said and adjusted his baseball cap. "The Blood Family wants me to pick up a car in Copenhagen and drive it to Stockholm."

Sven turned around in his seat so his shoulder ended up against the backrest and his upper body was angled toward David.

"I'm listening," he said and crossed his arms. "Who gave you the assignment?"

"Simon Hall," David said.

"I'll be damned," Sven said. "A luxury car?"

"The car doesn't seem to be the point this time. It's the cargo," David said.

"Drugs?" Sven asked.

David shrugged. "Simon was real fucking tightlipped this time. I just hope it's not a person, I can't deal with that kind of bullshit."

"Don't worry," Sven told him. "I'll take care of it. Let me know when you know more about the cargo and the when, where, and how, and I'll make sure we nab them before the handover."

David looked at Sven. Pondered whether telling him had been the right call.

"Make real fucking sure you get it right this time," David said. "I'm not being sent down for fucking trafficking or whatever this is, just because you don't have your shit together."

"You're not going to have to have deal with any of it. Go to Copenhagen and just keep reporting to me. Don't worry, I'll do the rest. Okay?" He patted David on the shoulder.

David opened the car door and climbed out. He did worry, but as ever, he had no choice but to trust Sven.

"That was a long smoke," Saga called from the living room when he closed the front door.

"I took a walk. Felt like stretching my legs," David said.

He desperately wished he could tell her he was doing something good. Pulling himself out of his life of crime while also helping the police to nail the kind of people who destroyed other people's lives. David just wanted a normal life with Saga. He dreamt of a house in the suburbs with a big lawn where he and Saga could host barbecues in the summers. He just needed to save up a bit of money, then he was out. After that, Sven would have to find someone else to be the police's errand boy.

"Hey, dad called. He wants us to come over for mom's birthday next week. They've invited all the relatives. My cousins are coming as well. They're doing dinner out by the pool if the weather's good."

"He invited me too?" David said.

She nodded slowly. "It feels to me like they're extending an olive branch," she said.

David couldn't hide his joy. It in no way meant he was accepted as part of the family, but at least they were willing to give him a chance. That was all he needed. He was going to go and show them he was the best boyfriend Saga could have. That he was taking care of her. Making her happy. They were going to realize they had been wrong about him.

He hugged her.

"Finally! When is it?"

"On her actual birthday, Thursday afternoon."

Fuck! That was the day he was supposed to pick up the car in Copenhagen. But the dinner wasn't until the afternoon. He was going to have to try to make both.

NINETEEN

"You're late," I told Vikki Dimberg as she came walking toward me.

I had texted her the address of the building in the Meatpacking District earlier that day and waited around for ten minutes before she finally deigned to show up. Annoyingly, she was ambling along, showing no signs of feeling rushed. It was already ten past ten at night, it was cold out, and I had no desire to spend more time than I had to in this neighborhood. Once she had handed over the money, I was going to go straight home and to bed.

When she got close enough, the security light on the building behind me illuminated her and I was able to see her face properly. She had a big black eye extending out toward her left temple and down across her cheek, a welt across her jaw on the same side and a cracked upper lip.

I stopped; we stood facing one another. She gave me a quick glance and lowered her eyes. I nodded slowly.

"I'm guessing you did your best to persuade your pals about the money," I said.

She pulled a pack of Camel Lights from her jacket pocket, winced slightly when she put a cigarette between her lips and lit it. Took a deep drag and exhaled with a nod.

"The guy who beat you up, is he the one who has the cash and the gold?" I said.

She nodded again and shoved the pack of cigarettes back into her pocket. Considering how tough I knew she was, he must have really laid into her, big fucking coward. I sighed. Realized my warm bed was going to have to wait.

"Come on!" I said and started walking toward my car.

She followed. Moving slowly. As if every step hurt. I unlocked the doors.

"Get in," I said.

Even though she stubbed out her cigarette before climbing into the passenger seat, the smell of smoke filled the car the moment she sat down. It's always been a mystery to me why people would choose to inhale that crap. Poison, straight into the lungs.

"Where does he live?" I said and put the car in reverse.

She didn't answer. When I looked at her she shrugged.

"They have a place in Råcksta. They're probably there now."

Råcksta. Fuck! It would take at least twenty minutes to get out there. Truth be told, I was too tired, but this couldn't wait. She had said "they." So this wasn't just some random guy; it was a gang.

After getting on Drottningholmsvägen and crossing the Traneberg Bridge, I sped up and turned on my sirens.

"Buckle up," I said.

As we zipped past all the other cars at high speed, lights flashing, I saw Vikki Dimberg smile for the first time. Neither one of us spoke. I didn't turn the lights off until we exited onto Råckstavägen. Vikki guided me from Råcksta town center to a residential neighborhood that looked like the projects. In the dark of the evening, the apartment buildings were shadowy gray blocks of concrete.

"Down there," she said, pointing to a building with a short set of steps leading down to a basement.

I drove past and stopped the car in a parking lot a few blocks down. Turned to Vikki.

"Now you're going to tell me who these guys are."

She should be smart enough to know she had no other choice but to give me their names. Instead of delivering the money she'd promised in return for being released from custody, she had come to me empty-handed and battered.

"It's T...and a few others," she said.

"Excuse me?" I said.

"Um, T," she repeated.

"What do you mean, T?" I said more loudly. "What's his name? His name, personal identity number, address, license plates, shoe size, anything!"

I opened the car door and got out. After sitting in a car filled with Vikki's smoky exhalations, the crisp night air was like a soothing balm for my lungs. I pulled open the door to the back seat and snatched up my laptop bag. From the sound of the door slamming shut, Vikki should have known I wasn't in a great mood. I got back in the driver's seat, unzipped the bag, and started getting my laptop out.

"You get that I have to look these guys up, right? I need to know who they are, what other crimes they've committed, who they're in with, what kind of weapons they might have, and all the other things I as a detective really need to have a handle on before I walk into a basement full of thugs who have just got away with a jewelry store robbery.

Under normal circumstances, this kind of bust would be unthinkable without planning or waiting for backup. Vikki didn't respond. Just sat staring into space. Fuck! Why had I got myself involved in this?

I smacked the laptop shut before it even had time to boot up and swung the bag back into the back seat. Started the car and reversed so suddenly Vikki's seatbelt locked as she pitched forward in her seat. Then I rolled up to the basement she had pointed out. I had more than half a mind not to bother with this whole thing, to just push her out of the car and drive straight home, but at the same time I just couldn't swallow that those idiots had first tricked Vikki out of the loot, then beaten her up when she came back to demand her cut. It pissed me off even more than Vikki's unbearable way of refusing to talk and give me the information I needed about them. It was so fucking typical that she, a girl, was loyal to some guys who clearly didn't give a shit about her.

I stopped right next to the stairs. I wasn't going to hide. Quite the opposite.

"How many are there?" I said when I pulled the key out.

Vikki shrugged.

"T's almost always there in the evenings. The others come and go."

"Let's go in!" I said.

The tough, cocky Vikki who had put up a real fight during her arrest and who had assaulted two detectives was nowhere to be seen. Now I had an insecure, gray little mouse with a battered face in tow.

I nodded for her to lead us into the place. She banged the graffiti-covered steel door with a specific series of taps I didn't bother memorizing. I had no intention of ever coming back here.

When no one opened, Vikki pulled out the same old junkie phone we had confiscated earlier.

"They always have music on. Probably can't hear. I'll send a text."

It wasn't long before a guy with a shaved head, wearing a hoodie and sweatpants, opened the door. The dull thudding of a baseline grew louder.

"What the fuck are you doing here?" he said when he saw it was Vikki.

"I wanna talk to T," she replied in a voice that would have made a mosquito sound loud.

He turned to me and looked me up and down. Then back at Vikki, eyebrows raised.

"It's my sister, okay?" Vikki said and pushed past him. He moved and let me by as well.

The place reeked of sickly sweet marijuana. After walking down another short flight of steps and down a hallway, Vikki opened a door to a room that looked like it had once been used for communal bike storage. It was furnished with coffee tables, arm-chairs, and two couches. A group of men were gathered around one of the couches, smoking. If the window hadn't been open, it would have been impossible to breathe.

The men stopped talking and stared at me and Vikki. A beefy guy with a shaved head and a big black beard nodded to one of the others, who stood up and walked over to an iPhone sitting on a speaker next to the couches. The music died. I heard footsteps behind us and saw the man who had opened the front door out of the corner of my eye. He stopped next to us. The man who had turned off the music looked nervous. Shot anxious glances at the bearded guy, who must be the one Vikki called "T."

I took out my police badge. Held it out in front of me like a shield. I wasn't going to try to hide who I was. They had probably already figured it out anyway. Guys like these usually had a good radar for things like that. They could spot a cop a mile away.

When the guy from the door saw the badge, he tensed up like he was going to bolt.

I drew my gun. Quickly. Pointed it at him.

"Nice and steady," I said through gritted teeth.

I nodded toward the couch where the other guys were sitting. "Sit down!"

The guy put his hands up and slowly walked over and sat down across from T. I rarely brandished my weapon, but this could turn ugly quick if I didn't make it clear who was in charge. Everyone was looking at me, except T, who was staring at Vikki with a look that could hardly have been any more menacing.

"And you," I said, and pushed Vikki toward the guys.

She slowly walked over and stood a little to the side, in a corner.

"Now you're going to listen goddamn fucking carefully. First, I hope none of you imagine I'm the only one who knows about this cozy little hidey-hole. The Inner City Task Force knows I'm here and wanted to tag along, but I told them it was fine, that I was just going to swing by and make sure everything looks okay. They're expecting a call from me in a few minutes."

The Inner City Police didn't have a task force of their own, but I assumed these guys weren't exactly up on the structural organization of the Swedish Police Authority. Once everyone stopped moving, I lowered my weapon.

"Let me introduce myself. As you saw, I'm an officer of the law, but I suppose you could say I work differently than my colleagues, wouldn't you agree, Vikki?"

All the guys turned to Vikki, who stared at the floor.

"Vikki has refused to give you up, even after hours of interrogation. She wouldn't bring me here until I put a gun to her head. But you have her to thank for not being in a holding cell right now."

I didn't want to drop Vikki in it with these idiots. She glanced up at me from under her bangs, which were hanging down, hiding her face.

"I'm investigating your little robbery on Kungsholmen. Things are looking pretty good for me, and bad for you, put it that way."

I fixed each of them in turn. They were staying calm. I looked around the room to make sure there were no other ways in or out. Didn't want to be surprised by someone bursting in from an unexpected direction.

"Robbery will get you locked up for a few years, at least. But I thought I'd stop by and have a chat with you before showing all the evidence against you to the lead investigator."

I addressed T.

"I'm going to give you an offer. I'm told you were given this information by Vikki earlier today, but I think you'll understand it better coming directly from me: you give me the cash, and I will make sure the investigation goes away, like it was never there. You can keep the gold."

I had neither the time nor the inclination to fence the gold on the secondhand market. My offer was a good deal for both parties. T was stony-faced.

"How do I know you won't nail us regardless?"

It was the first time I'd heard him speak. From his calm, deep voice, I guessed he wasn't easily agitated. For my part, I didn't feel as calm as I was hoping I seemed. I needed to relax. I forced myself to speak slowly. Lowered my voice to a deeper register.

"You're going to have to trust me. It's a fair deal."

The others looked at him. The man who in the next few seconds was going to determine their future.

"Your buddies here might have things they'd rather do with their lives than spend years and years in the slammer, just because you got greedy," I said.

T glared at me for a few moments before he nodded to the same guy who had turned off the music. I raised my gun again and backed up slightly. The guy held his hands up and slowly walked over to a wooden cabinet on the far side of the room. When he pulled the doors open, they revealed an unpainted safe. He punched in the code with casual movements clearly honed by frequent practice. Pulled out a black bag.

I looked at T.

"I know down to the cent how much money you made away with. Try to get one by me and you're going down, got it?"

That was a lie. I didn't have exact details from the jeweler yet. The guy started walking toward me with the bag in his hand.

"Stop! Throw it toward the door," I told him.

He slid the bag along the floor toward the exit. I backed away, still with my gun trained on them. Bent down and snatched up the bag with one hand. Seeing the wads of notes, I stood back up.

"I'll keep my word about the robbery, just like I told you," I said. "But Vikki behaved like a fucking asshole toward my colleagues. Several counts of threat against and assault on a police officer. I can't accept that. I'm taking her with me. She's going to be charged."

T glanced over at Vikki. She was still standing up, head bowed. Just as I had guessed, he shrugged and motioned with his hand to signal I was free to take her. She slowly started walking toward me.

"So, are we cool, T?" I said.

When he nodded, I slowly lowered my weapon and pushed Vikki forward so hard the bag of money smacked her in the back.

"Outside!" I said.

TWENTY

I had started on the coffee table. Spread out the documents from the file SÄK had sent over. When I ran out of space on the table, I moved onto the floor. At night I was happier working from home than staying at the office.

I glanced at the bag of money from Vikki's jewelry store robbery and sighed. It contained 21,500 kronor. Nowhere near the hundred thousand Armand demanded. If the money had been in my bank account, I could have transferred it to my online account with Pokerstars. But maybe relying on gambling to grow my funds wasn't the best idea. After all, you always ran the risk of losing everything. Larissa hadn't answered my text. I'd been hoping to borrow money off her.

My insomnia meant my eyes constantly felt full of sand. I broke off the tip of one of the little pipettes in the multipack on the table, tilted my head back, and squeezed a dose of soothing eyedrops into each eye. I had switched from a bigger bottle to single-dose pipettes after realizing they minimized the risk of bacteria and were therefore the more hygienic choice. I rolled my eyes and blinked rapidly to spread the drops evenly across my eyeballs. After blinking a number of times and wiping away the excess fluid that trickled down my cheeks, I went into the kitchen and turned on the kettle. I had done my stomach some damage, drinking all that coffee at work. It was tea from here on out. Chai was the only kind I could bear. It was spicy and had an unusually rich flavor for a tea. I made myself a whole thermos. There were going to be a lot of cups of tea before the night was over.

During the search of Fred's apartment, electrical tape, ammonium nitrate, electrical wires, nails, wire, and other things had been found, but nothing that gave any real clues as to the motive behind the recent bombing. Like most people I came into contact with through work, he had had a complicated childhood. Like many of them, he also had reason to be angry at the society that had let him down. Fred was perhaps simply a lonely, angry man, who wanted revenge for what he felt society had done to him. He might also, for the same reason, have elected to join a terrorist organization. There were gaps in the information we had on him that would trouble any detective.

Members of the French Foreign Legion lived in an alternate reality, that much I knew. His file said he had joined up in 1985 and stayed for nine years. No one I had ever heard of had lasted that long. Even though everyone who passed the entrance tests had to sign a five-year contract, hardly any of them stayed beyond a couple of years. The ones who tried to run away and were caught were thrown in the Legion's own prison.

I would probably never know which wars Fred had fought in. The reason he'd quit the Legion despite his recently renewed contract's still being in effect was a gunshot wound to the shoulder. After emergency care in the field, he had been transported to a French hospital.

Everyone who was accepted into the Legion, whatever country they were from and whatever their background, had to sever ties with everyone they knew. Parents, children, partners, friends, colleagues, everyone. They were then given a brand-new identity and a new passport.

I took a sip of tea and leaned back against the edge of the sofa. Turned it all over in my mind for a moment.

A new identity.

To become someone else.

Who wouldn't be tempted by that?

It was easy to see how that would draw a lot of young men who might have burnt their bridges back home and wanted to start over, but also people who wanted to test their own mental and physical boundaries. The knowledge that you might be killed in armed combat seemed to both terrify and attract.

Exactly what he had been doing during his time in the Legion was less interesting to me than who he had come into contact with and what he had been up to afterward. After completing service, all mercenaries were given the choice of keeping their new identity or reassuming their old one. They were also offered French citizenship and could stay in France if they wanted, which Fred seemed to have done for a few years. Once he got to France, he seemed to have more or less gone off grid. There was no documented information about where he worked or resided. Attempting a search for something SÄK had been unable to get from the French Intelligence Services was clearly futile. The explanation was probably that he had worked illegally and couchsurfed with friends. But there were also a lot of questions. Whom had he spent time with after the Legion? Could those unknown associates have something to do with the attack? Who had been the target, and had he done it of his own accord or had someone ordered him to? If I could find the answers to those questions, I would probably be closer to locating any potential second bomb. Was there even a second bomb? If there was, that would suggest he wasn't working alone.

I aimlessly rummaged through the papers. There was no indication Fred held any extreme religious beliefs. No radicalization of any kind was known to the authorities. But it couldn't be ruled out.

After a few years in France, Fred had returned to Sweden. There was no explanation as to why.

According to the case file, Fred had fraught relationships with his family. Both growing up and later on with his wife and child.

There were simply too many questions that needed answers.

An interview with one of his former work colleagues, Mirja Virtanen, piqued my interest. The interview was very brief. Reading between the lines, I got the feeling she knew more than she let on. Even though it wasn't my job to conduct additional interviews, I was going to ask Anette to contact Mirja and set up a meeting with her as soon as the cruise ship she worked on next docked in Sweden.

I pondered how to structure my interviews with Fred. Got up and paced around the room with my cup of tea in hand, as though that would help me think. It was odd, I had met Fred several times. Spent time in the same room as him, tried to talk to him. And yet we hadn't communicated. It was as if we hadn't even met until that last time. I sighed. This was not going to be quick.

I was going to have to adjust my approach.

Start slowly building trust.

TWENTY-ONE

His left eye. Temple. Panning down his cheek. Nose. I looked at the camera display again. Zoomed out slightly so I could see both of Fred Sjöström's eyes. He hadn't woken up when I entered, which meant I could record from the moment he opened his eyes.

Filming someone this close up was disgusting. I could see every pore, beard hair, blemish, and wound. I zoomed out a bit more, until I could see his chin and neck. Part of the pillow. His shoulders. Hair. Then I stopped.

A correctly recorded video interview was normally supposed to show both the interviewee and the interviewer, to make sure that any attempts at influencing the interviewee's answers through facial expressions or other signals were documented. But I didn't care. I had no desire to be in the video, and to fit us both into the shot, it would have to be so zoomed out it would be impossible to discern his facial expression. I wanted to be able to study him closely. Interpret his reactions to my questions.

His face was strangely peaceful when he slept. The wrinkles on his forehead and around his eyes and mouth had been smoothed out. He looked like an ordinary older man. Like someone's grandpa. A gray beard had sprouted on his cheeks, aging him. If you didn't know it, it would have been difficult to imagine that this man had recently tried to blow himself up.

This was going to be like a fresh start. My attitude and approach were completely different this time.

I gingerly moved the visitor's chair closer to the hospital bed. Sat down.

"Fred."

No reaction. He was probably sedated. I grabbed the bed frame and shook it gently.

"Fred Sjöström!"

His eyelids started quivering. As though he were struggling to open his eyes. Eventually, he started blinking. When he spotted me, he quickly looked around the room, as though to establish whether he was alone with me.

"It's all right, Fred. You can relax."

My voice was calm. He swallowed and his mouth smacked softly. He seemed to be trying to clear his throat. I reached for the water glass sitting on a cart next to his bed. Brought it closer to him and aimed the straw at his mouth the way I had seen the nurse do. When he gave me a suspicious look, I nodded and smiled as warmly as I could. He opened his mouth a crack and sucked down water.

I wondered if he had considered this possibility when he planned his attack, that he might survive. With disabilities that might make him dependent on others for the rest of his life.

"Fred, you and I got off to a bad start," I said. "I'd like to start over."

He looked at me expressionlessly.

"I apologize for how I behaved last time we met."

As a detective, it was annoying to have to start an interview by apologizing, but to have any chance at all of making him talk after my meltdown, I had no choice. Anyone who knew anything about interrogation techniques knew that the way to get information out of an interviewee was to create an atmosphere that was conducive to talking. Beating information out of a suspect only worked in the movies. If there.

"It had nothing to do with you; it was about me being over-burdened. Your case is time-consuming and I had been assigned too much work."

That might have come across as uninteresting ramblings to him, but I had to give him some personal information about my situation while still maintaining my professional status as an officer of the law.

He still made no answer.

"But that's no excuse," I continued. "I took it out on you, and I'm sorry. If you want to report me, you are well within your rights to do so."

When I looked at him, I was suddenly unsure he was even taking any of what I said in. I wondered what kind of pills they were giving him.

"I have explained to my superior that you are ready to talk now and she has relieved me of some of my duties so I can focus on your case. I'm here to listen to what you have to say."

He looked at the camera mounted on its tripod at the end of his bed. I calmly reeled off the usual rigmarole about who was being interviewed, personal identity number, date, time, current charges, and his right to have a lawyer present. He showed no signs of hearing me.

"Fred, what is your worldview?" I said. "Are you religious?"
He shook his head.

"What did you mean by what you told me last time I was here?"
Silence.

"Fred," I said again in a gentle voice. "You said the reason you're still here is that the first one failed."

He turned his eyes to me.

"I am still here, right?" he said quietly.

I nodded slowly. "But you wanted to die, is that right?"

"It's not about what I want," he continued.

"Is it about what someone else wants?" I said.

He didn't reply.

"The Security Service thinks you're part of a terrorist organization. There has been speculation about everything from the ETA to ISIS. Why did you choose Parliament?"

Still no reaction. I pulled his file out of my bag and started flipping through the pages.

"I've been reading up on you. There are gaps in your background information that make us think you're not in this alone."

He didn't even look at me.

"Fred, if there's something you want to tell me, you have to start—"

"Our society is broken," he said.

"In what respect? According to these documents, you have made quite a few peculiar life choices that ultimately led to your trying to blow yourself up. But you're saying society is the problem?"

"It's made me who I am," he said.

Society, sure, I thought to myself. So nothing was his responsibility. He was one of countless criminals who insisted on playing the victim. It was the go-to rationalization for anyone who considered themself a victim of circumstances beyond their control. Who supposedly wasn't in control of their own actions. He seemed, like so many other thugs, to blame his rotten life on others. Some might argue I was one of them, but I wasn't. I didn't blame my actions on anyone else. The choices I had made in life I considered completely my own and I accepted full responsibility for them.

"So you're not in any way responsible for your own actions?" I asked.

"No one cared about her," he said.

"...or maybe you're saying someone forced you to strap on that belt of explosives and go stand outside Parliament?" I continued. "As far as I understand, you had —"

"You don't understand shit, Leona. I was wrong about you."

I just stared at him. Not because he'd raised his voice, but because he had implied that he had had preconceptions about me and that he had now changed his mind.

"No one was there for her, get it?" he continued. "No one helped her when she needed it. But what the fuck do you care, you and all the other fucking pigs?"

I fell silent. He turned his head away.

"You can leave now," he said. "I'm tired."

"Oh no, Fred," I said and stood up, "that's not how this works. It's not up to you to decide when the interview's over. That's my call."

With a clenched jaw, narrowed, frosty eyes, and pursed lips, he breathed in slowly as though he were trying to suppress an outburst. Before I could stop him, he shoved the cart away so forcefully that water from the half-filled glass splashed across the bed and the glass shattered against the floor while the table shot off and slammed into the opposite wall. He ripped the cannula from his arm and knocked over his drip stand, sending it clattering into the chrome bed frame before it crashed onto the floor.

The door opened and one of my SÄK colleagues entered.

"Get someone in here," I called to him.

Seconds later, two nurses arrived. I backed away and watched them stop the bleeding on his arm and give him an injection.

Even though he calmed down fairly quickly, I was left wondering how I was ever going to get through to Fred. The task of conducting interviews with him seemed hopeless. When everyone had left the room, I said, "Fred, I want you to think very carefully about how you want to do things going forward. I will come back just one more time. It'll be your last chance with me. If you choose to continue down this path, I'm going to give up the task of conducting interviews with you."

He looked at me with weary eyes. I pressed on.

"I know you've been through a lot. How much, only you can tell me, but this isn't working. You and I aren't getting anywhere. If you choose to carry on like this, you'll go back to doing interviews with the Security Service."

When he closed his eyes, I packed up my things.

"I can't risk time passing and innocent politicians or other civilians being killed by explosives you or someone else has planted."

"There aren't any," he said grimly.

I turned to him. "No explosives?"

He slowly shook his head and looked straight at me.

"No innocent politicians."

TWENTY-TWO

David had just delivered a hand truck piled high with moving boxes to the apartment and was on his way down when his phone rang. Answering inside an elevator where there was virtually no reception wasn't a good idea. He declined the call.

"Cigarette break," David announced when he met his colleague Ior in the foyer.

He went out onto the street and walked past the moving van.

"What have you got for me?" Sven asked when David called back.

"Next Friday. Six pounds. From Riga to Stockholm."

David spoke quietly. Looked around. There was no one in sight, but it didn't hurt to be cautious.

"What time?" Sven said.

"Shouldn't you be able to find out the rest? You're the goddamn cops."

David was sick of them wanting everything served on a silver platter. It should be beyond easy for them to look up the boat traffic on that day. Ships didn't exactly roll in from Riga every two minutes. Sven didn't seem to have any appreciation of just how fucking dangerous it was for David to press people for details. If he didn't know Sven was a stubborn son of a bitch who would keep calling him again and again until David picked up, he would have hung up on him.

"I can't be running around asking things like that, okay?" he said.

"Drop the attitude, David," Sven said. "If you just tell me everything in one go I don't have to drag every word out of you. How many are they?"

"The Riga gang is big, but I think only two of them are coming over. Three or four Swedes meeting them here and selling it on."

"Weapons?" Sven asked.

"Latvians doing international cocaine deals, what do you think?" David said.

"And the cocaine?"

"I already told you. Six pounds. Maybe more."

Sometimes, David got the feeling Sven asked him the same question several times to check if David was telling the truth.

"Storage?"

"In some kind of special bag, I don't know. Probably surrounded by coffee. I heard someone say that would throw the dogs off. When do I get my money, by the way?"

"Keep on top of the cocaine deal. Let me know if they change the delivery date," Sven said.

David saw Ior come out the front door, step into the moving van, and attempt to unload a large cabinet by himself.

"I gotta go."

David hung up and put his phone back in his pocket while he ran up and grabbed the other side of the cabinet.

"I'm so fucking sick of people's crap," Ior said. "What do they need it all for? This cabinet is just going to be filled with more shit they never even use."

Ior was fifty-six and had been moving people's belongings for twenty years. He claimed to like it, but nevertheless always complained. Things were either too heavy or just ugly. Today, it was just the fact that people had possessions at all that had him riled. He was an old crank, but David kind of liked him anyway. He just didn't want to end up like Ior. Work for a moving company for another twenty years and complain about everyone and everything.

"You shouldn't ruin your young back doing this shit," Ior said.

"Hey, free workout," David replied and smiled.

"That's true, pushing papers around some office isn't a lot of exercise," Ior said and laughed. "It's good to feel you're alive. If you just help me out with this beast, I'll do the rest. Just bits and pieces left anyway."

"Sweet," David said and opened the elevator door.

Even with the hand truck, getting the cabinet out of the elevator was a challenge. It was really too wide for the hand truck and too big to turn inside the elevator. David squeezed past the cabinet into the corner to be able to hold it up and help tilt it. Ior put one foot on the frame of the hand truck and heaved as he simultaneously pushed his weight against the handles. Before David realized what was happening, the cabinet had slid sideways and was coming at him. He didn't manage to grab it in time. All he felt was a hard blow as the edge of the cabinet hit his forehead and a thud as the back of his head slammed into the elevator wall.

"Fuck!" Ior shouted and let go of the hand truck.

He pulled on the cabinet, which tipped back and landed on the elevator floor with a loud crash. David touched his forehead and felt sticky blood between his fingers.

"Stay here," Ior called. "I'll run down to the van and get..." Ior started running down the stairs.

David turned to look in the elevator mirror. It was hard to see how big the gash was. How could a cut eyebrow bleed so much? There was already a bump that would probably turn blue. Goddamn it! Now Saga was probably going to think he'd been in a fight. Hopefully it would heal enough before Thursday when they were going to her parents' for dinner.

TWENTY-THREE

7 p.m. Värtahamnen Port. Confirm.

I cursed inwardly at Armand's text and shoved my phone back in my pocket as I continued to pace around Aimi's office. Now I knew the time and location, as well as the sum he required. He also demanded I text him back to confirm. Delaying any longer was going to be impossible.

I had a hard time staying still. Sitting down felt restricting. As if I were confined to a two-square-foot area and on top of that had to remain absolutely motionless.

Aimi was probably busy trying to figure out what delusions I was exhibiting today, so she could note them down in her book.

I was no stranger to delusions. With a job like mine, I had seen plenty of people afflicted with them. Suspicious people who thought they were being watched, that someone wished them harm. Unlike those people, I *knew* there were people who wished me harm. Hardly a delusion. But if I were to tell Aimi an armed man had been lying in wait in my apartment when I got home from work, threatening to kill me and my daughter, that notebook would probably be filled with suggested diagnoses that could explain my new symptoms.

In a way, you could say Aimi wished me harm, too. She wanted to put me on par with disturbed, sick people.

I had toyed with the idea of telling her everything. What I told her was confidential, after all, though I wasn't sure to what extent. But that I was a police officer who committed crimes in my spare time was information few would be able to handle.

I wondered how many people in our society were seeing a therapist despite being completely healthy. Who were labeled with all kinds of diagnoses just because they didn't conform.

"You seem to want to stand up today too," Aimi said. "Are you anxious about something?"

I wasn't sure "anxious" was the right word, though I supposed it was fairly unsettling to be forced to deliver money to a lunatic while also trying to relax in an armchair that looked impossible to ever get out of again.

"I'm always sitting down at work, I want to stand up for a bit," I said.

I walked over to the window and looked out. That wasn't something I only did at Aimi's, it was pure reflex. I wanted to keep an eye on the goings-on in the area. Possibly a work-related tick that may have been exacerbated by my short stint in surveillance. I had already looked out twice, or was it three times, but I had no way of knowing if something new had happened while we were talking. If someone was lying in wait for me when I got out, I wanted to be prepared.

"Terrible weather today," I said and looked down at the cars parked on the street.

I saw a young man walking a bulldog on the other side of the street. He stopped and looked back at something. I couldn't see what from where I was standing.

"How did you sleep last night?" Aimi asked.

Why did she always ask me that? I had already told her I barely slept nights. I leaned closer to the glass to make out what the guy was staring at.

"Do you still have nightmares?"

I pushed a potted plant aside to see better.

"Leona!" Aimi said more loudly when I didn't reply.

"Uh...what?...Yes," I said. A girl was walking up to the guy. She took his hand and they walked on together.

I left the window. I wanted Aimi to write me a prescription for sleeping pills, but wasn't going to ask for it, because I realized that would jeopardize my chances of actually getting them. That was always the way when you wanted something from someone. You had to make it seem like it was their idea to give it to you. If you asked for it, you just seemed desperate and people immediately pulled back. Probably particularly when it came to prescription drugs. Because I had told her about my gambling, she claimed I had an addictive personality, which would probably make it even harder for me to get her to give me sleeping pills. Apparently, everything you said to a therapist had consequences.

"I only had a few hours last night," I said, trying to sound appropriately downbeat. "Working's pretty rough when you're sleep deprived," I added and glanced furtively at her.

She said nothing. Was looking down at her notebook.

"Peter is away, so I'm looking after Beatrice as well now. We overslept today," I said and rubbed one eye with the back of my hand. "Luckily, I have flexible hours at work, but it wasn't exactly a calm morning."

The kid thing usually worked like a charm. Peter wasn't away. He was looking after Beatrice, but if I mentioned her name and that I was unable to function as a mother without enough sleep, I judged my chances of getting sleeping pills would be greater. Aimi continued to write.

"And how do you feel about having Beatrice now?"

"She does a lot herself. Sorts out breakfast and stuff like that when I'm too tired after a night without sleep."

"But isn't she just five years old, Leona? She makes her own breakfast?"

"I guess it's usually just like a cracker or whatever, but it's great that she can help out when my head is pounding from lack of sleep. She says she helps mommy when mommy's tired."

Aside from a tiny frown, Aimi seemed remarkably unperturbed. She must have been desensitized by all her strange clients and the stories she'd been told. If I were a therapist, I would have reacted strongly to the information that a grown-up let a five-year-old make their own breakfast that consisted of a cracker or two. How she could consider that normal, and at the same time jot down a bunch of diagnoses in her notebook about other things in my psyche, was beyond me.

"Have you ever taken sleeping pills?" she asked.

Finally. Aimi had nothing to worry about. The risk of me getting hooked on prescription drugs was minimal. I didn't like pills. Couldn't understand how people were okay with swallowing whatever shit they could get their hands on without a thought about their health. I was no health freak, but I didn't see any reason to do more harm to your body than nature and time did anyway.

"I've never needed to. This is the first time I've lost a child while also going through a divorce and being buried in debt. I don't like taking drugs, but if you think I should give it a try, I guess I should."

My strategy involved being slightly reluctant. Pretending I didn't really want the pills.

"Do you have other recurring nightmares than the one you told me about before?" Aimi asked.

"Locked up," I said and walked over to the bookcase by the other wall.

She looked at me inquiringly.

"I dream about being locked up," I continued. "Like when I was little."

I studied the books on the shelf but didn't see the titles. I was unable to stand still. It was like my body was itching on the inside.

"Where were you locked up?" she asked.

"In the basement."

I raised my arms to the ceiling, stretching my back and sides from top to bottom. The feeling of extending my tendons was liberating.

"How old were you then?"

"Around five. I don't remember much before that."

I let my arms fall, tilted my head to the side, and rubbed my neck and shoulder.

"Tell me more about that. In what situations were you locked in the basement?"

"They made me go down there when they thought I'd been bad."

"Your parents?"

I changed sides. Felt blood rush to my neck where I was rubbing it.

"What had you done when they thought you were bad?" Aimi pressed.

For some reason I felt calmer after stretching my body and giving myself a massage. I walked over to the armchair and sat down.

"It could be anything. From fighting with my brothers to asking for a treat. Mom always baked delicious brownies."

"They thought you were naughty for asking for a brownie?" Aimi clearly had no conception of how unpredictable my parents were.

"Sometimes, when I came into the kitchen and asked mom for something to eat, she'd give it to me. Other times when I asked, I was yelled at. And sometimes she said nothing at all and just forced me down into the basement."

"So you never knew how they would react?"

It struck me that my parents were the ones who should be talking to a therapist, not me.

"What did the basement look like?" she asked.

"Concrete. More like a storage room. But my parents didn't want to keep anything valuable there, because it was cold and damp. Anything they stored down there was ruined, they always said."

She looked down at her notebook and wrote something.

"But there was a mattress and quilt down there, on top of some flattened cardboard boxes."

Couldn't she just write the prescription already? I wouldn't be able to stand being in here much longer. I checked the time again.

"You know I will tell you when it's been an hour, Leona. How long were you forced to stay in the basement each time?"

"Until I learned my lesson. I slept down there a lot."

"It must have been hard to learn since they were so inconsistent with their discipline," she said.

"I started studying them. Carefully. Always stopped in the doorway and never entered the room until I knew what mood they were in. It was easier to tell with dad. Mom was harder to figure out."

"So you got good at reading them."

Aimi wrote more things in her notebook. I couldn't muster the energy to care. She could write whatever she wanted. There were natural explanations for all the things she tried to label as deviant, but I had nothing to gain from arguing about it, since I couldn't support my claims with evidence, because I couldn't tell her the truth about how I was under threat and why.

"Did you read other people too?"

I wondered what she was getting at. What the significance of it was.

"Teachers. It was easy to tell what they wanted."

"How did you do in school?"

School had always been easy for me, but I had found most of it boring. I always finished before everyone else. To pass the time, I was given extra work that I also completed before anyone else was done. By that time, I was usually tired of sitting still and found ways of getting out of the classroom so I could do something else.

"It was easy to figure out what the teachers wanted you to study for the tests. I usually got top grades."

Aimi reached for the water jug on the low, round coffee table between us. Held it up to the glass nearest me and looked at me inquiringly. I declined. She poured herself a glass and took a sip. I checked the time again. Didn't have time to stay but wanted that prescription. I slumped deeper into my armchair.

"Was there any adult in your life you felt you could trust?"

"What do you mean?" I said. "You can't trust people. If you could, we wouldn't need the police. The whole legal system would—"

"I mean, was there anyone you could talk to about your home situation?"

It became clear to me Aimi had no idea how I functioned. Grown-ups couldn't be trusted. I had learned that lesson early. There was no point trying. No one ever understood me.

My only chance had been to become like them.

I realized I no longer had any use for Aimi. Granted, she had got me back on my feet, aside from the insomnia, but this was the end of the line for us. That being said, I wasn't leaving her office without my sleeping pills. I sank even deeper into my armchair. Closed my eyes. Raised my eyebrows and blinked a few times to make her understand I was struggling to stay awake.

"I mostly kept to myself," I said drowsily.

"Didn't anyone notice you were having trouble?"

"Aimi, you know what, I don't think I can do any more today," I said.

I sat up with my elbows on my knees and rubbed both my eyes. Grabbed the armrests and slowly heaved myself out of the chair.

"I have to pick up Beatrice from day care as well."

"Had you arranged to pick her up when we booked this appointment? It's only been twenty minutes," Aimi said.

I sighed loudly. It was a lie. I wasn't picking up Beatrice. I just wanted an excuse to leave.

"I don't know...things blend together...days and nights. No, I really do have to go." I stood up.

Just as I managed to get upright, I wobbled. Grabbed the chair's backrest, closed my eyes, and said, "Oh dear, it all went black there for a second. But I'm fine."

I held on for a while before straightening my clothes. Picked my bag up from the floor and started rummaging through it, mostly to give her time to write the prescription. I glanced at her furtively. She walked over to her desk and pulled out a drawer. Spotting a hair tie in my bag, I fished it out and started pulling my hair back to put it up in a ponytail.

"I'm going to write you a prescription for sleeping pills, Leona. You might feel a bit drowsy the next day, and they can affect your ability to drive a car, so you have to keep an eye on that. It varies from person to person, so you have to be the judge of whether or not you should drive.

I couldn't understand why it had taken her so long to decide to write the prescription. Some people were certainly not quick thinkers.

"Do you really think I need sleeping pills?" I said.

Why did I say that? I was home free. Sometimes it was like I had this strange urge to destroy everything I had worked for the moment I got it. I didn't know why. Maybe that could have been something to discuss with a therapist, but I wasn't about to bring it up with Aimi. At this point I should be thankful if she didn't rescind the offered prescription and refer me to some health food store to buy some kind of herbal tea that tasted like hay.

"I think it might be a good idea to try it for a while and then we'll see."

Before I got to my car, I had decided to stop seeing Aimi. Maybe I would feel a need to dig deeper into my psyche in the future.

But not now.

I was starting to get my energy back and now that I'd been given the means to sleep at night, everything else would work out.

She'd insisted on booking another appointment before I left her office instead of my calling later as I had suggested, but I would have no trouble canceling that session. Or postponing it.

Far into the future.

Without knowing how I would get the money, I pulled my phone out of my pocket and replied to Armand's text: *I confirm.*

TWENTY-FOUR

I was sitting in my car outside Österåker Prison, waiting. He should be out any minute now.

Johnny Timmer.

I knew he wouldn't have any relatives coming to pick him up when he was released after serving his two-year prison sentence, and so far, there was no one else either.

Compared to a lot of criminals, he was a bright guy who I felt deserved better than walking out those prison gates with no plans for the future. This kind of place, right outside a prison, was the ultimate recruiting ground for my business. Hopefully, his time behind bars had motivated him to learn more about how to avoid getting caught again.

There could be no doubt that a life of crime was what awaited him on the outside. He had no education, no place to live, and no family to speak of. I knew he had debts. At some point, I had seen him at the poker tables at Casino Cosmopol, but I knew he wasn't much of a card sharp.

We had some history together, him and me. The first time he featured as a suspect in one of my investigations, I had found him to be a pain in the ass. He constantly talked back in interviews. I would ask a question and he would answer something completely irrelevant. He kept that up until I couldn't bear talking to him anymore. But things got better every time we crossed paths until eventually we had started joking around with each other. But now I hadn't seen him in a long time. Since his last run-in with the police, he had been locked up.

I tapped my index finger against the wheel while I waited for him to come out. Figured it must be dreary being released on a day like this. Not a single ray of sunshine to welcome Johnny to his newfound freedom. The orange prison wall was the only splash of color in the area.

The drizzle had covered the windshield with a layer of moisture that looked like what you get when you spray something with a spray bottle. I turned on the wipers and let them drag across the glass once before turning them off again. Then I saw someone walking toward me. Probably Johnny, but he was too far away to tell for sure. The build and gait seemed right. He might be slightly thinner than I remembered, but prison had that effect on some. Dark, unkempt hair, white T-shirt, black leather jacket, blue jeans, and sneakers. It was him. When he got closer, I noticed his clothes hadn't been washed in a long time. That was fine. I had brought a change of clothes. I let him get fairly close before I opened the car door and stepped out. I pulled out my police badge and showed it to him.

"Timmer, I want to talk to you."

"Oh come on, give me a fucking break. I just got out. What could I possibly have done in the few minutes since I walked out the gate? I haven't even fucking called anyone."

"Chill out, Timmer, I just want a quick chat," I said.

"Cops always just want a quick chat. But somehow you always end up behind bars, chatting with yourself."

He kept on walking past me.

"You're free to go, but I have an offer for you. I want to give you a chance to make money. A lot of money."

He stopped. Turned around. I opened the passenger door.

"Get in and I'll tell you more."

He shook his head, his face blank, then turned around and kept walking.

"If you're not interested after you hear what I have to say, at least you scored a ride into town," I said. "It'll take me at most five minutes to explain. Five minutes."

He stopped and checked his wristwatch.

"Or are you in a rush to get somewhere?" I said and looked around.

The area was completely deserted. In one direction, the only road in sight led straight to the prison. In the other direction it continued away from it. On either side of it were flat stretches of grass. He turned to me again.

"Never in a million years am I getting into some goddamn fucking cop car, all right?"

"Calm down, this isn't an undercover car, it's my private one. No one knows I'm here to talk to you. I swear."

I stuck my index finger in the air, as if that would somehow show I was telling the truth. I usually drove my work car, but I realized that immediately after being released, he wouldn't be so keen on sliding into a police vehicle, so I had taken my own.

He studied me, eyes narrowed. I pulled a pack of Marlboro Lights from my jacket pocket. Lit one and managed to inhale and blow the smoke out without coughing.

"Sorry," I said, pulled another cigarette halfway out the packet and held it out to him.

He hesitated. Looked around like he didn't want anyone to know he was standing around talking to a cop. When he had reassured himself there was no one around, he came closer. Quickly pulled out the cigarette as if the rest of the pack was on fire, and backed up a few paces before putting it between his lips. I held up my lighter and once again forced him to come closer. After a couple of drags, he seemed to relax a little. He looked back at the prison.

"You know," I said. "I can make sure you never go back inside again."

His mind seemed to have wandered off. He wasn't listening.

"You could keep doing what you do, only better," I continued.

I was unsure if he even heard me. He didn't look at me again until I said his name.

"What the fuck are you on about? If you're trying to nail me for something, I'm going to fucking—"

"Shh...," I said. "Don't get yourself into trouble now, Timmer. It would suck for me if I had to arrest you for threats against a police officer."

I held the car door open.

"Five minutes?" I tried again.

He finished the cigarette like it was the last thing he was going to do in life. Ground the butt under his heel and got in the car.

"You and I have obviously met a number of times," I said after getting in and closing the door.

"And?"

"I know you've been committing crimes since before you were even in your teens. No matter how much people have tried, you just keep going back to that shit."

"Seriously, I was just released and I'm in a good mood. Are you going to try and get me down now? I mean, fuck," he said, slumping down in his seat and crossing his arms.

"You're always going to make your living by breaking the law, aren't you?" I continued.

I don't know why I asked. How was he supposed to answer that? He probably didn't think beyond getting the money he needed to get through the day. Somehow it was as if I was trying to make sure he wasn't going to lose out on something by joining my venture. I wanted to know how he viewed his future.

He shrugged.

"You didn't exactly see employers lining up outside the wall, fighting to hire me when I got out, now did you?" he said.

"I have a project I think might suit you," I said.

He didn't even look at me. Like the others, he had probably heard it all many times before. He had no way of knowing my project was fundamentally different from the offers he had been given before by the Prison and Probation Service or Social Services.

"Just drive me into town instead," he said. "You can dump me at Sergels Torg. I have to find a buddy of mine."

"I want to teach you how to commit crimes," I said.

Once the words penetrated into his conscience, he slowly turned his head toward me. Looked at me for a few seconds as though he was trying to read something from my facial expression. When all he got was a solemn look, he burst out laughing and looked around the car.

"What the fuck is this, some kind of sick setup or what? Where are the cameras?"

He turned down the sun visor and ran his hand across it. Felt behind the rearview mirror and touched the dashboard.

"Relax, Timmer. There are no cameras. I've selected you because I know what you're made of. I know your background. You've had a rough fucking go of it, but that makes you a survivor. You don't belong with the rest of the thugs on the street. You're smarter than that. I want to see you among the more sophisticated criminals. The ones who make big money breaking the law."

He stared at me, wide-eyed and silent.

"The ones who know how law enforcement works and who consequently don't have to spend half their lives in jail," I continued. "I want to help you with that."

He shook his head.

"If I didn't know you were clean, I'd assume you were having a bad trip or something. Let me see your badge again," he said and held out his hand to me.

"Come off it, Timmer. You know who I am," I said. "We've met loads of times."

He kept his hand extended. I took out my badge and held it up to him. He studied it closely. Took hold of one corner of it as if he were expecting parts of it to fall off. Like I had bought it online or something. Then he looked up at me.

"What the fuck are you?" he asked.

"I have new clothes and shoes for you in the back seat. If you want to give me a chance to show you what I'm talking about, you'll climb back there and change. They're in those bags."

He threw a quick glance at the back seat.

"I want to show you something that can change your life in a way that's never been suggested to you before."

He was still eyeing me suspiciously.

"Come on, what have you got to lose? If you don't want to, you'll get out and forget this meeting. If you choose to get on board, you can still change your mind at any time and walk away. You're a free man. You've paid your debt to society."

He threw open the car door and climbed out. Slammed it shut behind him. Fuck! His leaving would not be good. Not because I was worried about his talking about me—this guy's criminal record was so long no one would believe a word he said—but it would be a loss for both of us if he didn't want in. Candidates for my venture didn't exactly grow on trees. I was limited to the ones I could get, the ones I knew, and the ones I thought would be a good fit.

I looked at him. Hoped he had decided to get in the back seat, but he hadn't. I bent forward across the passenger seat to see where he was going and saw him stand a few yards away, typing on his phone.

I started the car and slowly turned out into the street, angling the rearview mirror to keep watching him. As I had thought, when he realized I was about to drive away, he came running. Opened the door to the back seat and jumped in before the car came to a stop.

"Fine, so drive me into town then," he said and closed the door.

I kept driving. In the rearview mirror, I could see him searching through the shopping bags I had left there.

"What the fuck is this? Men's Warehouse?"

"Just put them on," I said. "Your clothes are filthy."

"This is fucking embarrassing. I can't walk around like some goddamn Joe Six-Pack," he mumbled.

"Why not?" I said and smiled. "You're not wearing those old rags where we're going. And besides, who says no to new clothes? Especially if you've just been released from prison."

"Seriously? I mean, fuck! This is pretty goddamn twisted," he continued.

I let him get on with it. He rummaged around the bags some more, ducking every time he saw a person on the street.

"I suppose this could be okay," he said, holding up a completely run-of-the-mill white T-shirt. But I'm not wearing these fucking winkle-pickers, just so we're clear."

I had to pull it together hard not to burst out laughing. I liked Timmer. He was entertaining.

"How about we swing by McDonald's?" I said. "My treat."

Österåker Prison wasn't exactly known for its gourmet fare. I'd have been surprised if he'd said no to a Big Mac.

"Make it a drive-through," he said. "No fucking chance I'm walking into a Mickey D in these bullshit clothes with some cop bitch."

I drove out toward Globen. There wasn't a McDonald's drive-through for miles, but I couldn't be bothered to argue with him. When we got to the Globen City Mall, I gave him money and said I wanted a McFeast menu. He could buy whatever he wanted for himself. I explained he could certainly split and take the money if he wanted. That way, he'd gain two hundred kronor and lose the opportunity of a lifetime. I wasn't going to tell him about my venture until we got there. It was best not to tell him anything more specific, in case he did decide to split, but I had at least made him curious enough to tag along this far.

Even though it took longer than expected, he did eventually come back and seemed to have bought food for both of us. I laughed out loud in the car when I spotted him slinking toward me, hugging the side of the building, hunched over in his light khaki slacks, white T-shirt, light-blue shirt, navy sweater vest, his own grimy white sneakers, clutching a McDonald's bag in his hand.

"Drive!" he shouted the moment his behind touched the car seat.

I guess he realized how comical it was, or maybe my laughter was just contagious, because I saw in the mirror that he smiled as he wolfed down his french fries.

I drove down toward the Meatpacking District. The rain had started up again and was pattering against the windows. The whole area looked gray. Two of the letters in the neon sign at the turnoff had gone out. The Globen Arena peaked out between the buildings at the end of the street like a shining, light-gray sphere. The asphalt was wet and illuminated by the handful of security lights mounted on the buildings. I parked the car a few blocks away from the building I had rented but stayed in my seat and reached back for the bag of food.

"Was there change?" I asked.

"Right, sorry," he said and dug around his pocket.

He handed over a few coins with greasy, salty fingers. I ate my burger but didn't want the fries. He happily ate mine too and seemed careful not to spill in the car, which I appreciated.

"Whatever you think about what I'm going to tell you over the next hour, I want you to know that you were carefully selected."

"An hour? You said five minutes."

"Listen, Timmer. This is a very special business venture and I've only chosen a few guys to be in on it. I believe in you, remember that."

He glanced at me while he drank the last of his Coke.

"Bring your old clothes in those bags and follow me," I said.

I locked the car and we walked toward the building together. He looked around but didn't say anything. I led the way up the short flight of steps to the loading bay. Unlocked the door and turned the lights on. The fluorescent light bounced off the tiled walls, the stainless steel work benches, and the stone floor. I would have preferred a different setting, but places that were suitable for what I was doing were few and far between.

"What the fuck is this?" Timmer said, looking around.

"Grab a chair from over there and take a seat for now," I said and pointed to a stack of chairs by the wall. "There'll be more people coming in a bit."

"More cops?"

"Relax, Timmer," I said.

After walking past every barred window and peering through them suspiciously, he sat down on one of the chairs. The first of the others to arrive was Vikki Dimberg. To help her get away from the Råcksta idiots, I had offered her a spot. I was happy she had taken me up on it. This time, she was on time as well.

Timmer glanced at her and then shot me an even more surprised look.

The ones who had attended the first meeting dropped in one after the other. I smiled to myself. I got a kick out of seeing that I'd made them interested enough to come back. They were also supposed to have brought money this time. This was going to work out.

TWENTY-FIVE

"We have two new people here today, Johnny Timmer and Vikki Dimberg."

The others looked the two of them up and down. Both seemed uncomfortable. Vikki looked down at the floor. Her face was still bruised. Timmer seemed to feel awkward in his new outfit and slumped low in his chair. I quickly explained the nature of my business venture. Vikki and Timmer looked around at the other participants as if they wanted confirmation that what I was saying was true. The others sat there calmly with their eyes on me, which made Vikki and Timmer do the same.

"So if you pay attention, you'll be able, with my help, to make so much money you eventually won't have to break the law at all anymore. Today, I want to talk about the most important factors for avoiding being identified. But first I want to say a few words about the last thing we talked about at our first meeting."

I looked out at them.

"Has anyone given any thought to the perfect crime? Does it exist, you think?"

"I suppose it has to, since you've brought us here," Liam said.

"If you define the perfect crime as a crime where you leave no trace behind whatsoever, the answer is no. That's virtually impossible."

I sat down on the chair facing them.

"*But*, the most important thing is to make sure the traces you do leave behind aren't enough to get you arrested. If you do end up arrested anyway, they have to not amount to what the law describes as 'sufficient evidence to charge.' And they certainly shouldn't be verifiable 'beyond reasonable doubt,' which, as I'm sure you know, is what is required for a conviction in a Swedish court of law."

I'd have to get back to how to go about this later.

"The evidentiary requirements are considerable. But in order to avoid being singled out as a suspect in the first place, you have to avoid being identified and associated with the crime. Which is why today, we're going to talk about disguises and camouflage."

Identifying a suspect early on was often pivotal to the success of a police investigation. Criminals were often sloppy and made basic mistakes, which led to their arrest. I was going to have to break this down to beginner's level if I wanted them to understand the importance of it. Then I would be able to pick up the pace more and more. Teaching them how to plant evidence now, at the start, would be a complete waste of time if they didn't first get the hang of the fundamentals.

"Some of you, like Timmer, Zack, and Eli, have been arrested lots of times."

Timmer, who had been dealing drugs since he was a teenager, was actually lucky to have avoided a long prison sentence. Zack, who was primarily into selling explosives and guns, had also been busted for a variety of minor offenses. Eli burgled houses and sold the loot. Aside from being criminals, the three had another thing in common as well: they had all been arrested on days when they had *not* committed any crimes. As a result of routine searches.

"I have a question for you. Can you tell from looking at a person that he or she is a criminal?"

I looked out at them. Liam, who had a lot of tattoos and shaved one side of his blond head, spoke up. "Some people look like criminals even though they're not, others are criminals but look like regular family guys. So no, how could you?"

"Wrong," I told him. "Some police officers can. Or rather, we *think* we can. We'll say we can't, since it's prejudiced to suspect people on the basis of their appearance alone, but the fact is that most police officers are convinced they can tell from looking at a person whether he's a criminal. This is sometimes referred to as a 'gut feeling' but what it's really about is that we draw conclusions from our prejudices and our subjective experience. How many of you have been stopped by police for no reason?"

Everyone except Vikki raised their hands.

"In other countries, this is called 'stop and search,' and just like in Sweden, it's been the topic of a lot of debate since some people feel it allows the police to arbitrarily stop people they think look like criminals without there being reasonable suspicion. I don't know if you've ever given it much thought, but most people go their whole lives without being stopped by the police. I'd imagine you've all been stopped quite a few times?"

"Are you fucking kidding? The pigs are all over me all the goddamn time," Liam exclaimed.

"You may have had to give urine samples, we may have searched your clothes or just said hi and asked you a few general questions on the street. Why do you think we've singled you out?"

"Because you're fucking idiots," Marc said.

I leaned against the table behind me. Crossed my arms. If there was one thing I was used to, it was thugs who hated cops. If he thought I was that easily provoked, he was mistaken.

"I'm sure that's true of some of us," I replied calmly, "but that wasn't the answer I was looking for. Would you like another guess, Marc?"

He just glared at me without responding.

"It's quite simply because you look the way we expect thugs to look," I told them. "I know the way you dress, your tattoos, maybe gang tattoos, piercings, shaved heads, ripped muscles, gold watches, club emblems, swanky cars or old beaters, biker vests, pro-drug badges, and whatever are a big part of your identity. But a lot of these things are exactly the attributes the police are on the lookout for."

I was aware most people outside the criminal underworld figured all criminals were smart enough to hide things like that, but that was definitely not always the case. Often, the opposite was true; they wanted to display who they were, which gang they belonged to, and so on.

They looked at me in silence.

"So we're presumed guilty? Before we've even done anything?" Liam said.

"I guess you could say that," I replied. "At least in the eyes of a lot of police officers. But this is a bit complex, since a lot of the times, you have actually done something. It becomes a vicious circle where police officers keep having their preconceived notions confirmed. If we were to check people with different appearances, we'd find criminals among them too, but the thing is that we don't, because we think they look upstanding. Where we look for crime, we find crime, and that's how the upstanding-looking ones get away with things. Does that make sense?"

Some nodded, others stared at me stiffly. A few looked indignant.

"Don't blame me," I said. "It's not my fault. I'm just telling you what reality looks like."

I couldn't imagine that what I was saying was news to any of them, but it had probably never been explicitly stated and confirmed by a law enforcer before.

"This might sound stupid to you, but believe me, if you'd understood the importance of it, and used it to your advantage, you wouldn't have gone to prison half as many times as you have. And if you keep coming to these meetings and learn, you will reduce the risk to close to zero."

"Fucking pigs," Marc muttered.

"Marc, you should know this isn't just true of cops," I continued, "but of the general public as well, of regular people. They get suspicious around you too. If you think about it, you'd probably be the same. I could show you a picture of a tatted-up motorcycle guy in worn black jeans and a vest next to a banker in a white shirt, tie, and suit. If you bumped into them in an alley in the Old Town on a dark night, I'm sure you'd feel more at ease with the banker and be more wary of what the motorcycle guy was up to. The banker could be a serial killer and the motorcycle guy the world's kindest man, for all you know, but that's probably not how you'd see them."

"But aren't cops supposed to know better than regular people?" Vikki asked.

"You might think so," I said. "But that's not always the case."

I think it was dawning on them what I was getting at.

"What I'm describing now are, of course, extremes. I'm not saying you have to start dressing like bankers, but you have to be aware of this and try to understand the importance of it. If you really want to be able to make a living off crime, without being arrested all the time, you have to adjust your look."

I went around the room. Studied them.

"To be honest, all but two of you look like thugs. People like me would stop you in the street. The only people I wouldn't stop are Timmer and Vikki."

Everyone looked them up and down.

"Just so you know, these aren't mine," Timmer said and held his arms out at the others. "I would never buy these fucking bullshit clothes."

A few people grinned. I pointed at Timmer.

"I doubt any of you would guess that he was released from Österåker today, would you?" I said. "Slightly unkempt and unshaved, sure, but aside from that you look very upstanding, Timmer. Thanks to Men's Warehouse."

I turned to Vikki.

"Just the fact that you're a woman means people won't be as suspicious of you. Tough shit, guys. Because you've dominated crime statistics throughout history, at least in this context, we women have it easier."

Vikki smiled and made a V sign with both hands at the guys.

"There are a lot of simple things you can do to change your appearance, but those of you with dark skin will have the toughest time. Unfortunately, you're still considered suspicious. Research shows immigrants are discriminated against at every level of law enforcement. They are disproportionally reported and identified by witnesses and victims, get arrested more, are paid closer attention to by detectives, get charged more often, convicted more often, and given harsher sentences. This is structural discrimination that has actually been shown to be more prevalent among the police than among prosecutors and judges. Unfortunately, you need to bear this injustice in mind."

The guys had obviously already figured this out, but I wanted to make it clear to them that the discrimination wasn't in their minds, it was systemic and scientifically proven. I didn't tell them this so they could feel sorry for themselves or to make them disappointed about how racist and unfair the police or the rest of the world was, but because they needed to be aware of the importance of it and find ways to exploit it.

"Clearly, you can't change the color of your skin, so you have to find other ways to compensate."

"So you're saying I have to dress like that," Zack said with a queasy nod to Timmer.

Liam and Eli laughed. I walked over to a big easel pad standing off to one side of the room. I wrote: "Joe Six-Pack"

"Joe Six-Pack, in the sense of that regular, law-abiding, average person, that's the look we're going for. Preferably slightly upper class, but just normal works fine. This is about surface. On the inside, you can be whoever you want as far as I'm concerned."

I put my hand to my chest.

"The people who get away with crimes that can't wear or don't require a ski mask, do so because they're good at blending in. There's also a small group of seriously dangerous big-time criminals who are good at exactly that. Serial killers, for example, often look like regular family men. They might be married, live in a normal house, and have pets. No one ever suspects them because they look normal and live normal lives. What the concepts 'normal' and 'regular' mean is obviously open to discussion, but let's not overanalyze. I think you know what I mean."

No one spoke.

"You obviously also need to behave like upstanding people. Be polite and helpful to others, and don't be afraid to smile. Think of it as playing a part. We all play all kinds of roles in life, don't we? The roles of parent, son, boyfriend, employee, and whatever else. But this is for sure going to be your most lucrative one, if you can learn to play it well."

The reaction to this was slightly unexpected. The guys were glaring at me.

"I know many of you have fought prejudice your entire lives. This is about learning to use people's narrow-minded preconceptions for your own gain. It's about making it hard for my fellow police officers and others to suspect you."

"So you're saying we do have to wear a mask after all; what difference does it make, then?" Eli said.

"This is obviously not applicable to a bank during a bank job, but rather to places where you can't wear a ski mask and where you don't want people to notice you, like when you're going to and from a crime scene, when you're smuggling something across national borders, when you're doing recon for a heist or steal or whatever else. The method has to suit the crime."

As I was talking, there was suddenly a loud knock on the door. I looked at the others. Had someone run their mouth off about what I was doing here? A couple of them jumped out of their chairs. I reflexively put my hand on my gun. Walked over to a window some ways from the door. Peeked out from behind the plastic sheet. It was Lasse, the landlord. I went over to the door. Opened it just a crack.

"Hey there, I just wanted to make sure everything was all right for you," he said.

"Hi," I said and smiled. "Absolutely, everything's great."

He stayed where he was, trying to peer in through the door.

"We're in the middle of a...," I said with no further explanation.

"Ah, right, I didn't mean to interrupt," he said. "Like I said, I just wanted to check in."

"Thank you, Lasse, that's very thoughtful."

He stayed where he was.

I stayed where I was.

"We're just going to get on with it then," I said.

"Sure, right, of course, go ahead," he said, and stayed where he was.

I stared at him.

"See you," he said.

I nodded.

He turned around and started walking down the stairs. I closed the door and turned to the others.

"A good example of a witness," I said. "They'll pop up when you least expect. That was the man who rents this place out to me. What do you think he would have thought if I'd let him in and he'd seen you?"

I pushed back a few hairs that kept falling in front of my right eye.

"He'd hardly believe I was running a mindfulness workshop," I said. "He would probably have asked me a bunch of questions about what I was using this place for or maybe he would have just called the police to tell them he suspected some kind of criminal activity was going on here. Just from catching a glimpse of you."

I took a hair tie out of my pocket and pulled my hair up into a messy bun.

"And speaking of witnesses. You want to avoid them as much as humanly possible."

Witness statements could be ruinous for a criminal.

"Even if there is DNA, I want you to know that courts often consider witnesses' statements more important. DNA might tie you to the scene of the crime, but it might not prove you actually committed the crime. If, on the other hand, an independent witness saw you commit the crime, you're in a tough spot when it comes to trial. And remember, witnesses are everywhere. On balconies, in the house across the street, the shop next door, on buses and in other vehicles passing by, dog owners walking around the oddest places at all hours of the day and night. People see a lot, even if some of them have a hard time remembering and recounting what they've seen. The goal is to have any potential witnesses, especially ones that have happened to catch a glimpse of you, not remember anything particular about your appearance, because you look so nondescript."

It seemed like they were finally starting to understand how crucial this was.

"By the same token, a judge will have a hard time passing a guilty verdict if there are no witnesses. But *if* someone did see you, then what do you do?"

"You get rid of the witness," Liam suggested.

I'd been on the fence about recruiting Liam.

"What fucking gangster movie are you living in, Liam? Come off it, will you? Hurting an innocent person who has nothing to do with anything, who just happens to be in the wrong place at the wrong time, is completely fucking unacceptable. If you have a hard time accepting that, you're going to have to imagine it being your little brother."

I knew he had a younger brother he was close with. Over the years, I'd come to understand that most people have the ability to put themselves in someone else's shoes and empathize with their feelings. To me, it seemed implausible. As if you could just slip into another person's body. Think that person's thoughts. I had no way of knowing if these guys had that ability, but since the received wisdom was that most people were capable of it, I just had to cross my fingers it was true.

"To go looking up witnesses and threatening them with violence if they talk to the police is only viable if you're one hundred percent sure your threats will be successful. If they're not, and they report your threats as well, you could be charged with obstructing the course of justice. This is considered a very serious crime since it would undermine the entire legal system if people were too afraid to testify or report crimes to the police. This is most common in organized crime circles, in youth crime, and with crimes among family members."

I could sense I was getting too theoretical.

"All because you were incompetent and didn't use the appropriate disguise or camouflage. Going back afterward to threaten people isn't worth the risk. And whatever you do, never take hostages."

I looked at them.

"Have any of you ever done that?"

Marc nodded.

"And how did that work out for you?"

He rolled up his sleeve to the elbow and showed me his tattoo-covered forearm. Among the different signs and symbols was a clearly distinguishable number, an eight. I nodded slowly.

"Eight years in prison is not the best use of anyone's time, is it?" I said.

He muttered something inaudible in reply.

"You should be grateful you made it out alive. A hostage situation is one of the most dangerous messes you can get yourselves, your hostages, and the police into."

I checked my watch. Time to speed things up.

"We police officers obviously don't just stop people we think look like criminals, we also stop people who we know have committed crimes before. If you've been busted for a certain type of crime a few times, we actually recognize you. If you're hanging out in an odd location at an odd time of day, we're going to know something's going down. We know that almost only thugs will be in certain places at certain times. As soon as we see something unusual, we react. We're out on the streets all hours of the day and night and we don't miss much. Not to mention the people we have under surveillance, but that's a story for another time."

I needed to hit a few more points on the subject of looks.

"Is that tattoo on your neck finished?" I asked, addressing Liam.

He shook his head.

"One or two more sessions," he replied.

"Sweet, man," Eli said, studying Liam's neck. "Who did it?"

"A guy I know," Liam replied. "He's awesome. I can give you his num —"

"No visible tattoos," I broke in. "You've all been arrested for serious crimes and booked. That means the police have all your tattoos, piercings, scars, fingerprints, height, hair color, eye color, facial shape, and build registered. You get what that means, right?"

Before anyone could reply, I pressed on.

"It means all the cool and unique tattoos and piercings you felt compelled to have done over the years help us identify you. If a witness claims to have seen an eyebrow ring, a tattooed teardrop under one eye or a spider on a neck, you've helped us narrow down the possible pool of suspects considerably. We're always grateful for that. During trial, you're also in some deep shit if a witness has pegged their recollections on something everyone in the courtroom can see. If she, for example, were to say she saw a creepy-crawly on the perp's neck and you're sitting there with a big scorpion under your chin."

The guys had quite a lot of ink, but aside from Liam, none of them seemed to have any in places that couldn't be covered with clothes.

"And if that's not bad enough, you've all been swabbed as well, which means we have you logged in our DNA database. That means it's going to be important not to leave skin, hair follicles, or bodily fluids at the crime scene. If our crime scene technicians find any of those things and there's a match, it'll be tough for you to explain it. I'll get back to how you can avoid that."

I tried not to rattle off too many facts right now, since I might lose their interest, but I was on a roll; talking about crime was a rush. I also wanted them to know what kind of information the police had about them and how it was used. That the police often had the upper hand.

"Knowledge about crime scene technology could be very useful if you wanted, for example, to lead the police astray or plant DNA from someone else at the crime scene. But then you have to know how to go about it. You can't just dump a lock of hair randomly, but that's advanced stuff for later."

I was doubtful we'd get that far during the series of meetings I had planned. There were more important things to get to, but this was enough for today. I had covered a lot of ground, even for me.

"I think you should consider whether you're really committed to this. You should know that we keep pretty good track of individual thugs, criminal gangs, and the people operating on their outskirts. It's going to take a lot of work for you to get good."

This was our second meeting and even though I needed every one of them, I knew that if they weren't dedicated and didn't take the information in, my plans for them wouldn't work.

"Can't you tell us what to do if we get nabbed by the cops? I mean, to get away," Vikki said.

"The whole point is that you won't end up in that situation anymore, but I will also teach you exactly what to do if everything does go wrong and you end up arrested. If you want that information, you'll have to keep coming. We're done for today. Pay on your way out."

I'd been worried they would find my meetings redundant. A lot of criminals were cocksure and didn't think they'd ever get caught, but it seemed like they realized I was in a position to actually provide facts they found useful.

While I stacked the chairs, Timmer went to the bathroom. When he came out, he was wearing his own grimy clothes. He handed me the Men's Warehouse bag.

"Keep them," I told him. "Who knows, maybe you decide to start wearing them. If not, you can always sell them. That way, you can afford to attend the next meeting."

TWENTY-SIX

Last night's meeting in the Meatpacking District had made me tired enough to fall asleep without sleeping pills. But I'd taken one anyway, just to be sure. When I woke up, I was sluggish to say the least, but I actually felt rested during the day. The hours in the office went by without my head or body hurting.

Even though my new house keys had been rattling around my purse since last week, they were still shiny. I unlocked the door and went inside. The heavy burglar-proof door my landlord had bragged about when I moved in had proven pretty ineffectual against unwelcome guests. Armand had clearly found a contact with skills in that area and had keys made. The only locksmith I trusted was the one we used at work. Ten minutes after I called them on Monday, they had an employee at my apartment. She had changed the lock in minutes. If Armand was planning to send someone to pay me a visit again, I was at least not going to let them traipse in using the same key.

I had been trying to get hold of Larissa for two days, without success. I was starting to think something had happened to her. She wasn't the kind of person who didn't pick up her phone.

Before I took off my windbreaker, I went over to the living room window and checked the street outside. As usual, there were many unfamiliar cars parked down there. I tore a sheet of paper from the notepad in the bookcase, wrote down the license plate numbers I could see and left the sheet of paper on the windowsill. If I kept writing down every car I saw, sooner or later, I'd notice if there was a car that kept showing up wherever I went. I pulled the curtains closed and went into the kitchen. Same thing there. A new sheet of paper and a pen that I left by the window after writing down every car I could see.

I checked my phone. Armand had already given me all the information I needed, but I still wasn't able to relax. Didn't know how to get the money in time. It was dinnertime, but I wasn't hungry. I found Peter's number in my contacts while I walked back to the hallway and took off my shoes.

"I want to talk to Bea," I said when he picked up.

I had dispensed with "Hello" and "How are you" and other forms of polite chitchat. Ineffective nonsense.

"We're at the supermarket," Peter said. "Why don't you call back at bedtime and say good night instead?"

"I'll call then too," I said and took off my jacket. "Give her the phone now."

After a sigh and some crackling in my ear, I heard Peter's footsteps followed by him calling her softly.

"For fuck's sake, Peter! You don't know where she is at all times? Where did you say you were?" I said.

He didn't respond. Didn't seem to be holding the phone to his ear. I put my hand to my mouth to form a megaphone to amplify the sound and shouted even louder.

"*Peter!*"

Still just the sound of his footsteps and a scraping noise. He was out of his fucking mind, leaving her unattended somewhere in the store. I was unable to stand still now so I started pacing around the apartment. Didn't he get that all it took was one second of distraction and she could be gone?

"Bea!" he called out, his voice happy and carefree. "Mommy wants to talk to you."

Just as I was about to put my shoes on and run out to the car, I heard her on the other end.

"Mommy, I've found new crayons."

I sat down on the chair in the hallway with my head bowed and one hand on my forehead. Exhaled and felt warmth spread through my body at the sound of her tiny little voice. She loved to draw. Paper and a couple of crayons could entertain her for hours.

"That's nice, sweetheart. Are you having fun?"

"They're the same as Benji's crayons."

"That's great, Bea. Now listen to me, honey. You have to promise mommy not to leave daddy like that. Do you hear m—"

"Leona, we have to go now," Peter's voice was suddenly back.

"What do you think you're doing, Peter? You can't leave her unattended like that."

"What exactly is going to happen, Leona?" He replied in an aggravating drawl. "She wanted to look at the toys and I was just a few aisles away."

"You have no fucking idea what could happen. Every day, I see—"

"Ah, so she's going to get kidnapped, sold to traffickers to be a child prostitute in South America or what?" he said sarcastically.

"That actually happens, Peter."

"Leona, come off it, okay?" he said. "We're at Hemköp by Skanstull. Not in some bad action flick."

I couldn't bear to listen to his naive bullshit. Peter was an amazing dad in many ways, but when it came to safety, he was clueless. Like so many people, he lived in his little protected bubble, refusing to believe anything bad could ever happen. Blissfully ignorant of what police officers saw every day.

I was just about to hang up when he said, "By the way, a former colleague of yours asked about you."

"Yeah?" I replied.

"He didn't give his name, but he said you'd worked together about a year ago. Dark hair, wearing a shirt and sport coat. Actually looked more like an office monkey than a cop."

"So you met him. Where?"

"Calm down," Peter said. "He rang the door yesterday."

"At the apartment?"

Peter still lived in the apartment we'd shared.

"Where else?" Peter replied.

"But you know all my colleagues. Surely you know who it —"

"How am I supposed to remember all the people you work with? But Bea recognized him."

"*What?!*" I said, raising my voice.

"She ran up and said hi. I figured if she recognized him, then…"

"What the fuck, Peter, are you out of your mind?!"

"Look, we're at the checkout now. I'll have to call you back, Leona."

"But you can't —"

He hung up.

I threw on my jacket and shoes and ran out the door, car keys in hand. I couldn't let Peter be in charge of this. If anything happened to Beatrice I would never forgive myself.

The feeling of being watched returned when I got in the car, but no one seemed to follow me when I drove away.

After ringing the door to Peter's apartment on Allhelgonagatan on Södermalm three times without anyone answering, I sat down on the stairs and waited. I had called him several times, but he wasn't picking up. Even though I made myself as slim as possible, and there was plenty of room on the stairs, a neighbor groaned loudly and stomped his feet demonstratively as he walked past me.

Peter had said that they were just down by Skanstull, buying groceries. I checked my watch for the fourth time. Surely it shouldn't take this long?

"Mommy!" Beatrice shouted when the elevator door opened and she spotted me.

Before I could get up, she was running toward me with open arms. I hugged her close. Her innocent voice calmed me down. When I felt her little arms around my neck, I realized that for the first time since Benjamin died, I was able to hold her without it hurting. Without seeing Benjamin's lifeless little body in the hospital bed.

Beatrice was right there in front of me.

She was moving in my arms.

She was so full of life.

The overwhelming love I felt there on the stairs was intoxicating.

"Where's daddy?" I said and just then heard the elevator start back down.

"I can ride the elevator by myself," Bea said.

I felt irritation at Peter leaving her alone mix with my sudden euphoria.

"Leona?" Peter said when he opened the elevator door.

"We need to talk," I said curtly.

Overcome with emotion, I tried to make my voice sound normal. It was crucial to approach this with the right attitude. Communicating with Peter had become virtually impossible since we separated. I had avoided him as much as I could. Been succinct and matter of fact regarding joint decisions about practical matters.

While he unlocked the door, he kept glancing furtively at me, as though he was wondering what I was up to. I picked up one of the grocery bags he'd put down on the floor. Beatrice immediately took my other hand and went inside. I followed her into the hallway. She kicked off her shoes and kept pulling me farther into the apartment.

"Mommy, we can draw an elevator. Daddy bought me crayons. Like Benjamin's."

"You can bring the crayons, honey. We can keep drawing at my house."

Peter stopped dead and looked at me before turning around and bending down to Beatrice.

"Go to your room and open the crayons, Bea, I have to talk to mommy for a bit."

"But I want to show mommy…"

"I'll be right in, honey," I said and held out my hand. "Give me that."

She handed me her cardigan and disappeared into the apartment. The home Peter and I had been able to buy thanks to Peter's inheritance. All the furniture was where it had been when I moved out. I shuddered when I walked past the kitchen and looked into the bedroom.

"What is going on, Leona?" he said while he carried the groceries into the kitchen. "We've talked about how important it is that we plan pickups and drop-offs."

"I want more time with Beatrice," I said.

To start criticizing him for his lack of safety awareness would not be a constructive strategy; it would just set him on edge.

"Will you be able to?" he replied.

"I'm doing better, Peter. I miss her. I don't want to lose my relationship with my own daughter."

Without scraping its legs against the floor, I pulled a chair out and slowly sat down.

"I've needed time to myself, and I appreciate that you've given me that time. Before, I could barely look after myself, but I've come out the other side. My therapist has helped me. She says I've found new strength."

That wasn't exactly what Aimi had told me, but I no longer doubted that I was able to look after Beatrice for longer periods of time.

I looked around. There was something about this apartment that made me depressed. Peter's eyes, memories of a different time, thoughts of Benjamin, it was one big mess in my head. What had happened to my life?

No family.

No husband.

No children.

"I wake up in the morning and my home is empty. Without the children…"

As if from out of nowhere, my eyes filled with tears. Surprised by own reaction, I quickly wiped them away with the back of my hand. I had to look strong in front of Peter. I wanted him to know that I was capable of looking after Beatrice. That I had the strength. I had come over to make sure nothing happened to her. But now, saying the words, seeing her, hugging her, the emotion of it washed over me.

I wanted to look after my little girl.

My Beatrice.

Despite my best efforts, the tears kept coming. Peter tore off a sheet of kitchen paper and handed it to me. I wiped my cheeks on the rough tissue. Cursed myself for reacting this way. Now Peter would never believe I was able to take care of her.

The chair next to mine creaked when he sat down. I had to convince him. Between sobs, I tried to get the words out.

"You shouldn't think...just because I..."

"I think that sounds like a good idea."

Peter almost whispered the words. I had forgotten how gentle his voice could be. Comforting somehow.

"For the first time in a long time, you seem sincere, Leona," he said.

TWENTY-SEVEN

I walked down Allhelgonagatan toward Helgalunden Park with Beatrice's hand in mine. Scanning the people in the area. The cars. Checking if there was someone inside them.

"You're walking really quickly, mommy," Beatrice said.

Her voice was whiny. I didn't mind, was content just having her by my side. I opened the door to the back seat and let her get in. While I made sure her seatbelt was buckled properly, my phone rang. Unknown number. I let it ring.

"Pick up, mommy," Bea said.

Thinking it might be a journalist I'd have to fend off, I answered; to my relief, it was Larissa.

"My phone just died a few days ago," she said. "I have a new one now. I've been calling you, but you haven't picked up," she said. "Are you okay?"

"Can we meet up?" I said tersely, while I closed the door and walked around to the driver's side.

"I'm at the gym," she said. "Short break between sessions right now, but come over if you want. I'll be done for the day in forty-five minutes."

I opened the driver's door. Quickly made a sweep of the other side of the street and the rest of the area before getting in and pulling the door shut.

Larissa and I had known each other since our Police Academy days. She hadn't felt law enforcement suited her and had quickly turned herself into a personal trainer. Now she coupled that with teaching aerobics at one of the city's gym chains.

I glanced at Beatrice in the back. She seemed busy studying her own fingers. Made signs like the ones I remembered from Itsy Bitsy Spider.

"Bea, that man who came to visit you and daddy yesterday, do you remember him?" I asked as I looked at her in the mirror.

She nodded.

"The dog wasn't there," she said.

"What dog?" I asked.

"The man's dog," she said and kept on signing.

"He has a dog?" I asked.

"Really soft and cute," she said and moved her hands in the air as if she was petting it.

"Where did you meet that man and his dog?"

"Look, look, Mickey Mouse!"

Bea pointed out at the street where some kind of advertising event with red balloons and people dressed as cartoon characters was taking place outside the gym on Ringvägen.

"Bea, the man with the dog, where did you meet him?"

Bea turned in her seat, trying to see the cartoon character through the rear window as we went down into the Söderleden Tunnel.

"Bea!" I said again.

"At preschool. His dog could jump this high up the fence until the teacher told him off."

She waved her hands up and down.

"Bea, you can't talk to strangers outside your preschool, you know that, right?"

"Mommy, I want a doggie."

"Promise me, honey?"

She nodded firmly again. I'd never liked that preschool. Now it had been confirmed to me that they didn't know what they were doing. I wasn't going to let Beatrice attend anymore.

Larissa was still in her aerobics class when we got to the gym. I took up a position outside the glass door with Bea and waited. Even though the door was closed, you could hear the thumping of the music and Larissa's voice over the speakers. Bea watched with delight and stepped this way and that trying to imitate the movements. Larissa sounded professionally cheery and looked like a dancing gazelle at the front. Like all instructors, she was incredibly fit. She was slightly taller than me and didn't have an ounce of fat on her body. The class ended with a round of applause. The door opened and a horde of women with sweaty hair stuck to their bright red faces poured out of the room. Some looked like they were gasping for breath while others guzzled water from bottles as though they'd been wandering the desert for days without anything to drink. Larissa was standing in the front by the stereo, packing up her things. Bea and I stepped in through a wall of sweat stink. Bea ran right up to Larissa.

"Hi, honey, it's been so long," Larissa said and bent down to give Bea a hug.

"Jeez, how do you put up with it?" I said, waving my hand in front of my nose.

Larissa smiled and came at me with open arms.

"Apparently there's something wrong with the ventilation. It's not usually quite this bad. But you get used to it," she said. "Brave enough for a hug?"

"I don't have time to stay until after you've showered, so I guess we have to do it now," I said with a smile.

Hugging was not something I'd ever seen the point of. Granted, there were many aspects of social intercourse I didn't get and just went through the motions with because I knew I was supposed to, but throwing yourselves into each other's arms at the drop of a hat seemed particularly odd. Especially when one of you was half-naked and dripping with sweat.

"Is there somewhere we can talk privately?" I asked.

She nodded and checked my facial expression. While I fetched Bea, who was pressing the palm of her hand against the mirror, Larissa walked across the room and locked the media cabinet.

"You want coffee?" she said as we walked through the gym to a staff room with a few armchairs and a coffee table.

"Thanks, but we need to be on our way in a minute. Can Bea sit in there while we talk?" I said, nodding toward the next room, which looked identical to the one we were in but on the opposite side of the hallway.

"Sure, we might even have a piece of paper and a pen," Larissa said. She opened a couple of cupboards before finding a sheet of paper and a ballpoint pen.

"You can sit in here and draw, honey," I said and took her by the hand. "I'm just going to talk to Larissa real quick. Then we will go home and read a story. Why don't you draw someone working out?"

Bea shot the pen a look of disapproval but didn't object. I pulled up an armchair so I could see Bea from the other room. Larissa sat down with a glass of water in her hand. Looked at me inquiringly.

"It's about money…" I said.

I didn't want to drag Larissa into this, but I really had no choice.

"What happened? The divorce?"

I nodded slowly and lowered my eyes. Heaved a loud sigh.

"I owe Peter money and he's hounding me to no end. It's just been a lot lately, I can't take much more. The funeral, the divorce, I..."

I fell silent. What I'd said was true, I was feeling bad, but the money had nothing to do with the divorce or the funeral. Telling Larissa the truth was out of the question.

"God, I get it. You've really been through hell," she said. "What do you need?"

"A hundred thousand," I said, straight out.

There really was no way of sugarcoating the amount. I knew Larissa had inherited money from her parents after they passed away, but I didn't know how much.

"That's not exactly peanuts," she said and walked over to the window.

"I'll pay you back with interest, I promise, Larissa. We can work out a payment plan right now if you want, I'll do anything. I just can't quarrel with Peter anymore. I need to be free of him, both financially and mentally. Otherwise I'll never get through this."

Larissa sat down in the armchair across from me.

"If you need the money, of course I'll help you out."

"You really mean it?"

"You'd do the same for me," she said.

She was right. I would have done the same for her. Even though I had a hard time putting myself in other people's shoes, I knew what it was like to be in financial trouble. Larissa was going to get every penny back, and more. She had saved me for now. Before I went to get Bea to go home, I gave Larissa a big hug.

TWENTY-EIGHT

"Read *The Kids' Book,* mommy, please!"

Beatrice was standing on the little plastic stool in the bathroom, holding her toothbrush out to me. *The Kids' Book* was a story Benjamin had always wanted me to read. It was about four little creatures who saved the people and animals of the world from danger. I squeezed out a bit of toothpaste and grabbed her colorful toothbrush.

"I can do it myself, mommy," she said and clung to it.

For long periods, I'd not been in a place where I could have Beatrice stay at my house. Seeing her had hurt too much. She reminded me too much of Benjamin. Her voice. Movements. Words. I had talked to Aimi about it. She had told me it wasn't unexpected after everything I'd been through. I was skeptical, convinced she was just saying it to make me feel better. She would never even imply that I was a bad mother. But I knew it, I didn't have what it takes. A strong parent was supposed to be there for their other children, even if they had just lost one.

Ever since Benjamin died, Beatrice wanted to do everything he'd liked to do when he was alive. She wanted us to read the stories he had loved, eat the same gluten-free cereal he had eaten, watch the same children's shows. It was utter torture for me.

Repressing memories was a dangerous way of dealing with grief, Aimi had told me. The body remembers, she had claimed. When you least expected, it could all come flooding back, twice as violently.

"You forgot a tooth in the back, it's hard to get to. I'll help you," I said and reached out for the toothbrush.

She immediately let out a shriek so loud it made my ears ring, grabbed the toothbrush with both hands and pulled, howling, "Daddy always lets me brush myseeeelf!"

I let go. Turned abruptly and marched out of the bathroom, into the living room. Wore a small path from the couch to the bookcase and back again. Tried to calm down. I had never had Peter's patience with the children. Lately, things had got even worse. I would blow up over trivialities. Tiny everyday niggles could make me fly off the handle. It was strange. Of course, I had been annoyed on occasion before as well, but not like this. I felt nothing but love for Beatrice, and yet I flared up over nothing. Was this what it was like to have real feelings? They didn't show up one at a time, but doubled, contradictory, in a jumble?

I heaved a sigh. Sat down on the couch. Pulled my buzzing phone from my pocket. Unknown number again. I didn't pick up. Inhaled deeply through my nose. Slowly exhaled through my mouth and looked out at my apartment. Almost everything in my home was new. Every last piece of furniture. I hadn't wanted to take anything from my and Peter's apartment. Everything had been bought at Ikea, in one fell swoop. I'd almost given myself a stroke, walking around there amid all the families with yellow bags, enormous dollies, and screaming kids, even though I had carefully selected everything I wanted in advance online. But that was the way of Ikea. You found something in the catalogue or on their website and decided to buy it. Then, when you got to the store and saw the thing, you realized it was rickety, rock-hard to sit on, or completely the wrong color. I had had to force myself to make detours from the arrows in the main aisle and actually buy the furniture I'd picked out before going, otherwise

I would have risked leaving with nothing but a packet of napkins, two toilet brushes, and a hundred-pack of tea lights. But I was pleased. Aside from Beatrice complaining about her bed not being as soft as the one at daddy's house, the furniture did what it was supposed to. Which was all I asked.

The apartment wasn't big enough for Beatrice to have her own room, but that was no problem now since I wanted her as close to me as possible. All of this was just a temporary solution. This was not my forever home.

Armand clearly knew where both Peter and I lived. Even so, I felt safer with Beatrice at my house. I was careful not to let her catch a glimpse of the gun I now carried at all times. At night, I put it under my mattress.

The phone buzzed on the coffee table. It was Peter.

"How's it going?" he said.

"What do you mean 'how's it going?'" I retorted.

It annoyed me that he didn't seem to think me capable of looking after my own daughter.

"I wanted to say good night."

"Good night," I said.

"Cut it out, Leona, give Bea the phone."

"She's in the bathroom."

Through the cracked door, I could see Beatrice brushing her teeth, standing on the little stool that helped her reach the sink.

"By the way, I forgot to mention that she's going on a field trip tomorrow," he said as I heard Bea turn the tap up to the max.

The sound of the powerful jet spraying straight into the sink made me take a few quick steps toward the bathroom.

"She needs to bring—" I heard him say before I dropped the phone on top of the washing machine, picked Beatrice up, and turned off the tap, killing the gushing stream of water that had splashed up from the sink, soaking her top, face, and hair.

With a bawling Beatrice in my arms, I picked the phone back up.

"I'll have to get back to you tomorrow, Peter."

Without waiting for a reply, I hung up. I didn't care what he thought.

"You're all right, honey, it's just water," I told Beatrice while I wiped her face with a towel. "You're getting in your nightie now anyway."

I was still unaccustomed to taking care of Beatrice. After she had calmed down, I managed to get her into bed and lay down next to her.

Held her and kept soothing her.

Just as I'd used to do with Benjamin.

With tears in my eyes, I read her *The Kids' Book*.

TWENTY-NINE

"Oh my, is there a new little detective joining us today?"

Anette smiled at Beatrice as we stood in the door to her office. Anette was the kind of person you could always go see. Whatever she was doing, she would put it down.

Beatrice reacted by taking my hand and burrowing her face into the sleeve of my cardigan.

"A sleepy little detective," I said. "Beatrice, do you remember Anette?"

Bea nodded and peered at Anette from behind my arm.

"You don't have to be shy with me, I'm not dangerous in the slightest," Anette said and smiled.

"My wonderful little detective is going to be giving me a hand for a couple of weeks," I said and took a step into the room.

"A couple of weeks?" Anette said and looked up at me with concern in her eyes.

"Or...well, we'll see how long it ends up being. They're renovating her preschool," I said, and mimed the word "closed" to Anette.

Miss Stina had, as ever, been curt with me when I called with a song and dance about Bea having come down with chicken pox and needing to stay home for a few days, but I didn't care. It was none of her business.

"Preschool's not closed, is it, mommy?" Beatrice said.

"We're going to skip preschool for a bit, honey," I replied. "And we'll do some other fun things. Maybe we'll have time to go look at the police cars. Maybe, if you're lucky, you'll even get to ride in one."

Beatrice lit up.

"You probably have lots of saved-up vacation days you could use as well," Anette put in. "I can check how many—"

"I don't think Alexandra would let me take off right now," I said. "This is the only solution."

Anette nodded.

"I'm obviously happy to help out if you need," she said and looked at Beatrice. "By the way, Alexandra asked for you. I think she's in her office."

"I could use some admin help with my investigation, Anette." She nodded to the chair next to the desk.

"I was just sorting out the staff schedule for the police cruise, but I can do that later. Weird they're not sending you, by the way."

Everyone was talking about the cruise like it was the event of the year.

"Put my purse on the floor and have a seat," she said and smiled.

It was strange how the popularity of certain luxury handbags suddenly exploded sometimes. It was surprising that Police Authority employees were walking around with luxury handbags that cost several thousand kronor. If it had been anyone other than Anette, who was the most honest person I knew, I would have been suspicious. I carefully gripped the shoulder straps, closed the door, and made sure there was no gravel or other dirt where I put it down.

"You can sit, Bea," I said, nodding to the chair. "Right, so, I would need to know the schedules of the country's national politicians for the next three months."

"SÄK would have that information," Anette replied with a searching look.

"I don't have the energy to get into it with them. I don't need to know every individual politician's schedule, just when there are major meetings or conventions. In other words, events where there would be a lot of politicians in the same place. Especially the politicians who were in Parliament on the day of the attack."

Bea had found a small felt tip pen and had started drawing on her hand. I pulled a time sheet from Anette's bookcase, turned it over, and put the blank piece of paper on the desk in front of Bea. Without a word, she moved on to drawing on the paper.

"I'd also appreciate some help finding the identity Fred Sjöström used when he was in the French Foreign Legion. And I need to get in touch with this woman."

I handed Anette a note with Mirja Virtanen's name written on it.

"It's one of Fred's colleagues. Fred worked on a cruise ferry before the incident. Mirja has already been interviewed by SÄK, but I'd like to ask her a few additional questions."

Anette nodded and took notes.

"Can Bea stay with you for a few minutes while I run over to see what Alexandra wanted?"

"Of course," Anette said with a smile. "I could use an assistant. When you're done drawing, Beatrice, would you mind helping me with some forms that need filling out?"

Bea nodded and looked at me.

"I'll just be a few doors down, Bea. Stay here with Anette. I'll be right back."

I carefully moved Anette's purse before opening the door.

Anette stretched and stood up as well.

"Leona." She studied me. "How are you feeling? You look a bit pale."

"I do? No, I'm fine. I've been having some trouble sleeping lately, that's all."

Anette nodded and put a warm hand on my shoulder.

"I'm here if you want someone to talk to," she said. "You can call me anytime. You know that. At night too."

I nodded and left to go talk to Alexandra.

"Leona! Great. Give me an update on the suicide bomber," Alexandra said as soon as she spotted me in the doorway.

"There's not a lot to say, other than that he admits some of the circumstances."

"So he's admitting he was at the scene, or what?" Alexandra said.

"Mm…Better than nothing," I said.

"And why?" Alexandra asked.

"Society has made him who he is, he claims."

"And that's why he wants to kill himself by blowing himself up right in front of the country's most important political building?"

I nodded significantly at Alexandra.

"Keep at it and keep me up to date. It's good he's saying something at least."

I recalled that he had said a few words about a woman. From what I had read in his file, I assumed he was talking about his mother. Drug addict, according to the documentation. Father unknown.

"Hey, Alexandra, I was wondering…" I sat down on one of the conference chairs.

She shot me a concerned look. Could probably tell from my tone I wanted to talk about something of a private nature.

"...It's Beatrice. She's had a rough go of it what with our divorce and her losing her little brother at the same time. Preschool's not working out anymore and we're trying to find a different solution. During the transition, Peter and I both have to pitch in. I was wondering if it'd be okay for me to bring Beatrice to work with me for just a few days?"

Alexandra raised her eyebrows.

"That's all? Of course. Don't worry about it. Pretty much everyone around here brings their kids from time to time. Without even asking. I do feel your case is a bit special, given what your family has been through. And you only have the interviews to worry about at the moment, so it's no problem."

I nodded. It was true, my colleagues often brought their kids to work. Whenever their preschools were closed or they were under the weather and their parents were unable or unwilling to miss work.

"Great," I said, "I thought I might have to take time off..."

"That won't be needed," Alexandra said. "We're happy you're here. I'll let Anette know as well. She might be able to help you with Beatrice when you're out doing your interviews or whatever."

"Thanks, Alexandra, that means a lot," I said and stood up.

On my way out from Alexandra's office, my phone rang. It was Aimi Nordlund.

I didn't pick up.

THIRTY

"Leona Lindberg, VCD. I'm here to interview Ken Örberg."

Anette had promised to look after Beatrice while I went to the Kronoberg Detention Center. Now I was standing outside, talking to an entry phone on the wall. The woman on the other end had a tinny voice and sounded like she was holding her nose. The lock buzzed and the door opened. I walked down the long, narrow corridor. Every locked door I came to made the same buzzing sound as the first before opening. I wondered when I'd finally get away from all these locked doors.

It was always the same procedure at the detention center. Show identification at reception, put your gun and phone, both banned from being taken inside, in a locker, go through more locked doors, take one elevator and then another, go through another locked door and to another reception window. Explain whom I was interviewing again, wait for the detention officers to get him and lead him to a small, run-down, smelly, windowless interview room, and sit there with him for an hour or two before walking back out through all those locked doors again. And this was nothing compared to the Sollentuna Detention Center, which was a virtual Pentagon.

Even though I told them I was there to interview Ken, this was really a much less formal get-together. Ken didn't feature in any of my investigations. I knew him from before and word around the water cooler was that he'd just been arrested on suspicion of robbing a video rental store by Odenplan. He'd shown up clearly on the CCTV footage because his mask had come off during the robbery. Fairly inept, one might say, but it actually wasn't unusual for criminals to make simple mistakes like that. People often likened the police to the Keystone Cops, but they had no idea how inept the average criminal was.

This guy was unusual, though, because he wasn't like the cocky ones who were a dime a dozen. He might not be the sharpest member of the criminal underworld, but he quite possibly had the biggest heart. His physical capacity was greater than many other people's and he could probably look very intimidating when he wanted to. But he had never hurt anyone. Once, an investigation revealed that he had been armed, but had chosen not to use his weapon, even after being stabbed in the thigh. In the interview, he had said that he could never hurt anybody and that he only carried weapons to scare people off, "so he wouldn't have to fight," as he himself had put it.

Two officers opened his cell.

"Ken! The police are here to see you," one of them shouted.

I waited outside. I didn't like going into the cells. I heard him moving on the wall-mounted wooden cot, which was covered by a mattress wrapped in thick plastic. From the sound, I could tell he sat up and padded across the floor of the cell in his stocking feet. Shoes weren't allowed in detention, only plastic slippers he'd apparently declined. When he came out, he gave me a quick, surprised look. Didn't understand why I was there to see him. Neither of the detention officers reacted. They didn't keep track of which detectives were assigned to what cases. My badge number had been logged, but matching the right detective with the right interviewee wasn't the Prison and Probation Service's job.

Ken really was big. He had been tested for steroids, but was apparently clean. A mountain of muscle with pale skin and a shaved head.

The detention officers let us both into one of the little interview rooms.

"Are you expecting his lawyer?" one of the officers asked me.

"No, but she's been informed," I said. "I just spoke to her."

I caught myself behaving just the way a liar would. Giving more details and information than necessary. The officers didn't care whether Ken's lawyer had been informed. If anything, it was suspicious that I wanted to explain something like that to them. That the lawyer had been informed and invited to sit in on the interview was a given. The officers took no notice, but I admonished myself to get it together.

Ken stepped inside and sat down with his back against the wall. At the Kronoberg Detention Center, the interview rooms were arranged so that the suspect always sat at the far end with his or her back against the wall, while the interviewer sat near the door in case something went awry.

The room smelled unusually good. The officer seemed surprised as well.

"They've fixed the AC in the interview rooms," he said. "Actually seems to be working."

There was a notepad and a pen on the table. The detention officer shook his head and picked them up before walking toward the door.

"You know the drill, just press the button when you want us to come and get him," he told me and pointed to the button by the exit before closing the door behind him.

I sat down.

"How you doing?" I said calmly.

Ken shrugged and folded his hands in his lap, as if he were wearing invisible handcuffs around his wrists. His eyes looked tired. They were an unusual color. Green flecked with brown.

"Not exactly the first time you're in here," I said. "I've counted. So far in your life, you've been arrested five times. That's quite a lot, considering that you're only twenty-four years old."

He made no reply. Acted like he didn't care. Maybe that was true, but I knew these walls did something to people. It often baffled me that so many young men seemed clueless about what they were doing with their lives.

"I want to make you an offer," I said.

He looked at me wearily. I couldn't exactly expect him to jump for joy. To him, I was yet another representative of a penal system that claimed to want to straighten him out. It was sad to see how some people had given up. Figured they were useless and stuck living a certain way. I could relate to that feeling. I had been stuck living a certain way too. I couldn't compare myself to them, but I had been trapped in rigid notions about what my life should look like. I was going to give this guy a reason to be hopeful about the future. With the right knowledge and motivation, there was no telling what he could achieve.

"If I were to tell you that I could help you make money without working, what would you say?"

He shrugged. "That you're full of it."

It took me a while to persuade Ken. I told him what I knew about him. About his qualities and strengths. He almost looked bashful, didn't seem to be used to hearing good things said about him. I explained that I could do nothing about the ongoing investigation, but that given the circumstances of his case, I would be surprised if he wasn't released at his next detention hearing, which was scheduled for the day after tomorrow. I asked him to contact me if he was. If he got further detention, he would have to get in touch once he was out.

When we parted ways, I thought I glimpsed a tiny glint of hope in his eyes. He shot me a look over his shoulder as they led him into his cell.

Maybe he'd be in touch.

THIRTY-ONE

I studied their feet when they came ambling into our lecture room in the Meatpacking District, one after the other. They all wore sneakers. This time, I hadn't been as sure they'd all come back. Our last meeting had covered a lot of ground. A torrent of facts, not to mention the less than flattering information about the prejudice and racism that existed with the police force, which had raised some hackles. But here they were again, sitting in front of me. Their clothes were pretty much unchanged, but at least they had shown up. I was going to continue on the same theme.

"Eli, I gather you were sent down because of a footprint once."

Eli looked at the floor, embarrassed.

"I know, I was a fucking idiot."

"So now you probably know the police have a database with thousands of shoeprints from various crime scenes, which they match against the suspect's shoes. We also collect fibers from crime scenes. Which means you have to be smart about disposing of the clothes and shoes you had on. I've seen so much evidence dumped in trashcans, off bridges, and in shrubberies near the scene of the crime. A lot of people don't give it a second thought and might, for example, leave the shoes they wore during a robbery sitting on a shoe rack at home for when we come around with a search warrant."

One of them had mentioned masks during our last meeting.

"If you're pulling a bank job or robbing a store, you need a full disguise. A proper ski mask that hides your hair and face, not an old scarf and a hoodie that slips down on your way out."

I had seen things like that in CCTV footage several times.

"I suppose you want us buying masks from a costume shop, clowns and nuns and whatnot, like in the movies," Timmer said and laughed loudly.

"You mock, but people do that in real life, too, just so you know. You have no idea the kinds of things we detectives see on the job. Three years ago, I investigated a robbery where one of the robbers was wearing a bunny suit. In the middle of the robbery, a witness walked up to the robber and asked if they were shooting a movie. The robber had to fire his gun in the air inside the mall to get the witness to realize it was for real. Then he dropped a paw on his way out, which made my job a whole lot easier."

Everyone laughed. I was pleased the mood had lightened. This was our third meeting. They were getting to know each other a little.

"And speaking of malls, you have to hit the shops before you rob anything. Never use your own clothes. Never buy supplies near your home and don't buy brands you normally wear, unless they're very common. Go to big department stores and don't pay with a credit card, because that's registered. Always pay cash and don't forget to throw away the receipts and bags they give you when you shop. This also applies to any equipment you might need."

They weren't exactly taking notes, but they nodded their heads and seemed to be listening.

"As your new stylist, I'm letting you know it's dark clothes from here on out. Well-fitting gloves. Avoid thin latex gloves. Some are so thin you can leave traces of fingerprints through them, not to mention that they break all the time. Leather gloves are the best. Tape them to the sleeves of your jacket. Use black tape that really sticks. Dark jeans. Dark sneakers with generic sole patterns. Elegant and dashing," I said with a smile.

I realized I should say something about the stuff in their pockets too.

"Never bring any personal effects. They are easily dropped at the crime scene. I've had perps who dropped their wallets and driver's licenses. Others have left behind watches, jewelry with their name engraved on it, car keys, or cell phones full of contacts."

There were a lot of little details that criminals gave no thought to, but that could be pivotal to solving a case.

"But what about the CCTV cameras?" Zack said. "They're fucking everywhere."

I smiled. "I actually think I've seen all of you on tape in one investigation or another. No, strike that, not you, Vikki."

CCTV cameras were not much of a problem if you were dressed right and knew where they were located.

"Aside from in stores, they're all over the metro. Our new image and sound analysis unit has a direct line to the Transport Authority and can download video from them any time, twenty-four/seven. I would advise you not to use public transport at all since it's obviously better to avoid cameras, but if you have to, make sure you wear a baseball cap and hoodie. Where the cameras get in close and show your faces clearly, you have to put your hood up so your hair doesn't show. Keep your face down so the brim of your cap hides your face. It's a good idea to wear a baggy jacket to conceal your build."

This wasn't rocket science. And yet investigators could often trace a suspect's entire journey through the metro system using CCTV footage.

"There's even more advanced equipment at the Central Station and the City Terminal. There, we can get a high-definition image we can blow up many times over. If a person is having a burger, it's no problem to get close enough to tell what dressing's on it. That gives you an idea about the image quality."

I'd been impressed by the new surveillance system.

"Clothes that stand out, like a red baseball cap or a T-shirt with a unique print make it very easy to track a person from camera to camera. Do you know any other places that have surveillance?"

"Cabs," Liam said.

"Yep, every time the doors of a Stockholm taxicab open, a picture is taken. I've seen you in those, Timmer. And then there are ATMs, whose cameras sometimes show a large section of the street."

I was keen to bust the myth that crime was as easy as Hollywood made it seem.

"If you've ever considered taking out the CCTV cameras in a store with spray paint or by breaking them with a hammer, forget it. Finding all the cameras, which are often mounted near the ceiling, bringing spray paint or trying to break them, are all things you just don't have time for. It's more important to make sure your disguise and camouflage are good and suited to the situation, timeframe, and escape route."

The meeting continued in that vein. They asked more and more questions, which I was happy about. A lot of them were about what the police could and couldn't do, but also about details pertaining to their individual criminal interests. I started collecting the money. So far, no one was trying to get out of paying.

"What types of crimes you choose to commit is obviously very important. Next time, we're going to talk about high-risk crime, low-risk crime, and risk assessment. I'll see you then."

THIRTY-TWO

I slowly drove into the section of the Värtahamnen Port where I was supposed to meet someone. I didn't know who. Armand was hardly likely to show up in person. If it was anyone other than the man I had encountered in my living room, I was going to ask to speak to Armand directly before handing anything over.

Luckily, the money from Larissa had arrived in my account in time. I'd ordered and collected a hundred thousand kronor in cash from my bank and put the money in an unassuming tote bag for the handover.

I had dropped Beatrice off at Larissa's before meeting with my crew. If something were to happen to me, Bea would be in good hands with her. Larissa was, after all, an ex-cop and trained in various martial arts to boot.

Naturally, I had brought my gun. Carrying a weapon while off duty was only allowed under exceptional circumstances, but there was no way I was going to a meeting with these people unarmed. I was early. Parked the car a good way away and waited. Almost jumped when my phone went off in my pocket.

"I want to say good night to Bea," Peter said on the other end.

"She's asleep," I said.

"It's not even seven," Peter said.

"And?" I retorted. "She was tired, Peter. I'll call you back tomorrow."

He muttered something and hung up just as a car slowly came rolling toward me. I moved forward until my window was lined up with the other driver's. I rolled mine down. He did the same. It was the same man who had been in my apartment. I recognized his mustache and glasses.

"Where's Armand?" I said.

The man pulled out a cell phone, put it to his ear, and closed his window. After a few seconds, my phone rang. It was Armand.

"*Bonjour*, Leona. *Ça va?*"

As usual, Armand was smarmily polite and formal.

"I'm fine," I replied.

"*Très bien.*"

He instructed me to open my door and put the bag of cash on the ground. To park a bit farther down the lot and wait until the other car flashed its lights, then I could leave. Easiest for everyone involved, he said. That way, we didn't have to get better acquainted. It seemed like a good solution to me. I wanted as little as possible to do with the man in the other car.

"*Au revoir*, Leona, we'll be in touch again soon," Armand said.

I did as I'd been told. Opened my door and slowly placed the bag on the ground. Closed the door and moved along. Pondered his words about how we'd "be in touch again soon." If he had just calmed down, laid low for a few weeks, he could have had it all in one go. Unfortunately, I had to make sure I stayed on his good side. After his threats, I couldn't take any risks. By "we'll be in touch again soon," he had probably only meant that he was going to demand more money. Probably another hundred thousand. The question was when.

I waited for the other car to flash its lights before driving away.

THIRTY-THREE

I locked the car and started walking toward Larissa's house to pick up Beatrice. Larissa lived in an idyllic residential area in Enskede, not far from town. The neighborhood had become one of Stockholm's most expensive, but Larissa had inherited her house from her parents, who had bought it when prices were much lower. If not for the noise from a nearby freeway, loud despite the highway barriers, you'd think you were in a small town, not five minutes from the center of Stockholm.

On my way to Larissa's house, an orange tabby sitting by a shrubbery on the other side of the street caught my eye. It looked like it was eating something. I walked past the parked cars to get a better view. The cat kept tearing at whatever it was. Something brownish red. It looked too big to be an animal the cat had killed. And yet its nose was red.

I slowed down. Stopped. Was just about to cross the street to have a look when two cars came down the street. When they had passed, the cat was gone. Whatever it had been feasting on was still there, though, closer to the shrubbery. From a distance, it looked like it was red with blood. I quickly crossed the street. When I got closer, I saw what it was. The same kind of teddy bear Olivia had owned. The little girl who committed the crimes I had masterminded last fall. How had her teddy bear ended up here? And was that real blood on it? I studied it carefully where it lay, halfway into the shrubbery. Its nose had been ripped off and where one of the eyes had been a thread was dangling down toward the sidewalk. Olivia had loved that bear. Would throw a fit if she couldn't bring it someplace. I had a sudden impulse to pick it up and hug it. Comfort it somehow. I slowly squatted down and reached out for it.

"Leona!"

Larissa's sharp voice made me jump. She was calling me from the other side of the street.

"What are you doing?"

"Uhh…I just dropped an earring," I said and stood up quickly. Surreptitiously pulled the thin silver hoop out of one ear while I crossed the street and walked over to the house. Held it up and smiled.

"But I found it."

"Mom, we've had so much fun," Beatrice shouted as she skipped toward me. "I've had loads of pancakes."

"That's great, honey," I said. "Why don't you go get your things and we'll go home."

"Mom, I want to stay over at Larissa's!"

"Larissa has work in the morning, so you can't. Hurry up now."

I looked at Larissa to check how everything had gone.

"Like a dream," she said. "If I could just find a tolerable man to procreate with, I'd push two out in short order," she said and smiled. "At least if they were guaranteed to be like this little angel."

"You're a star, Larissa, you know that, right?" I said.

"Bah, it was my pleasure to have her today. Happy to do it again. Just say the word. So long as I'm not working."

I took Beatrice by the hand and started walking toward the car. By reflex, I looked back at the shrubbery, but there was no trace of the teddy bear.

THIRTY-FOUR

David was woken up at 5:30 a.m. by a knock on his hotel door in Copenhagen. He had set his alarm for ten to have plenty of time to have breakfast and get to the rendezvous by one.

No one knew him here so maybe it was someone from the hotel staff. The only people who knew he was staying at this particular hotel were Simon and Sven. He pulled on his jeans and went over to the door. When he opened it, two men in dark clothes pushed past him into the room. One of them was holding a phone. Without a word, he held it out to David. David slowly took it. Instantly recognized Simon's voice on the other end.

"David, they're paranoid, want to do the handover right now. Go with them and get it over with."

Fuck! Now none of what David had told Sven would be accurate.

One of the men took David's clothes from the desk chair, threw them to him, sat down and fixed him with a level gaze. The other stayed by the door. David got dressed in a hurry. These guys didn't look like they had the patience to wait around.

"I'd like to check out of room 239," David said. He left his key card at reception under the watchful eye of the two men.

One of the men walked ahead of David to a car parked on the other side of the street. The other followed behind. Held open the door to the back seat. David got in. Dug around his pocket and pulled out his phone. Before he could call anyone, though, one of the men held out his hand. David surrendered his phone.

David didn't know Copenhagen and had no idea where they were, but when he realized they were heading out of town, fear sunk its claws into him. Maybe all of this was about Simon figuring out who he was and sending him abroad to have him taken care of. He still hadn't been given any information about the car he was supposed to drive back to Stockholm. Maybe there was no car. No cargo. Nothing. Maybe in an hour's time, he'd have vanished. No one would know where he'd gone. Saga would never find out what had happened to him. That he had worked for the police and died for a good cause. She would think he'd relapsed and been killed in some gangster showdown. That's what it would look like. His stomach dropped. His heart was racing. He wanted to scream out his anxiety but instead he sat motionless, staring out at the landscape rushing past. As if frozen in the back seat. Practically apathetic.

It might be just as well, he thought. Who would even really care if he didn't come back? Saga, of course, but in all honesty, she'd be better off without him. Her parents would console her and explain to her that they'd been right about him all along. That she deserved someone different, someone better.

The men hadn't said a word to each other. David didn't know what they sounded like, what language they spoke, or what their nationalities were. Just that they weren't rookies.

The car turned off the freeway onto a smaller road. Stopped in a parking lot and waited. No one spoke. For at least five minutes. One of the men checked his watch, turned to the other, and gave him a curt nod.

Just as the men opened their doors and climbed out, David saw the headlights of another car cut through the morning fog.

The man who'd sat in the driver's seat in front of David opened the door to the back seat, grabbed David's arm, and pulled him out of the car. David's legs would barely carry him. He watched the other car slowly pull up in front of them. The driver opened the door and stepped out. He looked slightly older than the two who had picked up David. Without a word, the man walked up to David and his keepers, handed the car key over to the driver, and continued toward the car David had come in. The driver handed the key to David in turn, before both he and the other man who had picked him up went back to the car they had driven there and got in. Without a word, they started the engine and drove away.

David stayed where he was in the deserted parking lot. Watched the red taillights of the car disappear up the hill toward the main road. Tried to take deep breaths. Calm himself down. He was alive.

Just when he was about to start walking toward the car they'd left him with, he noticed their car stopping in the distance. It honked its horn. One of the men climbed out. Raised one arm in the air and then bent down to the ground by the side of the road. David understood what he meant. His phone. Then the man got back in the car and it disappeared over the crest of the hill.

David looked over at the car that was parked just a few feet away. It had tinted windows in the back, which made it impossible to tell if there was someone or something in the backseat. Heart pounding, he walked up to it. Looked in through the window. Empty. He opened the door and leaned into the back seat. Aside from a few old newspapers and a soda can, there was nothing there.

He exhaled. Maybe everything was how Simon had said it would be after all. A life of crime had made David distrustful. Maybe that was why his imagination was now trying to convince him whatever was in the trunk was going to put him in a very dangerous situation. He closed the door and walked around to the back of the car. He couldn't shake the notion there might be a person in there. A dead person? Or maybe still alive, but beaten to a pulp? Tied up? Unconscious? There was no sound coming from inside. He tried to formulate a strategy for what to do if that was the case, but he couldn't think a single clear thought. His entire life and future was going to be decided right here, right now. He took a firm hold of the metal handle and opened the trunk.

THIRTY-FIVE

Fred Sjöström's mother had not been out of bed all day, except to go to the bathroom to throw up. Little Fred had been out to buy bananas, rose hip soup, and bread for her in the supermarket on Blackeberg Square. The lady who always manned the checkout had told him he was a good boy for staying home with his mother instead of being out vandalizing things like the other thirteen-year-olds in the area. She even gave him a couple of bananas for free; they were going to go bad by the next day anyway. But Fred's mom hadn't eaten any of the things he'd bought. It was always like this when she decided to quit, it always made her sick.

That morning, when he went into her bedroom, she'd been so cold she'd been shivering in her bed. He'd given her his blanket as well, so she had two, but it hadn't helped. She was cold even though it was summer outside. That was a few hours ago. Now she had kicked both blankets off and wanted him to open the window instead. Told him she felt like she was in a sauna. Even so, her hand was cold and clammy when he held it. She liked it when he held her hand.

The print on the pink T-shirt she had worn all weekend had cracked, but Fred was proud; he'd bought it for her for Christmas, with his own money. Money she'd given him. He had hidden it, because he knew she would want it back when she ran out. He had wanted to buy her a new T-shirt, but they cost too much. This one was almost as nice, even though he'd found it at a flea market. Though it had fit her better at Christmas. She was so thin now.

Her knees were knobby. She said they and her back hurt. The needle marks and bruises on her arms and legs had multiplied, and grown. Fred didn't like to look at them. Thought they looked scary. Some of the needle marks on her feet were infected. When he wanted to put Band-Aids on them she said you weren't supposed to. That they needed air.

Fred hadn't told anyone about his mom. No one knew. He couldn't bring friends home after school, but that was okay. There were always a lot of people around anyway. The people who would come to their house. Granted, they were mostly men his mom's age or older. Some of the ones that came often called him "slugger" and gave him a friendly punch on the shoulder. Most were nice. Sometimes they brought beer and let Fred have some. The first time he took a sip, he thought it tasted gross, like yeast, but now he liked it. He would drink while they sat on the sofa, rustling their sheets of tinfoil on the coffee table. Afterward, there was usually no talking to them. Some of them became normal, though. His mom was one of those. Things were bad when she couldn't get drugs. When that happened, Fred would leave the apartment or lock himself in his room, because he couldn't stand being around her.

She often told him she didn't want to do drugs. She'd tried to quit many times. Each time, she got sick. Like now.

This weekend, she had told her friends not to come by because she was going cold turkey. Again. If she could just get through the first three days, the worst of the withdrawal would subside and she would be able to kick the habit, she said. That was yesterday. Today, she was even worse. Fred mostly thought it was hard to see her feel so bad. It made it hard for him to eat too. His stomach just hurt all the time.

He had opened the window now, like she wanted. Let some fresh air in. Sometimes when she'd been asleep or at work, he'd taken some of her drugs and hidden them, in case there was ever a crisis. Now he couldn't bear seeing her so sick. She refused to go to the hospital. Always told him they would take him away from her if they knew she did drugs and they wouldn't give her any help anyway. When he showed her the stash he had squirreled away, she said she wanted it.

He pulled the strap a little tighter around her upper arm. Looked at her to see if it hurt.

"Like that?"

She nodded so imperceptibly he almost couldn't tell if he was imagining it. He could see the blue veins in her arms protruding under her skin. Her pale skin was almost translucent. That was a good thing. It made it much easier to see the blood vessels. It usually helped if she opened and closed her fist hard several times in a row. That made the veins pop out even more, but she would never be able to do that in the state she was in. She was way too shaky and weak to inject herself, she said. Fred didn't really want to do it, but he'd do anything to make her feel better.

He had already mixed it, heated it with the lighter, and pulled the liquid into the syringe. He grabbed her thin arm and tried to find an unused vein.

"Try to stay completely still now, mom."

Her eyes were closed. She was on her back in bed, with her other arm draped across her forehead. Fred remembered when they'd been given vaccines in school and the nurse had injected his arm. He liked to think of this as a vaccine his mom needed to not be sick. He knew it wasn't true, that it was poison, but it was easier to think about it that way.

He felt along the vein with his fingertips. Where it felt a bit softer, he stuck the needle in a little and stopped. To make sure the needle was in the right place, he carefully pulled the plunger out further. When the red of the blood trickled in, mixing with the liquid in the syringe, he knew he'd hit the spot. When it looked like that, she'd smile and nod at him, but now she was just sprawled on her back, waiting. He removed the strap around her arm and quickly injected the contents. When she winced, he stopped for a second, then continued more slowly until the syringe was empty. Pulled it out and pressed down on her arm with a wad of tissue. There wasn't a lot of blood. He was going to throw the syringe out. She always said never to use them more than once. She had told him about friends of hers who had shared a needle with others and contracted serious diseases.

Fred looked at her. Her eyes were still closed. He let up on the wad of tissue. No more blood was coming out, so he removed it altogether. Got up and walked to the kitchen to throw away the syringe, needle, everything. He washed the spoon and his hands carefully. It wouldn't be long before she felt better. He couldn't wait. They'd be able to eat together. After that, he'd feel better too.

He was happy there weren't a lot of people at their house this weekend; that meant he could move around the apartment freely. He poured water into a pot and whisked in the rose hip soup powder. She liked it warm. While the stove warmed up, he got out the bread he'd bought. In a while, she'd be hungry. He made two cheese sandwiches for her and two for himself and took the pot off the heat before going back into the bedroom.

The curtains were flapping in the breeze when he got here.

"Mom, I've made some food," he said while he closed the window.

She didn't respond. She'd pulled the blankets so far up he could barely see her. She was probably cold again. The room was cool. But there was something else too. A feeling. His heart started beating faster as he slowly approached the bed. The feeling in the pit of his stomach was strange. He slowly grabbed the blanket. Lifted it up.

"Fred!"

Someone was calling his name from far away. A woman. He felt pressure across his chest, but he didn't care. Kept pulling the blanket away from his mom's face.

The woman's voice echoed in his head. He tried to ignore it while he stared at the top of his mom's head. Her light brown hair was stuck to her forehead in lank strands. Her face was gray. Clear liquid had trickled from her blue lips onto her pillow. He let go of the blanket. Backed away from the bed. Screamed...

"Fred!" the woman called again, louder this time.

Fred woke up in his hospital bed because someone was holding him. He was screaming, screaming. Just like that day forty years ago. The same terror. The same panic. He sobbed. Gasped for breath. The anxiety that had seized him forced all his anger and frustration to the surface.

"Fred!"

THIRTY-SIX

"Fred! Calm down," I said.

I had said his name several times, but he was still asleep. He was panicking. Had started screaming. He raised his head, propped himself up on his elbows, and was trying to heave himself out of the bed. I put one hand on his chest. The other on his shoulder. Then he stopped and was completely still for a short time. Looked around.

"You're in the hospital, you're okay," I said.

He slowly lay back down. I let go of him. He looked at me, his eyes darting this way and that.

"I'll tell the nurses to bring dry clothes and something to drink," I told him and walked toward the door.

While the nurses changed his sheets, I went out to my colleagues from SÄK, who were looking after Beatrice. She was sitting on the floor between them, drawing.

"Mommy, this is you and this is daddy, and that's Larissa," she said, pointing at her drawing.

"That's lovely, honey," I said, and barely had time to squat down and have a look before she had got out a new paper and started a new drawing.

I stood back up. Thought about what Dr. Nair had said. That Fred's behavior indicated that he'd been through trauma at some point in his life.

When the nurses left the room carrying a pile of linens, I went back in. Set up the video camera.

"Fred, as I mentioned last time I was here, this is the last —"

"She probably didn't even know who he was."

He cut me off. Spoke in a deep voice. I sat down on the visitor's chair next to the bed.

"Every day, I waited for dad to come. So he could save her."

Fred wasn't looking at me, he was looking straight into the camera I had set up at the foot of his bed. With tears in his eyes, he continued: "When mom was too sick to leave the house, I had to buy the stuff for her."

Fred was fifty-three. I had not planned to talk about his childhood, but right now I was happy he was saying anything at all.

"I knew exactly where to go. There was a man on Blackeberg Square. He sold to anyone."

"When was this?" I asked.

"The first time I guess I was six, seven years old. It went on until..."

He trailed off. Turned his head to look out the window.

"...that day. I was thirteen. She was going to quit like so many times before. I couldn't stand seeing her so sick. I knew what I had to do to make her feel better. The powder, the spoon, the lighter, the syringe, how to inject, I knew it all."

He heaved a slow, deep sigh.

"I just didn't know I was giving her too much..."

His voice broke.

"She always said she wanted to quit for my sake, but I wanted her to take the drugs. They made her normal."

As a police officer, I'd been told a lot of life stories. Each worse than the last. But to grow up with a single junkie mother whom you as a child had to buy drugs for and inject when she was unable to do it herself, and then, when you were thirteen, to watch her die of an overdose you had caused, that was definitely one of the worst I'd ever heard. I was speechless. The file had only said she'd died of an overdose. Nothing about Fred's involvement.

I studied him. An ex-mercenary, sailor, suicide bomber who was now confined to a hospital bed. Weak. Tearily recounting a horrific incident from forty years ago that had probably set the course for the rest of his life.

I searched my bag for a tissue and held it out to him. He looked at me through his tears. There was something about his eyes. They were full of pain and worry, but also a special strength akin to my own.

He raised a hand to his throat and looked at me.

"The necklace," he said in an unsteady voice. "Do you have my necklace?"

THIRTY-SEVEN

"Grenades!" David said loudly into his phone for the second time, but Sven didn't seem to want to understand.

David knew there was no point yelling at Sven, it was like water off a duck's back. Nothing could change the fact that at this moment, David was on his way from Denmark in a car full of weapons he had smuggled across the border to Sweden. Handguns, ammunition, and...grenades.

"Twenty hand grenades," David said.

"Goddamn it, David! You can't tell me things like that. I have a duty to report that now," Sven hollered.

"Then why did you ask, asshole? You're the one who got me in this fucking shit. You promised to sort it out," David shouted. "Then you and your fucking colleagues never even show up!"

"David, calm down. How was I supposed to know it was going down earlier than planned?"

"How fucking stupid are you? I gave you the name of the hotel. You should have had someone outside, you fucking dumbasses! I had no goddamn choice but to go along. Now Simon's waiting to take delivery. And if I don't deliver, I'm gonna be in some deep fucking shit, okay?"

Sven sighed on the other end. David had listened to Sven's bullshit a thousand times. David wasn't supposed to commit crimes, and if he did, he wasn't allowed to tell Sven because cops weren't allowed to be involved in criminal activity, which meant Sven couldn't cover for crimes David committed. But what the fuck was he supposed to do? Even the cops seemed to get how twisted the system was. As an informer, you sometimes had to do things to save your own skin.

"You can't fucking set the cops on me now," David said. "We both know I had to do this. You should be pretty goddamn happy if I make it to Stockholm in one piece so I can hand this shit over."

David saw in the rearview mirror that the car behind him was pulling up close. He let it pass. Was meticulous about staying within the speed limit. This wasn't the time to be caught speeding.

"But the grenades, who are they for?" Sven said. "This seems to be bigger than what the Blood Family usually gets up to."

Sven's tone suddenly changed and an exultant note crept into his voice.

"Good job getting that delivery, David. Very good."

"I'm glad you don't give a shit about me having to drive around in a death machine while you ponder how you can show off to your crooked fucking colleagues during your afternoon coffee break."

"Cut it the fuck out already, David. You sound like a whiny rookie. You signed up for this and you knew it might be danger-ous. Answer my question."

"I don't know who they're for. And if I knew I wouldn't fuck-ing tell you, because you'd probably fuck it up."

David hung up on Sven and tossed the phone on the passenger seat. It rang again immediately. He was too pissed to talk to Sven. But he still glanced at the phone. It was Saga. He picked up.

"How are you doing, sweetie," she said.

"I'm not going to make it, Saga."

No matter how badly he wanted a chance to make a new impression on her parents, he had to accept that it was physically impossible for him to make it to her family get-together on time.

"But...Where are you? Can't you..." was all she had time to say before he cut her off.

"I'm not going to make it, okay?!" he shouted.

He instantly regretted picking up instead of calling her back when he'd calmed down after his conversation with Sven. None of this was her fault. She hung up on him. He looked at the phone to call her back. Apologize. Explain that he was sorry he wouldn't be able to make it, which was true. It was at times like these he felt real fucking sick of everything. Was he ever going to get away from this shit and live the life he longed for? He glanced at the road while he found Saga in his recent calls list. Just as he was about to push call, he saw it up ahead. Cars parked in a row along the side of the road. Flashing lights.

Random police checkpoint.

THIRTY-EIGHT

Walking around toy stores was one of the things I liked the least about being a parent. I was jostling through a crowd of people in the basement of Butterick's, a gag-and-costume store on Drottninggatan, while Beatrice pointed to every single item. I had promised her she could pick one thing, if it wasn't too expensive. Even though the store and its whirlwind of masks, wigs, costumes, novelty items, makeup, toys, and gag gifts exhausted me, it was still nice to see her so elated.

I had left the hospital with a more nuanced view of Fred. His attitude had changed dramatically. The interviews were clearly draining for him; he couldn't handle long sittings. I had to accept that he would only talk at his own pace. I had explained the situation to Alexandra and could therefore relax a bit. She was the boss and paid to shoulder the responsibility. How she wanted to explain things to SÄK was her business.

Fred had asked about a necklace I'd seen in a picture in the seizure records. It had been found at the scene, but before he mentioned it there had been no way of ascertaining whether it belonged to him or if it had been present at the scene before the attack. It was relatively common for the police to bag and tag things that had nothing to do with the crime in question during crime scene investigations. I had planned to hold a special interview about all the confiscated items later, but his asking about the necklace had made it all the more urgent to find out more about it.

I had already explained to Alexandra that it was crucial for my continued communication with Fred that the prosecutor agreed to return some of the confiscated items to him. There was no reason to hold on to personal belongings, like the necklace, Fred's house keys, or his wallet. We didn't need to lift prints, DNA, or anything else from them, and his apartment had long since been searched. No one else had been in touch to claim the items either. The necklace seemed important to him, and I needed to figure out why.

I smiled when I saw a police uniform among the costumes. There were different versions. One for children and one that was supposed to be a female officer in a tight black miniskirt with handcuffs and a nightstick hanging from a wide belt, and a skin-tight, light-blue shirt with a plunging neckline. Turning back to where Beatrice had just been standing, I suddenly went cold.

Just froze, staring.

Unable to make a sound.

My ears popped and at the same time I heard a dripping sound. At first, I couldn't tell where it was coming from. I squinted and opened my eyes wide by turns to focus them. Blinked. No matter what I did, my vision was blurred. At the center of my blurry field of vision, a small blond girl I recognized appeared. Was it really her? How had she got there? I looked around. Saw the outlines of customers walking around the store like nothing was wrong. The dripping sound grew stronger. When I looked back at the girl, I knew it was her.

Olivia.

The seven-year-old girl who had committed the robberies for me. She was standing there, right in front of me, wearing some kind of thin, white dress. My eyes were drawn to her tiny hand, which was clutching her teddy. Blood was trickling from cuts on her arm, down her hand, onto the teddy, and to the floor, where a small puddle had formed. The sound of the dripping was echoing in my ears now. She slowly looked up at me with big, pleading eyes. Said in a tiny voice: *"Do you recognize me? Do you recognize me?"*

Her words reverberated inside my skull. I clapped my hands to my ears. Looked around. Did no one else see her?

"You didn't recognize me, mommy!" Beatrice exclaimed and tore off her blond wig, letting it land on the floor in a big, hairy heap.

She laughed delightedly.

"Be quiet, Bea," I hissed, once I snapped back in.

I quickly picked the wig up off the floor and hung it up on a wall rack.

"We're leaving now."

"But I wanted it, mommy, get it down."

"*No!* You'll have to pick something else," I said, and started walking toward a different shelf.

"I waaaant *that* one. I want long, pretty haaaaaiiir," she insisted.

"You either choose something else or we leave here with nothing at all," I said through gritted teeth.

She fell silent and went back to looking at the stuff on the shelves. I stopped. Breathed slowly in and out. Deep breaths. Tried to understand what I had just seen.

THIRTY-NINE

David had abided by every last rule of the road. Done everything to avoid drawing attention to himself or being stopped by the police. And yet here he was. By the side of the road. Just like the cars lined up in front of him, he'd been one of the ones waved over. Now he was waiting for the police to finish up with the other cars and come over to his.

David tugged at his hoodie a few times to cool down. Didn't know what to do. He picked up his phone. Called Sven.

"I've been stopped at a fucking police checkpoint. What am I supposed to do?"

"That sucks. Where are you?" Sven asked.

"What the fuck does that matter?" David hissed. "Too far away for you to get here. Just tell me what to do instead."

"Nothing. Do what they tell you," Sven said. "You're sober, right?"

"Fucking hell, I'm not up to this. I'm gonna bail," David said.

"If you do that, I'm done helping you, you know that, right? I can't—"

"I don't feel like you've done all that much to protect me either way. You might have tipped these guys off for all I know. Pretty fucking weird that they appeared right after we talked."

"David, listen to me. You won't get away if you just drive off. They have other cars out on the road. It'll just make them suspicious and they'll search the whole car once they get you to stop, and you know what they'll find if they do. Be smart about this. Stay cool."

David hung up on Sven again. The police officers had reached the car in front of David's. It struck him that he didn't even know anything about the car he was in. Whose was it? Where was it from? He opened the glove compartment and rummaged through the things in it. A calendar, a few pens and receipts. No registration.

One of the officers was on his way over to his car now. Was making a sign for him to roll down his window.

"Hello," she said, sounding almost cheery. "License please!"

David pulled out his wallet. His hands were clammy. His fingers left damp prints on the leather. His license always had a way of getting stuck behind the plastic pocket in his wallet. His sweaty fingers did nothing to help him get it out.

"Thank you," the officer said. "Blow into this."

She was holding out a breathalyzer.

"Gently and for as long as you can, please!" she continued jauntily.

David blew.

"I'll be back in a moment," she said.

She walked past the car in front of him and out of sight. He drummed his hands on the wheel. Maybe he was going to get through this after all. He started the windshield wipers to get rid of the drizzle that had settled on the glass. The officer came walking back toward him. Her expression was neutral. Maybe slightly on the happy side, he felt. She stopped before she reached his car. Looked at it. Nudged the male officer who was talking to the driver in front of David. He looked in David's direction. At him. At his car. They exchanged a few words. Nodded. David didn't understand.

The female officer walked up to him.

"Stone-cold sober. Lovely," she said and handed him his license back. "Thank you very much for that. Drive carefully now."

David nodded. Took his license and turned back onto the road. Looked in the mirror to make sure they weren't following him. He was afraid to smile but he couldn't wrap his head around the fact that he'd just made it through a police checkpoint with five handguns, piles of ammo, and twenty hand grenades in the trunk of his car.

FORTY

"A bit of silver polish on that thing and…," my colleague Fredrik said, looking at the grayish-black chain and pendant dangling from my hand.

I had collected Fred's necklace and was standing by the window in my office studying it.

"Mm, it seems to be real silver," I replied, squinting at the piece of jewelry, which despite the discoloration had a clearly visible hallmark stamp.

"Seized in the bomber case, is it?" Fredrik said.

I nodded. If there had been anyone else in the room, I wouldn't have said anything about the case, but I trusted Fredrik.

"It looks like it's been through a lot," he said.

The chain was broken in one place. Either the blast had severed it or the paramedics had decided to cut it off. The round pendant was badly scratched and blackened, but I could make out a hammered horseshoe like a crescent moon along the edge.

"Luck? Do you know if a horseshoe symbolizes anything else?" I said.

Fredrik shook his head. The letters *FS* were engraved in the middle of the horseshoe.

"What was his name again, the bomber?" Fredrik said.

"Fred Sjöström."

On the back of the pendant, I could see a few deliberate markings among the scratches. I scraped gently at the surface with my fingernail and angled the thing toward the light. There were hand-carved numbers, 3005 and 2301, it looked like. A small space between the two sequences made it possible to read it as one long number or two separate ones. I quickly wrote down the numbers on a piece of paper and slipped the necklace back into its bag.

"Hence *FS* I guess," Fredrik said and nodded just as Anette and Beatrice appeared.

"Hi honey, are you having a good time?" I asked Bea.

She nodded.

"I've stapled reports," she said and shot Anette a proud look.

"She's been so helpful," Anette said and handed me a stack of papers. "Here are lists of all political get-togethers during the summer and fall. Some of them are national conventions, some are smaller local and regional meetings. I put everything in for you."

"Did you manage to get hold of Fred's colleague Mirja Virtanen?" I said as I flipped through the pages.

"I set up a time later this afternoon. Just call ahead and she'll meet you on board the ship."

I perused the politicians' schedules. Say what you will about them, but they certainly seemed to sing for their supper. Some were traveling up and down the country as if it was an election year. I looked for any events that would draw a lot of politicians.

"Thanks, Anette," I said. "We'll head over right now. Do you want to go on a ship with me, Bea?"

"Yaaaay!"

FORTY-ONE

Once we were on board Silja Line's MS *Galaxy*, Mirja Virtanen took us through to the ship's staff common room. With a cup of coffee and a glass of water in front of us, we waited while she looked for a cabin where we could speak undisturbed. The coffee machine looked like the one the Police Authority had in all its break rooms. If I hadn't had a real hankering for the caffeine, I would have declined.

When Mirja returned, she looked stressed. We could talk privately in a cabin down the hall, she said. Taking Bea by the hand, I walked behind her down the narrow corridor. Being on a Finland-Sweden cruise ferry made me uneasy. It was cramped and smelled fusty but above all I knew too much about the things that went on there. If it wasn't smuggling alcohol and drugs, it was trafficking and prostitution.

The cabin she took us to was slightly larger than the ones I'd been in before. In addition to two beds, there was a desk and a small loveseat. Mirja had started talking about Fred before we even entered. Told me that like her, he'd worked there on and off for a few years. That she had appreciated having a slightly older colleague.

"He was probably the most decent guy around here," she said after we sat down. "Working on board these ships is pretty rough. Most people don't even try to be pleasant; everyone's in it for the money. But Fred was nice."

"In what way?" I asked.

"If anyone needed time off, he was always happy to cover a shift. He was older but worked harder than most. We used to talk on our breaks, him and me. There were rumors about us being an item, but it was never like that. We just talked. I don't know that much about him, even though we worked together for quite a long time."

"Did he tell you anything about himself?" I asked.

"He had no family," she said. "I remember one time when we were off duty and got drunk together. He told me he'd fought in a war of some kind. Other than that, he preferred not to talk about himself."

I turned to Bea, who was drawing on the politicians' schedules.

"Bea, why don't you have a listen now," I said.

I'd given her one of my old cell phones and together we had put music and stories on it for her to listen to while I worked. She got it out of her little backpack, put the headphones on, and pushed the buttons on the phone.

"What did his managers think of him?" I asked Mirja.

"Well, he always pitched in where it was needed. Never talked back. Worked all the major holidays without complaining. Everyone liked him. Everyone here was stunned when the Security Service turned up and questioned people about that bombing. Said he'd done it. And then it was in the papers as well. How's he doing now?"

"Relatively well, considering. He was lucky to survive. How did he seem to you before it happened?"

"Now that I think about it, he'd been looking pretty tired. He looked like he'd lost weight as well. Not enough to be really noticeable, but..."

She trailed off.

"He collapsed during loading once. It was about six months ago. Went to the hospital in an ambulance but was back at work for his next shift. Said he'd just been sleeping and eating badly. I think it's since then he's looked tired."

"Did anything else about him stand out to you?"

She leaned back in her chair. Looked down at the floor and slowly shook her head.

"I don't know…"

She fell silent. Her eyes darted back and forth. I knew what was going on. I'd read it between the lines when I went over the report from her previous interview with the Security Service. Little signs that she knew more. Loose ends the interviewer had missed.

I could almost see her mind turning. Unsure whether she should tell a detective what she knew, what repercussions it might have. That barrier between a police officer and a witness was always there. In one way or another, a process of persuasion was often necessary to get to the important things.

"Mirja, if you want, I'll keep what you say between us. I'm actually required to write down anything that's relevant for the investigation, but I understand if you don't want to say anything that could get other people in trouble."

She didn't seem to know what to do with what I was telling her, if she could trust me.

"It's very important that you tell me what you know, Mirja. Fred was on his way into Parliament with explosives. You realize how serious that is, don't you?"

"But I've already told the police," she said.

"The detectives you met before are the ones who have the overarching responsibility for the investigation. I'm only doing the interviews with Fred. I've met him several times by now and I know he's had a rough life. I have to try to understand why he did this terrible thing that could have hurt a lot of people. I need your help with that. No one will find out what you tell me. I give you my word."

She was silent for a while.

"He said he was going to do something...but...I don't know, it was incoherent. He was pretty drunk then, too. I was too. We're not allowed to drink on the job, but we did anyway sometimes."

She looked at me again as if to make sure I wasn't going to rat anyone out to their boss for drinking alcohol during work hours. I nodded for her to go on.

"I don't remember exactly what he said, but I had the impression he'd killed someone. Or was about to kill someone maybe. I didn't really understand. I thought it was just drunken ramblings, but now I don't know what to believe..."

She paused to think.

"He also told me he'd been a mercenary, but didn't want me to mention it to anyone. That would just cause trouble, he said. Maybe that's why he'd killed people?"

She looked at me inquiringly as though I knew the answer. This was not going the way I had hoped. Mirja had apparently been told something in confidence that she had not been sober enough to retain.

"For some reason, he seemed to really hate the police. Obviously, things do go down on these ships from time to time. The police come on board regularly to hold interviews. He always stayed well clear and claimed not to have seen anything, even though we both witnessed a guy being beaten up pretty badly once. When I asked why he'd claimed not to have seen it, he replied that he just hated cops. I said that it wasn't for their sake we told them what we knew. Then he just claimed he'd been focused on other things and hadn't seen exactly what happened."

"Did he ever mention a politician or a specific party by name?" I asked.

"We never talked politics. I'm completely uninterested."

That seemed to be the end of the line. The only thing I was going to get out of this interview was that Mirja remembered Fred talking about killing someone. Her information was very vague. His hatred of the police was hardly surprising. It was anything but unusual. I was just about to wrap things up when it struck me.

"Have you ever seen this before?" I said and pulled the necklace out of its evidence bag.

She nodded.

"He always wore it. I remember one time when a colleague was goofing off and grabbed the chain and pulled. Fred went nuts and gave him a serious beating. Didn't stop until another colleague intervened and pulled him off. We were all taken aback. Fred was always so nice, and never violent otherwise."

"Do these numbers mean anything to you?" I said and handed her the Post-it with the numbers that had been carved into the back of the necklace.

She took the note. Looked at it for a long time and then shook her head.

"Is it a code to something?" she asked.

I thanked Mirja for her help and left with Beatrice. As we were disembarking, I felt my phone buzz in my pocket. My heart started beating faster. As usual, I looked around. Took Beatrice by the hand and hurried toward the car. I didn't read the text until Beatrice was safely buckled in and I had sat down and closed the door.

8 July. 100,000. Confirm.

FORTY-TWO

"We're going to Skansen in three days," Beatrice said loudly at the lunch table at work.

"Is that right? So on Sunday?" Alexandra said and looked at me.

I nodded and plunked a dollop of wasabi into the soy sauce that came with my bento box.

"We've been talking about going there too, me and the girls," Alexandra said. "Maybe we could meet up there?"

The table went silent. I could tell my colleagues were listening closely to our conversation and Alexandra's suggestion. Even though she had led our division for almost six months now, people were still trying to figure out what kind of boss she was. So far, I hadn't heard any rumors about her playing favorites, which is why it was raising some eyebrows that she was suggesting the two of us socialize outside of work. Personally, I wasn't wild about hanging out with my boss in my spare time, but I realized it was socially impossible for me to say no.

"Why not?" I said. "The more the merrier, right Beatrice?"

Beatrice nodded and shoved a big piece of sushi in her mouth. None of our colleagues said anything.

"It's really great that you eat sushi, Beatrice," Anette said.

"We're going to see the lemurs and monkeys. And you know what? Lemurs are from Madagascar," Beatrice replied, dropping a few grains of rice into her lap.

"Bea, don't talk with your mouth full," I said and pulled her chair closer to the table.

She chewed eagerly to be able to get back to talking.

"Did you know that at Skansen, you can pet the sheeps?" Bea said and looked at Alexandra. "I'm going to get to. Mommy promised."

Alexandra smiled and looked at me. Cilla, who was always keen to get in good with her superiors, looked nervous.

"Maybe we should all go sometime?" Cilla suggested. "I'm sure everyone likes taking their kids to Skansen, right?"

She looked around the table. Someone nodded briefly. Alexandra didn't respond.

"Finish your food, Bea," I said and pushed her bento box closer to her.

"How's two o'clock for you?" Alexandra said to me. "Then you can meet my daughters, Beatrice. One of them, Sofia, is the same age as you."

Bea looked at Alexandra and grinned. Our colleagues watched us in silence.

"Great," I said in a tone that was neutral enough to be polite to Alexandra but not too ecstatic in front of our colleagues.

There was a degree of extra clatter when Beatrice helped me load the plates and cutlery into the dishwasher after we had finished eating. I heard someone sigh loudly as we walked back to my office.

"I want to sit on your chair, mommy," Bea said and ran to my office chair.

"You can sit here," I said and pulled the other chair up to the desk.

"Noooo! I waaaaant to!"

"Stop it, Bea!" I said sharply. "You can sit here or on the floor."

She went over and sat down on the chair. I got out some pens of various colors and a notepad.

"Maybe you could draw some of the animals at Skansen?" I suggested. "Maybe the sheep and lemurs?"

Bea got started straightaway. I opened Fred's case file on my computer. Went back to trying to figure out what the numbers on his silver pendant meant. I had considered showing the sequences to my colleagues during lunch and asking them if they had any idea what they could be. Sharing information about an ongoing investigation and asking for help or opinions was not at all unusual, but after Alexandra's Skansen question it hadn't been the right time to ask my colleagues for help.

I had already checked if the numbers could be linked to a safe deposit box, a code to a safe, a personal identity number, special date, time of day, log-in code, phone number, IMEI number for a cell phone, the serial number of stolen goods, a VIN number, and so on. But everything I'd found seemed too far-fetched. I looked at the Post-it with the numbers again. 30052301.

The obvious connection was that the first four numbers matched the date Fred blew himself up in front of the Parliament building, on the thirtieth of May. It should follow then, that the last four numbers were the date of a possible second bomb. That would make it the twenty-third of January, a date that had come and gone almost six months ago. That was not, in other words, a plausible theory. That Fred could have placed a bomb that was set to go off on that day next year, six months into the future, seemed unlikely. He must have realized there was a risk someone might discover the bomb long before it was supposed to go off.

I opened Webstorm, the database listing all field reports. I wanted to go over the incident reports to see if something relevant to this case had happened on the date in question. I scrolled down the list. As usual, it was a hodgepodge of incidents. An ongoing kidnapping, a car accident, a fistfight on a metro platform, a cat run over by a car, descriptions of three suspects from an earlier robbery. Going through the list for all of Stockholm County was going to take a while. I decided to bring my laptop home and consider it my nighttime reading.

Fred had asked for his necklace back after talking about his mother. Might she have given it to him? I did a new search on his mother and found a possible connection.

Fanny Sjöström, born 15/03/1940, deceased 30/05/1974.

So she had died on the thirtieth of May. I looked at the numbers from the pendant. 30052301.

"Mommy, look, I'm done," Bea said and held the drawing up for me to see.

"That's lovely, honey," I said without looking up.

Fred had decided to blow himself up and die on the same day his mother had passed away.

"You're not looking, mommy, look!"

It could hardly be a coincidence that 3005 was the first number carved on Fred's pendant.

"*Mommy, look!*"

"Okay, Bea, shh…" I put a finger to my lips. "You can't shout here."

"Then look, mommy," she whispered instead, and held the drawing up to my face. "I'm petting Bessi."

I moved the drawing back a little so I could focus.

"That's nice. And there's daddy," I said, pointing to a figure standing next to them.

"Noooo, that's Bessi's owner," Bea laughed. "And that's the fence."

I stared at the drawing. Felt my pulse starting to race.

"Bessi?! Is that the dog and the man from preschool?" I said. She nodded firmly and smiled. I grabbed her arm.

"You can never pet that dog again, Bea. You understand? Never."

"I know, mommy, you told me," she said and wiggled out of my grasp. "Mommy, I need to go to the bathroom."

FORTY-THREE

"My life fell apart completely after my mom died," Fred said, looking straight into the camera. "Foster homes, skipping classes, alcohol. I committed minor crimes and was caught. Fucking cops beat me up. I hated the cops. Hated social worker hags. Hated everyone."

While I listened to Fred, I kept thinking about how I had spent the night before analyzing the recordings from the interviews. Scrutinizing his facial expressions, voice modulations, emotional responses, which questions he had chosen to answer and which he had evaded. Even so, I hadn't been able to uncover any signs of his having planned a second attack. Still, I couldn't shake the thought that there might be another bomb. He didn't answer my questions on that subject. Had his plan always been to survive in order to make the right people listen to him?

He had started talking more now. Since telling me about his mother's death, he'd been more open, but we still mostly talked about how the world had ignored their situation.

I had to agree with him that it was remarkable that their neighbors, his school, social services, the police, and whoever else had failed to do something about the deprivation he lived in. However, according to his file, there were some people who had noticed that all was not well. It described, for example, that a school nurse had reported to social services that Fred often wore tattered clothing, looked skinny, and walked around without a warm jacket in the middle of winter. Knowing what was going on, it wasn't hard to imagine that his mother had spent the money meant for winter clothes on other things. No one had reacted to the fact that she was struggling financially, since she was a single parent, which, granted, had been less common back then, but not unheard of. She had a low-wage job. According to Fred, social services had made two planned home visits to their apartment. His mother had been high both times. Had told the social workers she had allergies the first time, flu the second. Social services had believed her. Other than that, their neighbors had called the police a few times to complain about noise coming from their home, but that was all.

Fred's case confirmed that societal neglect when a child is little can have dire consequences.

"What were you trying to achieve with all this?" I said. "To bring about change? The only thing your attack has changed is that the city is on high alert. Protected areas are lousy with cops, the Parliament building has been searched from top to bottom to make sure no one has managed to get in and plant something there, and all politicians have been given increased protection. The assassinations of Prime Minister Olof Palme and Foreign Minister Anna Lindh, the suicide bomber on Bryggargatan, and now this. Not to mention the costs. Do you have any idea how much this is costing the state? Money that could have been used to help people."

"Where was that help when we needed it? When my mom needed it?"

Even though I thought he was right about many things, he wasn't exactly the only person in the world with a tragic childhood.

"Everything's a lie, don't you get it? The Swedish people are a bunch of blinkered fools. They pretend to be good people who care about others, but they don't actually give a shit about people who are suffering. So long as they can ignore anything happening outside their own circumscribed little world. They actually look down on people who are less fortunate. Kick people who are already down. All the adults around me knew what life was like for me and mom. Teachers, classmates' parents, neighbors, *everyone*. Not a single one of them did anything to help. Instead, they mocked us."

"And how did you figure blowing up Parliament would change what you just said?"

"People don't react if all you do is write in to your local paper. No one listens to people like me, okay? But I've got their attention now."

It was hard to argue with him. Hearing Fred talk, you had to admit society had got off lightly. He'd really been a ticking bomb long before the incident outside Parliament.

I pulled the evidence bag from my purse, turned it upside down, and let the necklace fall into my hand. Held it out to him. Without saying a word, he slowly raised his hand and gingerly picked the chain up. Held it up with the pendant dangling in front of him. Turned it over and looked at the back as if to reassure himself it really was the right one. Closed his other hand around it and brought both hands to his chest.

"Where did you get it?" I asked him.

"My mom. I got it after..."

"After what?" I asked.

No reply.

"You got it after what, Fred?" I repeated.

"She always wore it. My grandpa had given it to her. He was a farrier."

So that explained the horseshoe. And *FS* was not for Fred Sjöström, but for his mother, Fanny Sjöström.

"What do the numbers on the back mean?" I said.

"It says right there," he said, nodding to the file on my lap.

It wasn't the first time he'd referred to the case file in answer to my questions. He didn't react at all to the fact that I had discovered the number sequence. That troubled me a little. Could it be that he had counted on the information on the pendant becoming known? If that was the case, this was a lot more sophisticated than I had expected. The numbers were not easy to spot, and could only be seen if you held the pendant up to the light at the right angle. He kept his eyes fixed on the file and repeated, "It's all in there."

FORTY-FOUR

Sitting at a desk in the Blood Family's clubhouse, David glanced to the side to catch a glimpse of the two guys who were somewhere behind him. It bothered him that he wasn't able to keep track of the people in the room, but he couldn't turn around. That would just make him look nervous.

Simon Hall was sitting on the other side of the desk with a bowl in front of him that he was stirring with a spoon. His bodyguard was seated in an armchair next to him, staring dully at David.

David had called Saga several times on the way, but she wasn't picking up. He knew her mom's birthday and family dinner meant a lot to her. It did to him too. He realized she must still be there, but he had to deliver the car to the Blood Family before he could join her. Turning up at Saga's parents' house in a car full of weapons and leaving it parked in the driveway while he socialized with the in-laws didn't seem like a good idea. Besides, he knew Simon would keep track of the time. The car keys were supposed to be delivered to him personally.

"Where did you find this?" Simon said and scrunched up his nose after taking the spoon out of his mouth.

"Down by the square," one of the guys behind David said.

Simon pushed the bowl away.

"Take it back. Goddamn it, I order soup and they give me some microwaved fucking dishwater with a few bits of carrot in it. Tell that guy to sort his food out."

The guy came over and removed the bowl from the desk.

"Bring me a salad instead," he said before the guy left with the soup.

Simon turned to David and shook his head. "Shit, bro, you can't find any decent food around here when you're cutting."

David didn't think the man in front of him looked like much of a healthy eater.

"You seem to have made good time, despite running into some trouble on the way," Simon said and smiled.

Did Simon know David had been pulled over by the police? Or did he mean what had happened in Copenhagen? David had no way of knowing for sure. He held out the car keys. Simon nodded to his bodyguard, who took them and handed them on to the third man in the room.

"Feel free to hang around from now on, if you want," Simon said with a nod to David.

David knew what that meant. Simon trusted him and was inviting him to join the Family's periphery. That meant hanging with gang members but above all that he could keep running errands for the gang. From that position, he would be able to work his way up and become a full member. For a person who wanted to join the Blood Family, what Simon had just offered was a great honor.

David nodded curtly and stood up. He didn't relax until he was back out on the street. On his way to the metro, he called Saga.

"I'm on my way now," he said.

"It was hours ago," she said. "I'm home."

David sighed.

"I don't get it, David," she continued. "Where have you been?"

"I told you. I had to help a friend with something."

David placed his wallet on the card reader on the barrier.

"Why are your friends always more important?" she said.

"You're the most important thing to me, you know th—"

David stopped talking. Saga had hung up.

FORTY-FIVE

"First they ask me to do the interviews, then they have the nerve to criticize my interview methods!" I said to Alexandra over the phone.

I glanced at the clock on the wall. Just after 8 p.m. The sounds on the other end of the line indicated that Alexandra was at home, too, and busy with evening routines. She had called me to say that SÄK had been in touch to demand a meeting with me regarding my interviews with Fred.

"You shouldn't assume they're going to criticize, Leona. They told me they'd read your summary reports and seen some of the footage. Overall, they were happy, but they wanted you to add a few questions. And then they wanted to go over your approach going forward."

"This was exactly what I didn't want —"

"Call me after the meeting tomorrow morning," Alexandra said and hung up.

The message was clear. I sighed. Was pondering what kind of nonsense SÄK might throw at me when I had a text from Johnny Timmer. He had called me after our most recent meeting to tell me about an old childhood friend of his he thought might be a good fit for my business. He assured me the guy was okay, that they had known each other since their early teens. Said they had committed crimes together before.

If the two of them were as good together as Timmer claimed, I'd be able to make good use of him. Timmer had given me his personal identity number and I had run a thorough background check on him in the Record of Suspected Offenders, the General Criminal Register, and the General Surveillance Register. In this context, I considered featuring in the Criminal Register a merit. If they had been sentenced to prison, that was a good thing. Then I knew they'd be more motivated to learn what I had to teach. The ones who hadn't spent time behind bars yet tended to think of themselves as invincible. Thought they were too clever to get caught. This guy had been convicted of a bunch of minor offenses and one major drug crime, which had netted him a long prison sentence. The Surveillance Register also linked him to a number of organized criminals. The interesting thing was that he had been questioned in a number of serious criminal investigations, but he had avoided convictions in all but one case.

As I sent Timmer a simple "OK" to let him know he could bring his friend to our next meeting, it struck me that I hadn't heard so much as a peep from the bathroom since I left it a little while ago.

I normally let Beatrice do tubs on her own, but I always kept the bathroom door open and didn't leave her unsupervised for long periods of time. She would usually sing, shout for me to fetch her a specific toy, or just ask me to come see how long she could hold her breath underwater, but now it was dead silent in there.

"Bea!" I said.

No reply. I turned the sound off on the TV and got up and started walking toward the bathroom. Felt my heart racing. The bathroom door was ajar, just as I left it. Everything was the same inside as well, except that the shower curtain had been drawn. Nothing seemed to be moving behind it. I took two quick steps across the room and swept it aside.

"But mommy, I want the curtain. It's like a fort."

Beatrice looked up at me with her big blue eyes. The foam that had almost been overflowing when I left had shrunk and was now level with the bottom of the tub.

"Didn't you hear me calling you?" I said curtly.

I tried to relax, but I was still on edge.

"Why didn't you answer, Bea?" I pressed.

"Didn't hear you, mommy. I had bubbles on my ears."

"It's late, let's rinse off the bubbles and get into bed," I told her.

I pulled the plug. There was a slurping sound as the water was sucked into the pipes.

I grabbed the showerhead. Tested the temperature on the inside of my wrist.

"Weee, cold, cold, mommy," Beatrice whimpered. She twisted away from the jet. I turned the temperature up and waited until she had approved it.

"Hold your head up," I said and rinsed the foam out of her hair.

I watched the water stream down her back. When the foam disappeared, I noticed some dark patches on her back.

Bruises.

I went cold. Where were they from?

"Sweetheart, what happened to your back?" I said and kept rinsing.

On her shoulder as well. I turned her body around so I could see her front and was paralyzed by what I saw.

Big lacerations.

The water was red with blood trickling from the wounds. Red rivulets that mixed with the white foam.

"But what...what...?"

I was speechless. Adrenaline pumped through my veins. What had happened to my little girl? I tried to wash the blood off. But the more I rinsed, the more bruises surfaced. I could feel myself breathing heavily. The room was foggy from the steam and damp. I inhaled but couldn't get enough air.

"But mommy, what are you doing?"

Everything stopped. It was like waking from a nightmare. Everything was gone. The blood, the bruises, the wounds, the fog.

"But…?"

"Do the other arm too," Bea said and gave me a questioning look.

It made no sense to me. I'd seen it with my own eyes. I inspected her back again. Not a trace of what I had just seen.

FORTY-SIX

"You want any?" Timmer asked.

David shook his head.

"I quit, Timmer. A long time ago," he said. "You know that."

This was exactly why David didn't like hanging out with his old friends. He didn't want to risk being dragged into something he couldn't control. Be tempted to do drugs or end up in the same situation as last time, when the police suddenly stormed a friend's apartment and found a lot of snow. But even so, he needed to see them. He tried to think of it as work. Because if he could choose, he'd rather take money from the cops to report what he heard and saw at parties than haul furniture for a moving company for the pittance they paid him.

Timmer had just been released from prison and had called to ask what David was up to. David, who had come home to an empty apartment after handing the car keys over to the Blood Family, had turned around and headed straight back out. When he'd told Timmer he was at a party at a friend's house, Timmer swung by.

David would have preferred to stay home with Saga, have a nice dinner, and watch a movie on the couch, but after missing the family dinner at her parents', he didn't know where she was. Probably at a friend's house. Explaining to Saga why he disappeared from time to time and came home late sometimes had become harder and harder. He hated having to lie to her, but he had no choice. He would never tell her the truth and risk both his and her safety. She seemed to think he chose other things over her and that he was out partying, when in fact it was the other way around; he did all of this so the two of them could have a better life someday. Lately, though, she seemed to have got it in her head that he had met someone else. It didn't matter how many times he told her he loved her.

Timmer disappeared into the bathroom, holding hands with a girl he'd just met. Seemed manic about getting laid. David knew they were going to snort Danne's cocaine in there. Danne was an old classmate who had been selling drugs since high school. David hadn't told Sven about him. But he had tipped him off about other people higher up the hierarchy, the ones Danne bought his stuff from. Sven had put surveillance on them and was waiting for the right time to strike.

"David!"

A dark-haired girl with a low-cut dress was standing in front of him.

"S'up...," David said.

He couldn't remember her name, but he did remember having sex with her one time a number of years ago. She had a glass in her hand but was so wobbly in her high heels her drink was about to spill. When she realized this, she took a big gulp and then smiled at him. He had no desire to talk or do anything else with her. Being sober made a lot of the things he had used to do for entertainment seem pretty uninteresting. He tried to find a way out of the situation. Looked around and spotted Timmer, who had already come back out of the bathroom; he was waving David over.

"I'm sorry...," David said.

Damn it, why couldn't he remember her name? He left her and walked over to Timmer.

"I want to talk to you," Timmer said.

David followed him. Hoped he wasn't in for another offer of drugs. Timmer opened door after door in the hallway of the big apartment they were in, but closed each one again when he saw there were people on the other side. In the end, he found an empty room with a desk and shelf after shelf of books.

"Look, I know you quit and all, but..."

David was starting to understand what this was about. He regretted not leaving the party sooner. Now he was going to have to wiggle out of Timmer's campaign of persuasion.

"...I have a thing you just have to get in on," he continued.

David sighed. He'd been right.

"You're going to like this, I guarantee it. What are you doing day after tomorrow?"

"I'm working out. Boxing."

"Blow it off. I'm picking you up. I've sorted out a car."

He smiled and pulled out his phone. Browsed through his pictures until he found one of a black sports car.

"A Honda," he said, "though you'd never believe it, right? It's an NSX. It's pretty sweet. I'm borrowing it until the end of the month."

David wasn't particularly interested in cars, but he agreed it looked pimp.

"Listen," Timmer said and shoved his phone back in his pocket, "this just seems incredibly goddamn good. You're going to see something you would have never thought possible. A cop teaching people how to commit crimes."

David raised his eyebrows.

"I know, it sounds insane, I barely believed it myself until I saw it with my own eyes."

"Seriously, Timmer," David said and sighed.

"I know," Timmer replied. "I've had a lot of stupid ideas, but this is one hundred percent solid. David, I swear. But you..." He glanced back at the door. "...you can't so much as breathe a word about this to anyone, got it? Only a few select people have been chosen."

"What the fuck did you take in that bathroom, Timmer? This sounds completely deranged," David said.

Timmer often got himself excited, but he was unusually agitated this time. He was pacing around the room, gesticulating as he talked. After David's comment, he walked up to him, stopped dead, and said, "Never mind what I'm telling you, David. Just tag along and you'll see for yourself. One time, that's all I ask. One time."

David had to smile. He shrugged. Timmer broke into a big grin and extended his hand.

"Good deal, brother, I'll be picking you up in my Honda."

FORTY-SEVEN

Hans Nilsson, head of SÄK, nodded while I ran through a quick summary of the current interview situation with Fred. I glanced at the clock on the wall of the conference room. Quarter past ten. I had promised Anette to be right back. She had brought her adorable little mutt to work today, which had sent Beatrice over the moon, but I didn't want to burden Anette more than I had to by making her look after both a dog and Beatrice.

"Leona, is this the first time you've met Fred Sjöström?" Hans asked and looked at me.

I frowned. Didn't fully understand his question.

"What do you mean?" I said. "I've conducted a number of interviews with him."

I could feel the three other detectives at the table studying me closely.

"I was just wondering if you ever crossed paths before this started? In an investigation or anything like that?"

His question was strange to say the least. If I had, SÄK would already know it. It was easily checked in DURTVÅ, the platform we used for logging investigations. SÄK and Alexandra could have checked that with a few clicks of the mouse. I had expected to be challenged about why my interviews with Fred were so short and infrequent, and had prepared an explanation about how his medical condition made it necessary. But what they seemed to want to know was whether Fred and I had ever associated outside of work.

"What is this meeting really abou—"

"Just answer the question," the detective who had introduced himself as Ulf Öhman cut in.

"What the hell is this?" I said and got to my feet. "Some kind of fucking interrogation?"

Hans stood up quickly.

"No, no, Leona, sit, sit. We just want to know. Want to make sure Fred's not being influenced by his interviewer. It's a good thing if you've never met before."

I glanced at him. Slowly sat back down.

"We want to talk about the interviews. You see, Leona," Hans said, "we've noticed they're going off on a bit of a tangent."

I raised my eyebrows.

"Ulf, explain to Leona," he continued and looked at Ulf Öhman.

Ulf cleared his throat and straightened up. Leaned back in his chair.

"You've asked a lot of questions about Fred's relationship with his mother in recent interviews. We consider that fundamentally uninteresting at this time."

He pulled a paper tissue from his pocket and blew his nose loudly before balling it up, getting out of his chair, and discarding it in the trashcan by the door. After slowly sauntering back to his chair, he continued.

"You see, we still haven't been able to rule out a connection with a terrorist network. You have to focus on what's important instead of yammering on about his relationship with his mommy."

I stared at him.

"Were you one of the detectives who did the initial interviews with Fred?" I asked.

"Yes, that's right," he said and cleared his throat.

"Who else?" I said and looked at the other two.

One of the two men raised a finger. Like Ulf Öhman, he was on the older side of middle-aged and of a girth that meant he couldn't pull his chair all the way in.

"And how successful would you say your interview method was?" I said and looked at them each in turn.

Ulf Öhman cleared his throat again. "Ahem...well, the thing is that Fred had not woken up yet when we conducted our interviews with him."

"A bit odd to call it an interview then, don't you think?" I said to Ulf. "It's certainly not in accordance with how the law defines an interview. The Code of Judicial Procedure states that —"

Hans cut me off. "I think what Ulf is trying to say is that it was unclear whether Fred was fully conscious when the interviews took place."

It was unclear to me why Hans felt what he said changed things. Whether he was unconscious or asleep surely made no difference.

"Exactly," Ulf agreed. "So we didn't get much out of him."

"Not much?" I said. "So you did get something. What was it?"

I looked at all four of them questioningly. My comment might be construed as petty, but I wasn't about to let them get away with their smug conviction that they had done a good job. After a few seconds, the fourth person, Kenneth Dahl, broke the silence in a slightly more subdued tone than Hans or Ulf.

"The main problem was really that he didn't want to say anything..."

I smiled inwardly. They were smart enough to catch my drift. They hadn't managed to get Fred to say a single word. At least nothing useful to the investigation.

"You could take over again, now that I've got him talking, then you can have it your way," I said.

They were acting weird. Exchanging glances without saying anything.

"What?" I said.

"Leona," Hans said. "Don't get us wrong. We're very happy with your interviews, but the focus has to be on his years in the French Foreign Legion and his foreign contacts. We have to be able to tell our foreign counterparts whether there is anything to suggest that this attack was part of a series, orchestrated by a terrorist network with cells in other countries."

I didn't respond.

"We all agree you're the right person to conduct the interviews, don't we?"

Hans looked at the other three, who muttered affirmation and nodded. Except Ulf, who glared at me from behind his crossed arms.

"You know the reason I was asking Fred more questions about his parents, don't you?" I said. "The necklace and the silver pendant…"

"That trail's cold," Ulf said. "We've checked out the number sequence, it doesn't seem to lead anywhere."

I nodded.

"Are we done here?" I said, looking at Hans as I started to get up.

"We have more questions for you, Leon—" Ulf started saying, but he was cut short by Hans, who raised a hand to silence him.

"That's enough. Let's thank Leona for her good work so far."

I got up and left the room.

FORTY-EIGHT

Just as I was checking the time, the first few started walking through the door to our meeting place in the Meatpacking District. It was Saturday and Larissa, who had the day off, had volunteered to watch Beatrice for a few hours. Larissa had no children of her own and liked looking after Bea. Bea had been ecstatic because Larissa always did fun things with her.

When I spotted Ken Örberg, I smiled and walked over. Shook his hand.

"Released pending trial, eh?" I said.

He nodded with a smile on his lips. He had sent me a text saying he was out. I had told him the time and place, but hadn't been sure he would show. He looked around.

"I'm glad you came," I told him. "Have a seat. You'll find out more in just a minute."

I turned around and saw Johnny Timmer enter with another new guy in tow.

"This is David, the one I told you about," he said and nodded to the new guy.

"David Lind," he said and extended a hand.

Even from just looking at his passport photo on my computer screen, I'd been able to tell there was something special about this guy's eyes, but it was even more obvious in real life. They were blue even though he had dark skin and short, kinky, dark-brown hair. His hoodie wasn't able to conceal his broad shoulders and ripped upper body.

His hand enveloped mine. Didn't he hold on just a little longer than common practice dictated?

"ID?" I said.

He pulled a driver's license from his wallet and handed it over. I booted up my laptop. His license checked out. I knew from previous searches that his dad had emigrated and his mom had passed away.

"Your grandmother lives in Kälvesta, I see. The same street as an acquaintance of mine. I've also seen that you hang around with some unsavory guys."

I was referring to the organized crime groups the Surveillance Register linked him with. I didn't give a shit. I was simply letting him know that I was well informed about who he was, whom he hung out with, and who his family members were.

David looked at Timmer, who spread his arms wide.

"I told you you'd be checked out."

I smiled. "This is just a fraction of the information I have on you," I said and fixed David with a level stare. "Have a seat."

The others had all arrived, carried chairs over, and sat down. As I quickly introduced myself, I could tell something was up. The guys were muttering and whispering to each other.

"What's going on, Liam?" I said.

"It's Marc. Haven't heard from him. Rumor has it he was taken in."

Liam and Marc seemed to be causing me trouble.

I checked the clock. Almost ten past. If there was one thing that irked me, it was people who didn't show up on time.

"None of you will be arrested by the police, not if you do as I say. If you're caught because you're sloppy or haven't listened, you can't count on my help."

I checked my laptop.

"There is no Marc Tidelius in detention, so that's not what's happened."

I moved on. That was all the time I was going to waste on a tardy participant.

"Ken Örberg and David Lind are new here today," I said. "This is as many as you're going to be in this round. Now let's get cracking."

I started writing on the big easel pad I'd found in one of the storage rooms.

"As I mentioned last time, these are the things we'll be talking about today:

Risk assessment
Planning
High-risk crime / low-risk crime

But first I want to say a few words about your choice of crime scene. It should be a different neighborhood or city from where you live. But not so far away that you have to buy a ticket or spend hours in the car to get to and from the crime scene. So choose a place at just the right distance from where you live. In some cases, it can be a good idea to choose a place where there's already a lot of DNA, or in other words, where lots of people have been. A store, a bank, a mall, an airport, you get my drift. Finding your particular DNA in one of those places is like looking for a needle in a haystack. Timing is obviously also important. You have to decide what time of day to do it."

It was time to talk about risk assessment. In a law enforcement context, this was part of a broader risk analysis that included a threat assessment. You considered the threat in relation to a person's vulnerability and the consequences of a threat being realized, and then made an assessment in order to decide on appropriate protective measures. But in my meetings, risk assessment was about something completely different. Here, it was about assessing the risk of being caught by the police. In order to make a correct assessment of that risk, an immense amount of knowledge was required. It was often complicated because any number of unexpected things could occur. A lot of criminals tended to routinely underestimate risk.

"You can make a lot of money from one job, but you have to put the reward in relation to the risk of getting caught. The risk is considerable if you don't know what you're doing. If you're not completely sure about your own abilities and you haven't found out all the facts, you'll have to instead consider whether you are willing to spend a few years behind bars, praying that you'll be able to cash out your share when you're released. A share that might not even be there anymore, depending on where you hid it or what people you partnered up with. Your own freedom is what's at stake. Once you start earning the big money, the stakes might get even higher. If you mess up and end up getting on the wrong side of the wrong people, it can literally cost you your life."

I was going to give them a few very simple examples of what I meant.

"Say you're stealing something from a store. Just to keep it simple, let's say a 7-Eleven. How do you go about it?"

"I guess you just go in and shove a chocolate bar in your pocket when nobody's looking," Eli said and grinned at the others.

Zack and Timmer laughed. I went over to my laptop. Did a quick search on Eli and clicked through to the General Criminal Register.

"You were busted for shoplifting four times as a teenager, I see," I said.

That made David and some of the others burst out laughing.

"Oh come off it, like you haven't all been busted doing shit like that. Check everyone else out too," Eli said defensively and looked at me.

"Shoplifting is one of the most common crimes among young people by far. You've all been busted for it. Even you, Vikki."

"Ooooh," the guys exclaimed mockingly and looked at Vikki.

"Big time criminal lady," Timmer said and gave her shoulder a shove.

She replied by giving him the finger. I smiled a little, knowing that Vikki could take several of these guys out if she wanted to.

"So, how many of you do a risk calculation before you commit a crime?"

Everyone nodded.

"I'm guessing some of you do it too late, when you're already at the scene. You might look around to see if there are security guards or police around. Laugh all you want, but that's how it usually goes when people steal cars, sell drugs, rob people, and the list goes on."

Sam raised a finger in the air.

"When are you going to start talking about real crimes, the kind that pay the big bucks?"

"That's exactly what I'm doing. If you pay close attention, you'll be able to apply this simple example to your particular field. I get that patience isn't your strong suit, but in this case, it's required."

He sighed.

I continued: "To make sure we're all on the same page, I'm going to give you this simple example. Why might it not be the best idea to stroll into the 7-Eleven at the City Terminal and pocket a Snickers bar, even though you've got a real hankering?"

"High risk," Timmer said.

"Exactly," I agreed. "There will be store detectives, CCTV cameras, members of staff, other customers, and so on. Also, negligible reward. I mean, a Snickers bar…"

By high-risk crime, the police usually meant crimes where the risk of the perpetrator continuing to commit crimes was high, such as robberies, grand theft auto, assault on police officer, or intimidating a witness. In contrast, I used the term to describe the kind of crimes where the risk of being caught and convicted was high.

"If, for example, you are planning a bank job, you need to know how much money you're going to get away with and put that in relation to the risks you take, which, by the way, are disproportionately high for bank robberies. Most are solved and in many cases the robbers don't even manage to get their hands on any real money. Many banks don't even handle cash anymore. You might think all bank robberies yield enormous profits. That's not true. In some cases, it's a handful of thousand-krona notes. Given how many years in prison you can get for robbery, the risk you took clearly wasn't worth it. If you've cocked up the planning, you'll get no money at all, just a lot of time behind bars."

Some of them nodded.

"Heavy criminals are sometimes arrested for a minor offense, which then leads to something bigger, and that brings us back to the question of appearances."

I had to give them examples to make it more concrete.

"Imagine the police stopping a male driver. We think he looks high and pat him down. We study his pupils, tell him to hold his arms still so we can roll up his sleeves and check for needle marks. Instead, he keeps sticking his hand in his pocket. That makes us suspect he has drugs in it and gives us the right to do a full search.

We look through his clothes and bags. If we find drugs in his pocket and maybe phone numbers to known dealers in his phone, we search the car. If we find anything else that indicates drug offenses, we move on to the guy's home, garage, basement storage, and so on. We might find a weapon he doesn't have a license for, marked bills, maybe even a description of a planned heist. Well, you can see what I'm getting at, one thing leads to another. The classic story of a broken taillight that ultimately lands you in prison for several years."

They were paying rapt attention.

"Again, it's all about making sure the police don't get suspicious in the first place. Driving a car under the influence of drugs or alcohol can come at a high cost for you. Not worth a few minutes' enjoyment of a couple of beers."

It was time to move on to the types of crime I was eventually going to use them for. In this context, I needed to be even more explicit about the risks.

"Bank robberies are among the most complicated of the high-risk crimes. You'll need to calculate the risks very carefully. As an example, we can use the robbery of the Östgöta Enskilda Bank in Kisa that ended with Jackie Arklöv, Tony Olsson, and Andreas Axelsson being sentenced to life for robbery and for killing two police officers in Malexander. The money they took, around 2.6 million kronor, clearly was not worth all the suffering that followed. If they had calculated the risks in advance and considered all the parameters, they would have known as much."

"The helicopter robbers got away with a lot of money," David said. "I suppose they had people on the inside too, and that was a really well-planned robbery."

"We also have to bear in mind that there were a lot of people involved in that robbery. Six were convicted but there were probably around thirty people involved in all. Thirty million kronor split that many ways doesn't make for a lot of money each."

Liam raised a finger.

"What happens if you end up killing someone?"

I stared at him.

"By mistake, obviously," he added.

His questions made me feel concerned, to put it mildly. Had he even been listening to anything I'd been saying?

"You don't accidentally kill people, Liam."

"But someone could trip and hit their head on something hard," he insisted.

"It's your goddamn obligation to make sure no one trips and hits their heads, got it? You've put those people in that situation, so you're completely responsible for what happens at the crime scene."

He didn't argue. I was clearly going to have to keep an eye on Liam.

"What's more, you could be charged with murder and sentenced to life in prison."

"Nothing's worth life," David said.

"Maybe the seriousness of what you're doing is starting to sink in. You have to know your shit."

"Don't a lot of people get caught trying to cover up what they've done? Like with murder," David said.

I nodded.

"Getting rid of a body is not easy. Murderers usually end up leaving more tracks trying to move the body and dumping it someplace than if they'd just left it where it was. Some things are best left at the crime scene. If, for example, you need to bring a weapon, say a handgun, and are forced to use it to fire a warning shot, you'd do better to leave it at the scene when you're done than to bring it with you or try to get rid of it later. Because where it's found, it will be easier to connect it to you. You have to cut all ties between you, the crime, and the crime scene."

My phone buzzed in my pocket.

"I'll be right back," I said and walked into the next room.

"Peter, what do you want?" I said.

"I want to talk to Bea."

"I'm busy, I'll call you back later."

"You keep saying that, but you never do. What are you up to? And where is Bea while you're busy?"

"Peter, I..."

I couldn't tell him Bea was with Larissa. Peter would never accept that she was there when I had demanded to keep her with me.

"This isn't working, Leona. You have to bring her home," Peter said.

"Home? She's at home when she's at mine as well, isn't she?" I said. I felt my irritation grow.

"You know what I mean. I've called several times and you never let me talk to her. I'm starting to wonder what's going on." Peter was raising his voice.

"I'll call you tomorrow and we'll talk about this. But I can't talk right now."

I hung up and went back into the meeting room. I couldn't let Peter have Beatrice now, it was way too unsafe.

"You have to understand the importance of calculating and minimizing the risks. Minimize, I say, because they can't be completely eliminated. Doing crime is taking risks. The most important thing is to have enough knowledge to make a sound assessment before getting involved in this kind of business. The next step is planning the crime."

"So what crimes are low-risk, high-reward then?" Vikki asked.

"Areas the police have a bad handle on at the moment include fine art trading and Internet-based crime. We're not, for example, up to speed with regard to large sections of the online world. But things like that are time-consuming and if you don't have the economic and technical know-how to generate large profits, those things are pretty uninteresting as far as I'm concerned. It would confine you to doing a lot of small stuff for pocket change, like tiny Craigslist frauds all day every day. Hardly the stuff of dreams. You'd do better to keep coming to my meetings and learning more."

I picked up the pen that had fallen to the floor when someone suddenly pounded on the front door from outside. I looked at Liam.

"It's Marc. He just texted me," Liam said.

I went over to the window and peered out from behind the plastic sheet. The pouring rain and dim lighting made it hard to see, but I recognized him from his bearing.

"Shit, I'm sorry I'm late, this weather fucking sucks," Marc said and pulled off his hood.

He tossed his jacket on a chair. I locked the door behind him. Waited for him to carry a chair over and sit down.

"You're aware, I hope, that this isn't some fucking playgroup where you can come and go as you please?" I said.

The room went dead silent.

"What do you think would happen if this were a job and you were picking everyone up in a car and you showed up..." — I checked the time — "twenty-three minutes late?"

He didn't respond.

"You get where the rest of us would be, right? Incarcerated."

He rolled his eyes and sighed as if I were his mother, bitching about him being late for dinner.

"Calm down. My train was delayed, what am I supposed to do about that?" he said, spreading his arms.

"Let me make myself real fucking clear: I don't accept bullshit! You should leave," I said.

He didn't get up, just sat there staring at me. I went over to the chair he'd thrown his wet jacket on. Snatched it up, opened the front door and flung it out onto the loading bay.

"The fuck you doing? Fucking cunt!"

He quickly got up and started coming at me. I stood my ground.

"Cut the fucking drama," I said. "You don't even have the right to be pissed; you're the one who was late and it's not the first time. You don't seem to get what this is about, so you might as well leave."

He looked around like he was expecting to be backed up. When no one said anything, he kicked a chair out of the way, cursing loudly, and stalked off. I pulled the door shut behind him and turned to the others.

"If anyone else has a problem with the minimal fucking discipline required to show up somewhere on time, you can join Marc right now, because you don't have what it takes to work in this business."

I looked each of them in the eye, one after the other, and waited. They all sat motionless.

"This is serious, okay? You might think I'm being ridiculous, but twenty minutes can be the difference between success and one of you spending half your life behind bars. If discipline and punctuality are beyond you, you're in the wrong place."

It was just as well Marc left before he fucked up something that could have serious consequences.

"If you're committing crimes with other people, you have to know how they function. Working with the wrong people can be a death trap."

I kept a close eye on Liam, who was tight with Marc. Decided to sound him out afterward to make sure he was still motivated enough to be part of this and also send Marc a clear message about what would happen if he talked out of turn about my business. I didn't want to make a big deal of what had happened so I needed to direct their attention elsewhere.

"Equipment," I said. "Depending on what job you're pulling, you'll need different equipment."

I pulled a folder out of my bag. These were the only materials I was going to give them. It was information that needed to be seared into their memory, but I couldn't be bothered to run through it all with them; this way, they could study on their own instead. I gave one of the stapled handouts to David, who was sitting closest. He took it and immediately started flipping through the pages.

"This contains information about how to open locks quickly. As I'm sure you know, there's no universal solution that always works; it depends on what kind of lock it is."

Everyone was eyeing the handouts I was giving out curiously.

"Some locks can't be opened quickly enough to be worth the trouble, because if there's one thing you're short on, it's time. Which brings us to part two of your handouts."

They immediately turned to the next section. The incident with Marc seemed forgotten and everyone was giving the handouts their full attention.

"This tells you how to break through any door."

I had collated the information in the handouts from police teaching materials and relevant Internet sources. I had carefully removed all police logos and anything else that meant it could be traced back to the police or me.

"Just so you know, a regular crowbar and a sledgehammer aren't enough to get into places anymore. These days, security companies sell products that even make it hard for the police and emergency services to get through certain doors."

The handout contained several pictures of locks and doors sold in Sweden, as well as the tools needed to open them.

"I haven't included balcony doors and such. Forcing that kind of door is easy, but in this group we're not in the business of breaking into people's houses. Remember what I've told you about close contact with the public. Besides, it's beneath us to bumble into people's private homes. This is about doors to commercial buildings."

I let them browse for a minute before moving on.

"A regular door shouldn't take longer than ten or twenty seconds to open. A steel-reinforced one forty-five to sixty seconds. Study this. You'll find a list of specialty tools and how to use them in there, too. You have to know, for example, which pry bar to use on reinforced doors that open in as opposed to out and vice versa, which metal brake is best for folding the metal lip covering the crack between a door and a doorjamb, and which tool gives you the most striking force in a cramped space."

This was our fourth meeting and I felt it was time to introduce a few things they would actually have to study. They didn't seem to mind; on the contrary, they looked really motivated to learn.

"The last few pages are about how to deal with various alarm systems. Study up on how they work and how you can disrupt or shut them down. There's also information about in what situations you would normally choose to silence an alarm that goes to a security company and the most common codes people give security companies when they call after an alarm is tripped. You'll also find the average response time for security companies and police for various locations, as a function of distance and time of day."

I closed the handout.

"That last bit applies to buildings you want to break into at night when no one's around. During the day, you'll have to make sure the staff in the store, bank, or wherever you may be, don't sound the alarm."

To get them pumped about studying the materials, I was going to tell them about one of the world's best-planned robberies.

"Have any of you heard of the burglary of Banco Central in Fortaleza in northern Brazil?"

A couple of them nodded.

"It was one of the world's biggest and best-planned bank heists. It took place in 2005. Three months before, the burglars rented a house a couple of blocks from the bank. They broke through the floor in the living room and dug a 256-foot tunnel straight into the bank vault."

"Two hundred and fifty-six feet?" David said. "How deep?"

"Thirteen feet below ground level, about two and a half feet in diameter."

I spread my hands to help them visualize approximately two and a half feet.

"That's not something you just grab a shovel and dig," David continued. "They must have had an engineer with them or something. And northern Brazil, isn't that close to the equator? Pretty warm there, no?"

I nodded and noted that David seemed clued up about the world.

"To excavate the very well-designed tunnel, which had a mean temperature of about a hundred degrees, they used sophisticated equipment and experts on architecture, mathematics, and excavation technique. The tunnel had both lighting and air-conditioning."

I obviously wasn't going to have this group pull a job like that on our first outing; this was about studying other heists to fully grasp the importance of planning.

"In order to move the enormous volumes of sand and soil from the tunnel without the locals becoming suspicious, they put a sign on the building they'd rented with a company name and fake information about them doing landscaping and selling lawns and plants. The burglars were also nice in general to their neighbors and were described as good people. During a weekend when the bank was closed, they managed to get through three and a half feet of reinforced concrete and into the vault, disarm the bank's internal alarm system, and transport three and a half tons of banknotes through the underground tunnel. The burglary wasn't discovered until the bank opened the following Monday."

"Several tons of notes?" Timmer said.

I nodded.

"It was a total of 164 million Brazilian reais, the equivalent of about 515 million Swedish kronor at the time."

My audience gasped.

"What can we say about this heist?" I asked.

"Well planned," David said.

"They had planned it for months. Think about all the things I've told you about. They had the right people, the right equipment, had chosen the right time, and had all the knowledge they needed to pull it off."

"What about the notes?" David said. "Aren't they usually marked?"

"They knew these were bills that were going to be destroyed and therefore were nonsequential. Because of that, they were almost impossible to trace."

"Did anyone go down for it?" Timmer said.

"A handful of them were arrested much later with money in various places, but only about twenty million of the 164 million reais were ever recovered."

It was almost time to tell them about my plans for them.

"Burglaries and robberies require planning. The police can gather a lot from how you get to the scene, how you break into the building, and what your escape route looks like. These things have to be decided well in advance and there has to be a plan B in case something goes wrong on the way out. You obviously also need a good safe house for yourselves and your loot. You have to give some thought to what that place should be like, since you might have to spend quite a long time there. There has to be water, food, and in some cases ammunition there, for example."

Since they were giving me their full attention, I felt it was time to start letting them in on my plans.

"I want you to listen carefully to what I'm about to say. I'm planning a big heist that's going to make some of us very rich. Those of you who are selected for this job are going to make so much money you won't have to work or commit any more crimes for years. If you move to a country that's cheaper to live in than Sweden, which I strongly recommend, you will likely never have to work again."

What I had planned was nothing like the Fortaleza burglary. Far from it. It wouldn't be very smart of me to use them for such an advanced hit. The strength of my plan was that we were going to commit a high-reward crime with relatively simple means. I had the requisite knowledge, now I just had to pick the right people to execute it for me.

"How is it going to go down?" David asked.

"We're going to go to the place in question, grab the money, and leave," I said briefly and smiled.

They looked at each other. Probably thought I was kidding.

"I'm guessing not a bank job, then, because you don't just stroll into a bank, take the money, and stroll back out." David again. He was full of questions.

"This is another important thing for you to bear in mind. Don't share your plans with anyone other than the active participants you know you can trust. Every person who knows has the ability to reveal or ruin your plans. You know what it's like in criminal gangs. Someone tells someone else and then everything falls apart. You should also know that disgruntled people, like people who feel they should get a bigger cut, or that they've been treated badly some other way, are dangerous to deal with. That's often how the police are tipped off about serious crimes. By someone on the inside who's unhappy and snitches."

I tore off the paper I had been writing on.

"And for God's sake, never rob someone you know. The first thing we detectives do is look for connections between the victim and the perpetrator."

After everything I'd said, I could see why they'd be curious about my plans.

"I'll let the relevant people in on my plan later. For those of you who are not chosen, there will be other opportunities, so don't worry about it. We just can't be too many on any one job."

If everything went as planned, there would be no more opportunities. But I couldn't tell them that, because I didn't have time to coddle the hurt feelings of the people who weren't chosen. I had a plan for how to solve that, but it would have to be dealt with later.

I walked over to my laptop and closed it.

I had noted that David had been studying me in a different way from the others. Every time our eyes met, he held my gaze. There was something special about him. He seemed more attentive and interested than the others. He was more clued up. The interview records I had read showed the same thing. He was sharp. I was looking for a person I could trust with more responsibility for future heists. A person I could be in direct contact with in the field and who directed the other people at the scene.

Maybe he was just what I needed.

FORTY-NINE

"Mommy, look, it's so cute!"

Bea called from inside a sheep pen at Skansen. She'd been talking about petting the sheep for days now and they were clearly living up to her expectations. I was standing outside the pen with Alexandra.

"Thanks for letting me bring Beatrice to work. It's been a tough time for us," I said.

Alexandra looked at me gravely.

"I'm glad you seem to be feeling better. Of course you can bring her. I know what it's like," she said, nodding toward her own girls in the pen. "You're the only one of my detectives who's even bothered to ask. Other people bring their kids in regardless, whenever the need arises."

Alexandra waved to her youngest, who was sitting on the ground with a tiny lamb in front of her.

"Your situation is unique," she continued. "I'm glad you feel strong enough to come to work. You're needed. How did the meeting with SÄK go yesterday, by the way?"

"As expected. They tried to tell me how to do my job."

"I think they're just trying to help, Leona. Did you come to an agreement?"

"Kind of," I said.

Alexandra looked at me inquiringly.

"I told them they could do the interviews themselves if they didn't like my methods," I said.

Alexandra sighed and rubbed her forehead.

"But for some reason they don't seem to want to do that, though I don't understand why."

Alexandra firmly explained that she would prefer if all contact with SÄK went back to being handled by her, which I had no qualms with. I was happy to avoid having anything to do with them. I was convinced the reason she wanted to maintain good relations with them was that she was a climber. A job at SÄK would give her a boost in terms of both status and salary. None of our managers knew what positions they'd be given in the new year, so a lot of them were angling for jobs in the divisions they were interested in.

While Alexandra talked about how it was important for our department to maintain good relations with SÄK because of potential future collaborations, I studied a person behind her. Far away among families, strollers, and frolicking children, I thought I glimpsed a man I recognized. I leaned to the side to see past a group of people blocking my line of sight. My suspicion was confirmed. I felt my pulse starting to race.

It was him!

Armand's crony. The one in the suit and glasses who had lain in wait for me in my apartment and aimed a gun at me two weeks ago. His clothing stood out among the families at Skansen. I turned to the girls in the pen and was struck cold.

Bea was gone.

I quickly scanned the area as I started climbing over the fence. I could see Alexandra's girls, but not Beatrice. I didn't get it. I'd been standing right outside and had only let Beatrice out of my sight for a few seconds at a time while I talked to Alexandra. I heard Alexandra calling out to me as I ran over to her girls.

"Where's Bea?!" I shouted. "Where's Bea?"

The older of the two pointed to the other side of the pen where there was a big tree stump. Bea was crawling around on the ground, in pursuit of one of the prancing lambs.

"*Bea!*" I shouted and ran toward her.

"Mommy, look how cute this one is," Bea called.

I grabbed her. Hoisted her up off the ground.

"We have to go!"

"Noooo, mommy, nooooo."

She thrashed about in my arms. I put her down, grabbed her hand firmly, and pulled her along. She struggled.

"Leona!" I heard Alexandra call after me.

Out of the corner of my eye, I saw her walking briskly toward me along the outside of the fence.

"What's going on?" she said with a frown when we met by the gate.

"We have to go," I replied tersely. "I'll see you at work tomorrow."

I looked toward where I had seen the man. He wasn't there now, but I knew he was around somewhere.

With a crying and struggling Beatrice, and with gawking parents all around, I left Skansen and headed for the car.

"Mean, mean mommy," Beatrice said over and over again, her cheeks wet with tears.

She refused to put on her seatbelt. I didn't argue. Locked the doors and drove off.

FIFTY

I studied the document in front of me. COASTAL RANGERS COMPANY KA1 was printed at the top.

It was Monday morning and I had decided to accommodate SÄK by asking Fred Sjöström different questions. Not because they had demanded it, but because from the point of view of interview technique, it was a good idea to branch out, now that he'd started speaking more freely.

"The mental and physical training meant I had no energy to dwell on all the shit I'd been through," Fred said.

After going through evaluation, Fred had been assigned to the Coastal Rangers company based on Rindö Island outside Stockholm. Along with the parachute rangers, it was the unit with the highest physical and psychological entry requirements. They were Sweden's most elite units, where strength, willpower, and motivation were put to the test.

"Were you close with the guys in your unit?" I asked.

"Some of them were idiots, but there's something special about going through a lot of shit together. It forges bonds."

"Did you see each other after completing your military service?"

"Me and another guy went to sea straight after. I worked for a couple of years until I met Sophia."

"The mother of your daughter?" I said, flipping through the case file.

He nodded.

"When we got married I thought I'd finally managed to turn my life around."

Even though I had to allow for the possibility that everything Fred said was part of his plan, I was glad I didn't have to drag the words out of him. I leaned back in my armchair.

"What did you do for a living?" I asked.

"I did casual work at sea. I looked for other things too, since I didn't want to be away from her, but I couldn't get a single goddamn job. I've never done drugs, they terrify me, but alcohol made life easier. We got married when Sofia got pregnant. When Ina was born it was just too much. Money problems, and I wasn't mature enough to care for a child. I'd started suffering from depression as well, had started thinking a lot about my own childhood and stuff like that. I ended up drinking more and more. In the end, Sofia couldn't take it any longer."

He lowered his eyes.

"Even though I probably knew, in my heart of hearts, the divorce still came as a shock...But that wasn't the worst thing..." He looked away from me, squinting at the camera. "...they took my daughter from me as well."

"Sofia was given sole custody?" I said.

"I was only allowed to see my own daughter in the company of a fucking social worker. You know?"

He looked me straight in the eye.

"As if I would ever hurt my own child. It was fucked up!"

He closed his eyes and inhaled slowly before continuing: "That's what the Swedish state has done to me. Our perfect Swedish utopia is not so fucking perfect, as you can tell. At least not for everyone. After that, I left everything and went abroad."

Fred didn't seem to reflect on the fact that his reasoning was inconsistent. He complained that no one had done anything to help him when he grew up with a mother with a substance abuse problem, while also castigating the state for having intervened when his own child risked growing up with a parent with a substance abuse problem. He didn't seem to see that he had repeated his own childhood experience. As usual, social inheritance loomed large, and even if he wasn't in nearly as bad shape as his mother had been, there were parallels there. I wasn't about to raise that with him, however. That wasn't my job. That criminals clung to inconsistencies was more a rule than an exception. They rarely recognized their own shortcomings and more often than not felt the world was against them.

Several of Fred's colleagues had described him as a very nice man in interviews. He was a hard worker, always there for his colleagues. And yet hardly anyone knew anything about his private life. Personable Fred had clearly been walking around thinking about completely different things while seeing to the loading and repair works on board the cruise ferry.

On my way out, I called David. He told me he had boxing practice in the afternoon. I offered to give him a ride home afterward. I needed to see him alone. I wanted to feel him out.

FIFTY-ONE

A fresh smell of shampoo and aftershave spread through the car after David climbed into the passenger seat. I checked my watch and was pleased to see I had plenty of time before Larissa was due to bring Bea back to my apartment. Larissa had the whole day off and had promised to bake with Bea.

"Want to grab a bite on the way?" I said and turned out from the parking space outside the boxing club. "I'm starving."

"I should probably get back as quick —"

"My treat," I cut him off before he had a chance to say more. "I was hoping to talk to you about something."

After he said okay, I stopped at a Chinese restaurant.

"What do you think of my project?" I said, flipping through the menu.

He smiled.

"I'm sure there are lots of criminals out there who'd like that knowledge."

I ordered chicken with cashew nuts, which was really the only thing on the menu I liked. He picked spring rolls and Chinese shrimp in sweet and sour sauce. Very odd choice.

"So what made you stop by in the first place?" I said.

He shrugged. "Johnny talked me into it."

I smiled. I'm glad he was honest. I wasn't particularly good at making small talk, but I was trying not to be too direct. I knew it worked better if you asked one or two questions about something else before you got to what you really wanted to know. When the waitress had brought our plates and he was a few bites in, I found a clear opening.

"How's the grub?" I said.

He nodded with a piece of spring roll in his mouth and gave me the thumbs-up. All right, enough chitchat.

"You're the only person in the group I didn't personally handpick. I saw from your record that you've been a suspect in several investigations and that you've talked yourself out of trouble."

He smiled bashfully.

"I was pretty out of control when I was younger."

"Still, you've done pretty well compared to a lot of people."

"I suppose I've figured out how you cops work," he said and shot me a dazzlingly white smile.

I had become curious about how he had managed to get several charges dropped, and had studied a couple of the cases. Read the records from his interrogations and been interested to see how he responded to the questions. It was plain to see the guy was sharp and knew what he was doing.

"How did you end up doing crimes in the first place?" I said and took a sip of the ice water in front of me.

"The usual way, I guess. I couldn't stand being at home so I started going out, skipping school, smoking, drinking, committing minor offenses. When it got bad, in my late teens, I went to stay with my dad in Ghana, but I had to start learning the language and all that stuff. I didn't get along with my dad either, so I moved back."

"What do you do now?" I asked.

"Casual work. For a moving company at the moment, and some other things."

Maybe that, coupled with the boxing, explained his ripped body. I couldn't help thinking it was a waste. David looked like an American actor I couldn't recall the name of. He would have done well in front of a camera. Was sort of naturally touched up with his smooth brown skin and light stubble.

"Some other things?" I said.

"Other assignments," he replied.

I got his meaning. I'd seen he had connections with organized crime.

"But I actually want out," he said. "It's a downward spiral, I know. I've seen it happen to several of my friends."

I nodded slowly. He was right. For most people, it ended badly. They either ended up shuttling in and out of prison for the rest of their lives, which made it problematic for them to have the things most people considered fundamental to a meaningful existence: real friends, family, and children. Or they ended up junkies. Or both.

"I really think this would suit you," I said. "This could be your way out."

He didn't seem entirely convinced. I considered that a healthy reaction. He was a person who weighed the pros and cons. Came to his own conclusions. Trusting a sycophant who just obeyed orders could be dangerous for me, if something did go wrong and initiative was required. I needed a person who could keep a clear head in a tight spot.

After talking for a while, he opened up about himself more. Said that he was single, and renting an apartment with his cousin but was looking for a place of his own. That he didn't like hanging out with his criminal friends anymore.

As I drove across the Traneberg Bridge toward Alvik, I felt more and more convinced he was the right person. But I needed to make him understand and believe if I was to risk giving him the responsibility I wanted him to shoulder.

He asked me to drop him off on the main road a few minutes from his house. He could walk from there, he said.

FIFTY-TWO

David had just shut the door of Leona's car when he spotted Saga watching him from the corner. He smiled and walked up to her.

"Who was that?" she said.

"Uh...who? Just a friend's sister," David said, but he could tell it didn't come off as believable.

Normally, David was good at lying, which had often come in handy, but Saga knew him too well.

She said nothing, just turned on her heel and started walking down the street toward their block. Ever since last week when David missed her family dinner, things had been tense between them. Saga had stayed over at a friend's and David had been out most of the weekend.

"Where have you been?" David said to change the subject.

Saga didn't answer. He caught up with her and tried to put his arm around her shoulders. She shrugged it off and kept walking a few steps ahead of him.

"What's wrong?" David said.

She still didn't answer, just walked even faster toward their house. Punched in the entry code and threw the door open. Instead of taking the elevator as she usually did, she stomped straight up the stairs. David followed.

"But Saga...," he said.

He heard her get her keys out and unlock the door. Before he reached their floor, she had slammed it shut behind her. David climbed the last few steps. Sighed. Realized the next hour was going to be given over to interminable discussions where he had to defend himself. Which wasn't easy since he couldn't be honest and tell her what he was doing, but instead had to lie to the person he loved most.

He opened the door, hung up his jacket, and pulled off his shoes. The apartment was silent. He went into the living room but Saga wasn't there. She was standing in the kitchen with a glass of water in her hand. She started speaking without looking at him.

"I've put up with so much while we've been together, David. More than you understand. I've defended you to everyone who didn't believe in our relationship, my friends and my family. Since you were released from prison, you've done nothing but lie and go behind my back. You've come home in the middle of the night, had secret phone calls, and told me you had to work when I know that's not where you were going. For a while, I thought you were doing drugs again, but what I've been suspecting recently was just confirmed to me: that you're cheating on me."

"Saga, it's not what you think..."

"No? What is it then?" she broke in and stared at him.

He sighed. Didn't know how to make her understand. When he didn't respond, she poured the rest of the water into the sink and smacked the glass down on the counter.

"I can't live like this anymore. Sometimes when I wake up in the night or the morning, you're still not back. I worry that something's happened to you. Don't know if I should call the police. If you're dead in a ditch somewhere. I call all your friends, but they either don't pick up or they're high at some loud party and I can't hear what they're saying. But no one ever knows where you are. Now I get why no one wanted to tell me."

David was just about to defend himself when she held her hand up.

"David, I can't take this anymore," she said with a deep sigh. "I want you to move out."

FIFTY-THREE

As I got back from giving David a ride home, I noticed someone sitting outside my building. It made me suspicious. When I got closer, I realized it was Peter.

"Where's Bea?" he said when I reached him.

"Hi. It's nice to see you too," I said.

"Seriously, Leona, what the fuck do you think you're doing? You don't answer my calls and when I call Bea's preschool, they tell me she's sick. That she wasn't there on Wednesday or Thursday or Friday last week, and that she hasn't been there today. Where the fuck is she?"

He had raised his voice. I looked around.

"Shh, calm down," I said. "She's at Larissa's. I was just running a few errands. Larissa's on her way over with her." I looked at my watch. "Should be here any second."

"Larissa? Why the fuck didn't you bring her to me?"

"We can't just pass her back and forth like a football. You're the one who's always going on about how she needs continuity in pickups and drop-offs. Bea loves Larissa, we've spent a lot of time with her."

That very moment, Larissa drove up. She honked twice as she slowed down on her way to a parking spot farther down the street. Bea waved happily through the window.

"See? Everything's fine," I said.

"This is unacceptable, Leona. So where is Bea during the day?"

"She likes being at work with me."

"What the fuck, you're out of your mind! You're bringing a five-year-old when you're investigating serious crimes? Have you lost all sense of reality?"

"It's fine, Peter. You're overreacting. Plenty of my colleagues bring their kids from time to time, when their preschools are closed or there's a situation at home. Nothing weird about it. Besides, she's safer at the police station than anywhere else."

Larissa had let Beatrice out of the car. She was happily skipping toward us.

"Daddy!" she called and ran up to Peter. He bent down and greeted her with open arms, picking her up and spinning her around.

"Hi, sweetie, there you are! How have you been?" he said.

"Good," she said. "Larissa and I made a raspberry cake."

"Hi Peter," said Larissa, who had reached us. "Nice to see you."

"Are those Bea's things?" Peter said curtly and nodded at the bag in Larissa's hand.

Larissa looked at me inquiringly. She didn't understand why Peter was being so brusque with her. That I had been forced to use her in an emergency lie to Peter about where all our joint savings had gone. A few hundred thousand that I'd actually pissed away on online poker, but that I told Peter I had lent to Larissa who was in financial difficulty.

"I don't understand either of you," Peter said. "I'm taking Bea home now."

Peter held his hand out for the bag. Larissa looked at me stiffly and gave it to him. Peter snatched it up and glared at her.

"Peter, you can't do this," I said.

"*Me? You* can't do this," Peter said. "Beatrice isn't supposed to be at work with you all day, that's what preschool's for."

Larissa looked at me.

"Beatrice hasn't been to preschool at all?" she said with surprise.

I glowered at her. She should know this wasn't the time for that discussion. If only she and Peter could understand that I was doing this to shield them from all my problems.

"Say bye to mommy," Peter told Bea and put her down on the ground.

I sighed and bent down. Hugged her hard. I could do nothing in this situation. Peter was clearly determined and the last thing I had the energy for was the custody battle Peter might initiate if I refused to hand her over.

"Bye, honey. It's okay," I said. "I'll see you again soon. Be nice to daddy."

Peter took her hand, turned, and walked away at a brisk speed. I stayed where I was, speechless.

"Leona! What's going on? What was all that about?" Larissa said.

"It's complicated," I said. "Thanks for looking after Beatrice. I have to go home and go to bed. Not feeling well."

"I'll come with you. I can make us something to eat and we can talk about it," Larissa suggested. "I could've looked after Beatrice more if I'd known."

"I'm all right," I said. "I'm just tired, been sleeping badly."

"Are you sure? It's no hassle for me, I'm off tonight anyway."

"I just need to rest," I said. "I'll call you tomorrow."

I couldn't bear having someone around right now. She gave me a hug before turning around and walking back to her car.

I slowly walked up the stairs to my apartment.

Feeling empty.

Inadequate.

I had yet again failed to protect my child's safety and security. Each step I took felt heavier. The steps seemed steeper. I rummaged around my purse for my keys. Unlocked the door, pulled it shut behind me and collapsed on the doormat. I was defeated. I couldn't get up, just sat there on the floor. Thought about Beatrice. Benjamin. Little Olivia and the strange visions I'd been having lately. Were the sleeping pills causing them? Or were these the delusions Aimi had written about in her notebook?

Was Peter right, had I lost all sense of reality?

FIFTY-FOUR

David opened the passenger door and climbed into Sven's car. Sven set off before he could even buckle his seatbelt. At high speed. Out of town. David didn't know why Sven was in such a hurry to see him. Friday, the day the cocaine was being handed over, had already come and gone. David hadn't heard from Sven since. Strangely, he hadn't heard any rumors about how the deal had gone down either, but then David had been busy with other things.

He had done everything he could to change Saga's mind. Explained how much he loved her. She had listened but cried and said she needed some peace and didn't have it in her to worry about him anymore. About him being beaten up or sent to prison again. When she told him how difficult their relationship had been for her, he understood. He wanted nothing more than to get her back, but he wasn't going to fight with her. Deep down, he agreed, she deserved better. But he was going to show her that he was able to turn his life around. He knew that was the only way. He was going to pay her back for the rent and bills she had covered. He was going to make enough money for the two of them to have a good life together. David was staying at a friend's house now but thought about Saga every second.

"What's up?" David said. "The coke deal didn't pan out, or what?"

Sven kept driving and made no reply. When they reached a turnoff, he stopped. Killed the engine.

"We got them. Get it? All of them. Thanks to you."

David stared at him.

"Really fucking well done, David. Everything you told us was right, except the amount. We seized fifteen pounds of cocaine, not six. The guys were caught red-handed, just as they were doing the handover. Not a chance of them talking their way out of it."

David straightened up in his seat. He had to admit, it felt good to finally get some praise.

Sven pulled out an envelope. Slightly fatter than the previous ones. David opened it. Looked inside. A number of five-hundred-krona bills.

"We've been discussing your situation. I'd like to upgrade you. It would mean a bit more money. Down the line, maybe even a monthly payment, if you keep doing this well."

David didn't reply. Didn't know what to say. What he really wanted was to leave that world. This way, he was just going to get more deeply entangled. It was like the law was forcing him to live like a criminal. It was an in-between kind of world.

"You could go to school at the same time, if you wanted. Apply to college and it's like a partial scholarship. After that, you can get a better job than the one at the moving company."

David thought about his colleague who'd worked there for twenty years. Ior was both worn out and bitter.

"Of course, it will require a bit more of you. You'll need to be available twenty-four/seven."

"How much money are we talking?" David wanted to know.

"For big busts like this one, you'll be paid extra. What do you say?"

"How much?"

"I can't promise you enormous sums, but enough to get by."

David needed more money. Saga wasn't the only person he owed money, he'd borrowed from friends as well.

He thought about how much they'd give him if he told them about Leona and her business venture. A detective teaching criminals how to commit crimes would probably net him quite a big bonus, on top of the monthly salary Sven was talking about. But in order to maximize his reward, he needed to know more about the heist Leona was planning. Date, time, method, and if other people were involved. He needed to find out more about her plans.

FIFTY-FIVE

I changed position in the visitor's chair. Slumped down a little. After spending so many hours in this chair, I was trying to find a new way of making myself comfortable. The camera was on as usual. I had asked Fred why he had decided to apply to join the Foreign Legion.

"I didn't really have a burning desire to go to war, it was more about choosing how I wanted to die. Whether I wanted to hang myself in a grimy suburban apartment outside Stockholm, where no one would miss me, or fall in combat in a foreign land, fighting for something."

He turned his head to look out the window.

"I was done with life, couldn't stand Sweden anymore. I was indifferent to everything."

"Let's take a short break," I said.

I turned the camera off. Grabbed the binder with all the information about the investigation and walked toward the door. Turned around.

"Do you want a cup of coffee?" I asked.

He looked at me in surprise, as though he hadn't imagined me capable of saying something nice.

"I'm getting one for myself anyway," I said.

He nodded. "Can you ask a nurse for a bedpan? I need to go to the bathroom."

I nodded and left the room. Even though I mostly kept my eyes on the floor, it was impossible to avoid noticing the specter walking toward me in the hallway. A pale, emaciated woman dragging a rickety drip stand on wheels behind her. She slowly looked up when I passed. I avoided meeting her eyes and quickly walked on, but I stopped when I spotted a nurse coming out of a room.

"Fred Sjöström in room nineteen needs to go to the bathroom," I told her.

"Leona?" she said, giving me a searching look.

I nodded. Looked her up and down. Couldn't remember ever talking to her before.

"Fred has been saying your name in his sleep. Several times. At first, I thought he was talking about a loved one, but I've been told he doesn't have many of those."

I nodded and made my way down to one of the cafés. Still keeping my eyes on the floor. I was used to people having accidents or being the victims of violent crime, but all these diseases that seemed to grow out of the human body, like tumors, were revolting to me.

On my way back, there was a vibration in my pocket. I pulled out my phone. Armand again. Same text as last time. As before, he'd written *"confirm,"* but I hadn't replied. I didn't know how to raise the fifty thousand I didn't have. I couldn't ask Larissa again. And even though my poker game had improved, I didn't dare risk it.

"Should you even be drinking coffee?" I asked Fred when I got back from the cafeteria.

I put one of the paper cups down on the tray by the side of his bed and sat back down in the visitor's chair. He tried to reach the mug, but couldn't. I pulled on the cart to make the tray swing in over the bed.

"Feel good to be able to drink without help?" I asked.

He didn't respond. Whether or not coffee was good for him might, granted, not be his biggest concern right now. I turned the camera back on.

"I've talked to Mirja," I said.

His eyes shifted from the camera to me. Held my gaze for a while, then shifted back.

"I heard rumors about the Legion during my military service," he said in a monotone. "A romanticized image. A few people talked about joining, but none of them were accepted."

He ignored my comment about his cruise ship colleague.

"So what was the Legion like? You and your buddies were taught how to blow things up all day long or what?"

For the first time, I saw Fred crack a smile. Not a big smile, not even using both sides of his mouth, just one. So tiny I wondered if I'd really seen it, but yes, one of the corners of his mouth had definitely curled upward. How he had learned to handle explosives wasn't important for me to know at this point. If the Legion hadn't taught it to him, there was endless information to find on the Internet. Anyone with enough motivation could find out what they needed to know there. I was more interested in whom he got to know in the Legion.

"You were there for nine years."

He shrugged.

"What did I have to go back to?"

"You legionnaires were probably pretty chummy, huh?"

"You ended up talking to the people from your own country for the most part. The Americans kept to themselves, the Germans to themselves, the Russians, Dutch, and so on. The only language spoken in the Legion is French. That meant the French soldiers had an enormous advantage. The rest of us had to take a lot of hard knocks because we didn't understand our instructions and did things wrong. I didn't know a word when I first got there and quickly realized the best strategy was to hang out with the French."

"You kept in touch after leaving the Legion as well," I said.

I said it like a statement, but it was really a question. He looked at me as if he was trying to figure out how much information I might have access to.

"When you joined up, you were given a new identity, new passport," he said. "You left your previous life behind. Most of the people there had nothing good to go back to afterward. After completing your service, you were offered French citizenship. I stayed in France."

"And your closest buddies too?"

"I was in the Legion for longer than most. When I left, the people I knew best had either destroyed themselves or moved away."

"You left before your second five-year contract came to an end," I said.

"War injury. Got shot in the shoulder. Spent a month in a French hospital."

"What kind of work did you do in France after that?"

"Me and another guy started our own business. We ran various semicriminal rackets. Money lending and laundering. He was a businessman, so he took care of the finances, I collected the money. We kept at it until we couldn't."

I drank the last of my coffee. Stood up and binned the cup.

"What happened?" I said.

"He crossed a line," Fred said. "Started using more and more gangsterlike tactics. Demanded I kill a man over a late payment. When I refused, he thought I'd collected the money and was keeping it all myself. He knew some unpleasant people and put a price on my head. I moved back to Sweden."

The timeline was slowly coming together. But I hadn't discovered any clear motive to explain why Fred had blown himself up and therefore had no clues as to whether there was a second bomb or not.

"What did you do when you got back to Sweden?" I said.

"It quickly became apparent that the Legion was not considered a merit, quite the opposite. I couldn't get a job. Sat around in a tiny suburban apartment in a dark, gray Stockholm without a job or family, with nothing but my war memories to keep me company. I realized I'd thrown away my life serving in the Legion, drinking, committing crimes, and a lot of other destructive things. The thoughts that had come and gone throughout my life surfaced more and more frequently. Grew stronger. I wanted to get back. Get revenge."

Finally we were getting somewhere.

"Who were you close with during this time?"

He looked at me with a weary expression.

"You're not listening, Leona. I keep telling you. I was alone. Always have been, always will be. I don't trust anyone and don't want anything to do with anyone. This is my thing."

I leaned back in the armchair. Enough already. SÄK could say whatever they wanted, but I was convinced Fred was telling the truth. There was simply not a shred of evidence that he was part of a terrorist network.

Besides — I could spot a loner from a mile away.

FIFTY-SIX

"Help me carry in the equipment!" I shouted through the half-open car window to the guys who were huddled on the loading bay outside our meeting place in the Meatpacking District. Even though I quickly rolled the window back up, water had got in all the way to the passenger seat. I rolled forward a few feet and then reversed up to the metal steps to get closer, opened the door, and ran back to the trunk where two of the guys were waiting. I threw them three big, black police bags which they lugged up the steps.

"Here!"

I tossed David the keys to the door while I parked the car under the eaves of the building across the way.

It was high time to let them try on the uniforms they were going to be wearing during my planned heist.

The police uniforms.

Before you put on a police uniform, you have no idea how the weight and heat will affect your ability to move around. My guys also needed to know where all the parts went and how to handle the equipment correctly.

Getting hold of the uniforms had been relatively straightforward. It was no problem for me to sign out new police shirts, pants, and jackets from the central stores. You just went over, told them what you needed, and were more often than not left alone among the endless shelves of clothing and equipment in both men's and women's sizes. Usually, you even filled out the form detailing what you had taken yourself. All police officers had several sets of clothing and since I'd been planning this for months, it'd been easy to go stockpile a few items at a time. Even though detectives like myself mostly wore civilian clothes, everyone had to go into the field for various assignments that required uniforms from time to time. When I entered the room, the gang had already got one of the uniforms out. Timmer had pulled on a pair of uniform pants that were at least two sizes too small. They were very tight across his backside and thighs. He walked straight down the middle of the room like he was on a catwalk, hips swaying, while the others whistled and laughed.

"For fuck's sake, get a grip!" I said, but I had to laugh and wonder how many of those sexy lady police officer costumes I'd seen when I took Bea to Butterick's were sold every year.

Liam pulled out a belt and uniform cap and put them on.

"Hand me the jacket, Timmer," he said.

Timmer, who had thrown the jacket over his shoulder and was now twirling it in big circles over his head like a stripteaser, threw the jacket to Liam, who only just managed to catch it before it landed on the filthy floor. Liam put the jacket on. After adding a belt and a cap that covered his half-shaved blond head, he was starting to look eerily like a police officer.

"Shit, dude, you look scary," Zack said as he put his hand in his short dreadlocks.

The others were also studying Liam with obvious fascination.

"Shut up you son of a bitch," Liam said and stared menacingly at Zack as he slowly advanced toward him. "You're gonna do exactly what I say, you hear me? Don't fucking piss me off, you miserable junkie shit!"

Zack looked nervously at the others and emitted an uneasy laugh while Liam kept advancing. Everyone knew it was a joke; Liam was just pretending to be a cop. But even so, the room went dead silent. The lighthearted mood had vanished. No one was laughing. It was clear they had all encountered that cop at one time or another. The aggressive, domineering cop who took his frustration and his hatred out on whoever crossed his path, whoever he considered criminal.

It was hardly news that uniforms changed the people wearing them. You put on a role. A position of power. Uniforms were dangerous on the wrong bodies. Seeing a criminal in police uniform and understanding, through his behavior, what police officers were like from his perspective was an eye-opener for me. I had to sit down. Was unable to take my eyes off Liam, who continued to move in on Zack.

Good versus evil.

Or?

The rest of the fitting turned out differently than I had anticipated. The atmosphere was heavy and subdued. I robotically demonstrated where the different parts went.

The belt. The holster. The handcuffs. The pepper spray. The flashlight. The tactical vest. Shirt tucked into the pants. Pants over boots. The cap on the proper way. Neat and tidy.

Everyone followed my instructions in silence. They extended their telescoping batons and aimed their fake guns, but no one seemed to think it was fun or exciting anymore. They took the uniforms off as soon as they were allowed, as if the clothes had thorns on the inside. What I had intended to be a longer runthrough of the equipment and tools available to the police as compared to the weapons criminals usually wielded, instead became a monotonous dressing and undressing. I was glad I worked in civilian clothes and found it hard to come to terms with the fact that, once upon a time, I had enjoyed wearing my uniform.

I was never putting one on again.

FIFTY-SEVEN

"Cheers! To change," I said.

David smiled and clinked glasses with me before taking a sip. It hadn't been difficult to get him to come home with me after the uniform fitting. I'd told him I could give him a ride home afterward, but since we were now drinking wine, it was clear there wasn't going to be any driving tonight.

Peter had insisted I take the wineglasses we were now drinking from in the divorce. I had no idea why. Peter seemed to think glasses and china were important to me. I was completely uninterested in those things. It was odd how after so many years of marriage, he still didn't seem to know much about me. Peter was an emotional person; he was ruled by his feelings and made decisions based on emotional impulses. He was often sad about things I didn't understand at all. Aimi liked to say I was more rational and Peter more empathetic. She claimed that people like Peter often had closer emotional ties with the children. She had so many theories, Aimi.

Formally speaking, our divorce wasn't final yet. I wasn't the one who had filed, but once divorce was inevitable, it was grating that it wasn't over. I didn't see the point of the six-month waiting period the state forced on people just because they had young children. If two people had come to a decision and separated, why would they ever start wavering and wanting to go back? And in what way would that be good for the children?

"Do you want something to eat with it?" I said and got out of my armchair.

"I'm good," he said. "I've eaten."

I opened the pantry and took out a bag of peanuts. Poured them into a bowl and went back to the living room. David had gone over to the bookcase. Was holding the one framed photograph I had on display there.

"How old are they?" he asked.

"Beatrice is five. Benjamin was two and a half when the picture was taken. Just before he had surgery. A surgery he unfortunately didn't make it through," I said.

He instantly turned to me.

"I'm sorry."

I nodded. Sat down on the couch.

"I wish I..." I trailed off. There was no reason to share details about my children with David. I held out my hand and he gave me the picture. I looked at Benjamin. Pale and skinny but still with a tiny smile on his lips. Beatrice was standing with one armed raised in the air. Full of life. Even though I was trying, I couldn't shake the feeling something might happen to her. I had also talked to a colleague in Surveillance, who had promised to swing by and check on things from time to time whenever they were out and about. He had obviously been curious about why I wanted him to keep an eye on my own daughter and ex-husband, but had just said it was cool, that I didn't have to explain and that they would obviously do what they could. I knew they couldn't be there around the clock, but I was grateful for their help. The most important thing now was for me to keep Armand content.

"Have some nuts," I said, holding the bowl out.

He moved closer. Took a handful of nuts from the bowl and sat down next to me on the couch. I raised my glass again.

"Which members of our little team did you know from before?" I asked.

"I'd heard of most of them, like Liam; everyone knows who he is. But Johnny's the only one I know well."

"I've been thinking about who to pick for the robbery I'm planning. Any thoughts?"

"Depends on how advanced it is," David replied. "How many people do you need?"

"It's going to be the heist of the century, trust me. Not spectacular and flashy like the helicopter robbery, but a lot more sophisticated, and with a ridiculous amount of money."

He smiled.

"I want you on board," I said.

He studied me with a look on his face I couldn't read.

"I was even going to put you in charge of what happens in the field. As I'm sure you understand, I won't be able to be there myself, but if you agree, you and I will be in constant contact and I will direct everything from right here in my apartment."

He kept chewing his peanuts as if he hadn't heard what I said. Took his time replying. When he was done chewing and about to throw some more nuts into his mouth, he said, "Okay."

I pondered how to interpret his flippant reply. Sometimes, I had difficulty reading people's cues. It almost seemed to me he didn't understand what I was offering. A ticket to a carefree existence where he would have money that he'd never even dreamt of.

"You'll be the one in charge at the scene."

Still no reaction.

"What are you planning to do with the money?" I said, and raised my glass again.

He chuckled and took another sip.

"Depends on how much I get. What kind of money are we talking?"

I went to the kitchen, fetched the wine bottle, and topped up our glasses.

"The best thing would be to move abroad. Then no one would think twice about you suddenly having all kinds of money. You don't have anything keeping you here, do you?"

"I've been thinking about maybe going to college," David said quietly.

"College?" I said and laughed. "Why? That's what you do to get a well-paid job. When this is done, you won't have to work."

FIFTY-EIGHT

David started feeling tipsy after just two glasses of wine. He'd told Leona he'd eaten already, but the truth was he hadn't had a proper meal since he moved out of Saga's apartment.

"You don't seem to get it. We're talking millions and millions of kronor, David. Do you understand what I'm telling you?" Leona continued.

"Sweet," David said and smiled.

"It's great you want to study, but if the goal is to get a well-paid job, it's a waste of time."

Leona seemed very agitated. He didn't really know how to approach her offer of making him her deputy in the robbery she was planning. He needed to know more. If it was as big as she claimed, Sven would probably give him a big chunk of change for preventing it. Far from millions, though. Doing the robbery without informing Sven would probably make more financial sense, but David just knew it would blow up in his face.

Because it would, right?

It was a vicious cycle. It was a vicious cycle. He repeated it to himself several times. He'd promised himself not to get dragged back into that shit again.

David knew there was no point going to Sven with incomplete information. What, when, where, how, and with whom were questions Sven immediately asked whenever David brought him anything new. Before he had the answers, there was no point talking to Sven. He would just be ticked off that David hadn't found out more and then the demands would start flooding over him. It seemed Leona was deliberately tight-lipped about certain details. Maybe she'd be more talkative after a few glasses of wine.

"The heist has been carefully planned. And you, you'll be my right hand. I believe in you. I'll be right back," she said and left the room.

He took another sip of his wine. Heard her close the bathroom door. He looked around. There were two boxes in the bookcase. He quietly got up and pulled one of them out. Looked through a lot of papers, pens, ChapStick, and other sundries. He didn't know exactly what he was looking for. Maybe blueprints or a written plan describing the heist she claimed was so well thought out. But there was nothing like that in the first box. He carefully closed it. Looked around. He hadn't heard the toilet flush yet, so there should be time. He slowly pulled out the other box. Lifted up a few power cords, a couple of paperbacks, a —

"What are you doing?" she said.

David whipped around. How had she returned without him hearing?

"Uh..." He quickly recovered. "...I was just trying to find a lighter."

She nodded toward the coffee table where two tea lights were burning.

"Ah, didn't think of that," he said with a quick laugh. "Is it okay if I smoke?"

"No," she said. "I think you should leave."

Fuck! She knew he'd been snooping around.

"I'm sorry," he said and moved closer to her. "I didn't mean to. I realize what this looks like, and to be honest, it's exactly what you think."

Her eyebrows shot up.

"I was snooping around. All of this just sounds really weird to me. I don't know if I can trust what you're telling me."

She nodded toward the couch. He went over and sat down. She took the armchair and eyed him suspiciously.

"What are you doing here? Why do you want in on this?"

"I want to quit crime, Leona. Just like I said. I want a normal life. That's why I'm going back to school. I want to get away from this shit, but I don't have any money. I want to seize the opportunity you're offering, but it all sounds too good to be true. So I wanted to check. To know who you really are. Make sure it's not a trap. If I have to go back to prison, I'll kill myself. I can't do it again."

He wondered if she'd bought his explanation. Everything he'd said was true enough, he'd just left out the tiny detail that he was a police informer. At first, she'd been looking at him gravely, but now her lips curled into a small smile.

"You want to stop being a criminal, and I want to stop being a detective. What a team."

He smiled.

"If I'm going to do this, it has to be absolutely the last crime I ever commit," he said.

"I'll make sure it is, David. But I have to be able to trust you, okay? Can I?" she said and looked him straight in the eye.

He looked back stiffly and gave her a slow nod.

FIFTY-NINE

Fred Sjöström pushed the button that made the top part of the bed slowly rise into an upright position. He had to do it slowly. Just a few degrees at a time to prevent a sudden drop in blood pressure that almost made him faint.

The interviews were more draining than he'd thought. He needed a lot of time to recover. In the Legion, he had withstood hour after hour of interrogation. It was different now. It was like his body had given up and just wanted to sleep.

Even though he'd been confined to the same hospital room for a long time now, he didn't know where he was when he opened his eyes. Sometimes when he woke up it was light outside, sometimes dark. He usually had no idea how much time had passed. Kept asking the nurses for the time and date. It was important. Both to stay sane and for his plans. Today was Friday. One step closer.

The nightmares tricked him. Sometimes he woke up as a child in his bed in his mom's apartment, or in the Legion during the Gulf War. Even though he was now a prisoner in his own body and completely dependent on the health care system, it was a relief to wake up from those dreams. The life he had lived before he ended up in a hospital bed had not been worth living.

The state between wakefulness and sleep he was sometimes in was pleasant. There, he could choose his own reality.

"Is it recording? The light's not on."

He nodded at the video camera.

"Don't worry, it's on," replied Leona, who had taken up position next to his bed.

"Fred, you told me before that your attack wasn't a matter of what you wanted. So who did you do it for?"

She had just arrived, but Fred had no trouble sensing that she was annoyed.

"For everyone who is or has been in my situation," he replied.

"Older men? Members of the Foreign Legion? Children with difficult childhoods? Who do you mean?" she said and pulled a binder out of her bag.

He cleared his throat.

"Have you ever killed another human being?" he said and looked her straight in the eye.

"I'm an officer of the law," she said and flipped through the contents of the binder.

"Was that an answer to my question?" he said.

"I'm asking the questions," she said.

It would be impossible for anyone who hadn't killed a person to understand what Fred had been forced to do. Because that's how he saw it. He had been forced to do it. Once he was standing there, in Iraq, the only way open to him had been forward. She would never be able to understand the feeling of returning from war. When you were supposed to readjust to a normal life. When feelings you had had to suppress while you were out there suddenly came welling back up. Before, he'd been numbed and had shut everything down, completed his missions, that was all that mattered. There were no questions. Not until afterward.

He would never be able to make people understand what he had seen, what he had been forced to do. That he had stood there with a dead man sprawled in front of him. A man he had killed, without blinking. Without thinking about the value of a life.

About how the man, who'd done nothing wrong, had fallen prey to him and his comrades. About how that man had been as alive as he was for seconds, minutes, and years, until that moment.

"…are you listening to me?" Leona said and stared at him.

Fred hadn't been listening. The only thing he could think about was the man lying in the reddish sand in front of him. But the blood pouring from his head and the unnatural position of his legs were not what had been etched on Fred's retinas, it was what he and the other soldiers had done afterward. What they had always been told to do if they killed a person by mistake.

"*Fred*," Leona said.

"How do I know what you're going to do with that recording? If anyone will ever even see it," he said and nodded at the video camera.

"You don't have to worry. A lot of people are interested in your story, trust me."

He couldn't trust her. It was time.

"I want to make a statement on live TV," he said. "The nine o'clock news."

She stared at him, eyebrows raised.

"Fred, your case is covered by investigatory confidentiality. We can't broadcast — "

"Make it happen!" he said.

Everyone was going to know his story. Know what he had been forced to do. Kill his own mother. Kill civilians and be told to conceal it. That he and the other soldiers hadn't even needed to say anything to each other when it happened. They had known what had to be done. Fred had gone about it in a trance. The man had lain motionless when Fred walked over to fetch the weapon from the vehicle they drove in Kuwait. A so-called drop weapon they had confiscated from some other person's home and put in their vehicle, as a backup in case a mistake was made. Mistakes were always made. It was inevitable. Civilians were killed by mistake. Fred had placed the weapon next to the body. As soon as it was in place, one of the other soldiers had photographed the man on the ground with the gun next to him. Fabricating evidence to prove that the body on the ground wasn't a civilian man, father, husband, killed by mistake, but a soldier.

He recalled the words one of the American legionnaires had said, which still echoed in his mind: "So long as you've got a drop weapon, you're solid." With a weapon like that and photographic evidence, they'd never be held accountable. No one would question them.

"I can't arrange a TV broadcast with you as the main guest, it's not in my power to do," Leona said.

"Time is running out, Leona," Fred said. "You have no choice if you want to hear the rest before..." He trailed off.

"Before what?" Leona said.

"Before it's all over," he said, his eyes locked on the camera.

SIXTY

After parking my car in the garage under my apartment building, I ended up just sitting motionless behind the wheel. Staring at the concrete wall in front of me. It was only quarter past eight at night, but my eyelids were heavy. I had talked to Alexandra about Fred's demand to go on TV and had a suggestion as to how to solve it.

I opened the door and stepped out. Got my bag out from the back seat, closed the door, and locked the car.

I'd only walked a few feet when I heard quick footsteps behind me. Before I could turn around, someone grabbed me from behind. I lost my balance and fell backward. He was holding me from behind. Choking me with his arm. Dragged me backward toward the row of parked cars. In between two of them. I instinctively grabbed his arm with both hands to ease the pressure on my throat. He was fast. Quickly pulled me down onto the asphalt. The moment he let go of my neck for a second to push me down against the ground, I pulled my arm down, trying to reach my gun. He was too quick. Straddled me. Put both hands around my neck and pressed me against the concrete floor. He was dressed all in black. Wore a mask. I twisted my body. Kicked out, but couldn't reach him. His grip around my throat tightened. I tried to grab his fingers to pry them open but couldn't get to them. His gloved hands felt like steel around my throat. I tensed the muscles in my neck as much as I could to expand my airway, but his grip was too firm. I couldn't breathe. I planted my heels against the floor and tried to arch my body to get him off balance, but I couldn't shift him so much as an inch off my chest and stomach. His grip around my throat tightened further. I could feel my mind start to flicker. I managed to turn my head. Glance to the side. From under the cars, I could see legs walking into the garage. With my last strength, I kicked out as hard as I could to reach the car next to me. The kick landed solidly. The car alarm went off and echoed loudly between the concrete walls. The man let go. Quickly got to his feet. Looked around before sticking his hand in his breast pocket and pulling out something that he dropped on the ground before sprinting off.

I rolled over onto my side. Curled up in the fetal position with my knees pulled up to my stomach. Sucked air into my lungs. Too quickly. Coughed. Spotted my laptop bag on the floor. The man had not intended to rob me.

"Oh my God, are you okay?" one of the women who had entered the garage exclaimed.

She came running over and helped me up.

"What happened? Was it that man who ran out of here?" she said while I kept coughing.

I nodded and rubbed my throat while checking to see what the man had dropped on the ground. It was a note. I bent down and picked it up between coughs.

"I'm calling the police," the woman said and starting rummaging through her purse.

125 000 8 July (25 000 for failure to confirm) A

The note was written in English.

"That's okay, don't worry about it," I said to the woman and cursed inwardly at Armand for getting physical over this.

Not to mention that he had increased the sum because I hadn't replied to his text.

"But it's important to report lunatics like him," she continued.

"Thanks, but I'll go down to the station and report it later," I said and hoped the woman would back off.

"I'll go with you," she said. "I'm a witness. He's not going to get away with this."

"Oh for God's sake!" I said. I pulled out my badge and shoved it in her face.

She watched me, bewildered, as I quickly walked away.

SIXTY-ONE

I had called my crew in for an extra meeting. Armand's warning to me in the garage couldn't have been clearer. I couldn't delay paying any longer. He demanded 125,000 kronor before the big heist, which forced me to alter my plans. My participants were going to be given their first assignment.

David barely looked at me when he entered our meeting place in the Meatpacking District. Sat straight down and talked to Vikki. She wasn't exactly a chatty girl. Not one for small talk. She looked like she was suspicious as to why he was talking to her at all, as though she figured he wanted something from her. Thinking about it, I'd never seen the two of them say a word to each other before. The others noticed too.

"What the fuck's wrong with you, David? Don't you have a girl at home?" Zack said.

"Relax," David replied calmly. "We're just talking."

"*You're* talking," Vikki said. "What do you want?"

"Wow, okay, hostile," David said and got to his feet.

He stalked off to the far side of the room. Picked up a chair and sat down away from the rest of the group.

"Are you going to pout now, Davy-boy?" Zack said, tilting his head and trying to catch David's eye.

David looked at me.

"Are we starting or what? Everyone's here."

I noted that Zack had said David had a girlfriend. I could have sworn he'd told me he was single.

I waited until everyone had stopped talking.

"You're robbing a jewelry store next week."

I let that sink in for a moment.

"Now I want you to listen up and memorize what I tell you. No written notes anywhere."

Not that they had been taking notes until now, but still. There could be no physical evidence of this conversation.

Having the gang rob a jewelry store hadn't been part of my original plan, but everything had changed now. Besides, it was good practice and would serve as a dry run for the big heist later. I would be able to observe who followed my instructions and kept their wits about them under the pressure a robbery entailed.

"You have to learn to handle the adrenaline rush you'll experience. If you can do that, there's no telling what you can achieve. The important thing is that you stay focused on the task at hand and don't react with anger, regardless of what happens. No matter how provoked you get. Anger makes you even stupider."

Before anyone could start bitching about my implying they were stupid to start with, I pressed on: "The thing is, that's how we humans function; anger makes us stupid. I can give you a simple example of this. I'm sure you've all kicked your foot or toe into the leg of a table or chair? It hurts and your adrenaline starts flowing. You fly into a rage and want to kick back. You know the table or chair wasn't trying to hurt you, but you still want to get back at it. Not so clever, is it? That's how we humans function."

I could sense a certain degree of recognition among them.

"It's important you're mentally prepared and stay calm. Make sure you follow my instructions without embellishment."

It was useful for me to see how they reacted in this high-pressure situation.

"Ken and Liam, you will be putting on masks and walking into the jewelry store in the morning, right after it opens."

They eyed each other. Even though all I had talked about in our meetings was crime, it was as if they only now woke up and realized it was serious.

"There's only going to be one person in the store, the owner. An older man in his sixties. You, Liam, will walk right over and point your gun at him. A fake gun, of course, but the man won't be able to tell the difference."

Liam nodded with a smug look, as though I'd just given him the coolest job.

"Not one fucking scratch on the owner, Liam. Is that clear?"

I stood up and looked out at them.

"You realize this is real now, right? If you make so much as one little mistake, you're jeopardizing everyone's safety. You can think of this as a test. Before we pull our next job, which will be much bigger and involve a lot more money, I want to know if you're sharp enough to do this."

I sketched out a bird's-eye plan of the store.

"The entrance to the shop is here. The alarm, two buttons the owner has to press simultaneously, is over here, under the counter."

I drew a red cross by the cash register.

"Liam, you need to get to the man in no more than a second or two, while he's still off guard. He mustn't get to the alarm buttons. Then you take him down this little hallway here, and into the staff room."

I turned to Ken.

"Ken, you pull the door shut as soon as you're in, lock it from inside, and change the sign with the opening hours. We don't want to risk having a witness banging the door because the store didn't open on time."

"Aren't there any cameras?" David said.

"There's a surveillance system," I said, pointing to the plan. "I'll get back to that. Ken and Liam, you have to get away from the window as quickly as you can. You don't want to draw attention from passersby. There's a big safe in the staff room, here, in the corner. You're going to force him to open it. You're going to be quick and methodical. Give him short, clear commands, but otherwise keep the talking to a minimum. With your gun against his head, Liam, he will follow your instructions."

I sat down on the table.

"You have to keep your adrenaline under control and be sharp enough to keep an eye on the man's reactions. He will be in shock. We don't know anything about his health, if he has heart problems or anything like that."

Ken raised a finger. "What happens if he faints or even…"

"Listen to me!" I broke in. "Just do exactly as I say. Liam will keep an eye on the man while you, Ken, shove everything from the safe into the bag you'll have brought with you. It's going to be gold jewelry and cash. I happen to know that this man has extremely valuable jewelry in his safe and a lot of cash. Don't touch the cash register or the jewelry in the displays. It's too risky, given how visible you'll be, and besides, there's only trinkets in there compared to what he keeps in the safe."

I wrote the number eight on the easel pad.

"You have eight minutes. I don't want you in there any longer than that. When you and the store owner hear sirens, you grab the bag and head out. Are you with me? What we want is for the store owner to see you trying to escape but being arrested by the police."

They both nodded. I continued.

"David, Vikki, Timmer, and Zack. After eight minutes, you drive up in a patrol car, dressed in your police uniforms."

Now they were starting to see where I was going.

"Timmer and Zack, you arrest Ken and Liam. Shove them and the bag into the police car and get out of there. Then you meet up with me and hand over the patrol car, the uniforms, and the bag. Any questions?"

Vikki cleared her throat.

"Won't the owner of the store think it's weird that the police are leaving with the gold?"

I frowned. It was the concern of someone who didn't know how this kind of investigation was conducted.

"The bag has been used in a robbery and is part of the investigation. The items in it have to be analyzed, photographed, and their value has to be assessed, pending charges against the robbers. Once that's done, the jeweler would normally get his gold and cash back, but this usually takes its sweet time. Let me worry about that part."

She nodded.

"David and Vikki, the two of you stay behind and play the police officers who calm the store owner down. He will be in shock and that can manifest itself in a range of ways. You will speak calmly, be friendly but firm with him. You will pretend to write an incident report and take his statement. He should feel safe having had the police there to help him, arrest the robbers, and initiate the investigation. You will explain that the gold will be returned to him in due course, but that it may take a few weeks. Give him my number and I'll take care of things when he calls."

By then, we should have completed the big heist and I should be able to pay the man back for what we took and then some.

"I just need six of you this time. The rest of you will have to wait. Questions?"

The room was silent.

"Whatever you do, never Google the crimes you're about to commit. When the police search a suspect's home and seize a computer, they put it through a process called mirroring. If they find lots of searches for 'robbing jewelry store' or 'best sledge-hammer for burglary' or even worse, 'dismember a body,' that obviously won't do the suspect any favors."

"Oh, come on, everyone searches stuff like that," Liam said.

I sighed. He was missing the point.

"Obviously your browsing history doesn't prove that you committed the crime, but it gives the police a sense of your special interests and what you may be planning to do in the future. They can also re-create things you've deleted. So stop Googling and do as I tell you instead."

Then I turned to David and Vikki.

"The last thing you'll do after taking the jeweler's statement is confiscate the CCTV footage of the robbery. Explain to him that you need it for the investigation."

SIXTY-TWO

David stayed behind when everyone else left. He studied Leona while she stacked the chairs by the wall. She turned and spotted him.

"David?" she said and smiled as she stacked another chair on the pile. "You want a ride home?"

"Nah, I'm good. I'm going to a friend's house."

Leona unplugged her laptop and closed it.

David cleared his throat. "Hey, this jewelry store robbery..."

She instantly cut him off.

"Yes, I know I told you there was only going to be one job, but I have to find out who's got what it takes before we saddle up for the big heist." She walked up to him. "I know you do, but I'm not as sure about the others. And I need someone to sort of stay on top of them and report to me. I need you there."

"But won't the police find out about this? That there's been a robbery, I mean?"

"Who's going to tell them?" she said. "This is a small, independent jeweler. The few people in the area who may see something will think the police have already been there. If no one reports it, the police will never know. If the press catches wind of it and writes about the robbery in the papers, they would say the police responded within minutes and took care of it."

She slipped the laptop into her laptop bag.

"The Police Authority is a large organization. No one there is going to sit down and compare press clippings with actual incidents. If you stick to my plan, very few people, if any, aside from the jeweler, will know there's been a robbery. And no one will realize that the people who were there, sorting it out, weren't real police officers. If there's one thing the Police Authority is grateful for, it's when things clear themselves up, which in this case, they will."

She smiled. Stepped in closer.

"The most important thing is to make sure no one phones it in, which is why you have to get there so quickly. You're going to make a fine police officer. The uniform looked best on you."

David couldn't stop a smile. He had to admit her plan was clever.

"Which jewelry store is it?" he asked.

She turned and walked back to the table where she'd left her bag.

"I also wanted to show all of you that what I've been telling you in our meetings isn't made up or empty words. You'll see for yourselves that it's possible to make money fast. I know several of the guys are very hard up and I take that very seriously. I know what it's like to be broke."

"When are we doing it?" David said.

"I'll tell you more nearer the time," she said and started walking toward the exit. "Sure you don't want a ride?"

David nodded. She stopped and turned to him. Tossed aside a strand of hair that had fallen in front of one of her eyes and down her cheek.

"So, can I count on you, David?"

"Mm," he replied, but he wasn't convinced.

SIXTY-THREE

When David stepped out of the boxing club a few days later, he paused under the roof at the entrance. The rain was pouring down. He looked up to see if it would be reasonable to expect it to clear up in the next few minutes, but the leaden clouds smeared across the sky made him decide to head out. He thought about Saga, how she had used to hand him an umbrella when he was leaving the apartment. He had always said no. Walking around with an umbrella wasn't his thing.

He pulled up his hood and walked briskly toward the metro. Cars were splashing through puddles. The flashing hazard lights of a car were reflected in the wet asphalt. David looked up and recognized it. He quickly glanced back at the club in case someone had come out and could see him before angling across the street toward the car. He opened the passenger door and got in.

"Why aren't you answering your phone?" said Sven, who was in the driver's seat.

"I've been busy," David replied. "I have a life too, you know."

"You have a life because we helped you out of that shit you used to do before, are we clear on that?" Sven said. "If not for us, you'd probably be back in the slammer."

Sven snorted derisively and looked out at the street. David said nothing.

"What's happening with the Family?" Sven asked.

David hadn't had much contact with the Blood Family since

the Copenhagen road trip. True, Simon had been in touch, asking for David's help with a few minor errands, which David had completed and been paid for, but that wasn't something he was going to discuss with Sven.

"I haven't had time to hang out with them. I've been working for the moving company."

David wanted to know how much money he was going to get if he was upgraded as an informer and how much his tip-offs would be worth then.

"Suppose I knew about plans to commit two serious crimes. If I were to give you exact info about when and where, how much money would I get?"

"I can't say unless you tell me what it's about," Sven replied. "Have you given any thought to my offer?"

"One is about a really big heist. Multimillion sum."

David could see that what he'd said had got Sven excited. But David needed more money and wasn't going to do just anything without guarantees of income.

"What kind of crime? Drugs? Robbery?"

"Crimes orchestrated by a government employee."

Sven raised his eyebrows.

"A current government employee?"

David nodded.

"Which government agency?" Sven wanted to know.

David looked at him without answering.

"I have to do a risk assessment," David said.

"A risk assessment?" Sven repeated. "Aren't we just pulling out all the fancy vocab today?"

"I'm not going to take any more risks without assurances," David said.

David still hadn't been told how much he would get if he

agreed to Sven's deal. He wasn't going to let himself be tricked into thinking it was a lot of money. Sven shook his head.

"That's not how it works, David, I thought you knew that by now. You can't set the terms."

"I need more cash," David said. "I can't stand living like this anymore."

"I gave you cash the last time I saw you. What the fuck did you do with it all? Have you started—"

"I don't do drugs, but I have debts, okay?" David broke in. "Saga has had to pay my share of the rent and utilities for months."

"Where did you tell her the money came from?" Sven said.

"I know the fucking rules, Sven, come off it already! I haven't told her anything."

"That's not what I was asking," Sven said. "She might be starting to suspect something."

"I told her I finally got the payment the moving company had been withholding."

Sven studied David thoughtfully.

"Is Saga still asking questions?"

David shook his head.

"We broke up. She threw me out because I'd been doing things behind her back for too long. I was always talking to you on the phone and I was out at night and stuff. She thought I was cheating on her."

"Hey, those crimes you were talking about just now," Sven said. "Tell me more about them."

"For fuck's sake, I don't have time for this," David said and opened the car door. Before Sven could say anything else, David slammed the door shut behind him and set off toward the metro.

If he'd been wavering about whether to take part in Leona's jewelry store robbery before, now his mind was made up.

SIXTY-FOUR

With a book in my hand and a carton of strawberries next to me, I was sitting on a blanket in Vasa Park, glancing out across Odengatan toward Lindström Jewelers. The name was printed in cursive on the green awning that hid half the window and revealed that the store was one of the older of its kind.

I checked my watch. Two and a half minutes since Ken and Liam went in. From the outside, everything looked peaceful. The reflections in the windows made it impossible for me to see what was happening inside. In five and a half minutes, David, Timmer, Vikki, and Zack were going to pull up in a patrol car.

I was too agitated to eat my strawberries. My eyes were glued to the store window. It annoyed me when buses and trucks blocked the view as they went past.

After four minutes, I suddenly spotted a man approaching the door to the jewelry store. He yanked the handle, but the door was locked, as planned. Without checking the hours sign that Ken had changed, he walked up to the window to the left of the door. Hopefully they were already in the staff room, but there was no way for me to know what he could see from where he was standing. I had to do something. I was just about to get up when I heard a small voice behind me.

"I loooove strawberries."

A little boy was standing behind me on the blanket, ecstatically eyeing my strawberries.

"Viktor!" a woman with a stroller called from a few yards away. "Come here!"

I left the blanket, book, and strawberries on the ground and ran toward the pedestrian crossing.

"Excuse me! Hello!" the woman called after me.

I zigzagged between the cars to get across the street to the jewelry store. The man, who had pulled out a phone, was putting it back in his pocket. Just as he had moved in close to the window and put his hands up to the glass to look in, I slowed down, pulled my sunglasses down onto my nose, and said, "Excuse me!"

The man turned around and looked at me. "Yes?"

He was in his fifties. Wore a thick Byzantine gold chain around his neck.

"Could you tell me where the Stockholm Public Library is?" I said.

He raised his arm and pointed down Odengatan.

"Sure, if you go straight down this street — "

"Oh!...I'm sorry, but I'm visually impaired, would it be possible for you to go with me part of the way and show me? If it's not too much trouble. Is it far?" I said.

"Oh, of course. No, it's not far at all. This store apparently doesn't open for another hour anyway," he said and looked at the sign Ken had changed.

We started walking together. I glanced in through the store window. Couldn't see anything unusual. When we were a block away, I heard sirens and a police car came roaring down the street. When it zoomed past us I saw my crew inside. I looked back and saw it mount the curb outside the jewelry store as the man and I continued our walk.

SIXTY-FIVE

David, Vikki, Timmer, and Zack quickly climbed out of the patrol car Zack had parked outside Lindström Jewelers. Before they could reach the front door, it was thrown open by Ken, who made it a few steps out onto the sidewalk with the bag in his hand before David grabbed him, opened the door to the store wide, and shoved him back inside. Vikki, Timmer, and Zack rushed in after David and continued toward the staff room. The door closed behind them.

"Police! Put your hands up!"

David pulled Ken to the middle of the store so he could see down the hallway and into the staff room. Ken was a lot bigger than David but moved with him. The owner was standing by the back wall in the staff room. David didn't think he'd ever seen so much fear in a person's eyes.

"Did you get all of it?" David whispered behind Ken's back while he cuffed him.

Ken nodded and looked at the bag that was now on the floor just inside the door. Timmer and Zack came out of the staff room with Liam in handcuffs.

"We're just going to put these two in the car," Vikki told the jeweler. "We'll be right back when that's done. You're safe now. Why don't you have a seat?"

"Fucking pigs!" Liam shouted on his way out of the store.

"Shut up!" Zack yelled back.

As David stood there in his police uniform, having manhandled Ken into the police car, closed the back door from the outside, and watched Zack drive away, he suddenly remembered that as a child, he'd dreamt of being a police officer.

SIXTY-SIX

"I want to see as much as I can before I completely lose my eyesight," I told the man while we slowly continued down Odengatan.

"Then you have to see the Royal Dramatic Theater as well, now that's a beautiful building. Have you been there?" the man said.

Before I had a chance to respond, he added, "And Drottningholm Palace, you just have to see that."

The conversation continued in that vein. The man suggested one building after another. Explained how to get to them, when the best time to go was, and how I could get the best camera angles. Even though my mind was elsewhere, I was fascinated by how enthusiastic some people were. They loved giving advice and showing off their knowledge at the same time.

"The Public Library is over there," he said and pointed. "If you walk down toward Sveavägen and turn right, you'll be approaching it from the right direction and you can take photographs from the main steps up toward the library."

I turned to him and was just about to thank him for his help when I saw a police car go past at high speed. It was my crew, driving away from the jewelry store. If all had gone as planned, Zack, Timmer, Ken, and Liam should be in it. David and Vikki were supposed to stay behind and hold a fake interview with the jeweler. Just as the police car was about to turn right onto Upplandsgatan at the intersection, another car came at it at full speed. The sound of car tires screeching against asphalt and the crash from metal hitting metal made people turn around and look.

"My goodness, what a crash!" the man said. "Was it the police car?"

SIXTY-SEVEN

With a small notepad and a pen in his hands, David was pretending to write down the jeweler's incoherent statement.

"They stormed in here like two hooligans and forced me...I'd only just opened for the day. They came at me with a gun...And I couldn't remember the code...And the safe."

The man was loud and gesticulated wildly. David's and Vikki's attempts at calming him down had not been particularly successful. They had managed to make him sit down for a while, but he kept jumping back up and insisted on pacing back and forth between the store and the staff room.

"And then they dragged me in here before I could even get to the alarm. And, and...then they asked me for the code to the safe. And, and...I at first couldn't remember the code. It was so strange. I've punched that code in every day for thirty years...but suddenly it was gone."

The man walked over to the table. Leaned against the table top and stood motionless for a few seconds. David went over to him. Put a hand on his shoulder.

"I think it would be a good idea for you to have a seat again. Try to take a few deep breaths."

David pulled out the chair closest to him. The man grabbed the backrest and slowly sat down. Vikki went over to the small kitchenette at the other end of the room, filled up a glass of water from the tap, and put it in front of him.

"Have a few sips," she said, "you'll feel better."

The man took the glass in his trembling hand and put it to his lips.

"Did you recognize either of them?" David asked and looked up from his little notepad.

The man shook his head. "I've never seen them before in my life."

"There's a welt on your cheek. Is that from this incident?" David said.

"What, really? There is?" The man put a hand on his cheek.

"One of the men hit me," he said. "Because I couldn't remember the code. He shouted at me that I was lying to them, but I swear, I couldn't remember. No matter how hard I tried..."

"Which one of them was it?" David said.

"I don't know, I could barely tell them apart. No, actually, it was the smaller of the two. The one who held a gun to my head the entire time."

David and Vikki exchanged a glance. Of course it was Liam who had lost his shit and hurt the man.

"We noticed you have a CCTV camera here," Vikki said.

"They installed it a few years ago. I don't really know how it works, but apparently it saves the video on that thing."

The man pointed to an old-style computer screen in the corner of the room. Vikki stared at it as if she'd never seen anything like it before. She nodded to David, who walked up and managed to get it started. After he fiddled with it for a while, the footage appeared on the screen.

"*There!*" the man exclaimed. "There they are!"

He got up and walked over to the screen.

"And there's the one who hit me. Oh my God!"

David turned it off. Realized it was traumatic for the man to see it all again. He managed to eject the floppy disk and made sure nothing was saved on the hard drive.

"Everything seems to have been caught on film. Very good," David said and turned to the man. "We will need this for our investigation, so we're going to take the disk with us."

"Of course, of course," the man said. "My God, I'm so lucky you're here. And that all my gold is safe."

"Everything will be returned to you, there's no need to worry about that. It's just going to take some time. We'll be working as fast as we can."

"How long will you be keeping it?" the man said. "I do have a business to run."

"It doesn't seem like they took anything from the store itself, so at least you have that for now," Vikki put in. "We're happy you got away without any major injuries, that's the most important thing. You did the right thing, doing what they told you to do. Otherwise, it could have ended badly."

The man nodded.

"You will be given details about when and where you can collect your gold," Vikki said. "We may even be able to arrange a delivery. I'm sorry this happened to you, but it really could've been a lot worse. Some perpetrators are never caught."

"I'm glad you got here so quickly." The man was quiet for a moment, then added, "You must have been just around the corner?"

Vikki glanced at David. He rolled with it.

"A witness noticed suspicious activity through the window. She called the police and since we're always out and about in the city center, we could get here in no time."

The man held his hand out to David.

"Thank you so much! People always complain about the police, but you've done fine work today."

SIXTY-EIGHT

"Is anyone hurt?" I enunciated into the phone to Timmer.

I'd left the man who'd shown me the way to the Stockholm Public Library and run into a parking lot behind the building.

"What the fuck...what are we going to do?" Timmer hissed. He sounded confused. I heard shouting in the background.

"Timmer, answer me! Is anyone hurt?"

"It's a man and a woman. They seem okay, but they're pissed."

"Listen to me! Make sure they're okay. Take their IDs, license plates, and contact details. Photograph the damage to their car quickly with your phone and tell them to take pictures when they get home as well. Tell them to expect a phone call from the Police Authority in a couple of days and that everything will be resolved. Explain that you have two crime suspects in the car who need to be taken to the detention center."

"There's a man standing here, shouting at Zack that we're completely fucking incompetent," Timmer said.

"Don't say your names out loud! And make sure you calm him down. He's just in shock. Tell him calmly but firmly that they can leave and that you will take care of everything. Ask the other person in the car to do the driving. Do it. *Now!*"

Timmer hung up. I felt like what I'd told him hadn't registered. Too many instructions at once. Fuck!

Returning a crashed car to the station commander would require an explanation. For a detective to sign out a patrol car was unusual enough in itself. We usually opted for unmarked vehicles. But if there were patrol cars available and you explained what they were for, it normally wasn't a problem to borrow one, as I'd done.

I stopped at a safe distance and observed what was happening. They were going to have to move out soon, before the intersection clogged up. The worst thing that could happen now would be for a couple of my colleagues to happen by, notice the commotion, and stay to help out. I didn't want to expose Timmer and Zack to a meeting with real police officers.

I stepped out into the street and looked toward the cars. Walked a few steps closer to see better. A man and a woman were gesticulating wildly while more and more people congregated. Traffic was starting to build up in the intersection; drivers were mounting the curb to get past. They were clearly not going to be able to handle the situation on their own.

I walked over at a brisk pace. Had to push through the crowd.

"Police commander!" I called out loudly and brandished my badge. "Let's move along here and let people get by."

I addressed Timmer and Zack loudly: "You two, take the suspects to detention and then head straight back to the garage for repairs. I'll take over here."

"I'm glad there's finally a sensible police officer in charge," exclaimed the man who seconds before had been waving his arms around.

"And what's your name?" I said.

"Martin Holmlund, that's me, and this is my wife, Linda. We came from over there and were just about to turn…"

"Martin, I saw what happened. You've done nothing wrong and we will cover the damage to your car. Are you okay?"

I looked at him and the woman standing next to him. They looked at each other like they hadn't stopped to consider that.

"Neither of you has visible injuries. Are you experiencing any pain?" I said to help them out.

It was sheer luck I didn't have to call an ambulance. That would have complicated matters further. Linda, who looked more composed than Martin, slowly shook her head.

"Good," I said. "The car's been dented, but is definitely drivable. Linda, do you have a license?"

"Yes," she said firmly.

"Then I want you to drive the two of you home now. I want you to go straight home and rest. If you experience any discomfort tonight, go to the hospital and get yourselves checked out. Okay?"

They nodded; both seemed to have made it through surprisingly unscathed. I took their IDs, license plate numbers, and contact details, and explained that it could take up to a week before they heard from us. I watched them drive away before I left.

I'd counted on there being enough cash from the jewelry store robbery to pay back Armand after giving my gang their cuts. That was the most important thing to me right now. If it wasn't enough, they would have to fence the gold before the end of the following day. My delivery to Armand was scheduled for tomorrow night.

Same place, same time.

SIXTY-NINE

"The car didn't 'come out nowhere,'" Timmer said and glared at Zack. "It came from the left in the intersection and had a green light. You just didn't notice the lights changing, why lie about it, you fucking moron. I mean, shit, did you buy your license online or what?"

"That's enough," said Leona, who'd spent the last half hour going through what had gone wrong during the robbery. "Let's move on."

Timmer kept fixing Zack with a level stare, as if to show that he wasn't going to forget that everything could have fallen apart because of him.

David had told Leona about Liam punching the store owner.

"Consider this a test," Leona continued. "You've been given your cut of the profits this time, but in the future, if you fuck up and fail to follow my instructions, you won't get so much as a penny of what we bring in."

She looked at Liam and Zack.

When David's phone buzzed in his pocket, he pulled it out and saw it was Sven. Again. Sven had called several times since David walked out on him outside the boxing club. He needed more money than Sven seemed able to offer. He had to sort out his own apartment. Leona's way of getting money had been faster. But the big heist she was planning was different. If the job was as big as she was saying, he didn't dare risk it. It was, after all, safer to let Sven take care of it. But he needed more information.

He had been over to her house again last night. Trying to find out more. But she was difficult to figure out, Leona. Just like last time, she'd opened a bottle of wine, but this time he had spent the night. Even though she was only about thirty-five, she was older than anyone he'd slept with before. She had been very much in charge. Told him what to do in a way he found exhilarating. He liked not having to initiate.

"Do as I say, and you won't get caught," Leona continued with her lecture. "But at the same time you do have to learn to calculate risk. Which is why I'm now going to spend some time on a subject you've been asking about. What to do if everything goes wrong, or in other words, if you have in fact ended up in the back of that police car on your way to detention."

David had been interviewed many times. Had seen cops with very disparate approaches. Some were almost over-the-top cor-rect and formal while others seemed to do as they pleased. This was an extremely interesting subject for all of them. Yet even so, he caught himself thinking about the night before instead.

"What you should do if you get caught by the police can really be summed up in one sentence: Don't fight, do as you're told, and shut the fuck up," Leona said.

David had never thought about Leona's voice until now. That commanding tone was there even when she was talking to the group. He just hadn't realized how sexy it was. He remembered how aroused it had made him when she whispered instructions in his ear. He'd been sitting on her couch, drinking the wine she had poured him, she had been in an armchair next to him. But then she had got up and walked over to the couch. Sat down on the coffee table right in front of him.

"If we arrest you at the scene, it's because we have a right to do so. There's no point arguing about it. You'll just end up being charged with more crimes, such as threat against or assault on a police officer. We might be forced to use pepper spray, which will make your eyes sting like hell. Plus, we might have to put you down on the ground and cuff you."

Leona had put her wineglass down on the table behind her back. David had held his in his hand.

"If you know you have trouble controlling you temper, just put your hands in your pockets when we grab you by the arms to lead you away. Which happens after the body search. No hands in pockets before then, because that'll make us think you have weapons or drugs. So avoid wriggling about, waving your arms around, or kicking your legs when we take you to the car, and you won't get charged with assault on police officer. And for God's sake, don't scream and shout all the way to the detention center. We're so incredibly sick of it and have already heard all the rude words you can come up with. Nothing you say will change the fact that you're being taken in."

Leona sat down on the table at the front of the room with her legs spread wide. Just as she'd done on the coffee table in her apartment with David sitting in front of her on the couch. Without looking away for a second, she'd started undoing her black blouse. One button at a time. When David had looked away to put his glass down, she'd caught his gaze, held it, and just said "sit."

"But what if you're innocent, are you supposed to just sit there in the police car like an idiot and not say anything?" Ken asked.

"Everyone claims to be innocent, you know," Leona replied. "We've heard it a thousand times and we honestly don't give a shit. It's not like the trial hearing's starting right there in the car, you know. Like we're about to fold our seats down and swing by to pick up a judge and a few jurors in the middle of the night so they can determine whether you were the one holding the gun or not."

David couldn't take his eyes off Leona. Sharp chicks were hot. She was razor sharp. On the coffee table in the dimly lit apartment, she had moved on to unhooking her black lace bra in the back. Had let the straps fall down her shoulders and exposed her breasts.

"No one wants to hear about whether you're innocent or guilty in the patrol car," she continued. "We're busy pondering whether we made the right career choices, since we have to deal with people like you."

She had looked David right in the eyes. The dim lighting had made her blue eyes dark. Seductive. He'd just been about to take a sip from the wineglass in his hand when she took it from him.

"If anything, ranting and raving in the police car can get you in trouble," Leona said. "If the police officers hear you say anything they think might be relevant to the investigation, they will write it down in a memo that will follow you all the way to court."

She'd taken a sip from his wineglass and put it down on the table. She put her palms down on the table top between her spread legs, leaned back, and slowly shook her head to make her dark, wavy hair tumble down her back. She had stayed in that position and let him study her naked upper body. He hadn't been able to take his eyes off her bare breasts.

"The only thing you should say is that you want a defender assigned to you, and make sure you suggest a really good one. And you should be polite to the cops."

"So now we have to be all buddy-buddy with the cops as well," Liam said.

"If you knew how a police investigation works, you'd get that there's nothing to gain from..."

David's thoughts began to wander. He remembered how she had slowly got up from the table. Kneeled on the couch, straddling his legs. One knee on either side of his thighs. When he'd grabbed her hips and pulled her toward him, she had slowly lowered herself until she was sitting on top of him. While she had grabbed the back of his neck with both hands, he had leaned forward toward her naked breasts. Had closed his eyes as he sucked her hard nipple into his mouth...

"David, are you listening?" she suddenly said.

David hadn't noticed that his eyes were glued to the floor.

"Huh? Yeah, of course."

He looked at her slightly inquiringly, as if to gauge whether she was showing any signs of having thought about what had happened between them. He was unsure. She obviously wouldn't want to let on in front of the others. But maybe there was in fact something there.

Leona was the polar opposite of Saga. She was cool and a bit weird in a way that aroused him. Few guys would turn her down.

He hadn't been able to get any more information about the big heist out of her. Nor had he found any clues in her apartment.

"We can't make you talk in an interview," she continued. "We have a legal right to use force to get you into detention, but we can't make you talk. On the contrary, it's our duty to inform you that you have the right to remain silent. I can't emphasize this enough, never speak during an interview, unless you're one hundred percent sure you know what you're doing. That's pretty much an unbreakable rule."

"When a buddy and me got arrested once," Liam said, "a cop told me my buddy had confessed to everything and been released. If I did the same, they would let me go too."

"An interviewer is never allowed to lie to you in an interview," Leona said.

That got them all fired up. Everyone was protesting loudly. David, too, was convinced the police lied through their teeth all the time.

"Oh come on, are you stupid or something?" Leona said. "First of all, you can't really mean that you, who do whatever the fuck you want and don't give a shit about laws and rules, demand that others follow them?"

"But, it's like, the police," Liam said.

"This is a fucking joke," Leona continued. "I've told you the police can't lie in an interview. That means we can't tell you your buddy's confessed to the crime you've both been arrested for, unless it's true. But if there are detectives who break that rule, you people bitch about it? Don't make me laugh. Come on! Do as I say and just keep your mouths shut in the interview room, all right?"

"But the cops always keep coming at you till you start talking. Why can't we just say we weren't there?" Vikki wanted to know.

"Because if you've been arrested, you've made a mistake. If that mistake consists of, for example, a CCTV camera showing your face in a picture somewhere and you've claimed you weren't at the scene, well, consider how credible you'll sound in court."

Leona didn't seem to be in a very good mood.

"Be aware that the police know what they're doing. We've done our homework. We know in what situations it makes tactical sense for us to tell you things we know in an interview, and when it's better to hold on to the information because we want to get something out of you first. We have a big advantage since we have usually already talked to the victims and witnesses and collected technical evidence. Don't think you can outsmart the police. We know what you're doing, even if the evidence isn't always strong enough to get you convicted."

"They always ask you how you plead," Ken said. "What are we supposed to say to that?"

"You have to know when to deny and when it makes sense to confess. Ken, if you're a suspect in a robbery case, and charged with possession of illegal drugs, you have to confess to the drug charge. In other words, you have to admit to the crime that's easily proven. Because when your urine or blood sample clearly shows what substances are present in your system, you don't help your credibility by claiming someone must've drugged you, that you've been exposed to secondhand marijuana smoke, or that you accidentally took the wrong syringe to treat your diabetes. You have no idea the kind of bullshit we're told every day."

"I've heard it's better to just deny everything," Liam put in.

"If you are guilty beyond doubt, a denial will only make you look bad. It's just another sign you can't be believed, get it?"

"But you might be able to sort out an alibi," Liam said.

Leona burst out laughing. "You have no idea how many bogus alibis we've disproven using only the most basic interview questions."

"But if you say you were at a friend's house, they do have to check it out, don't they?" Liam said.

"That's correct," I said. "A detective is obligated to investigate both things that can be advantageous and disadvantageous to you as a suspect. That means that if you say you were at Betsy's house at the time of the crime and that Betsy will confirm it, we have to check if that's true, since that would mean you're innocent. But after asking Betsy a few simple questions about what you did that night, we quickly discover that Betsy's version is different from yours. It almost never fails. So stay away from stuff like that. I've even seen slightly more advanced attempts at fabricating an alibi, where a suspect paid for a ticket to another town with his credit card, booked a hotel without CCTV, and claimed to have been staying there at the time of the crime. I saw through that too. So, again, keep your mouth shut during interviews unless you're absolutely certain you know what you're doing."

"But you have to talk during trial, right?" Vikki said.

"Once the investigation has been completed, you, the suspect, have a right to read the whole investigation report. Make sure you do. That's crucial. The report will outline the evidence against you. Only after reading the report will you know exactly what you're going to have to defend yourself against in court. Which is to say that only in the courtroom will it be time for you to start talking, because you have to know what the hell to say first, get it?"

David sensed Leona was losing her patience with them.

"A lot of people think the point of a trial is to find out the truth about what happened, but that's not what it's for. A trial is about what can be *proven* to have happened. Do you understand the difference?"

They nodded.

"On the force, we talk about a crime being 'solved,' which means we know what happened and who did it, but not necessarily that we've been able to prove it sufficiently. You know from your own experience that people aren't convicted of every crime they're reported for. That's not because you've managed to hoodwink the police — in most cases, we know the score — we just haven't been able to prove it. So walking around thinking you're smarter than the police is just ridiculous."

"What about during trial?" Vikki said.

"In the courtroom, you have to make a good, polite, honest impression; make it hard for the judge and jurors to believe you've done what you're accused of."

"But can't they tell if you're lying?" Vikki said. "Aren't there ways of telling? How can you lie without it showing?"

"There's been quite a lot of research in that area and the conclusion is that with our current understanding and measuring equipment, there's no reliable way of telling whether someone is lying or not. It's not like all people always scratch their nose, glance to the left, get sweaty palms, or whatever else when they're not telling the truth. There could be many other explanations for those behaviors. Disease, age, and other things affect our behavior and body language."

"But you could use a lie detector," Vikki put in.

"As you may know, lie detectors, or polygraphs as they are also known, are not used in Sweden. Besides, they don't measure whether a response is true or not, but rather a person's physical reactions to a specific question. Those reactions then have to be interpreted, so it's always a question of reliability."

"So you're saying you have no way of knowing if we're lying?" Zack said with a smile.

"We can't tell for sure if you're lying. That being said, we detectives can infer that you're being less than honest if your story doesn't add up, and all evidence points in a different direction."

"But what do you say to avoid being convicted?" Vikki said.

"Does anyone know what it takes to convict a person of a crime?" I said.

No one replied. I wondered if they had ever actually thought about why they'd been convicted, or if they were just pissed off and didn't care.

"In order to convict someone of a crime in Sweden, the prosecutor has to prove that they acted in accordance with the course of events presented to the court, and that this can be established 'beyond a reasonable doubt.' Those are stringent requirements and the whole burden of evidence is on the prosecutor. Think about that for a minute. Beyond a reasonable doubt. If the evidence is not up to that level, you'll be let off. Maybe now you understand what you and your lawyer need to do?"

David raised a finger. Leona nodded at him.

"Create doubt," David said.

"Exactly. One way or another, you have to come up with a story that makes it possible to doubt that you did it. Are you with me? You don't have to prove that you're completely innocent. Making it slightly uncertain you're guilty is enough."

She made it sound easy, but David realized it wasn't that simple in practice.

"So, how do you go about doing that? Well, you give a reasonably believable alternative version of events. In order to pull that off, you have to have read the investigation report. Carefully. You have to know your case backward and forward. Know what every witness said, what technical evidence the police have collected, and what the law says. From that information, you can create your own version of the course of events."

David looked at the others. They were looking at Leona as if she'd asked them to climb Mount Everest barefoot.

"Put differently, your version has to match the facts uncovered by the investigation. It's not an easy task. It requires that you know about the probative value of evidence, among other things. If, say, the police have found your shoeprints at a crime scene, that doesn't prove you committed the crime, just that your shoes were there. Not who wore the shoes. You have to come up with an explanation that sounds plausible."

"Isn't that what a lawyer's for?" Liam said. "They're supposed to sort all those things out."

"You can't tell your lawyer you're guilty if you are planning to deny the charges in court. The Swedish Bar Association has rules and guidelines. According to those rules, a lawyer owes his or her client loyalty and must act in his or her client's best interest, but a lawyer is also obligated to resign from your case if you behave that way. I'm sure there are some lawyers who don't give a shit about the rules, but you don't want to risk your lawyer resigning since it would be obvious to everyone what had happened. In other words, you can't even mention your plans to your lawyer. If you are going to deny the charges brought against you, you can't tell your lawyer you're guilty."

David heard the others sigh.

"So, the best option would be not to get caught, wouldn't you agree?" Leona continued and smiled. "But you can relax, if you ever were to end up in this situation while on one of my jobs, I will obviously help you out," Leona continued. "But remember, you can't expect any help from me if you've committed any violent crimes. If you've hurt another human being, you're on your own. If that's the case, I suggest you confess and use your time in prison to think about what you've done."

SEVENTY

"You've been cleared to make a statement on television, Fred," Leona said. "On Wednesday, just like you asked. Not in the evening, that wasn't possible, but during the morning news."

Fred heaved a sigh of relief in his bed. Maybe he'd been wrong about Leona after all; she did seem to get things done. They'd finally grasped that he had an important message.

"I want you to know that this is highly unusual," she continued. "It wasn't easy to get my superiors to agree."

Time was interminable in the hospital. Every minute felt like an hour. Now he had something to look forward to. It wouldn't be long now before all of this was over.

"The lead investigator has asked me to tell you that you—"

Leona was interrupted by the door opening to admit the head of one of the Security Service officers.

"Leona, would you mind stepping out for a second?" he said.

Leona stood up and placed her notebook facedown on the visitor's chair before following the man out into the hallway. His neutral expression made it impossible for Fred to guess what was going on.

Fred's eyes were drawn to the small notebook Leona had left. Had he been more mobile, he could have reached it and flipped through it. It would have been interesting to see which of the things he told her she chose to write down. But the chair was too low for him to reach the notebook. The back cover was facing up. Fred could see something written on it. He had decent eyesight and even though the notebook was upside down, he could make out a name and a phone number. He stared at it, hardly believing his eyes. He recognized the name all too well. Before he could think any further, the door opened and Leona entered.

"You're going to be moved again, Fred," she said. "We'll have to continue this later."

She picked up the notebook from the chair and slipped it into her purse.

"I've made sure you'll get your chance. Make sure you say everything you want said. And don't oversleep. I'll be here with a camera team before 7:30 a.m."

It wasn't the first time Fred was moved from one room to another. It was always a big to-do, because it had to be organized by the police. Leona had told him earlier that the officers guarding his door had already stopped at least two unauthorized persons trying to get into his room. One of them had been armed.

When the police set off alongside the nurses pushing his bed down the corridor, he thought about how ironic it was that they were there for his protection. The police had never protected him before. Or his mother. His strongest memory of the police was from when he saw them with his mom outside the supermarket at Blackeberg Square. He had been eleven years old and his mom had asked him to go into the supermarket.

"One gallon of milk," she'd told him and put two one-krona coins in his hand. "I just have to have a quick chat with someone I know."

Fred had gone into the supermarket. Just inside the doors, he'd turned around and seen his mom walking toward those people. The ones who always sat on the park benches. Fred had continued into the store. He hadn't noticed the police car parked in the square and the two police officers holding a person down on the ground until he came out again. When he heard his mom's screams and saw her maroon jacket and brown hair, he'd realized she was the person on the ground. He'd stopped dead. Dropped the milk and the change he'd been given. His heart had pounded in his chest. He hadn't known what to do. Just as he'd been about to run up to his mom, he'd seen Erik and his mom out of the corner of his eye. Erik was one of Fred's classmates. Erik and his mom had stopped like everyone else, staring and pointing at Fred's mom and the police. Instead of going over, Fred had turned around and dashed in behind a shrubbery a bit farther away. His mom's purse had been open on the ground with all her things scattered in a circle around it. Fred hadn't gone up to her. Hadn't wanted Erik to see him.

Not until the police car had left and Erik and his mom had moved on had Fred gone over. There on the ground, discarded, he'd spotted his mom's silver necklace. The pendant had been so scratched up, Fred had felt sure one of the police officers had stepped on it. He'd picked it up, blown off the dirt, and put it in his pocket.

When his mom had returned home several hours later, she'd been beaten black and blue. Ugly scabs on her cheek, a swollen lip, and a bump on her forehead. Fred had known it was the police officers' doing; he'd seen it with his own eyes. Since that day, he knew police officers were dangerous.

"Fifth floor," the nurse said to the Security Service officer standing closest to the buttons in the elevator.

Fred wasn't comfortable lying in a hospital bed in a cramped space together with two male police officers.

"The room's ready," a nurse from the new unit announced when Fred was rolled out of the elevator.

SEVENTY-ONE

David, Vikki, Zack, Ken, and Timmer were sitting in front of me. They were the ones I had chosen for my big heist.

Granted, Zack had messed up the driving last time, but I needed his explosives expertise. Vikki and David were going to do the driving instead. Liam was the only person I had rejected after the jewelry store robbery. He clearly had trouble adhering to one of my cardinal rules: to not physically hurt anyone.

Thanks to the jewelry store robbery I had directed my posse to commit, I'd managed to raise the money I needed and deliver it to Armand on time. It had been the same procedure as last time, except this time he'd changed the location for our meet-up at the last second to an industrial estate near Telefonplan. Armand had been present in person. When he declared he wanted another hundred thousand in a week's time, I had explained to him that my big heist was only two weeks away. That instead of a hundred thousand, he could get the full amount owed, plus interest, if he could just hold off for one measly week. He had agreed, but made it clear to me in no uncertain terms that he wouldn't wait any longer than that.

I started handing out secure mobile phones to my guys, to be used for all conversations about the robbery, however short. I realized I hadn't brought up the issue of cell phones before.

"You all know we can both tap your phones and locate them." They nodded.

"If I haven't told you earlier, please remember never to document your crimes. When we seize cell phones, we routinely find pictures and videos of fights, burglaries, rape, weapons, drugs, graffiti, shootings, even murder. You have no idea what criminals do to save, brag, and show off about their crimes. You've done half of our work for us if you've recorded it all on your phone. And again, deleted pictures can be re-created."

The time had come to prepare them for my big heist.

"You might have heard about the Arlanda Airport robbery in 2002, and the three-hundred-million-yen robbery in 1968."

We had studied a number of other robberies during our meetings, but I had deliberately held these two back.

"In terms of pure cash, the Arlanda robbery is the biggest robbery in Swedish history. The robbers made away with forty-four million kronor. In two weeks, there will be a cargo flight from Hong Kong Bank and Royal Scottish Bank, just like back in 2002. Except the cargo this time is mostly cash. The money will be delivered to Forex, Swedbank, and the Swedish Central Bank. On the way from Arlanda, we, or I should say you, will stop the transport. One of you will be doing explosives. I'll tell you more about how it's going to work in a minute."

They were listening attentively.

"In the three-hundred-million-yen robbery in Japan, a large armored car was stopped by a single robber dressed as a police officer who escaped with all that money. We're going to do a mash-up of these two robberies. It's going to be a calm affair and no one's going to get hurt."

Before telling them exactly how it was going to go down, I had to make sure I could trust them.

"How much money is being transported?" David said.

"I'll let you in on the exact sum later, but I can tell you it's going to be several million each."

The armored car was going to contain notes of various denominations, but I hadn't decided how I wanted to divide them up yet and so chose not to say anything about it.

"I hope you understand that I'm giving you a unique opportunity to become millionaires, so don't waste it. I've chosen you over the other people in the group because I know you're capable of pulling this off. It's crucial that you don't say a word about this to the others, but I know you know that already."

I was going to explain the circumstances and then give them a chance to back out. I needed to know they were one hundred percent in.

"As I've said before, no one can get hurt. Assault is only permissible in extreme situations and even then only to disarm a person or fend off an attack. Anyone who uses more force than strictly necessary forfeits their share of the profits."

I looked at each of them in turn.

"You may have to go into hiding for a while afterward. Not disappear entirely, but keep a very low profile. And I'm hoping it goes without saying that you can't start buying cars or rounds of champagne in fancy bars or flaunt your new wealth in any other way."

They smiled as soon as I mentioned the money.

"Whatever your thoughts and opinions may be, I'm the one giving the orders. The robbery will be executed exactly as planned. If there's any aspect of the plan you don't like, keep it to yourselves. If there's any aspect of the plan you feel could be improved upon, discuss it with me in private. No deviations without discussing them with me first. Understood?"

Unlike last time, I wouldn't be present at the scene for this.

"I want to be in direct contact with one of you, in case you run into trouble, and that person's going to be David. If you've done exactly as I said, but something still goes wrong, I will take full responsibility and cover for you, just so you know. The absolute worst outcome for you is that the police seize the money and you walk away with nothing. That's it. I'm shouldering all the risk here."

I meant it. I wasn't going to drag them into serious crime and then leave them high and dry if there were flaws in my plan. That was where I drew my ethical line in the sand.

"So the worst thing that can happen to you is that you're no better or worse off than you are right now."

They didn't seem to find that too terrible.

"You have one minute to think about this. If any of you want to back out, that's okay. This is your chance to let me know. Just stand up and walk away. But if you stay, I'm going to trust you completely."

I fell silent. Looked at the clock. No one moved. I was going to give them exactly one minute.

"All right, so you're all in," I said when the minute was up. "Let's go over the plan."

I stood up.

"You, Zack, will plant explosives in the garage of security services company G4S. A bomb set to detonate a week before the robbery. That's going to draw a big response, with police, media, and the whole shebang. You and I are going to go through all of that very carefully."

I looked at Zack.

"I'm familiar with G4S's routines," I continued. "I've worked with them a lot. I'll make sure the timing's right. As I'm sure you understand, you can't just walk up to a heavily guarded security company and plant a bomb. How quickly can you get your hands on explosives, Zack?"

"I need blueprints of the place so I know how big it is and where to place the explosives to get the best effect. I'll make the explosives myself."

"I want the bomb to go off but I don't want any injuries," I said. "This is about putting all G4S staff on edge before the robbery.

"A week later, on the day of the cash transport, I will requisition a patrol car from work. In it will be two uniformed cops. That's going to be you two."

I pointed at David and Timmer. Timmer brightened up and looked at David, whose face was impassive.

"I need one more car," I said. "Do any of you have access to a car that's safe to use?"

Timmer held up his phone with a picture of a vehicle.

"Will a Honda NSX do?" he said. "Does zero to sixty in three seconds."

I looked at the picture.

"Good, but it needs to be a car that looks like the ones our technicians drive. Preferably a Multivan. Vikki, you were the driver for a job recently. Could you get us a van like the one you were using for that? Without contacting T?"

Vikki nodded.

"You get what I mean by safe, right?" I said. "It has to be stolen and have new plates."

She nodded again.

"Great! I want you to set that up straightaway. We need to be able to use it on short notice later. Give me the details and I'll check it out in our databases. I'll take care of the cost of the van. In that van will be three bomb technicians, Vikki, Ken, and Zack. I'll fix you up with clothes and equipment."

"Just don't let Zack drive," Timmer said. "He can't tell the difference between red and green."

"Shut up," Zack retorted.

"I want Vikki behind the wheel," I said.

In hindsight, I should have let her drive last time too.

"G4S will provide the armored car from Arlanda. On the way from the airport, you're going to stop the armored car. There will be two security guards inside. You will inform them that you, which is to say the police, have received a tip-off saying there's explosives in the car and they have to evacuate it as quickly as possible so your bomb technicians can search it. The security guards will agree, no problem. With the bomb in their garage a week before fresh in their memories, they'll be happy you're there to help them out."

I carried on describing exactly how the robbery was going to happen. They were clearly amused by my approach.

"You will be courteous, correct, and respectful to the security guards. We want no drama, apart from the dramatic acting talent you all have to pull out to come off as plausible officers of the law."

After going over the robbery in detail at two more upcoming meetings, I believed they would be sufficiently prepared to execute the biggest heist they, and I, had ever attempted.

SEVENTY-TWO

"The mic's in the shot," the camera man said.

The sound guy holding the microphone raised the handle a lit-tle higher so it disappeared from the screen of the monitor placed by the foot of the hospital bed. I smiled to myself. They were good actors. It wasn't the first time a suspect had demanded to appear on live television. It seemed to be the wet dream of every weirdo out there. I was glad Fred seemed to believe it was really happen-ing. In reality, it would never have been approved. I would have absolutely no control over what he said.

Alexandra had put me in touch with very professional peo-ple at the public broadcaster's news desk. They had supplied everything I needed. They had also recorded the start of yester-day's news and after that filmed a short clip in which the same newscaster introduced Fred's appearance, and then a thank-you from the newscaster, which was followed by the rest of the regular news.

Fred's restrictions prohibited him from watching or listen-ing to the news, so he would have no way of knowing we were showing him yesterday's news. I had the help of two guys from Surveillance, who'd been given a fifteen-minute introduction to how a camera works. I didn't want public broadcast employees in the room, in case something happened. SÄK still had two guys on the door, but since this was Fred's initiative, we were taking all possible precautions.

SÄK had sent over an additional officer who was going to watch Fred's performance and could call in a team immediately if he gave us any information about the location of a second bomb.

Fred was sitting relatively upright in his bed. He'd been helped to shave and had asked the staff to lend him a shirt.

It was 7:58 a.m. I nodded to the camera operator and my colleague from SÄK to let them know everything was ready to go. Even though the whole thing was prerecorded, it was important that we made it seem to Fred like he was in fact going to be on the eight o'clock news.

"Fred, after they introduce you, you have three minutes," I said. "Choose your words wisely."

As usual, the news started with a brief summary of the headlines and then went on to cover each story in more detail. I watched Fred. His eyes were glued to the TV. I was also filming with my video camera. It was time. The newscaster changed the subject.

The man who detonated a bomb, strapped to his own body, outside the Swedish Parliament in Stockholm just over three weeks ago, survived with serious injuries and is now recovering at Karolinska University Hospital in Solna. The man has been reticent in police interviews, but now his demand to appear on live television to give a statement has been approved by the Security Service.

They read the words I had written out for them verbatim. When live footage of Fred appeared on the screen, I nodded for him to start. He'd pulled out a note he'd kept hidden under his blanket. I could see through the paper that the text on it was neatly organized, like a list.

My name is Fred Sjöström. I'm not a perpetrator, I'm a victim.
A victim of the Swedish social system.
The system that is supposed to help orphaned children.
Supposed to help drug addicts.
The system that is supposed to save children from growing up in homes with parents who are drug addicts.
That is supposed to protect you from police brutality.
The system that never strips a person of all their hopes for the future.
That doesn't force men to fight meaningless wars.
The system that is supposed to encourage contact between a child and its parents, not take people's children away from them.

He was speaking loudly and clearly. He had obviously rehearsed his speech. He held the note in his hand but he didn't look down at it a single time; his eyes were fixed on the camera as he spoke. Not until his three minutes were running out did he say:

I, and many with me, are victims of all these circumstances.
But the one who suffered the most was my mother.
I'm doing all of this for her.

Time was up. Fred looked at me. I nodded to the camera operator, who also handled the monitor. Fred was allowed to watch the newscaster thank him for his statement and move on to the weather forecast to make it more believable.

I was disappointed. It was a woe-is-me speech. Nothing of what he'd said was of interest to the investigation. He hadn't said a word about a second attack. A nurse came in and took the monitor away while my colleagues packed up their equipment. I followed them out, shrugged and sighed.

"I'm sorry that's all it ended up being," I said.

"That's how it goes," one of them said. "It was worth a shot."

"Thanks for helping out, guys."

I immediately called Alexandra.

"I'm sorry, nothing new," I told her over the phone.

"All right, Leona. I'll let SÄK know. I think it sounds like we've reached the end of the line with our dear suicide bomber. Stop by this afternoon and we'll discuss what's next for this case. I'm about to head into a meeting with the national police commissioner."

She hung up. I leaned back against the wall in the corridor. Turned things over in my mind. Had I overlooked something? Was this really how it was going to end? It was obviously great if he hadn't planned any more attacks, but my gut told me it wasn't that simple.

I must have missed something.

SEVENTY-THREE

"Are you done with that?" said a young man with the word "intern" on his nametag.

He pointed to the tray with the remnants of my breakfast. I nodded and grabbed the mug with my half-finished latte to keep it from being cleared with the rest of the tray. I would have preferred a coffee shop somewhere other than at the hospital, but if it weren't for a few sickly-looking customers, you'd actually never have known you were on the hospital campus.

It had been almost two hours since Fred had given his little victim speech. I was sitting by the window with his case file spread out across the table. The young intern hadn't shown even the slightest interest in the documents on the table; he'd looked as blasé as all tired, indifferent teenagers do. There were only a few customers in the shop, but I still made very sure none of them could see what the classified documents said. I'd gone over these pages countless times. And I still had no idea what I could have missed.

I pulled out my phone and found the recording of the speech Fred had just given. I put my headphones on and listened as I watched him on the screen. What had he really said? *"Orphaned children...drug addicts..."* I'd heard all of that before in our interviews. *"Save children from growing up in homes with drug addicts..."*

I studied his face closely. His expression was neutral. He moved his head a little when he talked, but was otherwise perfectly still, except for a few times when he touched his necklace. I went back to the start and watched it again. The first time he did it, it looked like he was adjusting it. He lifted the chain up as though it was too tight or chafed. It was when he said the sentence "*That is supposed to protect you from police brutality.*"

Police brutality?

He'd never mentioned that before. Or had he? He'd said he hated cops, but I hadn't thought much of it since it was a common trope among suspects. And the police hadn't been singled out, he'd also professed to hate the Social Services and others. I couldn't recall him mentioning police brutality. The bomb outside Parliament had been intended as revenge on politicians, that much was clear, but the police?

The second time, he didn't touch the chain, just grabbed the pendant and kind of rubbed it between his fingers as he spoke the last words about his mother.

I looked through the pictures of all the items found at the scene. Item BG-803335-9 showed the chain photographed from above against a white backdrop. I studied the picture closely. The unassuming chain looked even more scuffed in the picture than in real life. The back of the round, scratched pendant had been photographed as well. As I held the picture closer to my face, I was able, since I knew where to look, to make out the tiny numbers carved into it by hand. 30052301. I had utterly failed to decipher the meaning of those numbers.

"It's all in there," Fred had repeated. I looked through the file again to see if there were any numbers that might hold special significance for him. His mother's death on 30 May could explain the first four numbers since they were also the date of Fred's suicide attack. But the other numbers didn't match anything I'd seen in his file. That in turn made me unsure about what the first numbers meant. I searched among the dates of his other known life events, but to no avail.

After checking my watch, I drank the last sip of my latte, got to my feet, and gathered up the papers on the table. I had put it all back in the folder, except the picture of the necklace, which had ended up by the window, upside down. I was reaching across the table to pick it up when I saw the tiny numbers again. This time from a different angle. I froze, lowered my head so the light hit the tiny numbers on the pendant. One of the numbers looked different. The number 1. Suddenly, it looked like there was a line through it. I picked up the paper and held it up to the light. Still upside down. The scratches on the pendant made it difficult to determine what was deliberately carved and what was just scratches, but there was definitely a line across the number 1. I turned the paper the right way up and now saw the same thing. The 1 with a line across it now looked like it might be a 7.

I started searching through the documents again. Tore them out of the folder. I knew I'd seen several dates in the file that had almost matched the sequence, off only by a number or two, but that I'd dismissed because they weren't a perfect match or because they seemed unlikely to be related to the attack. Birthdays, area codes, street numbers, criminal codes, page numbers, phone numbers, vehicle registration numbers, I considered every number I came across. Some were a match if you jumbled the numbers or put another number in the middle. Then I reached the documents about Fred's mother.

And there!

There!

I pulled out an arrest report from 1973. Concerning one Fanny Sjöström, Fred's mother, who had been arrested for possession at Blackeberg Square. Date of crime and arrest: 23/07/1973.

2307.

I looked at the number sequence again: 30052301.

I felt my heart starting to race. If this was true, it could mean that the first four numbers on the pendant, 3005, matched the date of Fred's mother's death as well as the date Fred blew himself up outside Parliament. And if the one was actually a seven, the last four numbers were 2307 instead of 2301, and would thus match the date Fred's mother was arrested at Blackeberg Square, plus...I looked at my watch:

Today's date, 23 July: 23/07.

I snatched up the folder and my bag and ran toward the elevators. I had to get up to Fred to check his necklace. Before I went running to Alexandra and SÄK, I had to be sure the number wasn't just a scratch on the paper. I pushed the button for the elevator. Paced back and forth while I waited. My mind was racing. If I was right, another attack would likely happen today. What kind of attack? And where?

I ran down the corridor and threw open the door to Fred's room. Dropped my bag and the case file on the floor and walked right up to him where he was sleeping on his back. Reached out for the necklace around his neck.

In the blink of an eye, he'd swung his arm up and grabbed hold of my wrist. I jumped. Was unprepared for his quick movement. He held my wrist like a vise.

"Nice and steady, Leona," he said. "I'm an old disabled man, but I'm stronger than you, now that I'm feeling better. Don't think you can storm in here and do whatever you want."

As soon as he let go, I pulled my arm back and rubbed my wrist with my left hand.

"Show me your necklace," I said testily.

He picked up the pendant and put it in full view on his chest.

I reached over and took it in my hand. Turned and angled it toward the light so I could see the numbers on the back. Squinted.

3 0 0 5...2 3 0 7.

I let go. Paced around the room. Thinking. Today's date. Could he have planted a bomb that would go off today? If so, where?

Think, Leona, think!

I went to stand by the window.

"What are you pondering, Leona? Could it be that you've thought of something you think might solve —"

"Shut up!" I said.

"Why are you so aggress —"

I tuned out his nonsense. What had he actually said? He wanted to get back at politicians and the police. His mother had been arrested on this very day in 1973.

The police...

If he wanted to get back at the police, he would surely want to do it where he would get as many police officers as possible, like the politicians at Parliament.

Could it be the Police House? No, it had to be a place Fred could smuggle explosives into. Which buildings had he had access to before he blew himself up? I started pacing around the room again. What had he been doing before he blew himself up? Worked. On the cruise ferry.

The cruise ferry!

Fuck!

The police conference!

"*What the fuck have you done!*" I shouted at Fred.

"Took you long enough, Leona," Fred said with a revolting smirk on his lips.

He clutched the pendant with both hands, closed his eyes, and said, "Mom, this is for you. It's their turn to be victims."

I snatched up my bag and the case file, pulled the door open, and ran out into the corridor.

"Come see me afterward, Leona, I've got more things to tell you," I heard him call from his room.

I checked my watch. It was already 10:30. As far as I knew, the ship had left Stockholm last night en route to Åbo and was expected back today. It was probably in the middle of the Baltic by now. I called Alexandra as I raced toward the stairs.

Fuck! She wasn't picking up.

SEVENTY-FOUR

On my way down the stairs at Karolinska Hospital, I dialed Alexandra's number for the third time. There was no point calling Anette or Åse. Or Fredrik. They were all on the cruise. Out in the parking lot, I managed to get hold of Gunvor, an older colleague who was not always the nimblest.

"Gunvor, where's Alexandra? I need to get her right now."

"She's in a meeting with the national police commissioner and a few others from the top brass. They're in the Citywide Operations conference room on the ninth floor. I think they'll be done in forty-five minutes or so."

Fuck! I was so rattled I couldn't remember where I'd parked my car. I jogged along the rows of cars, frantically pressing the key button. Stopped and spun around to see if any lights were flashing.

"Leona, what is this about? I could go up there and give them a message if you want. But it'd have to be something very import—"

"Never mind, Gunvor, I'll take care of it."

I hung up. Telling Gunvor about this was out of the question. Besides, it'd probably be quicker to head over there myself. When I finally saw the flashing indicator lights I ran over and dove into the car. I let out a string of curses when I had to slam on the brakes for a car blocking my way out of the parking lot.

"*Get out of my way!*"

I shouted loudly, leaned on my horn, and waved at the man behind the wheel. He moved aside and I screeched off toward headquarters. Without blinking, I mounted the curb outside the entrance and stopped. I ran in, through the security checkpoint, down the corridors, and up to the elevators. Swiped my card through the reader and punched in my code. In, turn right, and down the hall to Citywide Operations.

Out of breath and frazzled, I pulled open the door to the conference room. The national police commissioner and the other seven or eight superintendents looked up at me.

"I'm sorry to interrupt, but a serious situation has developed. I believe there may be a bomb on board one of Silja Line's cruise ferries."

Alexandra looked up at me, nostrils flaring. The national police commissioner got out of his chair.

"What are you saying? Silja Line? Don't we have a lot of colleagues on board today?" he said and looked out at the others.

I nodded.

"The police conference!"

Alexandra got to her feet.

"Oh my God, there's over two hundred and fifty police officers on that cruise," she said.

"You!" the national police commissioner said and pointed his whole hand at me. "Who are you?"

"Leona Lindberg, VCD," I said.

"Leona, how reliable is your source? Is there a concrete bomb threat?" he continued.

"Uh...As you know, we have a suspect who blew himself up outside Parliament a couple of weeks ago and is now being treated at Karolinska Hospital. He's implying that he has planned another attack and I believe it consists of a bomb on that ship."

He turned to Alexandra.

"Has SÄK been informed of this?"

"This is completely new information," I said. "I tried to call Alexand—"

"I'm suspending this meeting," the commissioner told the others around the table. "If you have nothing to contribute, please leave the room. And not a word about it until we can establish whether there is any truth to this."

A few seconds later, the only people left in the room were me, Alexandra, the national police commissioner, and his secretary. The commissioner turned to me.

"You said he's hinted at having planned a second attack."

I nodded.

"He's a former member of the Foreign Legion who is angry at societ—"

"An attack, you say," he broke in. "How do you know it's a bomb?"

"Many things indicate that he—"

"Indicate?"

The commissioner fixed me with a stony-faced stare. Fred hadn't said it in so many words, but if you put the puzzle pieces together as I had, the bigger picture emerged.

"And how do we know it's that particular ship?" he continued.

He was addressing Alexandra too now. She didn't reply, just looked at me inquiringly.

"He's worked on that ship. He also had a necklace with a pendant with numbers I believe are dates relating to his late mother and..."

I could hear how outlandish it sounded, but the commissioner hadn't spent hour upon hour interviewing Fred. He hadn't heard Fred talk about the society that had destroyed his life, and he didn't know how the numbers matched important dates. Today's date.

"Are you saying that just because he worked on that ship, he would want to blow it up?" the commissioner asked. "What is this?" he said, turning to Alexandra again.

"I'm wondering whether we shouldn't take this seriously, Carl," Alexandra replied with a glance at me.

Alexandra rarely showed much emotion, but I could hear an unusual tone in her voice now.

"Fredrik, Cilla, Åse, and Anette are on that ship, along with two hundred and fifty officers from other divisions. And members of the public."

"They should be evacuated," I said.

The commissioner stared at me and continued: "We don't know if there are any explosives. We haven't even got a concrete bomb threat against the ship. You're saying we should frighten the wits out of thousands of people and create complete chaos based on what you've told us? And let's not even talk about the costs."

I just stared at him. He was out of his mind, doing cost/benefit calculations with people's lives. Normally, I didn't care overly much about what the Police Authority got up to, but talking about costs in this context was absurd. Besides, Silja Line was a private company, so the commissioner hardly had to worry about the cost. But I was smart enough to realize his reasoning was based on other considerations.

The national police commissioner was newly appointed and had, during his short tenure, had time to make quite a few controversial statements in the media, criticizing the police, saying more caution was needed in the interpretation of threats, that patrolling officers had to stop needlessly harassing private individuals and not assume that all crimes were acts of terrorism.

Not unexpectedly, he had been castigated both internally and externally. He'd also had harsh words to say about the Police Authority's expensive procurement process, claiming tax money was recklessly wasted on things like costly IT systems that ultimately had to be scrapped and thousands of laptops that were never used. Things that had already been sharply criticized.

Even so, I was speechless.

He continued: "We usually want something that at least bears some resemblance to a bomb threat against a somewhat specific target before we go in guns blazing."

"I think we have to do this by the book, Carl, and inform the head of Citywide—" Alexandra started to say.

"Maria, contact the ship," the commissioner told his secretary. "I want to know where it is. Let me talk to their security staff."

I looked at Alexandra. She gave me a look back. We both knew this wasn't the regular chain of command. An event of this magnitude was supposed to be reported to the director of Citywide Operations, whose job it was to assess any incoming bomb threat. Even if we didn't have an explicit threat in this case, I was fairly convinced the director would, off the back of my information, deem Fred's hints as highly credible. SÄK, who were in charge of the case, had at this point not even been informed. The national police commissioner had no operational authority whatsoever and was very well aware he was skating on thin ice, stepping in like this.

I was at least going to be clear about how I saw this situation.

"My opinion is that the ship should be evacuated," I said. "For all we know, it might be about to blow up."

He hadn't asked for my opinion, but what difference did it make? He looked at Alexandra like he was shocked she had let someone like me within a hundred feet of this case.

"I can inform the head of Citywide, it's not a bother," I ventured.

The commissioner held his hand up and raised his voice.

"Are you having trouble understanding? I'm going to talk to onboard security first. Maria?"

Once Maria had established contact with the ship, she handed the phone to him.

"This is National Police Commissioner Carl Magnusson speaking," he said into the phone.

I looked at Alexandra. She was usually unflinching and voiced her opinion in most situations, but now she was standing there in silence. I didn't have much respect for authority under the best of circumstances and had no intention of obeying the commissioner, but first I wanted some more information about the ship.

I walked over to the computer and went to a site called Shipfinder that immediately showed me a map displaying the location of all ships on the Baltic, which country they were from, their ports of origin and destination, and much else besides.

"We've had information there may be a concealed device on the ship," Carl said into the phone. "What's your location?"

I'd already found the position of Silja Line's cruise ferry MS *Galaxy* on the map and could see that it had left Stockholm last night at 7:30 p.m., turned around in Åbo during the night, left Mariehamn, and was now on its way into Stockholm's archipelago.

"We have very little information right now," the commissioner continued. "Unfortunately no word on the size of the item either...I see...needle in a haystack, you say...I understand."

I signaled to Carl that I had something to say. He looked at me.

"Could I speak to Security for a minute?" I asked.

The commissioner handed me the phone after a chastising look that meant I should choose my words carefully. I asked if there were any spaces on the ship where a person could easily hide something. The man on the other end laughed out loud.

"There are endless places where a person could hide things on a ship like this one. It's impossible to keep an eye on everything."

"Is there CCTV everywhere on board?" I said.

"Hm…Yeah, more or less."

"Are there places where there are no cameras at all?"

"Between the hulls, I guess. The space between the outer and inner walls."

"Who can get in there?"

"No one. Except crew members, I guess. To get in there you have to unscrew the massive bolts on the hatches. Then you have to crawl inside. It's a narrow, empty space."

I wanted to ask more questions, but I couldn't without explaining that we were suspecting explosives. I put my hand over the receiver and turned to the commissioner.

"We have to let Security know it's about explosives. I need to ask specific questions before it's too late."

The commissioner was sitting with his head in his hand. He waved at me to let me know I could tell them.

"We're interested in what options there might be for someone to hide explosives on the ship," I said. "We don't know if anyone has, but we want be safe and check this very carefully."

Not a sound on the other end.

"Are you there?" I said.

"I'm sorry, did you say there might be explosives on board?" he said. "I have to report that to the captain immediately."

"We're far from certain, which is why we wanted to check with you first. If you wanted to place a bomb between the hulls, as you just told me, how big would it have to be to have an impact? If the aim was to sink the ship?"

There was silence. The commissioner stared at me. Took a few steps across the room and snatched the phone out of my hand.

"Hello, this is the national police commissioner again. We have *no* indication at all that anyone is looking to sink the ship; Leona's questions are entirely hypothetical."

The commissioner put the phone on speaker.

The man from Security said: "Very big, I think. At least one hundred thirty pounds would be my guess. Not something you can bring on board in a normal backpack, that's for sure."

"Am I right in thinking a person who wanted to do something like this could," I said, "theoretically speaking, drive a vehicle onto the car deck and bring explosives into the ship using a dolly? Or bring it in a little at a time over a longer period?"

The other end went quiet again.

"If such a person had extensive knowledge of the ship, access to all areas, and wasn't caught in the act by one of us, then yes, it would be possible."

I'd heard enough. I left the room without another word.

SEVENTY-FIVE

"What the fuck is this?" Director of Citywide Operations Stefan Bäckström said, staring at me.

"Look, I don't want to rat out the national police commissioner, but he doesn't feel we have enough to go on to view this as a serious threat," I said.

"And how is that his fucking call?!" Bäckström said. "I'll be making that assessment. Going off what you just told me, plus the fact that the man has detonated explosives outside Parliament, I don't doubt for a second that he's serious. I judge this to be a very serious threat."

Bäckström got to his feet and was pulling his phone out before he was even out of his office.

"I'm getting in touch with the on-duty superintendent. He will decide whether to classify this as a 'major incident,' which I'm convinced he will. Once that's done, we have to assign a task force."

I quickly followed Bäckström into the hallway.

"Assign a task force? But we have to respond immediately. I don't know how much time…"

"I'm with you, trust me. That work will be done in parallel with my appointing a task force commander to oversee our response in the field."

Bäckström walked over to the conference room. Without so much as a knock, he threw open the door to where the commissioner, his secretary, and Alexandra were sitting.

"Bäckström, director of Citywide Operations" he said. "What's going on?"

"Oh right, hi. That's...great," said the commissioner.

"I've just been told about a bomb threat against a cruise ferry with thousands of passengers. Why was I not informed?" Bäckström demanded.

The commissioner cleared his throat.

"Ehm...There was some question as to the genuineness of the threat..."

"That's for me to assess!" Bäckström retorted.

I raised my eyebrows. Was happily surprised by Bäckström's way of just stepping in and completely bulldozing the national police commissioner.

"I was just about to contact you, but...someone seems to have beaten me to it," the commissioner said with a scowl toward me.

"It's a good thing someone here had the wits to inform me. I assess this threat as highly credible. We'll take over from here, Carl."

Bäckström walked out and over to the open-plan office that housed the division's operators. Each had three screens in front of them and large monitors covered one of the walls of the room.

"We have a bomb threat against MS *Galaxy* and need to contact the ship immediately," Bäckström told the operators.

Some of them raised their hands and nodded to him. Others were busy on calls, staring at their screens. Bäckström turned to a dark-haired girl who didn't look a day older than twenty-two.

"Anna, let me know when you have the commander of the ship."

It wasn't many seconds before Anna had got hold of the captain and handed over her headset to Bäckström.

"This is Stefan Bäckström, director of the Citywide Operations Division of the Stockholm Police. It has come to our attention that there may be explosives on the ship and we deem the threat credible. I don't know your exact position, but you should consider an immediate evacuation."

This was a highly unusual situation and I doubted even Bäckström had relevant knowledge of the rules pertaining to the ship's position, whether it was in Swedish territorial waters or not, and which laws and chains of command applied. That the captain was the one who ultimately decided whether to evacuate was clear to everyone, but since this was a private ferry company, there were probably a number of parameters that impacted on the captain's decision. With the captain still on his headset, Bäckström called the task force commander on his cell phone and mimed and motioned for the operators to inform the Harbor Unit, Sea Rescue, and Coast Guard. I was amazed by his multitasking ability. When there was a brief lull, he even managed to say a few words to me.

"It's been really quiet today. We had so little going on, we were actually planning to escort the cash transport from Arlanda Airport. But we can forget that now."

"A cash transport?" I asked.

"Oh, nothing, an international delivery that got moved up recently. It was supposed to happen next week but it's going to be today instead," he said and turned to the operator again. "Anna, make sure we get a direct hookup to the ship's surveillance system so we can get it up on the big screens."

What was he on about? Could he be talking about my cash transport? As Alexandra, the commissioner, and his secretary came in to watch Bäckström and his operators work, I walked over to a free laptop sitting open on one of the desks in the room.

"Listen up everybody! The ship is still on open water, but closing in on Furusund," Bäckström called out and moved toward the far end of the room. "The captain is discussing what to do with his staff captain, what options they have for emergency anchorage and evacuation."

I searched the list of events scheduled in Stockholm that day to see if my cash transport was on it.

Following an uptick in armored car robberies in Sweden, a rule had been established that all major cash transports had to be registered with the police. They were run without police involvement by security companies, but the police had to be informed in advance so they could be prepared in case something happened. As the security companies had improved their routines and the robberies had become less frequent, the attention paid by the police had waned. Official policy was still that the police were on standby, but in practice those resources had been reallocated as priorities had changed.

My cash transport was not due for another week. I scrolled down the list but found nothing. I didn't see it until I was almost at the end.

It was true.

The plane was landing at Arlanda at 1:15 p.m. Today!

"*Fuck!*" I inadvertently exclaimed so loudly one of the operators looked up from her screen.

I smiled back at her. Checked my watch. 11:07.

"I'm sorry, I'll be right back," I said and set off down the corridor.

SEVENTY-SIX

I rushed over to the restrooms. I felt like I was walking oddly. Like I wasn't able to gauge how far away the floor was. It was as though it was rising up to meet my feet. I stumbled. Quickly walked up to one of the restrooms. Held on tight to a doorjamb while feeling around for the lock. Fumbling in the dark, I grabbed hold of the sink and sat down on the toilet lid. Put my head between my knees. Breathed. Deep breaths. By focusing on the sliver of light at the bottom of the bathroom door, I tried to get my bearings. Control the vertigo.

"Fuck! Fuck! Fuck!" I whispered to myself.

How had this happened? I'd planned everything, down to the smallest detail. For months. And then the cash transport gets moved up a week.

Was everything over now?

What would happen if I couldn't pay back the rest of the money I owed Armand? Without the money from the cash transport I didn't stand a chance. I thought back to everything I'd done and sacrificed to be able to start a new life. The previous robberies, my marriage to Peter. My darling Benjamin. My new business.

Was it all going to have been for nothing?

I sat in the dark, hunched over with my head in my hands. Listened to the beeping sound of a police radio. Colleagues walking by in the hallway outside. Someone rattling off the address of a crime scene. A person stabbed. Just listening to them talking made me exhausted. The thought of living like this for the rest of my life made me feel sick.

I looked down at my watch. The fluorescent dashes marking the hours formed a circle underneath the glass. A dot on each hand marked the time.

11:10 a.m.

Like so many times before, I was at a crossroads. Before, I'd always chosen the safe, well-traveled path. But I had strayed from that now. Or…I had started turning away from it but only made it halfway. Now, it was as though it was calling me back. Scaring me and forcing me back into the rigid, robotic life again. But turning around and walking back to my old life was impossible. That life no longer existed. All that was left was some kind of in-between existence. An unsettling vacuum.

11:12 a.m.

Why was I really wavering? Had I reverted to the same risk-averse thinking as everyone else, the thinking that had used to control me before? The thinking that kept you from taking a single step in a different direction in life because you were afraid of losing something. Better the devil you know, how many times had I heard people say that? People who talked about how important it was to take charge of your life, but who nevertheless always put up barriers for themselves and never implemented any real changes. The people who were all talk and no action.

Maybe that was exactly what I was doing right now. Putting up barriers. I knew I had to take risks to get to where I wanted to be. I had expected to have more time, but what did I really need that time for? I'd already prepared my crew for the job. We had run through the plan again and again. They had already used their police uniforms in the first robbery. And a patrol car. I obviously wouldn't have time to bomb the G4S garage, but that was really a supplementary measure anyway, to make the security guards more nervous at being told there might be explosives in their vehicle. It wasn't reasonable to make that the be-all and end-all of this heist. It wasn't that pivotal. Most people tended to take bomb threats seriously, even if a bomb hadn't gone off the week before. Especially if the bomb threat was relayed by the police and they were told the explosives had been planted in the very van they were in. Of course they were going to take the threat seriously.

I quickly got to my feet. Turned on the lights. Enough dithering. I was never going to get a chance like this again. Cash transports carrying this kind of money were rare and I would never be more prepared than I was now. I just had to change gears mentally.

I splashed my face with ice cold water and squinted at myself in the mirror with water streaming down my cheeks and chin. I had made my mind up.

Nothing could make me back out now.

SEVENTY-SEVEN

"David, listen up. Okay, things are going down."

I was whispering into my phone as quietly as I could while also trying to enunciate so David could hear. The disabled toilet was echoing and I had no idea who might be standing around outside.

"It has to happen today. I repeat, we have to do it today. The cash transport has been pushed up. The plane is landing at Arlanda in exactly two hours."

I didn't know what he was doing on the other end, if he'd even been awake when I called.

"Get the group together and do exactly as we've planned, okay?"

David sounded shocked. Barely answered, just made some noises into the phone.

"Hello!" I whispered. "Wake the fuck up!"

"Can we really do this? It's going to be really tight," he said.

"I've done the math, we have time. We can't blow this, David. Everything's planned and ready to go. We just have to reset our brains. We'll follow the plan, except for the G4S bombing. I've already figured out the time frames. Just do as I say and we'll have enough time."

"All right!" he said.

"I'll get the police car and equipment," I said. "You and I will meet at the rendezvous point in forty minutes. Call the others and get them ready to go."

After one last determined look in the mirror, I left the bathroom. When I came out, they had established a link to the ship's surveillance system; the monitors showed a jumble of narrow hallways, staircases, restaurants, and people everywhere. On one monitor, they'd pulled up a passport photo of Fred.

Bäckström and his operators were working flat out. Alexandra was talking to the national police commissioner. There wasn't really much for me to do at the moment, but I still needed an excuse to leave for a while. I went over to Alexandra.

"I'm going to step out for a while to call the hospital. I figured if I tell Fred a little about what we know, maybe he'll give us a clue to help us get somewhere."

"I just talked to SÄK," Alexandra said. "They want us to be cautious about what information we give Fred, so only tell him what you absolutely have to, but do what you can."

"It's worth a shot," I said. "Send me a text if you find out anything I should know when I talk to him. I'll be right back."

SEVENTY-EIGHT

Timmer sounded like he was on heroin.

"Are you asleep?" David said to Timmer over the phone.

"Unh...huh?" Timmer drawled. "Why are you calling this phone?"

"Leona called," David said. "We have to do it today instead. I'm on my way to yours."

"What?"

"Change of plan. We're in a hurry. I'll be right there."

"I mean, shit! Seriously?"

"Timmer, get it the fuck together!" David shouted.

"All right, all right," Timmer said.

"Call Vikki, she has to get that van ready now."

David hung up. Dialed Sven's number on his regular phone. Fuck! He still hadn't told him anything about Leona, since he thought he'd have more time. This was his last chance.

Sven whispered on the other end.

"I'm in an important meeting."

David could hear someone talking in the background.

"Sven, I have information about a big heist that —"

"Look, I'll call you back in an hour," he broke in, still in a whisper. "Try to get me more details about that and we'll meet up later today, okay?"

"But I —"

Sven had already hung up. David didn't even have time to put the phone back in his pocket before the other one rang. It was Vikki.

"David, Timmer called me, sounded completely nuts. Is he tripping or something? Babbled on about me picking up the van because we're doing it today instead."

"That's right. I just dropped Leona off at the police station. She had some sort of snag there, but we're going to follow the plan. I'm on my way to pick up Timmer."

"Fuck me! Right now?" Vikki said.

"We're in a hurry. Get the car and pick up Zack and Ken. Make sure your phone's on. I'll see you at the rendezvous."

Timmer hadn't been able to find a place to live after being released from prison so he was staying at a friend's house. He'd asked David to wait a few blocks away. Didn't want to get picked up in a police car outside his friend's building.

Driving a police car was actually no different from driving a regular car. Leona had showed them the most important features. How to turn on the lights and sirens and whatnot.

David spotted Timmer when he pulled up. He stopped, but Timmer stayed where he was, huddled next to the building. David had already changed into his uniform and had to get out of the car and take his hat off before Timmer dared come closer.

"Fuuck, I wasn't sure it was you, you fucking cop asshole," he said and laughed. "Wouldn't want to jump in the wrong police car."

"Get in the back and put your uniform on," David said. "You'll have to change in the car."

They had both had trouble with their uniforms when they were trying them on in the Meatpacking District. David slowed down when he saw Timmer thrashing around in the back seat in the rearview mirror. The important thing was that he managed to get it all on. Hopefully, they'd have time to sort out the finer details at the rendezvous point. Timmer was surprisingly sharp when push came to shove. He'd gone from being asleep in bed a few minutes ago to being almost overhyped now. David watched through the mirror as he wriggled into his vest, sweater, pants, and belt.

David stopped the car briefly so Timmer could get into the front passenger seat. When he had sat down, they looked at each other. They were amped up, but in the middle of all the stress, they started laughing loudly. Hysterically. David would never have thought he and Timmer would one day be sitting in the front seat of a police cruiser wearing full police uniforms. He looked at Timmer.

"Shit, man, you look like hell."

"Holy shit, David, let's do this! We fucking rule!" Timmer yelled and drummed on the dashboard with both hands. "Come on, fire up those sirens!"

"Cut it out!" David said. "Not yet. We cannot fucking blow this now, okay?"

As he sped up, he tried to compose himself, but it was difficult with Timmer whooping next to him.

"This is so fucking cool, David! So damn awesome!!! We're fucking coming for you, Stockholm! Woohooo!!!"

SEVENTY-NINE

In an hour and eight minutes, I had managed to requisition the police car, hand it over to David, along with the uniforms and equipment, and make it back to headquarters. I ran down the hallway, slowing down to catch my breath before entering City-wide Operations.

The national police commissioner, Alexandra, and the head of SÄK were having a heated discussion that ended with the head of SÄK storming out. Alexandra looked at me, eyebrows raised questioningly.

"Any news?"

I shook my head. "Unfortunately nothing of value. How are you getting on with the CCTV cameras inside the ship?"

"They're still trying to find Fred in the footage. They're going through the recordings from the last few days he worked there."

I walked up to the monitors. The surveillance cameras showed the ship's narrow hallways, staircases, people streaming past. After about a minute, I spotted the hallway and staff room where I'd interviewed Mirja, Fred's colleague.

"Do we have a list of the police officers on board?" I said. "I'm thinking it's not out of the realm of possibility there might be bomb experts among them."

"There's one on board, but we need to get the ship evacuated and do a proper sweep with bomb-sniffing dogs," Alexandra said.

She seemed stunned by the whole thing.

"A lot of our colleagues were approved to go at the last minute."

We exchanged a look. Had the same thought. What a fate to have been given last-minute approval to go on a cruise ferry with a bomb on board.

EIGHTY

David and Timmer were sitting in the patrol car, staring at the traffic rushing past on the E4 freeway from Arlanda. David looked down as his phone started flashing in his hand. It was Vikki calling from the van.

"They're off," she said. "We're right behind them."

David pulled on his police cap.

"We're up," he said to Timmer.

David wished he'd had more time. His plan had been to decide what to do about Sven before they went ahead with the robbery. Now it felt like he'd been thrown into this without enough time to think things through. No one had made him do this, but stepping out now, when they were sitting there in police uniforms and everything was on the move, would be difficult. But he had to. A life of crime was not a life worth living. But when was the best time to back out? He cursed inwardly at Sven for hanging up on him. When he needed him the most, he wasn't there, as usual. That's how it had always been with Sven. If only he'd been able to offer some advice. To tell him what to say to pull out deftly, without the others catching on. Now he was going to have to back out in the middle of a robbery, of his own volition.

What would it mean for the others? Timmer, his childhood friend. Vikki, Zack, and Ken, they were all going to get in trouble because of him. They'd become his friends. Being an informer sucked. You lived in two different worlds with friends and obligations in both. Even though he knew he was doing the right thing, that the gang was in fact breaking the law and causing problems for a lot of people, walking away was still a betrayal of people who cared about him. Who were there for him.

"Here they come," Timmer said.

David saw the white G4S van approaching with Vikki's silver VW Multivan a few cars behind. He started the police car and got on the on-ramp.

Vikki called again.

"I see you," she said. "Head on out, I'll get in behind you."

David let the G4S van pass and drove out behind it.

When they were a mile or so from where they had planned to stop, David turned on his beacons and pulled up alongside the van. No sirens, Leona had cautioned, it drew too much attention. Vikki drove up behind the van. David signaled to the security guards to take the exit for Norrvikenleden and turn into the industrial estate Leona had selected. He pulled up next to the van. Vikki stopped in front of it. David killed the engine. Looked at Timmer.

"Let's do this!" he said and opened the door.

EIGHTY-ONE

We were all watching the screens at Citywide Operations. The captain had just ordered an evacuation of Silja Line's MS *Galaxy*, and we were witnessing exactly what the national police commissioner had foreseen. Panic had erupted. People were running from their cabins, fighting their way through the corridors, falling over each other on the stairs on their way up to the outer deck, where life vests, life rafts, and so on were located. Maybe they thought the ship was sinking. Given the 1994 *Estonia* disaster and other recent cruise ship catastrophes, people's reactions were understandable.

The surveillance footage had no audio, so we couldn't hear what was being broadcast over the PA system.

The national police commissioner clapped a hand to his forehead while we all stared at the chaotic scene before us. Bäckström called the ship again, but loud interference now made it difficult to hear the captain.

"Our helicopter should be with you any minute," Bäckström shouted.

"We're having trouble with one of the engine rooms," the captain replied from the speaker phone. "Lights in the control room indicate that something's gone wrong down there."

The commissioner looked at me. I shook my head. Any sign of irregularity had to be considered alarming.

"Are you there?" the captain said just as the screen began to flicker.

"Yes. We are monitoring events from here—"

Before Bäckström could finish his sentence, the screen went dark.

EIGHTY-TWO

"Police! Turn your engine off!"

David and Timmer had stepped out of the patrol car and walked up in front of the G4S van. David was shouting through a megaphone to the two male security guards. He noted that one of them looked relatively pudgy, while the other seemed fitter. With David's boxing skills, however, it shouldn't be a problem for him to take them both out. Later on, the security guards were going in the same car as Vikki, Ken, and Zack, who together were enough to physically overpower most people.

Zack started getting out his tools. The driver did as David told him and turned off the engine.

"We've had a bomb threat," David called out. "According to the threat there are explosives in your van. Now listen carefully. Without touching anything else, calmly and slowly open the doors and come out."

Both security guards looked stiff. Had a brief discussion. David was usually good at reading lips but he couldn't make out what they were saying. He waved for them to come out. The pudgy security guard in the passenger seat slowly opened his door and stepped down onto the ground. The athletic driver did the same.

David lowered his megaphone and called out to them.

"Don't slam the doors shut. Leave them open and move toward me as quickly as you can. Don't worry. It looks like everything's going well. What are your names?"

"Per," one shouted back.

"Andreas," said the other.

They quickly covered the distance to where David stood.

"Okay, Per and Andreas," David said. "Good job. You can wait in our bomb squad's van over there while we do a sweep of your vehicle. They will want to move away a little farther, but that's only a safety measure. You'll be able to see everything that's happening from there. We'll do a quick sweep. If we don't find anything, you can pick up where you left off. Hopefully it'll only take a few minutes. If we do find something, we'll give you a ride from here."

They both nodded, looking a little jumpy.

"We'll need the keys," David said.

The driver handed over the keys to the armored car. It was insane! Seeing them do exactly what he told them to was a kick. David would never have been able to talk to a security guard that way. From the look Timmer gave him, David surmised he was as thrilled about what was happening as David was.

Vikki took the keys and handed them to Zack, the bomb expert. Zack put his tool bag down and assembled the vehicle inspection mirror.

"Come with me to the van," she told the security guards.

David went up to Vikki and said softly, "They seem calm but be careful, I don't trust security guards."

The security guards obediently sat down in the van with Vikki and Ken. Vikki slowly moved the van a bit farther away. She now had to get the van at exactly the right angle so the guards could clearly see the front of their van but not the trunk of the police car, into which David and Timmer would transfer the security cases.

Once Vikki had come to a full stop, David nodded to Zack to get going. Zack demonstratively, almost too demonstratively it seemed to David, walked over to the armored car with his inspection mirror to check under the vehicle. He slowly walked around the whole car with the long handle in his hand.

David could see the security guards watching his work from Vikki's van. The security guards didn't have the keys to the security cases, so they were simply going to swap in substitute bags Leona had got for them. They were identical to the real ones and together weighed exactly 141 pounds. The money was supposed to be split across three cases.

When Zack gave a clear nod, meant to be seen by the security guards as well, it was time for David to open the armored car's back doors.

Everything suddenly seemed surreal to David. Granted, he'd committed crimes before, but never anything like this. Nothing this carefully orchestrated. It was like he was on a movie set. When he put the key in the back door lock and turned it, he had a feeling everything was about to go wrong. That the armored car might actually be completely empty when he opened the doors. The way it often happened in movies, to create suspense.

He turned the key. Slowly pushed the handle down and opened the doors. There they were. The security cases. David and Timmer stayed by the side of the van, letting Zack pass to go in first for his fake sweep. After a while, Timmer stepped into the van while David moved over to the trunk of the police car. He opened it and positioned himself so Timmer and Zack wouldn't be able to see him from the van. He pulled out his phone and dialed Sven's number.

David whispered his words to Sven into the phone.

"Sven, listen the fuck up now, because I don't have much time. Me and some other people are in the middle of robbing an armored car on its way in from Arlanda. We're talking millions. You have to stop this."

"What the fuck are you on about? *Now?*" Sven said.

"David, where the fuck did you go?" Timmer called from the van.

"Coming!" David replied.

He quickly peeked out from the other side of the car.

"We're going to be coming down the E4 going into town within the next ten minutes. We'll be driving a patrol car, wearing police uniforms. I repeat, a patrol car and police uniforms."

"Can you stall for a couple of minutes?" Sven asked. "I'll get into it right now, but it obviously takes time to get th—"

"For fuck's sake, Sven!" David whispered.

"Lay low for a while if you can," Sven said. "We'll be there, I promise."

"What's taking you so long?" Timmer suddenly materialized next to the car and stared at David. David quickly slipped his phone back into his pocket.

"What the fuck are you up to?" Timmer said and stared at David. "Who were you talking to?"

"Uh…It was just Leona," David said.

"She called your private phone?" Timmer said.

"Let's get on with this," David said and pulled out one of the cases from the trunk.

It was heavy. Full of newspaper. He walked up to the van. Timmer and Zack had lined the cases up on the left. David put his on the right as per his instructions, and went back to get the next one. They weren't allowed to take any of the original security cases back to the police car until the three fake ones were lined up on the right, to avoid mix-ups.

David worked as slowly as he dared to give Sven more time. According to the plan, David was supposed to carry the fake cases to the van and Timmer was supposed to unload the real ones, but

Timmer snatched up the last fake case and started walking it over to the van after giving David a long stare. Then Timmer started unloading the real security cases and carrying them back to the police car.

Timmer was fast. Fuck! David started regretting telling Sven. Regretting having anything to do with the police at all. Why was he always sticking his neck out for them when they always fucked everything up? He was trying to live his life right, but everything kept going wrong because he was surrounded by idiots. The only person who seemed professional and like she knew what she was doing was Leona. That the cash transport had been pushed up was beyond her control, but aside from that everything had turned out exactly as she'd said it would. He had no trouble understanding why she wanted to get away from the world of policing.

They shut the van doors. David called Vikki. Aware that she had hers on speaker so the security guards could hear.

"The entire vehicle has been searched. False alarm. I repeat, false alarm. No explosives found. Bring the security guards around so they can be on their way."

"The security guards want to report the incident," Vikki said. "Do they need to?"

"We've already informed G4S about pulling the cash transport over. I just spoke to their superior and let him know it was a false alarm. They are expecting delivery, so I suggest the security guards get back on the road as quickly as possible. We apologize for causing delay. Thank them for their patience and for doing a good job. We're leaving now. You can head back as soon as you've made sure the security guards are safely on their way."

For his part, he felt he'd sounded believable. He climbed into the driver's seat, Timmer slipped in on the passenger side. Zack, who was riding with Vikki and Ken, stayed by the armored car.

David slowly drove away. Kept his eyes peeled for Sven. Not a sign of his car. Timmer said nothing but kept glancing over at David.

"Hello? Turn on the beacons and speed up!" Timmer said once they were on the freeway.

David didn't respond. He knew that was what Leona had told them to do. Fuck! Where was Sven? Timmer kept looking at him. Before David could think any further, Timmer's phone went off.

"Ken, what's up?" Timmer said into the phone. "*What?* What the fuck! Are you completely fucking retarded?"

David looked at Timmer. Timmer's nostrils were flaring.

"You'll have to circulate until we've delivered the goods, I'll be in touch soon. Lay low and for fuck's sake, stay calm," Timmer said and hung up.

"The security guards were making trouble, wanting to report the holdup. Vikki freaked out and pointed her gun at them. Now the security guards are tied up in the back of Vikki's van and they're getting out of there.

"Fuck!" David shouted. "Fuck! Fuck! Fuck!"

"What's with this fucking car behind us," Timmer said. "It's been following us for a while now. It looks suspicious."

David didn't respond. Just sat there stiffly, staring straight ahead. Didn't know what to say. He glanced up at the rearview mirror. The car behind them had come closer. He'd recognize it anywhere.

It was Sven.

EIGHTY-THREE

"Oh my God, it's fucking plainclothes!" Timmer shouted and stared at the unmarked police car following them. "How the fuck did they find out..."

David didn't respond, just stared straight ahead at the road.

"David, are you listening to me?" Timmer continued. "The cops are after us! Speed up!"

David didn't know what to say. Kept both hands firmly on the wheel. Stared into the rearview mirror. Instead of speeding up, he slowed down a little. Felt Timmer staring at him.

"What the fuck are you doing, David. *Faster!*"

David slowed down even more. Timmer stared at him, looked back at Sven's car, and then at David again.

"What the fuck...David, did you snitch?" he said.

David couldn't bear to answer. He could see in the mirror that Sven was indicating for them to pull over. He slowed down even more.

"Fucking hell, David! I can't believe this!" Timmer roared and put a hand to his forehead.

David felt paralyzed. He could feel his heart pounding.

Timmer raved on: "Fuck, fuck, fuck, David! What have you done?!"

David's phone rang.

"What are you doing," Sven said on the other end. "Pull the fuck over!"

"What about me?" Timmer screamed at him. "And Vikki and Ken and Zack. What's going to happen to us? You don't give a shit, is that it? Answer me, David!"

"You're going to get me out of this, right?" David asked Sven.

He didn't care that Timmer could hear him. After all, he already knew.

"I don't fucking believe this!" Timmer bellowed again. "David, we fucking went to school together! And now you want to send me down for doing the same things as you. This is completely goddamn insane."

David was trying to hear what Sven was saying.

"The other guy in the car, who is he?" Sven said.

"What's it to you?" David said. "Are you going to help me?"

"We can talk about that later. You have to understand that right now, I'm taking charge of thi—"

"*Fucking answer me!*" David shouted into his phone.

Sven fell silent. After a second or two, he said in a calm, deep voice: "David, if what you're saying is true, that you've taken part in an armored car robbery, my hands are tied. We can't allow you to commit crime in our name, you know that, but we can make sure this stops now, to keep you, your friend, us, and all the other people on the road as safe as possible."

That wasn't what David had wanted to hear. He should have seen this coming. He was furious with himself. Because he knew. Had always known. Cops were not to be trusted.

"*Fuuuck!*" he screamed at the top of his lungs and banged the steering wheel.

Was this how it was going to end? He was going to be sent down for robbery. Spend a hell of a lot of years behind bars. There was no way back after that. His life would be ruined.

David looked up the road. An open lane. The police were on his tail. The people who kept messing up his life. The people he'd agreed to help, but who were just using him. Claimed they cared, but in their eyes he would always be one of the thugs. "Once a thug, always a thug," as a police officer had put it to him when he got caught one time. And then there was the rest of society. The society Saga's parents represented. They were never going to accept him. Whatever he did, no matter how much he straightened himself out, they would never think he was good enough. He would never be worthy of their daughter. David was exactly where everyone thought he belonged. Why fight against it, trying to prove them wrong? What was the point of striving to be accepted and always feeling terrible because you weren't good enough? Better to stay in the role he'd been cast in from the start and walk the path set for him. At least among other criminals he was accepted.

He looked at Timmer who was shouting next to him. Saw the fear in his eyes. David suddenly realized how selfish he'd been. This wasn't just about him anymore. The others, Timmer, Vikki, Ken, and Zack, they were just like him. Were also fighting for a better life. He was going to destroy them. To achieve what? For society's sake, the society that didn't give a shit about them and just threw up obstacles for anyone who tried to quit crime?

Their lives were his responsibility now, too. Sure, they'd made their own choices, but David had lured them straight into a trap that was going to ruin their lives. Was he going to be able to live with that?

"Now take it easy, David," Sven said on the other end. "I'll do what I can for you."

David hung up. Turned to Timmer.

EIGHTY-FOUR

"What's the goddamn problem?" Bäckström said. "Get us back online with the ship."

The screen was still dark.

My phone buzzed in my pocket. The display let me know it was Timmer. I walked off and found an empty room. When I hit accept I heard a loud, piercing sound that was all too familiar. Sirens. The last sound I wanted to hear right now. I shut the door tight.

Timmer was screaming into his phone: "Fuck, Leona, things have gone real fucking sideways!"

"Calm down," I said sharply. "Why are your sirens on?"

"The cops are after us!"

"*What?*" I hissed. "Is it their sirens?"

"No, no, ours. But a plainclothes is on our tail. What the fuck do we do?" he screamed.

A plainclothes police officer. How was that possible? No one should know about this.

"Are you sure?"

"Leona, don't you think I can spot an unmarked police car! He just appeared behind us on the freeway. What the fuck do we do?"

"Do you have the cargo?" I said.

"Yes, yes, it's all in the trunk, but fuck, Leona, tell us what to do!"

I felt like the whole building could hear him, but the door was closed and I could see through the window that no one was reacting, so it was probably just my imagination.

"Try to calm down," I said as quietly as I could. "Tell David to keep going with the sirens on. Other cars will move for you. He's going to have to do a quick exit and immediately turn off the sirens. Then you drive on with just the beacons and get to your car as fast as you can. Move the cargo and change your clothes, just like we planned."

"David, we have to find an exit," Timmer shouted in the car.

"Calm down, Timmer, it's going to be fine. Just do as I say."

"It's not just that. Vikki and Ken have taken the security guards hostage."

"*What?* What the fuck? No one was allow—"

The call cut out.

I had to get out of here. This was getting completely out of hand. I would have to explain to Alexandra why I'd left afterward.

I opened the door and quickly walked out into the hallway toward the elevators. The national police commissioner and Alexandra were standing in the hallway and spotted me coming out. The commissioner waved me over.

"Leona! Exactly what has this man told you in your interviews, and why did he demand to have you be the interviewer?"

"What?" I said, turning to Alexandra. "Fred asked for me specifically?"

Alexandra replied by shooting the commissioner an annoyed look. He seemed to realize his mistake and started clearing his throat.

"Ahem...I might have misunderstood."

I just kept staring at Alexandra. She nodded slowly.

"Why didn't anyone fucking tell me that?" I said.

Alexandra heaved a sigh. "It was Fred's demand in return for saying anything at all. SÄK didn't want you told since they had to check out the connection between the two of you. That's all

I know. As you're aware, they don't exactly like to share their information."

"If I'd known, I would have taken a completely different tack, Alexandra. I might have been able to prevent all of this. This is insane! I'm going to have to interview him again, about this, specifically." I saw a chance to get away from the station.

Alexandra didn't seem to know what to say.

"I'm going to go see Fred at the hospital right now," I continued, watching to gauge their reactions.

Alexandra frowned. "I think we should check with SÄK first," she said.

"You think we have time for that?" I hissed. "They're doing absolutely everything they fucking can to slow us down. Not that they've gotten anywhere with the case, either."

"They very well may have, Leona, we don't know anything about that."

"Exactly, because they won't fucking tell us anything. I can't work like this. Either I head up to the hospital and try to avert an impending disaster, or I go home. Then you can mess some other interviewer around. It's up to you, Alexandra," I said.

Seconds ticked by. I didn't have time to linger. I stared at her. She looked at the commissioner, who also seemed annoyed by how the case had been handled.

The moment she nodded to me, I turned around and ran toward the elevators.

EIGHTY-FIVE

When I got through to Timmer, he and David had managed to shake the police and were on their way to the place where Vikki, Ken, and Zack were holding the security guards. I had to get there fast. I'd have to dig into why Fred had requested me to interview him and how he even knew who I was at a later date.

I spotted Vikki's van and the police car, from afar, parked with my crew standing next to them. From where I was coming, you couldn't drive all the way to where they were, so I got out and started jogging toward them. The two uniformed G4S guards were standing next to them, handcuffed. I was just about to shout to them that they had to let the security guards go when I heard sirens. Two patrol cars were approaching behind me.

They'd seen me, seen my car, and probably already knew criminals were driving around in a patrol car, dressed in uniforms. If the security guards had managed to trigger the alarm, their GPS would have shown where they were.

My fellow officers were pulling up behind me.

In front of me were my uniformed robbers with the security guards in handcuffs.

And I was in the middle.

I had no choice. I pulled out my police badge, raised it in the air and shouted to my colleagues that I was a detective.

Then I drew my gun.

And aimed it at my robbers.

Then the worst imaginable thing happened. When my crew saw the police come running at them, Vikki and Zack each grabbed a security guard, pulled their fake guns, and put them against their heads.

No! No! *No!* I thought to myself. If they only knew how much they'd just escalated this already dangerous situation. Mostly for themselves, but for everyone around them as well. They obviously knew their guns were fake. They were meant to intimidate victims and witnesses. But from my colleagues' point of view, there was now a clear, concrete threat of lethal violence against the two security guards, a threat that could be carried out instantly. They would do everything in their power to prevent it, even if that required shooting and killing the perpetrators.

"*Police! Release the hostages! Drop your weapons!*" the police officers bellowed as they ran up from behind until they were level with me.

All four of my colleagues and I had our guns pointed at my crew.

Seconds ticked by.

I had to do something.

Now!

I lowered my weapon, put it down on the ground where they could see it, and ran toward David and the others with my hands in the air, screaming loud enough for everyone present to hear: "*Police! Release the security guards and take me instead!*"

As soon as I got there, David grabbed me, put his gun to my head and dragged me backward into Vikki's van. Timmer ran over to the driver's side. When Vikki, Zack, and Ken got close enough, they shoved the security guards away, threw themselves inside, and Timmer burned up the road.

EIGHTY-SIX

Fred had learned to recognize the sound of the doctors' and nurses' footsteps coming and going, even if he was facing away from the door. Leona's footsteps too, even though she often swapped between heels and sneakers. That was why he woke up abruptly when he heard two unknown individuals enter his room. Fred turned over as quickly as he could. One of the men stopped next to the bed, while the other went straight to the window, pulled the curtain aside, and looked out both ways.

"*Bonjour,* Sergei. Or should I call you Fred?" one of the men greeted him in French. "So this is where you're lying about these days?"

Given the media frenzy over his attack, Fred had counted on them finding him sooner or later. Considering who they were, there was no point pondering how they'd got past the members of the Security Service guarding his door.

"Armand, what took you so long?" Fred said in French.

Armand pulled out a pocket watch. Put a cigarette between his lips.

"*Ah, excusez-moi,*" he said, pulling another cigarette halfway out the pack and holding it out to Fred.

Fred shook his head. Armand's eyebrows shot up.

"So you've become interested in clean living in your old age? *Très bien.*"

He held the pack out to the man by the window. The man shook his head almost imperceptibly.

"*Ça va*, Sergei, how are you doing?" Armand continued and lit his cigarette. "That doesn't look good."

He pointed with his lighter to Fred's stumps and blew smoke at the ceiling.

"I appreciate your concern," Fred said. "What do you want?"

"Sergei, Sergei, Sergei," Armand said.

He insisted on addressing Fred by the name he'd been given in the Foreign Legion and that he had kept while he lived in France. Fred looked at the other man, who was still standing by the window, occasionally glancing down at the parking lot.

"So this is one of your new minions?" Fred said.

Armand broke into a big smile.

"There have been many like you, Sergei. That being said, most have been more biddable and have done what they've been told to do. First and foremost, they haven't stolen money from me."

The smoke Armand was exhaling was quickly filling the room.

"Goran, meet Sergei. We founded RDT together once upon a time. Unfortunately, he pulled out before the company had a chance to grow really big."

RDT stood for Rue de Toulouse, the street in Paris where Fred and Armand had started their company together, many years ago. They charged to lend and launder money, but after Armand had grown suspicious of Fred, he'd put a price on his head. Fred had fled to Sweden and had since been told that Armand had carried on without him and expanded into several European countries.

Goran gave Fred a sluggish stare, then turned back to the window.

"He's not very polished," Armand said, referring to Goran, "but he does what he's supposed to. Sergei, no matter how much I would love to stay and chat, we have to go. You know why I'm here. Don't make me ask Goran to take care of it."

Fred knew. He pointed to the wardrobe on the other side of the room.

"My house keys are in the bag on the floor in that wardrobe. I have money there. For obvious reasons, I no longer trust banks."

Armand laughed out loud.

"Come now, Sergei, you wouldn't want to insult us bankers."

"Feel free to take whatever you want," Fred said.

Armand raised his eyebrows.

"You're giving me your house keys?"

"As I'm sure you understand, I won't be needing them for a while," Fred said and looked down at his legs.

Fred had no intention of ever returning to his apartment.

Armand nodded to Goran to look in the closet.

"I'm almost starting to wonder if there is something fishy about this, Sergei? You wouldn't trick an old colleague, would you?"

"Look at me. What could I possibly do to you, Armand? I'm a cripple. Now take the keys and get out. I want to sleep."

Goran held up Fred's key ring and gave it to Armand. Armand weighed it in his hand. Rubbed it as though it were a crystal ball.

"Well, I know where to find you if anything is amiss," he said.

Goran started walking toward the door. Armand stayed put.

"By the way, I saw that little police cunt outside before," Armand said. "I've been told she's in charge of your investigation. She owes me things. I'm starting to lose patience with her."

"You're messing around with cops now, too?" Fred said. "Wasn't it you who always used to say that —"

"I never turn away a paying customer, Sergei. That being said, I'm afraid she's proving to be too much trouble. But we are keeping an extra eye on her." Armand glanced at Goran as he stepped in closer to the bed.

Before Fred could even fling a hand up for protection, Armand had aimed a gun with a silencer at him.

EIGHTY-SEVEN

I'd called emergency services. Told them who I was, given them a song and dance about being taken hostage by unknown assailants and then dumped by the side of the freeway.

I used my phone to study the black eye and scrapes I'd forced the robbers to give me before dropping me off. With the dirt I'd rubbed into my pants and the blouse I had ripped myself, I felt it looked pretty real.

While I sat by the side of the road, waiting for dispatch to send a patrol car to pick me up, I called Alexandra.

"Leona, where the fuck are you?" she said.

I couldn't recall ever hearing Alexandra swear before. I modulated my voice to sound shaken, but not too weak.

"I ended up in a hostage situation on my way to interviewing Fred. Was beaten up and dumped on the freeway. I'm okay, but I'm waiting to get picked up. They'll have to drive me to the hospital so I can talk to Fred. I have to have my injuries documented as well. Do it at the same time."

"Hostage situation? What are you talking about? *You* were taken hostage?"

"I'll tell you more later, Alexandra. The car's here now. I'll call you from the hospital."

"But Leona—"

I hung up. Didn't have it in me to answer any more questions.

The police officers who picked me up didn't say much, just turned on their beacons and headed straight for the hospital.

Amid all the confusion, I suddenly had a feeling everything was going to work out.

I leaned my head against the headrest in the back seat and closed my eyes. I needed a few minutes of peace. I listened to the crackling sound coming from the police radio and the alarms being radioed in. If my head hadn't been so full of thoughts, I would have drifted off. But then one particular alarm woke me right up:

Calling all cars. A bomb has exploded on board the Silja Line MS Galaxy, a cruise ferry with approximately two thousand passengers. Two hundred and fifty of them are police officers attending the annual police conference on board. Sections of the ship have already been evacuated following a tip-off. No perpetrator has been identified. We need a number of patrols at the terminal. Paramedics and emergency services are on their way. Report in if you're free to respond. Over.

EIGHTY-EIGHT

"Hello!" I said into my phone, sitting in the back seat of the police car on my way to Karolinska Hospital.

I'd been trying to get through to my VCD colleagues, Fredrik, Åse, and Anette, on the ship, but to no avail. Now someone seemed to have answered on Anette's cell phone, but all I could hear on the choppy line was some kind of klaxon, a speaker voice, screaming people, and clatter.

"Anette!" I shouted.

"Leona, can you hear me?! I'm on the ship. We're listing badly. It's utter chaos here."

"Are you okay?" I shouted back as we approached the hospital at high speed.

I was happy to hear her voice. With the phone pressed against my ear, I looked out toward the main entrance to the hospital and realized it was swarming with police. Two armored police vans and two regular patrol cars were parked outside.

"What the hell—?!" I said loudly to no one in particular. "Stop the car!" I shouted to my colleagues. They slammed on the brakes. I threw open the door and ran toward the entrance. The helicopter hovering above the hospital made it hard to hear what Anette was saying on the other end of the phone.

"There was a big blast, the whole ship shook," she shouted while I pushed past reporters, photographers, and a lot of other bystanders who had congregated outside the doors.

"Anette, you have to get off the ship," I shouted back and flashed my badge at the four uniformed officers who had their hands full holding the crowd back.

They gave me a quick nod and let me pass. In the eerily empty lobby, I ran over to the elevators, quickly pushed the button, but changed my mind and ran toward the stairs instead.

"I'm by the lifeboats now. The evacuation seems to be going okay, but people are panicking," she continued.

I climbed the stairs to Fred's floor two steps at a time.

"Leona, it's him, isn't it? It's the suicide bomber who did this," she said.

"Just get yourself to dry land, Anette, I'll have to talk to you later," I panted, starting to feel the lactic acid in my thighs.

"I have to find…"

The call cut out. I threw open the door to Fred's floor. The hallway, normally full of patients and staff, was now empty. I hurried on toward Fred's room. I slipped on the polished floor going around a corner, but regained my equilibrium and pushed on. When I turned the corner by the elevators, I could see a group of people at the end of the hallway, outside Fred's room. In the backlighting from the large window, I could only make out their silhouettes, but I could tell they were uniformed officers. Rushing forward, I shoved an open door closed to get past a nurse pushing a hospital bed. I didn't see the police cordon until I was already there.

"Leona Lindberg, VCD," I panted and showed them my badge.

I stayed outside the cordon.

"He's dead," one of them said. "The two officers from SÄK who were guarding him as well. Shot at close range and dumped in the storeroom over there. We're waiting for the technicians.

And I assume you heard about the cruise ferry? Twelve dead so far and a lot of injuries."

I didn't look at him; I was staring into Fred's room.

"But…"

My mouth was dry. My mind was spinning.

The door to the room had been propped open. My eyes followed the trail of blood. It grew more prominent closer to the bed where two rivulets of blood had formed a large pool on the floor. I couldn't see Fred's head from the hallway, but the angle made it possible for me to see parts of the bed and his body. The blood smeared across his chest and bed, coupled with the shoeprints in the blood on the floor indicated that a lot of people had been in and out of the room. Probably hospital staff who had tried to save his life, police officers, the perpetrator or perpetrators.

I wasn't about to storm in and mess things up for the technicians by contaminating the crime scene. There was no point going in there, he was already dead. But who had killed him?

I turned to look down the other hallway. Four more uniformed officers were guarding another police cordon around an open door some ways down it.

"Goddamn executions…"

"Coroner and technicians are on their way…"

"Informed the families…"

My colleagues' voices mingled with the beeping of their police radios and echoed up and down the hallways.

I couldn't make the pieces fit together. It was too much. I had to get out. Away from the hospital. Clear my head. My colleagues said something to me when I turned and walked back up the corridor, but I didn't catch what. When I was almost at the elevators, I heard a woman's voice behind me.

"Leona!"

A nurse came running toward me. When she got closer, she glanced back at the cluster of police officers outside Fred's room and said in a whisper: "Fred Sjöström gave me this. I promised to give it to you if anything happened to him."

She handed me a letter. I took it and immediately started opening the envelope.

"I could clean that up for you if you want," she said, looking up at my forehead.

I gingerly touched my hairline; my fingers came away bloody.

"Thanks, I'll be right back," I said.

She handed me a tissue before I walked off toward the elevators. I pressed it against my forehead.

I left reddish-brown fingerprints on the white envelope on my way down the elevator. I didn't manage to get it open until the elevator had already reached the ground floor. When the doors opened, Alexandra was standing there.

"Leona! My God, you look terrible!"

"Alexandra, I was just about to call you. He's dead," I said and stuffed the envelope in my pocket.

"I know," Alexandra said. "And two of our colleagues from SÄK as well. And the cruise ferry. I tried to tell you about it when you called, but the call cut out."

"Police dead there too?" I said.

"We've had no reports of dead officers, but twelve civilian passengers so far. We don't know how many injured. The evacuation seems to be going okay, but the passengers are panicking and the media are going crazy. I have to go upstairs and talk to our colleagues from SÄK."

I nodded and took a few steps toward the exit.

"Where are you going? We need you upstairs. Besides, that needs to be seen to," she said and looked at my forehead.

"I just need some air. I'll see you up there in five minutes."

I started walking toward the exit.

"Could the killers still be inside?" a journalist asked as soon as I stepped through the doors.

"I have no comments," I said and quickly walked past the reporters and onlookers, who were even more numerous than when I first arrived.

I walked around the corner of the building and found a park bench. Pulled out the envelope Fred had left with the nurse, and read.

"Leona! Ronni told me you were the right person."

Ronni? My mind was racing. Olivia, the seven-year-old girl who committed the bank robberies last fall, was Ronni's daughter. I hadn't been in contact with him since then. That being said, it wasn't unthinkable that Fred and Ronni knew each other. But what I took from this was that Ronni hadn't been able to keep his mouth shut and had walked around spreading all kinds of rumors about me. Fucking typical.

As I was reading, my phone buzzed in my pocket. The display told me it was Peter. I pushed accept and continued reading Fred's letter: *"You delivered my message."*

While I read I could hear Peter breathing heavily on the other end. I had a hard time understanding what he was saying.

"Leona, they just called from the preschool. It's Beatrice..."

"Now I want to give you a word of warning. Armand does more than launder money," the letter read.

"What about Beatrice?" I asked Peter.

"...she's missing! They've been looking for twenty minutes. What the fuck are we going to do, Leona? Call the police?"

The world stopped.

Swirled around me.

It had to be Armand. I didn't get it. I'd started the payments. Done everything he'd asked for. If that fucking asshole had taken Beatrice, I was going to deal with him once and for all.

"Peter, I'm going to take care of this. Do you hear me? Do nothing until you hear from me!"

"Armand is going to destroy your life."

I stared at the letter but was too distraught to understand what it said. Was just about to get up from the bench when rough hands grabbed me from behind.

Something big and dark was pulled over my head.

Everything went black.

EIGHTY-NINE

The first thing I felt was my body being shaken. I opened my eyes to complete darkness. The top of my head was knocking against something hard and sharp and my neck was being compressed by the weight of my body. The surface I was lying on was hard, uneven. I couldn't orient myself. The floor was moving. Loud traffic sounds reverberated through my skull. I tried to find something to hold on to, but my hands were tied behind my back. It wasn't until I pushed myself up into sitting that I managed to get my bearings.

I felt drunk. Dizzy. Parts of my body were numb. I was in a vehicle, probably a van. On my way to somewhere I wouldn't have agreed to go. If my arms hadn't been tied behind my back, I would have tried to open the doors and throw myself out when the car slowed down. Without my arms free, I didn't stand a chance. I found it hard to judge what speed the car was going.

I tried to cut through the strap around my wrist by pushing myself backward and pressing my wrists against the sharp thing that had hurt my head before. After a while, I could feel them starting to give way. At the same time, I was trying to hear where we were going. It was impossible without the use of my eyes. I carried on. The angle of my hands made my wrists ache. The vehicle came to a full stop. Stayed put for a while, then drove on.

The strap was hanging on by a thread now. When it finally snapped, I quickly freed my hands. I undid the cord wrapped around my neck and pulled the cloth bag off my head.

Aside from me, the back of the van was empty. They'd taken my private phone but missed the phone I'd been using for the robbery. I pulled it out of my bra and browsed through the apps to try to find out where I was. The battery was flashing red. The car turned again and the road surface changed from asphalt to gravel. I managed to pull a map up on my phone and see where I was. As the car slowed to a stop, I took a quick screenshot with a blue dot where I was and sent it off just as the doors opened.

Two men stepped in.

One of them grabbed the phone, threw it on the van's metal floor and stepped on it. I watched it break into pieces under his boot.

They manhandled me over the edge. I landed awkwardly on the ground. My legs buckled. They pulled me up by the arms. Hanging between the two men, I tried to get back on my feet. My body was weirdly numb. They dragged me over to a small yard between two buildings. A larger house with an adjacent barn. I was hauled into the house and down a flight of stairs to a basement, where they dumped me on the floor before going back upstairs.

I lay flat on my stomach, trying my best to push up off the ground when I heard a faint voice that made my insides go cold.

"Mommy!"

Beatrice was looking at me with her worried little eyes. She was wearing her pale green dress and holding her favorite bunny and a tube with pictures of candy on it. I was feeling nauseous. Wanted to throw up but did everything I could not to. I was relieved to see her, that she was okay, but also knew that her being here was the worst thing that could possibly happen.

"Honey," I said and grabbed hold of her.

I found new strength. Got to my feet and hugged her, probably a bit too hard. Let go when I heard her whimpering.

"What happened to your cheek, mommy?"

The left side of my face had been feeling tight. I touched it. Yet another swelling. Strangely, it wasn't particularly tender.

"I just tripped and fell, I'm all right, Bea. Have they been nice to you?"

She nodded.

"One of the men gave me candy," she said and shook the tube to make it rattle. "You want some, mommy?"

She held it out to me. Even though candy was the last thing I wanted right now, I opened the tube, turned it upside down in my hand and angled it slightly to make three pieces of candy roll out into my palm. One rolled over the edge by my thumb and onto the concrete floor. Bea quickly picked it up and put it in her mouth, shooting me a mischievous look. Her behavior convinced me Armand's men had been able to make her go with them without scaring her.

"They let me eat as much as I wanted while I waited for you," she said. "When can I see the police cars, mommy?"

"What police cars, Bea?"

"He said I was going to see the police cars at your work."

So that was how they'd lured Bea away from her preschool. I wanted to shout at her that she shouldn't have gone with them. That I had told her a thousand times that she must never go anywhere with a stranger, but that ship had sailed.

"We'll do it later, honey."

"I want to do it now, mommy."

"Soon."

I was looking for a way out for us. Peered up at the narrow basement windows. The only thing I'd managed to see when they dragged me in was that there was forest all around us. Even if I managed to get out, I would have to run through the woods with a numb body and a five-year-old in tow. Still, if I saw an opportunity, I would seize it. Staying here was riskier. Before I could search for more plausible escape routes, the basement door opened and Armand came down the stairs.

"Leona, *bienvenue*, lovely to see you," he said in his French-accented English.

He shot a quick glance at Beatrice and started walking toward me. I stood still. His shiny shoes and smart suit made him look very out of place in the basement. He came closer and kissed me once on each cheek. Looked me up and down and said, "Oh dear, you seem to have hurt yourself on the way here."

I smiled at him. Had to play along for Bea's sake. Then he turned and walked over to Beatrice, who was holding her stuffed bunny and chewing chocolate candy.

"So this is the little miracle," he said in broken Swedish and squatted down in front of her. "My name is Armand, what's your name?" He poked her in the ribcage to make her smile.

"Beatrice."

Armand laughed.

"Why are you doing this, Armand?" I said in English. "I've paid you. I've done everything you've told me to do."

If we stuck to English, Bea couldn't understand us. So long as we used a pleasant tone.

"Where's the money, Leona?" he said.

I hoped the text with my GPS position had been sent before my phone was crushed against the floor of the van, but I had no way of knowing. I thought about the letter Fred had left for me. That said Armand didn't stop at anything. If I told him where the loot from the robbery was, they would have no more use for me. Then what would they do to me and Beatrice? At the same time, I didn't know what they'd do if I didn't tell them. I had to play for time.

"You'd really hurt a child, Armand?" I said in English. "Are you that desperate?"

"I wouldn't be the only one who does cruel things to children," Armand retorted.

I realized he was referring to little Olivia, who committed the robberies I had investigated.

"I've never hurt anybody," I said.

Armand laughed loudly.

"You keep telling yourself that, Leona. As far as I know, that little girl isn't doing too well."

"What the fuck would you know about it?" I said through gritted teeth, but changed my tone when Armand glanced over his shoulder at Beatrice.

"Maybe we shouldn't raise our voices just yet," he said and smiled at me. "You were supposed to contact me after the heist."

He checked his watch.

"It's been several hours now. I couldn't risk having you vanish with the money, could I? Give me the address now, or your little girl will experience things little girls…"

"Torpängsvägen 35 in Huddinge," I said quickly.

He squinted at me.

"I don't suppose I need to explain to you what will happen if that is the wrong address?"

"There's a small shed in the yard," I continued. "It's locked, but you obviously have no problem getting through locked doors." I looked at the mustachioed goon who'd just walked a few steps down the stairs. The same man who had pointed a gun at me in my apartment and left behind a photo of Beatrice.

The address was fake, but I hoped it would take them some time to realize that, since it was on the other side of town.

Armand nodded for the man to leave. He disappeared without a word. Armand lingered. Walked around the basement looking pleased, studying Beatrice as though she were a nugget of gold that belonged to him. The sight of him was revolting.

"Fred told me about you," I said.

He laughed.

"Ah, you mean Sergei. Doesn't talk too much anymore though, does he?"

He left the basement with a smirk on his lips and locked the door behind him.

I walked around the basement, looking for something stable enough to stand on among the junk.

"What are you doing, mommy?" Beatrice asked.

"Just moving around a little, honey."

It was all empty cardboard boxes and debris. I squatted down in front of Beatrice.

"Bea, I want you to listen carefully. The men who gave you candy. They're not nice men. They want us to stay here even though we need to go home. Do you understand?"

She nodded.

"Remember the Pippi Longstocking book we read together? Remember how Pippi has to do all kinds of really brave things all by herself and be really strong?"

"Mm, picks up her horse."

"Exactly. I want you to be as brave as Pippi. I want you to sit on my shoulders and climb out that window. When you get out, I want you to run into the forest so no one can see you. Do you think you can do that?"

"But mommy, aren't you coming with me?" Bea said.

"I'm too big to get out through that window, honey. Only you and Pippi can."

She looked at me with big eyes.

"Then I want you to go through the forest to the road. On the road, you should wave to a car to make it stop and then say the thing we've practiced before in case you ever got lost, remember?"

"I've lost my mommy whose name is Leona Lindb—"

"You're going to have to say daddy instead, honey. Tell me again."

"That I've lost my daddy whose name is Peter Lindberg and who lives on Allhelgonagatan..."

Hearing how well she knew it made my eyes tear up. She even knew Peter's phone number.

"If you see any of the men from here, hide behind a tree. You know, like when we play hide and seek. You can't let them see you, honey. Do you understand?"

"But mommy..."

"Come on, Bea. You're brave and strong like Pippi. And you have to promise to watch out for cars. You can't cross the road. Promise?"

She nodded.

I walked her over to the wall beneath the window. Lifted her up and put her on my shoulders.

"Try grabbing the wall so you can stand on my shoulders," I said.

Bea managed to open the small basement window and climb out. Once outside, she turned around and looked down at me.

"Mommy, I—"

I put a finger to my lips to show her she had to be quiet. She stopped talking but didn't move, just kept looking at me. I whispered to her.

"You can do it, Bea. You and Pippi."

I waved for her to go. I was glad I hadn't been an overprotective mother. That she hadn't been raised to be scared of everything. This required strength and courage, and she delivered. I was proud. If only she could get out of this area and get to the nearest road without Armand's men spotting her. I was pretty sure that if she could get that far, she'd be out of danger. That she would happen to wave down a car whose driver was a trafficker or some such was just too implausible. Hopefully, some nice person would call Peter and then drive her back to him. Sending her away was a risk, of course, but it was more dangerous for her to stay here. Armand was capable of anything.

I sat down on the floor by one of the walls.

Fifteen minutes later, the door was thrown open and a man walked up to me where I was sitting. He grabbed me by the hair and roughly pulled me to my feet. My legs were steadier now, even though the pain in my scalp made me scream and flail about reflexively. But he was physically superior. Dragged me up the stairs, out of the house, and across the gravel yard to a copse of trees on the other side of it. I looked around to see if there was any sign of Bea or anyone else who might have come looking for me, but saw nothing to indicate either. I was happy Bea was no longer in the area, but I felt enough time had passed that they should be out here looking for me. Maybe my text hadn't been sent after all.

The man opened the door to the barn and gave me a hard shove in the back before closing it behind us. The smell of wet hay pricked my nose.

He nodded to the only piece of furniture in the barn, a wooden chair in the middle of the room. I realized there was no point struggling, so I went up to it and sat down. He followed me and I noticed him pulling a bunch of zip ties from his pocket. He forced my hands back and zip-tied my wrists behind the back of the chair and my ankles to its front legs. Then he left the barn.

I noted that he didn't bar the door from outside. As soon as he was gone, I pulled my arms up over the back of the chair so they rested against my back instead. I felt around for something sharp on the outside of my pants that I could use to sever the zip tie, but that kind of plastic was hard to break. Pulling it apart with just my hands was out of the question. It would only carve deep gashes in my wrists. I looked around the room. Random junk lined the walls. If I could just get to one of the walls, tip the chair over, and look for something sharp to cut the zip ties on. Since the man hadn't tied all of me to the chair, I could stand up. Then I started to move my feet. The chair followed my every movement. With tiny steps, my feet spread well apart, I managed to shuffle across the floor to one side of the room. Prodding things with my feet was virtually impossible since I had to bring the whole chair along whenever I moved either of my feet. I wanted to avoid toppling over. That would leave me in a very vulnerable position. Right now, though, I couldn't see any other options. On the floor, I would have a better chance of writhing around looking for something useful. I squatted down and leaned as far as I could to the left to pull the opposite chair leg up off the floor. I knew it wouldn't be a soft landing so I twisted my body as I fell, landing hard on my shoulder and back. Then I pulled myself along the floor toward the wall. Just as I was getting close, I heard the barn door open.

"What the hell is this? Get her up."

It was Armand's voice. The man who had shoved me into the barn came over and started tugging at me. Pulled both me and the chair upright. Then he grabbed the back of the chair, tipped it backward, and dragged it back to the middle of the room, where he set it down. Armand came to stand in front of me.

"Leona, Leona. You don't seem to want this to end well for you," he said. "You do understand that we've found out that the address you gave us was wrong, don't you?"

"What are you going to do, Armand, kill me? Or are you coward enough to torture a woman? That's not beneath your dignity?"

"Dignity? I don't think either one of us should throw around such lofty words, Leona. I think we both crossed that line a long time ago."

"Don't compare your primitive methods to me and how I work," I said. "Sending a goon to break into my apartment to intimidate me is like some kind of old-timey gangster crap. Use your fucking imagination, please...So you're going to hit me with that rope now. Go right ahead."

I was so furious I didn't have the sense to be scared. Armand was an asshole, that much I'd figured out. Way too late, unfortunately. But right now, I didn't care about anything.

"And kidnapping my daughter, how fucking low can you get?" I continued.

He made no reply. It occurred to me that he hadn't mentioned that Bea was missing.

"I believe I've been more imaginative than you think, Leona," he said and walked over to the door and stepped outside.

The door soon opened again and he entered slowly. He was holding his arm out behind him. As if he were dragging something behind him. And so he was. He was holding Beatrice by the hand.

The air was knocked out of me. It was as if I'd been punched in the gut. My chest constricted. I had to gasp for air.

"What happened to your tough and cocky attitude, Leona?" Armand said.

I wasn't able to respond. Couldn't look up; my head dangled limply with my chin on my chest. My body wouldn't obey anymore. The sound of his voice echoed in my head while my ears buzzed and howled.

"Why're you...sitting so...weirdly, mommy...," I heard Beatrice's thin voice say.

I couldn't speak. Tried to move my legs and arms, but was unsure if I had managed to shift them even an inch. All my energy was being used to suck air into my lungs. I only managed to inhale a tiny, tiny amount before I had to exhale again. Inhale again. With whatever strength I had left, I managed to straighten up and raise my head. I felt a stinging lash across my chest and heard Bea scream. I doubled over with pain. If my arms hadn't been wrapped around the back of the chair, my chest would have slammed into my thighs. My head drooped. I tried to form words. Wanted to console Bea. Tell her everything was all right. That she didn't have to be scared. I wanted to tell Armand where the money was. He could have it. All of it. It wasn't worth this. Bea shouldn't have to see her mom like this. At someone's mercy. Weak. Battered. I wanted to scream but couldn't get a sound out. Couldn't inhale properly. The air got stuck. Before I could think more, I heard a crack and my shoulders and neck stung. Bea kept screaming.

NINETY

I woke up to men shouting. At least two men.

"Police! Get down on the floor!"

I'd never been more relieved to hear those words. I must have fainted. Managed to open one eye. My head was too heavy to lift. I was lying in an awkward position with the chair still strapped to my ankles and my arms still around its back. My right shoulder, which was pressed against the floor, was twisted into a position that didn't feel normal. It was like my shoulder had ended up on my back. I managed to turn my head ever so slightly to the left so I could open my other eye. I saw one of Armand's men facedown on the floor. Uniformed arms were snapping handcuffs around his wrists. Someone screamed on the other side of the room.

My first thought was Bea. I couldn't see her. Couldn't hear her. Where was she? The police officer leaning over the man on the floor turned his head to me. As if he could hear my thoughts, he said, "It's okay, Leona, Bea's safe."

The blue police uniform was unable to hide his warm gaze. His voice was calm. Safe. I relaxed. Looked into his eyes. All of a sudden, I was crying. I was in pain, but that wasn't the reason. Seeing David standing there in his uniform, saving me and my daughter, made tears drip from my eyes onto the ground. I couldn't keep my eyes open any longer. I'd been given the information I needed.

NINETY-ONE

"Mommy, mommy, mommy, mommy, mommy, mommy, mommy, mommy, mommy…"

When I opened my eyes again, I was in the back seat of a car traveling at high speed. At the same time, I became aware of Bea's voice repeating the same word over and over again. In a tone I'd never heard before. Not like screaming but rather some kind of monotonous talk-crying.

My head was in her lap and a police jacket was spread over me like a blanket. She didn't seem to have noticed that I had opened my eyes. I could see that she was looking straight ahead and that she was having trouble sitting still on account of the speed. She seemed to be looking for something to hold on to. I suddenly had the horrifying thought that she might reach for the door handle.

"Push the…lock button…"

I was giving it all I had, but I could tell she couldn't hear me. My voice was so faint and the noise level in the car was so high. I wanted her to lock the door. When she didn't hear me, I tried to reach up to lock the car door myself, but I didn't even manage to get my hand out from under the jacket. My whole body ached.

"…seatbelt, Bea," I shouted as loudly as I could, but she still didn't react, just continued her repetitive droning.

While the car swayed this way and that, I tried to turn so I could see who was driving. I spotted David behind the wheel between the two front seats. He was looking around frantically. Bea noticed that I had started to move.

"Mommymommymommymommy...," she continued.

"It's okay, Bea," I said in a steadier voice. "Calm down. Put your seatbelt on."

She finally seemed to hear me. She turned her body to reach the belt. Her movement stretched my neck and made the pain in one of my shoulders radiate up and down my spine.

I could tell we were getting close to the city, but the drive still felt endless.

"You have to drop me off near the hospital," I said as loudly as I could manage. "And drive Bea home."

He shot me a worried glance over his shoulder.

"You can't even stand up, Leona."

"You have to," I told him. "You have to."

NINETY-TWO

David pulled up near the main entrance to the emergency room. Climbed out and opened the back door. I took a deep breath and grabbed his shoulders when he leaned in across the seat to help me out. My shoulder seemed to have ended up in the right position, but it hurt really badly. My whole body ached. Even my feet were sore. Once I managed to stand up straight, I stood still for a while with his arms around me. Closed my eyes for a moment to keep the vertigo at bay. He took a firmer hold around my back and waist. Even after I regained my balance, I didn't want him to let go. I stayed where I was. Felt his breath against my neck. My cheek was lightly touching his. There was something about that moment. A special feeling. Unlike any I had felt before. Every part of me was in pain, and yet a strange warmth flowed through me. David seemed completely focused on getting me to stand upright. Our eyes met. He nodded, as if to say that I was okay, that I'd found my balance. But I didn't want to let go.

"Mommy..."

Bea was pulling on my pant leg. She started crying again when I told her David was going to take her home and I wasn't going with them, so I let her come.

"You can do it," David whispered in my ear.

I could hear sirens approaching.

"You have to go now," he said and gently pushed me away. "Go!"

Knowing that he was there, I turned away from him. Bea nudged her tiny hand into mine. Staggering, we made our way toward the entrance. The more I moved around and made blood pump through my body, the dizzier I felt. I squeezed Bea's hand tighter. The ground was shifting under my feet. I wanted to throw up. I stopped. Let go of her and doubled over. Rested both my hands against my knees with slightly bent legs. Took shallow breaths. I hated that my daughter had to see me like this, going through all of this. At the same time, she was the only thing that made me keep fighting right now. Without her here, I would have collapsed on the ground. Indifferent to what happened to me. I summoned my strength for her. I took her tiny hand again and started walking, my back hunched. One step at a time. Up onto the curb. Just a few more steps to the doors. It felt like a mile. Suddenly it hit me.

The money!

I turned around. David was standing by the car, watching us. He pointed at the entrance to say I should go inside. I was too weak to shout, but I mimed it as best I could: "The money?"

Even though we were several yards apart, I could see his face fall. Having looked stressed before, he now turned grave. Looked down at the ground. I didn't understand. Stood frozen to the spot, trying to read him. Bea pulled on my arm. When he looked up again he slowly shook his head and mimed something back. I couldn't make out what. Mama? No, why would he be saying mama? I didn't understand the context. I didn't get it until he mimed it a third time. My stomach lurched when I saw what word he was forming. It was a name: Armand.

The air was knocked out of me. I swayed precariously, which made the automatic sliding doors at the entrance open. After two

Acknowledgments

First of all, thank you, Micke—there are no words to describe how much you mean to me.

A big thank you to my Swedish publishing house, Wahlström & Widstrand, for believing in me and Leona. A special thanks to my publisher, Christian Manfred, and my editor, Joen Gustafsson, for your insightful input and for understanding the ideas and vision behind my series.

Thank you to my U.S. publisher, Other Press, and to translator Agnes Broomé.

Thank you to my former colleague, Police Inspector Peter Wittboldt for your help and for letting me discuss police work and the law with you.

Thank you to sailor Jonas Kemi for facts about ship design and safety at sea.

Thank you to my literary agents for bringing Leona on breathtaking trips around the world.

Thank you to friends and colleagues who follow my literary journey with enthusiasm.

Thank you to my family for being there.

And finally, a big thank you to all the readers who have contacted me with thoughts, encouragement, and praise. Your warm words mean more than you know.

31901064128699